RAYGUN CHRONICLES

SPACE OPERA FOR A NEW AGE

RAYGUN
CHRONICLES

SPACE OPERA FOR A NEW AGE

edited by Bryan Thomas Schmidt

**Every
Day**

BOOK DESIGN BY CAMILLE GOODERHAM CAMPBELL

TYPESET IN ZAPF RENAISSANCE ANTIQUA BOOK
WITH HEADINGS IN SAUCER BB & WORLDSATWAR BB
AND DIVIDER ACCENTS IN ASTROBATS

PRINTED AND BOUND BY LIGHTNING SOURCE
IN THE UNITED STATES AND THE UNITED KINGDOM

EVERY DAY PUBLISHING
VANCOUVER, CANADA

WWW.EVERYDAYPUBLISHING.CA

Contents

To EE "Doc" Smith
and the others who paved the way,
with gratitude

and to Ann Crispin,
mentor, friend, inspiration
and favorite author,
you went too soon
but your legacy will last forever.

Introduction

Bryan Thomas Schmidt
Editor

I'm not sure when my fascination with the speculative began but from an early age, my favorite stories always involved the fantastical. From Mother Goose to Grimm, *The Nutcracker* to *The Wizard of Oz,* the stories that captured my excitement were always stories with elements beyond this Earth. Then in 1977, my cousin took me to see *Star Wars* and that was it. Soonafter, I was watching *Star Trek* and *Space: 1999* reruns every night before dinner, and I went to movies like Disney's *The Black Hole, Journey To The Center Of The Earth,* the animated *The Hobbit* and *The Lion, The Witch and The Wardrobe,* and then shows like *Battlestar Galactica* and more. I read Jules Verne, H.G. Wells, C.S. Lewis, J.R.R. Tolkien and tie-ins by James Blish and others. I devoured whatever I could get ahold of. And the stories that most moved me were almost always those set "out there" beyond this world we know.

Somewhere along the way, space opera became my first love, and I began imagining my own stories. My debut novel, *The Worker Prince,* which won honorable mention in 2011 from Barnes & Noble's Science Fiction reviewer, was conceived during that time. And I continued to expand my horizons and imagination, studying science, astronomy, space travel, NASA, and so much more.

Now here I am many years later, editing the first of what I hope is a series of anthologies collecting stories with similar elements. Stories more closely related to old school pulp science fiction wonder stories than more modern space opera, perhaps, but stories intended to both entertain and inspire, from top authors. Some were written brand new for this book by people I admire like Seanan McGuire, Allen Steele, Kristine Kathryn Rusch, and David Farland. Others have been published at a now short-lived zine called *Ray Gun Revival* which you'll learn more about in our opening essay. While in part, this anthology exists as a tribute to that fine effort, it also marks the launch of something new for myself and Every Day Publishing. We want to bring you the type of stories you can read and share with your family and friends again and again; the kind of stories that made us fall in love with science fiction and space opera.

Put aside what you know of this world and its limits, and open wide the doors of your box for a moment to the journeys that lie in these words. From talking bears to thieves and secret agents, from space warriors and soldiers to explorers, school teachers, and even giraffes, the stories here are diverse and fun, packed with action, tongue-in-cheek humor, and larger-than-life characters.

It was fun to read and edit them and fun to assemble them into a coherent body as we present them now. I hope it's even more fun allowing them to inspire your own imaginations, fantasies and sense of wonder, because when science fiction stops doing that, it will have lost its core purpose: asking what if and making readers want to find the answers or at least imagine what they might be.

That exploration, adventure, and excitement is what *Raygun Chronicles: Space Opera For A New Age* is all about – bringing a sense of the old to the new and taking us all back and away again. I hope to places we'd all like to go or wish we could. Whatever the case, I hope you enjoy the journey! Up, up, and away we go!

ESSAY:

TAKING BACK THE SKY

Johne Cook
co-editor, *Ray Gun Revival* magazine

WASH: [imitating Dino 1] Ah, curse your sudden but inevitable betrayal!
WASH: [imitating Dino 2] Ha ha ha, mine is an evil laugh, now die!
— FIREFLY, SERENITY VALLEY, 2002

I can't talk about *Ray Gun Revival* magazine without talking about Space Opera, and I can't talk about Space Opera without talking a little about *Firefly* (2002). Let's start there.

Lee S. King and Paul Christian Glenn and I started *Ray Gun Revival* magazine in July 2006 fueled by *Firefly* fervor and the desire to share our love for the genre with a new generation of readers and authors. We called ourselves 'Overlords' with a nod to Flash Gordon and Ming the Merciless as an indication that this was supposed to be fun, and as a reminder not to take any of this all that seriously. I recently looked back at the editorial from our first issue and our mission statement was clear even then: "Space Opera has fallen on hard times, and we intend to revive it."

But we knew we couldn't go it alone. We would need to start a community and grow our numbers. We needed not just a group of niche fans, we needed a revolution.

We can trace Space Opera back to E.E. "Doc" Smith and *The Skylark of Space* in 1928. By the time he wrote *Triplanetary,* the first in the *Lensman* series, he already knew what he was up to: "...in which scientific detail would not be bothered about, and in which his imagination would run riot." We've seen that in practice. Since then, Space Opera has come to be known for its massive scale, adventurous stories (in space!), grand or epic conflict set in the distant past or the far future. Space Opera is all about the sensawunda, about hope, about blurring genre lines. But that's not all.

As I was thinking again about what I love about Space Opera, it occurred to me there's something else. Space Opera is, in part, about overcoming: overcoming incredible odds, overcoming immense distance or technological gaps, overcoming physical or psychological limitations, overcoming fear, overcoming one's own self.

RGR was spawned from our desire to publish a genre that had fallen out of favor (again). For us, it was also about overcoming a lack of funds to pay for stories and art, and a lack of interest from the readers who simply didn't know any better. We started as a by-your-bootstraps outfit and slowly, carefully built something that never reached millions, but did reach the people who cared about such things.

There's something else, a shift in the culture. In the summer of 2006, there wasn't a hint of Space Opera in the blockbuster movies of the year:
- *Pirates of the Caribbean: Dead Man's Chest*
- *Night At the Museum*
- *Cars*
- *X-Men: The Last Stand*
- *The Da Vinci Code*

So far, 2013 has been a great year for films with Space Opera elements:
- *Star Trek Into Darkness*
- *Man of Steel* (the first 20 minutes are epic and detail the last days and hours of an advanced race with mind-blowing technology on the brink of total planetary collapse)
- *Pacific Rim* (has been compared favorably with the original *Star Wars*, a classic Space Opera)

And that doesn't even include *Riddick* and *Ender's Game*. Clearly, we've come a long way since 2006.

Johne Cook

Aside from fighting obscurity, more trendy genres, and a downturn in readers and reading overall, one of the biggest challenges facing writers of short Space Opera is simply self-control. If one of the primary hallmarks of Space Opera is massive scale, how does that translate to short stories?

The larger the story, the tighter your focus has to be. Yeah, it's hard, which makes the tales told by our best authors all the more impressive. They manage to evoke a far larger universe while telling stories that are personal and relatable.

Ray Gun Revival magazine closed shop in October 2012, after starting our seventh year of publication. I thought we'd said everything we'd wanted to say, accomplished everything we'd wanted to accomplish. But there was one last surprise - this anthology. Through the years, we've worked with a Who's Who of up-and-coming authors, editors, and publishers. This anthology represents some of the best selections from the virtual pages of *RGR*, as well as original Space Opera commissioned for this volume by Bryan Thomas Schmidt and Every Day Publishing. Reading through these stories has reminded me of just how far this formerly disreputable genre has come.

In 2002, they took the sky from us. In 2006, we decided to do something about. As I write this, the year is 2013. As I look at all the big name authors writing Space Opera, all the directors making Space Opera movies, and all the up-and-coming authors trying their hand with the genre, this much is clear - we can take back the sky. Who is 'we'? The answer is me. The answer is you. And the time is now.

"You can't take the sky from me." – SERENITY, 2005

RAYGUN
CHRONICLES

Given the inspiration for Ray Gun Revival *, it seems appropriate to begin our journey in a similar place. I told known* Firefly *fan Seanan McGuire this was her chance to write a totally original tale that captures the series' feel. She jumped at it, and then proceeded to blow us all away with this amazing story of generational warfare and the need for devoted teachers...*

FRONTIER ABCs:
THE LIFE AND TIMES OF CHARITY SMITH, SCHOOLTEACHER

Seanan McGuire

A IS FOR AMMUNITION

There are no banks to rob in this painted doll of a dustbowl fantasy town; the money is all bits and bytes stored in a computer vault no human hands can open, whether they belong to banker or bandit. But there are other forms of thievery to be practiced by the quick and the clever, and Cherry is both, when she sees call to be. So when word goes out on the down-low that the Mulrian gang is planning a heist and needs bullets to get them to the finish line, Cherry's one of the first to the cattle call, her guns low and easy on her hips, her hair braided back like an admonition against untidiness. They're surprised to see her – aren't they always, when she shows up in places like this? – but they're willing enough to let her on the crew once they've seen what she can do.

She doesn't brag much. Doesn't talk much either, outside of a classroom or a courtroom. But oh, that little lady in the worn-out britches and the red flannel shirt can shoot like she made a bargain with the God of All Guns.

Some folks say as she was a sniper in the last war. There have been wars upon wars since she showed up on the scene, and it's always "the last war." No one knows how old she is, no one knows the name of her home world, and no one's sure when she's finally going to snap and take out her allies along with her enemies. But they keep taking her on, because she makes the bullets dance to her tune. Could shoot the wings off a fly, the flame off a candle, and the fat off of a hog.

The raid begins at local midnight. Four techslingers, four gunslingers, a pilot, and Cherry herself, all walking into town from different directions, all heading for the places they're supposed to be. The first shot is fired at two past the hour, an old-fashioned gunpowder bullet smashing through the window of city hall. That's the signal. The gunslingers commence to shooting up the things they've been approved to shoot – mostly foliage and buildings and the police bots that come swinging down the sidewalks like they stand a chance against flesh and lead and practice – and the techslingers slide their clever wires into the datastream, bleeding off billions in less time than it takes for Cherry to reload.

That's her, up on the roof of the library, stretched flat with her scope circling her eye like a wedding ring. Every shot she takes is true, and she takes a lot of them. Nobody dies, but there's enough damaged as to take the edge off. Then the bell rings in her ear, and she rolls away from the edge of the roof, vanishing into the shadows. Fun's over.

Tip to tail, they took six minutes to bleed the beast, leaving shattered glass and frightened townies behind like a calling card. Cherry will check her bank balance later and find a healthy payoff from an uncle she doesn't have, on an outworld that may or may not exist. It doesn't matter to her. She's worked off a little of her aggression here, in the shadows and the dust, and that leaves her head clear enough for the real work to begin.

C IS FOR COVER STORY

"Now, can anyone tell me the origins of the human race? Where did we begin?" The one-room schoolhouse is ringed with windows, letting in so much light from outside that the overheads don't need to be turned on for most of the year. By the time the weather turns sour, the schoolhouse solars will have fed enough into the local grid that they won't have to pay a penny for the power they use. There's value in self-sufficiency.

The kids are a surly bunch, growling and glaring as they squat at their desks like so many infuriated mushrooms. These are the children of asteroid miners, farmers, and artisans, not rich enough to go to the fine boarding schools on Earth or Io, but not poor enough to be restricted to home schooling and play dates. They get the bulk of their lessons on their personalized terminals, but they're here for the social contact with their peers, to learn how to get along and how to form connections that will serve them for the rest of their lives. There are fourteen teachers working this part of the solar system, and Miss Cherry is a newcomer here, arriving at the start of the term. They still don't trust her. They still don't know whether they should.

She leans back against her desk, resting her weight against her hands, and smiles winningly at them. They do not smile back at her. She's hard to measure with the eye, a wisp of a thing in a blue dress printed with white daisies, her long dark hair hanging loose and sometimes getting in her eyes when she gets excited and begins waving her hands around. They're generally good at telling someone's age by the way they move, these children of the regen generation – when your grandfather can look like your little brother if he finds the scratch, you learn to read a body for the years it's seen – but Cherry is a book of riddles, one moment as open as a kindie, the next as closed-off as a three-time regen. Her face puts her in her early twenties, by far the most popular age with women trying to survive in the outer moons.

"Anyone?" she asks, and there is a sharp, sweet disappointment in her tone, like she can't believe they wouldn't know the answer to such a simple question. "I suppose I'll have to recommend that all your consoles be set to remedial human history for the rest of the term, then. I hate to do it – "

"So don't!" shouts a voice from the back of the room.

Cherry's head snaps up, and those sweet and easy eyes turn suddenly cold, the eyes of a predator searching for its prey. "Who said that?" she asks, scanning the crowd.

They've been in this schoolhouse a lot longer than she has; every child in the class knows how to hunker down and look like butter wouldn't melt in their mouths. They shift and look away, avoiding her gaze.

"You." Her finger stabs out like an accusation. "Why not?"

Her target, Timothy Fulton, squirms, but only a little. He doesn't bother denying that he was the one who spoke: she's got him, fair and square. Instead, he shrugs and says, "Because we've been over all the remedial stuff. We don't want to do it again."

"Well, then, you can spare yourself and your classmates a lot of boring scutwork by being a hero and answering my question." She isn't smiling. This is the first time since she arrived at the start of the month that she hasn't been smiling. "What was the origin of the human race?"

"Earth, ma'am. Humanity began on Earth."

"Very good. When did we move on to bigger and brighter things?"

"The Twenty-Second Century, ma'am, after we figured out how to adapt ourselves to other planets, and how to adapt other planets to ourselves."

Miss Cherry nods encouragingly. "Very good. What was the first great war after colonization? Anyone?"

Ermine Dale has never been able to sit by while other children were praised and she was not. She puts up her hand, waiting only for Miss Cherry to point at her before blurting, "It was over what makes a human, ma'am. Whether Jovians and Neptuneans were still people, given all the modifications they'd gone through."

"That's right." Cherry pushes herself away from her desk and walks around it to the chalkboard, an archaic piece of set dressing that nonetheless seems to help students learn and retain information. In a bold hand, she writes the number "10," and circles it before she turns back to the class and says, "This is the average number of years between wars since

6

humanity stretched beyond a single planet. This is how long we have to rest, recover, and learn to do better. That's what I'm here for."

"To rest?" asks Timothy, and his confusion is the class's confusion.

Miss Cherry smiles. "No. I'm here to teach you to do better."

I IS FOR *INEVITABILITY*

She's been here a full season, eight local months stretching and blending together on this farmer's paradise of a Jovian moon. Ganymede has taken well to terraforming, and Earth's crops have taken well to Ganymede. Half the moons of Jupiter get their food from here, and that makes it a bright and glittering target in the nighttime sky. When the next war comes – and there's always a next war – she expects the sides to fight mercilessly to own the sky's breadbasket.

The children have accepted her. They bring her apples and icefruit from the fields, and some of them have started to shyly tell her what they want to be when they grow up. Someday most of them will be farmers, but some of them may be explorers, or diplomats, or poets, if they get the chance to strengthen their roots on this good soil until the time comes for them to bloom. She likes these pauses maybe best of all. They remind her that the human race has a purpose beyond blowing itself to cinders against the stars. "We can be something more than fireworks, if we're willing to put the work in," that was what her long-dead lover told her once, when they were lying naked to the unseeing eye of Jupiter on the barren, rocky soil of this selfsame moon, barely cloaked then in its thin envelope of atmosphere, still an experiment on the verge of going eternally wrong. "We can be anything."

That wasn't true then and it isn't true now, but oh, weren't they pretty words?

The fact that she's thinking of him at all isn't a good sign. Means she's getting restless, and when she gets restless, she either needs to move on or find something that can bleed off a little of that energy. So she sends out a quiet query to her contacts, lets them know that she might be available for a little pick-up work if the price is right and the location is far enough from Ganymede. Maybe something out-system. Summer break is coming soon, and her kids will be needed in the fields. Easy then for a schoolteacher to slip away on errands of her own. As long as she makes it back before the apples come in, she'll be fine.

She's still teaching her classes and waiting for a job to present itself when the choice is taken away from her. Choices are like that. Some of them exist only for as long as it takes not to make them.

They're in the middle of a comparative theology lesson when the first shots are fired, big, loud things that boom through the still-thin atmosphere like the world itself is ending. Miss Cherry drops the book she was reading from and bolts for the door. The children are still sitting frozen at their desks, too stunned to react. By the time the book hits the floor, she's already gone.

Ermine starts to cry.

Then Miss Cherry is back, and there's a light in her eyes they've never seen there before, something wild and cold at the same time, like Io, like the stars. "Get to the cellar!" she shouts. "Now!"

She's the teacher, and so they obey her, running like rabbits for their bolt hole under the building. It's not until they hear the lock sliding home behind them that anyone really realizes she hasn't followed, that she's still out there.

In the dark, hesitantly, Timothy asks, "Was Miss Cherry holding a gun?"

No one's really sure. They hold each other close and listen to the distant, terribly close sound of gunfire.

K IS FOR *KILLER*

Children are like seeds, only they all look exactly the same; there's no way to look at them and say "this one's a flower, this one's a tree, this one's a strain of tangle-vine designed to break up ore deposits on the moons of Neptune." All you can do is water them, feed them, give them good soil, and watch how they grow. Be careful what you give them, because it'll change what comes out the other side. Something that could've been a rose may come out all thorns and fury if you plant it wrong.

It wasn't just one thing that went into growing Charity Smith. No one even agrees on what soil she was first planted in. She was Earth-born, she was a Martian, she was one of the first settlers on Ganymede, she was altered Jovian and then back again after the war started, when she realized that heavy bones and thick skin didn't suit a sniper. She was an Ionian mermaid, she was an asteroid miner, she was everybody's daughter and nobody's wife. No one claimed her, not at the beginning and not after. But we do know this much:

One of the places she put down roots was Titan. Her name's on the first settler manifest, pretty as you please, writ down proper in her own hand. She came in as an educator, fresh from Mars – and there's some will say this supports the idea that she was Martian born, while others say she couldn't have gotten a release from the red planet if she'd been a citizen, with the threat of war so close and them so very much in need of trained instructors. It doesn't so much matter, because she was just a teacher then, with none of the scars or patches that would come after. Titan was newly terraformed back then, and they needed people like her. People who knew how to work for their keep.

There is one surviving holo of the time that Miss Charity Smith spent as a schoolteacher on Saturn's largest moon. It shows her in one of the sundresses she still wears these two hundred and fifty years later, her hands clasped in front of her and a smile upon her face as she stands with her students in front of the Titansport schoolhouse. It was just one room, one of the first frontier schools built out past Mars, and she couldn't look prouder if you paid her. There are twenty-seven children in the shot, all of them looking at the camera with varying expressions of boredom and mistrust. They were the sons and daughters of bankers, miners, and farmers; they had no one to speak for them but their parents and their teacher. They were seeds looking for good soil, and Miss Cherry was their gardener, as wide-eyed and idealistic as they were themselves.

All that changed on the night the ships arrived.

There had been rumbles of war in-system for months. Earth fundamentalists thought the modifications of the Neptune settlers had gone too far; said that the Neptuneans were no longer human, and hence had no claim to their home world's rich mineral deposits. The Neptuneans didn't take too kindly to that, and had responded with threats of their own. As for who fired the first shot, well, that's just one more thing lost to the mists of history, which are fond of obfuscation, but not so fond of being cleared away. Someone struck first. Someone else responded. And before most of the solar system even knew that we were at war, the great ships were flying in search for strategic bases to use in their quest to obliterate the enemy.

Titan was well-situated for a lot of purposes. It was a good refueling station, and a better supply depot, with its farms and its farmers and its ready supply of livestock in both clone and field-grown forms. That was why the ships raced each other there; that was why the first real battle of the Great Earth-Neptune War was fought, not in the safely empty depths of space, but in the sky over Titansport.

It was local winter. All the children were in school, as was one young and frightened schoolteacher who had never tried to defend the things she cared for. She was still a seed herself, in many ways; she was still growing.

We don't know the full details of what happened on that day. Only one person does, and she's not talking. Here is what we do know: that the school burned. That the children died. And that Charity Smith walked away, someone else's rifle in her hands, and all the blood of a generation nurturing her roots.

We made her. We earned her. It's coming on three hundred years gone from that night, and we're watering her still. May all the gods of all the worlds that are have mercy on our souls.

M IS FOR *MURDER*

Everyone has heard the stories, of course; they're part of the two-bit opera that is the history of the Populated Worlds of the Solar System. No one believes that sort of crap, not really, not until they've come skimming through the thin atmosphere of a fresh-terraformed moon and found a woman with dark hair and cold eyes standing on the bell spire of the church with a disruptor rifle in her hands. They're coming in fast and hot and there isn't time for course correction, so the order is given: ready, aim, fire. Blow the stupid little gunslinger wanna-be back to the dust that spawned her, and prepare for the payday.

Cherry's been to this rodeo before. If the pilot had been one of hers, he would've pulled up, no matter what his captain told him. Her presence is a warning and a promise – "This town is mine," and "I will end you," both wrapped up in one denim and flannel package. She's shown her face. She has no regrets, and she never wants them. She buried her regrets in the soil on Titan. So she pulls the trigger and leaps clear before the ship's engines can realize what she's done to them. EMP guns are illegal on all the settled worlds, but so is killing children, so she figures her accounts will balance in the end.

The ship goes down hard in the middle of town. It takes out the church as it descends. It misses the school. That's all she's ever cared about. Adults are grown; their seeds are sprouted, and for the most part, they're past the point where they can change what they'll become. Children, though, children are still capable of domestication. They can learn from the errors of their past.

Cherry takes her time as she saunters down the street toward the wreckage. Faces appear in windows and doorways, gawking at her, taking note of her face and her place in the community. She'll have to move on after this. She always does. That's all right. The kids here are good students, and they've learned their lessons well. They'll grow up a little better than their parents, and when she makes her way back here to teach their grandchildren, some of them may smile at her in the streets, duck their heads and touch their hats, and never say her name out loud.

The hatch of the ship is rocking back and forth when she gets there. She sighs, sets her engine-killer gun aside, and pulls the smaller, more personal revolver from her belt. She's standing patient as the stone when the hatch creaks open some minutes later, and the face of a green-skinned Ionian appears in the opening.

He pales when he sees her. "You're supposed to be dead," he says.

"That makes two of us," she replies and pulls her trigger. The gunshot echoes through the town, followed by the sound of windows slamming shut and doors being locked. Curiosity has killed a lot of cats in its day, but it's left the pioneer folk for the most part alive.

Her gun speaks three more times before the ship is a graveyard. She steps away and scans the skies. There's never just one. It's not a battle if you're shooting at shadows. Finally she sees it, a cloud that moves just a little too quickly, skirting against the wind instead of with it. Cherry's sigh is a wisp of a thing, heartbroken and tired.

Earth, again. Why must it always start with Earth?

Charity Smith is going home.

N IS FOR NO QUARTER

"Are you sure, Miss Cherry?" The governor's voice is an electronic sine wave that caresses the whole room with its vibrations; the governor himself is a Jovian, genetically engineered to thrive in the seas of liquid metallic hydrogen that cover the planet's surface. He was born on Jupiter, and came to Ganymede as a young man, seeking his fortune. He can never go home now. He's been on this world, in its lighter gravity, for far too long.

His daughter has been in Cherry's class, born of a surrogate; he has never touched his more Earth-true wife with his bare hands. It was the governor who recognized Cherry's name and approved her hiring. He knows as well as any how important such gardeners are to a world just getting started.

"They saw me, Mr. Galais, and while I'd be just as happy to go back to my class, you and I both know that's not the way to keep the peace." She even sounds a little sorry. She likes this world. She likes these kids. "I'll need my ship and the pay you promised me. In return, I'll keep the war from your doorsteps, and I'll only contact you if I need an employment reference."

The governor chuckles despite himself. "You'll have it, rest assured; you've done nothing but good here. The children will be devastated."

"Tell them this is the cost of war. They should know that well enough already, from our lessons; you'll just be giving a reminder." Cherry shakes her head. "I have to go, or someone will come looking. Now. My ship?"

"Ready at the port. But tell me, Miss Cherry... where will you go? What will you do?"

Cherry smiles. It's a thin, wistful expression, broken and beaten down by more years than anyone who's seen it cares to count. "I'm going home. As for what I'll do when I get there, well... I suppose I still have a few lessons left to teach. And some folks clearly haven't been learning."

The governor had never considered double-crossing her; there's looking for a better deal, and then there's taunting a dog already proven to bite. In his tank of pressurized hydrogen, he shivers and turns, his long fins draping over themselves, and for the first time, he is glad Miss Cherry will be leaving them.

Some things are too dangerous to be allowed to take root for very long.

O IS FOR OUTWARD BOUND

There's always a moment of heart stopping joy when the pull of gravity lets go and her ship is running free and clear across the open sky. Cherry sits behind the controls, tied to the ship with optical wires and catheters and a dozen other cold connections, and she laughs for the sheer beauty of the images being beamed into her brain by the ship's exterior sensors. Her hands clutch the controls, and she soars across the brilliant blackness of space like a comet on a collision course with the cradle of mankind: Earth itself, that big blue, green, and brown ball of polluted seas and overpopulated soils that gave birth to the human race. She hates it there, how she hates it there, but sometimes, she has no choice. Sometimes, there is nowhere else to go but home.

After an hour in the air she punches in the final coordinates and keys up her med systems. It's time for another rejuve treatment. Wouldn't do to look anything but her best when she meets the relatives.

Q IS FOR *QUESTIONING*

Cherry's ship is small enough to fit through any hole in the security nets, and her autopilot is clever enough to find them, driving her on a clean, traceless route until she reaches the outer edge of Earth's security net. The auto wakes her then, and she yawns and stretches and activates an ID beacon older than most of what's left in Known Space. Alarms blare seconds later, in rooms too dark and far away for her to see. Cherry hangs there for a moment, a red bell on the collar of the cat, and then she hits the burners and she's gone, gone, away across the sky, and their tracers are following, and no one dares to press the button; no one dares to take the first shot. She is a fairy tale, a legend, a lie. She is a schoolteacher, and the daughter of a President, and the girl who gave everything away to grow in poisoned soil. She is a ghost story, and this is her frontier.

When she reckons she's taunted them long enough she stops, gives their guns the time they need to lock onto her position, and presses the button that will begin broadcasting her words across the heavens. "I thought we talked about this," she says. "You promised to leave the outworlds alone. You said you were done grabbing for what's not yours."

(And somewhere far away, a com jockey turns to his supervisor and asks, "What is she talking about, sir?" There is no answer. The bargain she refers to was struck fifty years ago, and the man who struck it with her has long gone to his grave. But where one side stands, the deal holds. That's the only honest way of doing business.)

She hangs there in the air, an easy target, and maybe that's the point; maybe she's more tired than she lets on. "Well?" she asks. "No response?"

("We have to say something, sir.")

"I suppose that means the deal's off. I suppose that means I'm setting myself against you."

("Tell her this.")

And then the words on her com, not spoken, but burning before her all the same: "We're sorry, Miss Cherry."

And Charity smiles.

T IS FOR *TEACHER*

She doesn't miss Earth much. The Earth that's there now isn't the one she left behind, not by a long shot; it's been too long, and there are too many bullets and too many bodies between here and there. She made her choices and the people who stayed planetbound made theirs, and regrets have never changed the past. She's invested her money and her time well since then. Generations have grown up knowing Miss Cherry as the quiet voice of reason, and knowing Charity Smith as a bogeyman used to frighten naughty governments into behaving themselves a little better, at least for a little while.

Six hundred years is a long time to pinch pennies and buy bigger guns. She's better armed than most planetary governments these days, and she makes sure they know it, even if they don't believe she's really who she claims until her ship's ID blazes on their screens like a warning from a disappointed god. She hasn't fired as many shots as people say she has. She hasn't needed to.

Maybe one day they won't need the firm hand anymore, and she'll be allowed to go back to the girl she was on Titan, the one who'd never held a gun or killed a man. Maybe one day the last of the poisoned fruit will fall, and all the children of all the worlds will be able to grow up safe and unspoiled. But until that day, she has a job to do, and if it's not a job that anyone gave her, well. Sometimes it's the jobs we take for ourselves that matter most of all.

The schoolhouse is not new; the desks are worn and marked with the initials of those who came before. But the chalkboard is clean and gleaming black, as dark as the hair of the woman who stands in front of the class. "Hello, Io," she says, and smiles. "My name's Miss Cherry. I think we're going to be good friends. Now, who here can tell me the origins of the human race?"

Kristine Kathryn Rusch is one of my favorite authors. Her Retrieval Artist *books combine mystery, detective noir, and space opera beautifully. And her* Diving *novels evoke classic space opera of a bygone age. In her story for us, a corporate bounty hunter is taken captive by men with a surprising connection to her past, and finds herself once again face to face with the last man she ever wanted to see again...*

RICK THE ROBBER BARON

Kristine Kathryn Rusch

Kita woke up tied to a wooden post with real rope cutting into her wrists and ankles. At least her ankles were crossed demurely. The last time she went through something like this, the idiot had tied her ankles behind the post like he'd tied her wrists. She'd slid down to her knees before waking up and had bruises for weeks – even though that had been a virtual simulation, just like this was.

When would these marauders figure out that the holocapabilities of her own ship were crummy? The edges of this entire vision sparked slightly, and even if they hadn't, she still would have known she was in a simulation.

The air was wrong, for one thing. The marauders had punched up one of those desert planet simulations, the things she used to distract herself from long days on a tiny vessel. But she hated heat and she hated dry air, so she'd made the air humid and the temperature no higher than seventy-five degrees.

Plus the ground was wrong. The yellow, sandy dust should have swirled with the breeze. Instead, it lay flat, like some kind of badly designed carpet. And even if she had believed all of that, she wouldn't have believed the post.

The marauders had put her in a bra-thing that should have cut into the skin under her breasts, but didn't. They had given her matching panties as well, which made her giggle. This particular outfit wasn't quite out of the marauders playbook: if they really wanted their prisoners to have no access to weapons hidden in clothing, they should have removed all clothing.

The fact that they'd left her only partially naked actually told her what flavor of marauder she was dealing with. Most likely the religious branch. They'd split off from the main branch over such minor things as murder and the kidnapping of children. Weirdly, the religious believed those things should be allowed. But God forbid if anyone got naked for any reason.

Instead of contemplating the vagaries of the marauders, she needed to applaud this clear sign. Because, if she could get the hell out of here, she knew how to defeat them.

She struggled to move her demurely crossed legs underneath her body instead of tastefully to one side. The stupid marauders had put particularly uncomfortable shoes on her feet. The damn shoes had heels, so she had to bend her legs at an awkward angle to get them directly beneath her. Then she stood upright on her toes, of course. Heels never allowed the foot to remain flat.

Plus, getting upright took another point off the verisimilitude scale: She should have gotten splinters in her naked back with that move. Instead, she slid up that pole as if it were made of some kind of slick polyfiber.

Lazy bastards. Laziness always counted her in favor.

She sighed, recited three numbers in three different languages, and then said, *failsafe escape stop,* in a fourth. The simulation winked out, and she stood in blackness for a moment.

Then the power came back up, and sure enough, she was in the simulation room, the thing that she had insisted on when she bought this rust bucket, the thing that made the price of this stupid ship five times what it would have been if she just wanted some kind of out-and-back zip vessel.

The room was small and boxy, and aside from the wall with the controls and all of the supplies, it had no distinguishing features. Without a simulation running, the room was very uncomfortable.

And it was too damn easy to hack. This was the fifteenth time marauders had tried to imprison her in her own entertainment room.

The first time was the only time that freaked her out. It had taken her forty-five minutes to escape, and she'd had to flee the room quickly because she had stupidly used the same passcodes for her failsafe in the simulation room that she had used in the cockpit.

She had arrived just as that particular marauder was using her codes to override all the security she had put into place. She'd shot him with his own laser pistol and taken back her ship.

Now she just used different passcodes in different areas of the ship. So much smarter that way. And she had separated the simulation's controls from the cockpit. That had been a smart move. Because now, the fact that she was free didn't register on any device in the cockpit.

No one would know until she burst in there, pistols blazing.

She grinned, lost in the fantasy, and shook herself out of it. Always a hazard in this room. Her brain was ready to relax.

But it couldn't, because something was still cutting into her wrists and ankles. She looked down at her feet. The shoes were real after all, but the ropes weren't. These marauders had used the plastic doodads that came with the simulator. The doodads could turn into anything needed on the body, because the body was the one thing that really didn't lie about reality and unreality – at least in this cheap a virtual simulation.

She had figured the marauders were religious, but she was beginning to wonder. They would have had to strip her and then touch her privates to put this sad little outfit on her, which wasn't something the religious would do. She could imagine them wrapping her in the flat plastic sheets, then removing her clothes without looking at her body, and finally, cutting some of the sheets into the proper squares.

The sheets were like the doodads; they turned into whatever the virtual simulation made them become – at least for the duration of the simulation. Right now, she should be covered in badly cut sheets of plastic, not actual clothes.

At least, if the religious marauders had done this.

Plus, changing her outfit seemed truly unnecessary from a take-over-the-ship-and-escape point of view. If someone wanted to see her in a sexy pose, why not leave her naked?

She sighed. She really needed hazard pay on this job.

Oh, wait. She did get hazard pay. Although it wasn't called hazard pay. It was a bonus. When those cargo ships she was defending made it to McQueen Primus with their precious minerals and other raw materials intact, she got a ten percent bonus. Ten percent of the full payment for the cargo, not ten percent of her measly little base salary.

And if she took out some of the major marauders and could prove it, she got a bounty for them as well.

So far, she was owed nineteen bounties. She'd love to make it an even twenty.

She stretched her wrists apart, and the plastic broke off just like it was supposed to. Then she bent down and pulled it off her ankles, nearly tipping over in the process.

The outfit was ridiculous, and now that she thought about it, she had a hunch she knew not only why, but who was waiting for her out in that cockpit.

Rick the Robber Baron. Joy of joys. Her life was now complete.

Or at least, her revenge would be.

Although, if she were honest with herself, the fact that he was even here was all her fault.

He'd been so cute when she met him. Six feet tall, golden blond hair, a whisper of a goatee that looked perfect on him. In fact, it made him look a bit like a pirate, which (if she were honest with herself) was something that she had always found attractive.

Maybe that was why she had become so disappointed in her work. Marauders weren't pirates. Marauders were greedy bastards without a sense of romance in them, out for profit and nothing else.

She took them down not just because they were thieves, but because they were usually very bad thieves, the kind whose very existence offended her.

But that night, she'd been hoping to meet a higher-end thief. The kind who was smart enough to attend a company party on McQueen Quintus, particularly when some unthinking executive decided the party would be not just a costume gala, but a best-selves costume gala, held in the virtual ballroom of corporate headquarters.

The Odolpho Corporation had hired guards, beefed up the security systems, and made a show of just how strongly they guarded their fortress. Of course, stupid them, they didn't bother guarding their mouths. And smart thieves should have shown up, just to have conversations.

Kita wanted to see how many smart thieves there were in this part of the universe. She had inserted a chip before she arrived, one that would strip the best-self glamor off the person, so that she could see their actual face. Then she'd do some internal face-recognition to see if any known criminals had bothered to attend.

The ballroom was huge and done in an art-deco theme, very Old Earth, very glitzy. Of course, the ballroom was just like her simulator, except it was a more expensive version (hell, probably the most expensive version) placed in a much larger location. The location wasn't on a ship; it was on the only continent in McQueen Quintus, in the valley where the Odolpho Corporation had once upon a time set up its mining base and now had its headquarters.

The building that housed the ballroom was part of those headquarters, although not a main part. But like most outpost headquarters, everything was hooked together. McQueen Quintus had a toxic environment, so the inhabitants of the Odolpho Corporation headquarters needed to be able to flee from one part of the headquarters to another with a moment's notice. Even the best built habitats failed, especially when the outside environment had an acid base. She had no idea how much money the Odolpho Corporation spent on constantly rebuilding and shoring up this monstrosity, but she figured it had to be a lot.

The Odolpho Corporation was worth more than any other in this sector and spent money like it meant nothing at all. It meant something to her. She was trying to take as many credits out of this corporation as she possibly could as quickly as she could, because she had learned over the space of her career (if you counted what she did as a career) that business relationships could go south in the blink of an eye.

She didn't even tell the Odolpho Corporation that she had come to this little event. Her handler (he called himself her boss) for the Odolpho Corporation thought she was dispatching bad guys a few light years from here.

If he attended this event, he wouldn't recognize her anyway. She had gone in with her best self a little thicker, a little bustier, a little taller. She'd lengthened her nose and raised her cheekbones, shortened her hair and darkened her skin. She looked different enough to be a best self, even though this wasn't the best self she carried in her head. That best self was private and certainly not for showing off at parties, especially parties where she was working.

This party was filled with beautiful people in beautiful clothes. Best-selves were always beautiful. Even the band was beautiful. She couldn't tell if the skinny glimmering folk who played ancient instruments near the entrance were real or a recreation, but even if they were a recreation of some famous music group from some long-lost era, they still probably didn't look like their original selves. Real people came in all sizes. Best selves seemed to come in tall, skinny, busty (female), built (male), and perfect.

But she could see through the best-selves to the fat, short, lumpy, imperfect real selves below. She wasn't even surprised that several of the best-selves were just tweaks of the real selves. Rich people spent money on enhancements. Enhancements often didn't work as well as advertised (in other words, they didn't make a person perfect), but they did work to some degree.

That was why, when she meet Rick the Robber Baron, who was presenting himself as Richard the Mineral Rights Investor, she believed what she saw.

Tall, handsome – but not quite as handsome as the best-self portrayed – those dark intriguing eyes, that not-quite-perfect form underneath the long silk(ish) suit coat, the trousers that hugged muscular legs.

She was a sucker for muscular legs. Most spacers, no matter how in shape they were, couldn't develop muscular legs. They were lucky to have good muscle tone at all.

She'd circled the room more than once, danced with a few of the company men who had no idea who she was, danced with the prettiest woman in the room. She'd been about to leave. That was when Rick spoke to her, in one of those hybrid accents that she found so sexy. His smile was perfect, with just the right amount of self-deprecation, and the next thing she knew, she was dancing with him.

They bantered, they danced, they danced and bantered, and they – well, she – had fun.

So much fun that she let him take her to the room he'd rented from the hotel attached to the headquarters. It wasn't as fancy as she had expected – surely someone connected to the Odolpho Corporation should have received a better room – but that detail only gave her a moment's hesitation.

She'd since learned to pay attention to those moments of hesitation. Something in her subconscious had been sending her a message. And she hadn't paid enough attention to receive it.

Although she got it the next morning, when she woke up next to a lumpy spacer with no muscle tone at all. He had the goatee, but it looked grotesque on his fleshy face. Best-selves dissolved after twelve hours. But his best-self had had a second best-self beneath it. That was why she hadn't seen him for who he really was at the party.

She damn near fell out of bed in surprise, and that ungraceful move had awakened him.

He grinned at her, extended a hand, and said, "Rick the Robber Baron at your service. I'm so honored to meet Kita Ogude. So, honey, you want to join forces?"

"No," she said, unable to keep the horror out of her voice. She got out of bed and groped for her clothes, unnerved that he had seen her naked, unnerved that he had done things with her naked, unnerved that he knew her name.

How had he known her name?

He propped himself up on one elbow. "You've heard of me, right?"

"Sorry, no," she said, and then wondered why she said *sorry* in the first place. She wasn't sorry.

"I'm the best thief in this entire sector." His grin got wider, making it look like his mouth was going to take over his face. "I even stole something from you."

At first, she had thought he meant that he had stolen a sexual encounter from her or maybe a bit of DNA. But no DNA went on the market, and no matter how she looked at it, he hadn't stolen that encounter from her. She had acquiesced.

In her most quiet moments, she even admitted to herself that she had initiated the hotel room part of their relationship. Which she wouldn't have called a relationship at all if it weren't for the fact that she couldn't let this incident go.

And that was when she realized what he had stolen from her.

He had stolen her confidence.

And she wanted it back.

So she'd hired on to the Odolpho Corporation's bounty program. She escorted ships all by herself, got them to their destinations in the McQueen system without any help, fought off various groups of marauders all alone, and no one thought twice about any of it.

She had more bounties than anyone in the program, and she had taken out more thieves than anyone in the history of the Odolpho Corporation. She even won a crappy little award from the Odolpho Corporation honoring her for "making the spaceways safer," whatever the hell that meant.

And she never saw Rick the Robber Baron again, even though she imagined him in every marauder she shot, every ship she destroyed.

Take that, you creepy bastard, she would mutter whenever she succeeded. *Take that.*

So now he was in the middle of her ship, and he was probably laughing at her. He hadn't realized that he had slipped into a trap.

There was a reason she caught all of those marauders, and it wasn't because she did the traditional thing. She didn't track them or hunt them down or go after them with righteous fury.

Nope. All she did was glitz up her ship a little, then leave it wide open to any passing netbot so that the marauders could see she carried a small fortune in rare minerals in the cargo hold and traveled alone.

And her ship wasn't defended at all.

Well, that part wasn't true. It was defended. Just not in any obvious way.

Before she left the simulation room, she had only one moment of hesitation – and she paid attention to this one. She had initially thought she'd change clothes. After all, that bastard seemed to have some sort of need for sexual dominance.

She initially thought she would thwart the need by dressing again, but that would only point out to him that she had momentarily felt out of control. She would go into the cockpit still wearing the stupid bra-thing and the ridiculous panties.

The only acquiescence she'd make to comfort would be removal of the shoes. Shoes like that weren't made for walking. They were made for – well, she didn't want to think about what they were made for in a sexual context. She didn't want to have a sexual context, at least not with Rick the Robber Baron. Not any more.

Because she'd done some research on good old Rick the Robber Baron. He only stole enough minerals or raw materials or commodities to make a comfortable living. Mostly, he stole intangibles.

Like peace of mind.

She stopped at the door of the simulation room, and using three different types of passwords, two of them coded to non-traditional body parts, she set the simulator's loop function into motion. She'd changed that after her first imprisonment in this room as well. Now there were two loop functions: the one that came standard with the room, and the one she'd modified to show the last simulation on a 2-D security screen in the cockpit.

She uploaded that now, so any time Rick checked on her progress, he would see her still tied to that pole. She altered the image just a little so that it looked like she was fighting her bonds.

She let herself out of the room, not through the main door, but through a side hatch that she'd also added after that first debacle. Sometimes marauders – real marauders, the organized types that paid protection to the truly smart marauders – stationed a guard outside the simulator room. She doubted Rick had a guard because he liked to travel alone, just like she did. But she left through the side hatch just in case he changed his standard practices just for her.

The corridor that she had converted from public to private (as if there were a public on this ship besides her) had gotten a bit funky since she last used it. She hadn't been kidnapped and stuffed in her own simulator for more than two months, and it showed. There was a thin level of grit on everything, primarily because she had unhooked all of the ship's systems from this little passageway.

Even the environmental systems were non-traditional, hacked through one of the lower level control panels so that the usage wouldn't show up in the cockpit.

All of this worked to her advantage. Sometimes she could just shut off the environment in all other parts of the ship, and let the marauders suffocate to death. Sometimes she hastened it with a bit of McQueen Quintus atmosphere (she thought that poetic justice for some of these thieves), and sometimes she just opened all the exterior doors and jammed the airlocks.

Not sometimes on that last. She'd only done it once, and then cursed herself afterwards because not even her cleaning bots were up to the task of clearing the goo. She'd had to travel for two days in that crap, and then hire a service to clean it all away.

Never again, on that one.

Not even for charming old Rick. Or not-so-charming Rick, as the case may be.

She had other plans for him.

She made her way from the simulation room to the cockpit. Before she opened the side hatch, she removed the laser pistol she kept primed and ready just inside the hatch's door. She double-checked it, saw that it was fully charged, and grinned.

Then she slid the top half of the door open so fast that it slammed against the side of the cockpit wall.

Rick whirled. He looked older than she remembered, and the goatee was gone. But his piggy little eyes glinted and a frown severed his forehead.

"Hey – !" he started, and she shot him.

He spun over backwards, unconscious. She had one of the cleaning bots nudge him just to make sure. He didn't touch it. Nor did he touch his weapon.

She let herself out of the side hatch and walked over to his body. She removed his weapons. His flesh spread out sideways just a bit, enough to make her realize carrying him would be hard.

She sighed. She didn't ever want to touch this creep again.

So she went to the nearest supply closet and removed a pair of gravity boots. Then she shut off the gravity throughout the ship. Her boots remained anchored to the floor, but Rick's fleshy body rose.

She used the pistol to push him forward, letting the doors open as she went.

When she got to the main corridor, she paused. She could do a couple of things: she could just send him back to his ship – via space, without a spacesuit; she could put him in her brig; or she could steal from him.

She put him in the brig while she checked his ship.

He came to briefly.

"Hey, honey," he said, already pissing her off. "You look good in that."

She'd forgotten she was half-naked and barefoot in an outfit of his choosing.

"I came here to talk to you," he said.

"Some conversation," she said.

"Well," he said. "I figured you'd be a bit pissed at me, so I wanted you calmer."

That worked, she thought, but didn't say.

"I've been thinking about you ever since that wonderful night," he said. His grin was unfortunate. It was more accurate to call it a leer. "We work alone. We both know a lot about a lot of things, but not everything. And if we pool our resources, one of us could work for the Odolpho Corporation while the other one stole from it. Wouldn't that be fun?"

"Not as fun as this," she said, and shot him again.

He made her decision for her. In truth, it was a pretty simple one. She blew up his ship, after taking all the pertinent registry information, and reclaiming what few tangible items he had stolen from the Odolpho Corporation.

With that, she would collect the bounty on his ship. She only got bounties for obliterating things.

So she wasn't going to get a bounty for him, even though she would turn him over to Odolpho's security forces on the nearest starbase.

She wanted to steal from him instead.

She didn't strip him down. She left him fully clothed. She didn't even tie him up with plastic doodads, although she did seal off the simulation room. It would be impossible to leave without knowing the new passcodes and using some of her DNA, plus a retinal scan from the eyeball of an old pirate she kept around here for inspiration.

She let Rick the Robber Baron loose in the only simulation she had actually designed. It wasn't for her. It was for cowards who believed they understood how the human brain worked.

Usually they didn't.

And judging by the screams that punctuated the cockpit's sound system like good music, Rick had no idea what was happening to him.

He'd figure it out later.

When he realized he no longer had peace of mind.

In the first of our Ray Gun Revival *reprise stories, A.M. Stickel gives us the tale of recruits on a tough planet, earning their metal through grit and sheer willpower as they struggle to survive and conquer the alien world of Triple in...*

TO THE SHORES OF TRIPLE, LEE!

A.M. Stickel

"Aw-right, Defectives, fall in! Welcome to Camp Alpha. I'm Sergeant Lee... That's 'Sir' to the likes o' you greenies."

"Sir, yes Sir!" we sang out, hating Lee already with all that was in us.

Still groggy from our passage through the light gate, we raw recruits looked around, entranced by the stark wilderness. *Triple* was a planet aptly named, being only marginally larger than the furthest of its double-moon sister bodies. Both visible by day, they hung in the blue above almost close enough to crush us. Unofficially dubbed by us *Cue* and *Eight,* our scientists had named them *Primus* and *Secundus* in a language older than the game of pool.

After Lee finished putting us through pointless drills to check what he called our 'cellular reintegration', we got the "At ease, Troopers."

The red-and-brown striated rock where we'd made camp looked to me like saltwater taffy frozen in mid-pull. My buddy, Reston, said it reminded him of old chewing gum gone mad. But our relaxation was brief.

"Hor – USS! Guard duty."

I yessir'd Lee and quickly took up my position opposite Private Solberg's on the high rocks above the camp, becoming part of Triple's sculpted landscape in my red-brown camo.

Reston was assigned to dome-setup. After saluting Lee, he slouched off halfheartedly with the others and a mumbled, "See ya' later, Horse."

We did meet again a few Terran hours later in the chow line, where I intended to do right by my nickname. Private Wolfe, across the table from me, dug into her share and honored her own handle, ignoring Reston and I as we elbowed each other and winked. Finally, we just gave up and carried our trays outside into the warm sunshine.

"When do you think the Dryl and the E-Lur will join the party, Horse?"

"With the Dryl, you can count on their shamans making a big ceremonial hoo-ha first. The E-Lurians always consult their computers to make sure they have everything exact down to the last nano-dot. Both races worry more about losing face than we Terrans do. Nope, we'll always stake first claim because we don't wait for permission from the Great Invisible, or from some inanimate hunk of bio-metal either."

Reston chuckled and added, "N' we don't give a half-chort for face!"

Suddenly, we were in cool shadow. I flinched, expecting Lee to be there. But when I looked up, Wolfie stood over us wiping the gravy off her chin. "Horus, Reston, mind if I join you?"

Without waiting for a reply, she plunked her pretty behind on a nearby rock. "Ouch!" Her tail scorched, Wolfie was up again in an instant.

"We were going to warn you about that, but you were too fast for us," I said. "These rocks'd make this place too hot for E-Lurian comfort, and the Dryl are too superstitious to deal with two moons hanging around so close."

"I still think there'll be a fight," said Wolfie, crossing her arms. "Well, they'd better show up for the showdown before I get tired of the synth-grub."

Reston gave his wheezy laugh, and agreed in his own way. "They're going to try to save face, just like they always do. Then *we're* going to wipe some more of it off when they try."

Wolfie fanned herself, mopped her brow and took a swig from her canteen. "With a whole galaxy as our genetic swimming pool, we end up on the rim of the pool with two other humanoid races! What are the odds of that? Maybe there really is a Great Invisible."

31

I looked around and lowered my voice. "Don't let Lee hear you joking about it. Solberg told me Lee's grandma was Dryl. I think that's how he comes by calling us pureblood Terrans 'Defectives' like the Dryl do."

Reston held his sides and hee-hawed, "How about that – a *Dryl* Sergeant!"

And so Reston's big mouth got the three of us stuck on permanent latrine duty. Why? Because the next shadow over us *was* Lee.

The three of us made a great team. Between us, we worked out a way to rig our blasters in tandem so that they dug the latrines faster than our laser shovels had. We figured we might never see action, so why not make use of our weapons in a practical way.

Lee was proud of our ingenuity, meaning he was not as mad at us for wasting blaster power as we'd thought he'd be. He'd watched us sweating out our shift, showing up when we least expected, solemnly saluting and asking, "How's the Dryl-Team doing today?"

"Sir, fine Sir!" We never said anything to our comrades, too ashamed to admit to our private joke. And Lee honored our silence with his.

As day after day passed, under those mismatched moons, we saw no sign of our rivals in the humanoid race for territory. Sergeant Lee, though, took their absence as a purely temporary oversight. "It's not like you've seen in holo practice, Troops," he'd say. "When it happens, it really happens. War is blood, stinking guts, and frying flesh. The Dryl will freeze-ray you with cold ceremony, and the E-Lur will vaporize you with hot frag. After it's over, and they've found face, they'll parlay and exchange hostages. With them, the order is always: (1) shoot to kill, (2) talk it over, and (3) kiss and make up."

The day *they* came, latrine duty – and Lee – saved our lives. Many in the troop were caught out in the open. Lee was with us. "Get into the hole, NOW!"

He didn't have to repeat the order. The E-Lur and the Dryl, while they were strafing each other, just couldn't pass up the chance to catch us with our shields down. When the shields went up, we four found ourselves on the wrong side, and, literally, in deep doo-doo, but alive. The real fun of the fight for first rights to the world of Triple had begun.

Our refuge, fortunately, was one we'd blasted out that day and had only used ourselves. Wide enough for the larger two of us – Lee and I – to stand on the bottom, the latrine hole was deep enough for Wolfe and Reston to stand on our shoulders without head exposure. Surrounding blaster-hardened walls helped brace us, as artillery shocks rocked our world.

Trooper indoctrination had included the details of our rivals' torture methods. Dryl grilling called for chemical drugging; the E-Lur injected captives with nanites. Then they'd simply wait.

We Terrans reversed the strategy by letting the enemy waste their firepower against our impregnable shields. Said enemy tried hard not to damage property they were after so as not to alienate their taxpaying, procreating public. Since they did a lousy job of protecting the landscape for the proletariat, their governments were forced to call in Terrans to repair the damage and public sentiment. The fanatic Dryl and the ascetic E-Lur disliked cleaning up their own messes.

BRAK-AK-AK-AK-AK! POW! The sky glowed crimson.

After that close one, Reston was first to break our unspoken no-talk pact. "I think I'd rather be Dryl-drugged than stay down here much longer. Horse, I don't know how you guys can stand it where you are."

Wolfe and Reston had their arms around each other with her head on his chest. And here he had the gall to complain! I waited for a pause in the blast noise before I growled at Reston, "Sarge is meditating."

"Go ahead and climb out, Reston, if you're not anxious to celebrate your nineteenth birthday or see your buddies enjoy theirs." Lee always did look on the bright side for his solutions. I abetted him by gripping Reston on the shin above his right boot top and squeezing hard.

"Okay, okay, you guys. I'm sorry I said anything," Reston whined.

"I think I'm gonna barf," admitted Wolfe, shifting.

"You wouldn't want to do that to us, Wolfie," I said, reaching up and giving her leg a gentler squeeze than I had Reston's, adding, "Reston, give her one or two of them fizzy chews you always carry."

Pretty soon I heard crunching sounds and ungraciously blamed Wolfe. With a closer look, though, I realized that the crunching was marching feet. Too soon, the feet were poised on the brink of our prison. What I saw, before a bright light blinded me, made me wonder why I'd ever left my nannies in the crèche to become a soldier. It also convinced me how absurd the rumor was about Lee's grandma being Dryl.

While the rest of us stood gaping, wetting our pants and trying to shrink into them, Lee's blaster was out and fired. A terrible howl and a thud told me I'd heard my first Dryl join the Great Invisible... not any too soon for me.

The next thing I heard was my beloved sarge saving our lives for the third time: "Out! On the double! Head for the shield and don't look back."

We'd almost reached Camp Alpha's shield when Lee yelled, "Duck and roll, Troops!"

I heard the shrill blast of a whistle, and recognized it as the one Lee used to single out one of us for discipline. Only, this time, there was an answering echo from the shield, which forced us to cover our ears as we rolled *under* the wall.

Mama Hen Shield had just lifted her feathers for her chicks. We felt the electrical itch of the energy field brush across our bodies, and then heard the satisfying *splat* of those pursuers who had been a little too hot on our heels.

Catching our collective breaths, Reston, Wolfe and I finally found enough air for questions. Lee answered us patiently, one by one, in order. The troopers not monitoring the shield, or otherwise occupied, gathered around to hear what their sergeant had to say.

"Reston, the enemy troops couldn't follow us because they have the wrong biosignatures. A signal-addressed shield only recognizes Terrans."

"No, Wolfe, our Dryl discoverer, with nothing on but boots and a freeze blaster, wasn't the usual breed of warrior. All that bare, see-through skin signifies the suicidal warrior-priest caste. Yeah, the sight of internal organs was yucky, but the stink when they came out was worse, wasn't it?"

"Right, Horus, they were looking to take prisoners. They keep hoping to discover enough about our technology to even up the score with the E-Lur, and then breed enough Terrans for a homegrown slave population, so they don't have to pay for our clean-up work anymore."

Solberg's reedy voice piped up from the rear, "Why didn't you guys run for the shield in the first place?"

Lee narrowed his eyes and shook his head at the stupid question. "We had to wait until the strafing from above was over, and they had their own troops on the ground. You greenies still have a lot to learn."

I chimed in, "Would it make sense for them to risk hitting their holiest warriors with friendly fire, guys?"

"What about the E-Lur, then, Horse?" Solberg retorted, smirking. I could see he thought he'd put both Lee and I on the spot.

Lee winked at me and motioned for the group to follow him into the dome where the shield monitors were hard at work with their equipment. We were treated to a rare sight on the big overhead screen covering a huge section of our central dome. There sat the shiny, heavily-armored E-Lur ground troops, lounging among the rocks, watching and waiting for the Dryl to finish wearing their warriors out, before taking the offensive themselves.

Besides hating the heat, E-Lurians were used to much lower gravity. Despite their best efforts, they hadn't been able to design effective armor that protected them from both unusual heat and uncomfortable G-force. Our screen also showed the Dryl, unbothered by the heat, wasting most of their time gesticulating skyward in warding motions they thought protected them from the evil of *Cue* and *Eight*. Every now and then the sluggish E-Lur would rouse enough to vaporize a Dryl who came within range.

The dome show went on. After checking the bodies of those fallen in the initial onslaught, the Dryl freeze-rayed the dead Terrans, as if disappointed about not getting to us live ones, or to the safely armored E-Lur.

With a "Show's over!" Lee called everyone to order and assigned new tasks all around, saying, "From now on, for at least awhile, your biggest enemy is going to be boredom, unless you keep busy."

The Dryl and E-Lur had moved their fight to Terran Camp Beta, a short distance from us, on open, sandy ground. Having learned our lesson, Alpha kept her guard up while our shield techs worked on shifting the field to cover the new latrine we'd dug. It also gave them a chance to vent the area under the shield, preventing toxic buildup.

"Horus, I want you and Reston to help the botanist expand our camp's greenhouse. That way we won't have to shift the shield so often. The well we're over seems like it can support some pretty decent hydroponics."

"Sir, yes Sir!" I saluted and went to work immediately. I knew Wolfe had been reassigned to the nanite-detection squad, and trusted in her ability to prove that our area remained relatively uncontaminated.

Arriving at the greenhouse dome, I encountered Reston, who took me aside. "Camp Beta's in trouble. They got careless, and some mean nanites crept into their fresh food supply; they had to vaporize the greenhouse, slag some latrines, and go back on synth-grub. Still, a whole bunch of them had to be light-gated to emergency quarantine facilities."

"Looks like one or more of us will be making some fresh-food runs to Beta. Who do you think Sarge will pick, Reston?"

Reston shifted uneasily, "You don't hear me volunteering, especially after I peed in my pants out there under the boots of a see-through warrior."

I put my hand on his shoulder. "We all did, good buddy. Let's put our bad scene behind us and tackle the hydroponics maze, okay?"

We set to work, both of us quiet and preoccupied. I hoped the E-Lur would realize that contaminating Triple for us Terrans and their Dryl rivals meant they were only making more messes for their colonists – if they won – which the colonists would probably pay us to clean up, as usual. I wasn't as worried about the present hexes and future taboos the Dryl would inflict. They only affected the Dryl faithful, not infidels like us.

The hydroponics worked almost too well, and we produced a bumper crop. So Lee decided to let two of us pair off. Only eight were committed enough. I wanted to continue missions out in the galaxy, as did most of the troops. Four couples put their names in the helmet, two to a card. Wolfe and Reston won. The next drawing was for two fresh-food runners. Lee and I won that one.

Although everyone else was surprised Lee'd put his name in, I wasn't. I was also relieved not to be making the run with a chort like Solberg.

Thanks to the nearby moons, night on Triple was almost as bright as day, but Lee and I did have good camo, and shared a miniature stealth generator. Although not impervious like a shield, the generator's field would dampen our heat signature, scent, and noise.

The night of Reston's and Wolfe's pair commitment ceremony, Lee and I set out for Beta Camp leading an anti-grav sledge loaded with delectable garden goodies. Instead of a honeymoon, the newlyweds were posted at the shield-interrupt site to guard our exit.

All was going according to plan as we left with our cheeks burning from Wolfie's kisses. I manhandled the sledge down-slope onto the sand. Lee kept an eye on both the multi-viewer and the nanite-detector. When he said, "Hot spot: veer!" and pointed, I jumped to it. I didn't want to end up in quarantine.

There's an old Terran war rhyme about a soldier returning home to his sweetheart, ending with: "Lips that touched nanites will never touch mine." I didn't want to find out the full implications of the old verse, but suspected it had a lot to do with almost all Space Corps offspring being brought up in crèches. Corps couples rarely lived long enough to reproduce, let alone spend any time with their kids. I hoped Reston and Wolfe could beat the odds.

We were relieved to find everything calm outside Beta's shield. They knew we were coming, but neither the E-Lur nor the Dryl did. A low dune hid the Dryl transport, although the call to prayer was being broadcast loudly from it. The faithful wanted to find favor with the Great Invisible. Between the E-Lur encampment and Camp Beta, a sacrifice had been staked out to appease the moon demons. E-Lur braves, not busy recharging their armor like the rest, were having fun turning the sand around the Dryl female to glass. Some were making obscene gestures. (We *had* learned about those before being light-gated.) From the sound of her, she wasn't going to go down easy.

"She's screaming, 'Curse you, unbelievers!' and other things not meant to be translated for tender ears like yours," said Lee. Lee twiddled the control on the viewer and grunted in dismay. "We've got a problem."

"Sir, I already know you have to whistle us under Mama Shield Beta."

"We've got more than one mama here, Trooper."

"Let me have a look." Sure enough, the viewer was focused on the naked sacrifice's glassy belly, and it showed movement of a tiny body within.

"That's barbaric. Why would they sacrifice her?" I gasped.

"We'll find out after we rescue her."

"Just how are we supposed to accomplish such a rescue?"

"Greenie, leave that to me." Then he blew the whistle. When the shield went up high enough, we dumped everything out of the sledge, and he called to the surprised faces within, "Sorry we can't stay to chat. Enjoy the chow. We gotta run along now." The shield slammed down.

The next thing I knew, we were in the center of the makeshift sacrificial grounds ready to load up the struggling Dryl lovely and thereby convince unbelievers of her Great Invisible's omnipotence.

Lee proved remarkably fluent in Dryl-speak, and finally succeeded in calming down the would-be sacrifice. Realizing we wouldn't turn her over to the nonexistent mercy of her own kind, she agreed to come along peacefully, sworn on both her honor and by her Divine Protector to behave.

Arriving back at Camp Alpha, Lee whistled up the wall and went in alone, leaving me with the transparent lady. I tried not to stare, but she eyed me boldly as if she could see *my* insides. Shame for the prejudices most recently acquired from my time in the hole made me blush. Compared to me, she was brave, even if for the wrong reason.

Finally, Mama Alpha blanked her shields for our prisoner long enough for me to hustle her inside. She seemed to enjoy riding on the sledge. We brought out a translation unit so that the Dryl-speak could be turned into Terran for the curious troops. She answered our questions as patiently as had Lee.

"You've asked who I am. I was a warrior princess of the Dryl until I was given to an E-Lur prince as an experiment in peacemaking. No, our names are not important. More important is that, despite our differences, we found love. The child I carry is our child. Dryl science made him possible. Most E-Lurians, however, still refuse to be one with the Dryl. Those Dryl who feel the same killed my child's father. I heard the call of the Great Invisible to join my prince. Even though this night I escaped, I have lost the will to live. If you choose to save my child by providing a host mother, then you might yet accomplish what his father and I have failed to do. Have you a candidate?"

Wolfie came forward and put her hand on the princess's shoulder. She didn't need to say anything. They just looked at each other and nodded. Reston followed his bride, for once not twitching nervously, but standing tall and proud.

Lee motioned to one of several anxious medics. "Medic, prepare three for light gating," he ordered.

"Sir, yes Sir!" said the medic, helping the Dryl princess from the sledge.

She gazed at us, one by one, as she was led away, saving me for last. I felt a ripple of understanding sweep through me that needed no translation.

Later, when I asked Lee about his familiarity with the Dryl language, he winked and answered, "Why not ask my grandma some day?"

I stood at attention and saluted him, singing the song he most loved to hear, "Sir, yes Sir!"

And that, Your Majesty, is how you came to be raised in the crèche like me, and why I was chosen to take you to visit your other two home worlds, since now you're of age. Seems like only yesterday I was eighteen, myself. Inside, I still feel eighteen. I think High Commander Lee does, too.

Next, Texas resident and 2013 Sidewise Award nominee Lou Antonelli takes us down to West Texas in a story with a retro feel wherein two characters get taken for a ride – in outer space – and wind up getting far more than they bargained for aboard...

THE SILVER DOLLAR SAUCER

Lou Antonelli

Chance McMurphy and Cisco McAtee would have been hanged from the nearest tree – if there had been one between Sanderson and the Mexican border.

They had robbed the Fort Davis stage just outside the West Texas town. It wouldn't have been so bad, but there was an undercover Pinkerton man on board who decided to act like a hero.

They had originally planned to head to Laredo after the robbery – where they had accomplices who would help them dispose of their saddlebags full of Double Eagles.

After leaving the detective dead in the dust, their plans changed. They made straight for Mexico. "Things are fixin' to get real hot real fast," said Chance as they spurred their horses due south. "Let's get to the damn border first," he added, "and worry about where we're going later."Cisco just nodded.

By nightfall, they made it to some rocks on the edge of the desert, halfway to the border in the foothills of the Davis Mountains.

They bedded down with no campfire, in case they were followed. For dinner, they chewed on some jerky.

The pink quartz outcropping cooled quickly after sunset, and they slept fitfully in the cold.

Cisco sat up when he saw the glow on the horizon.

"Thank God," he muttered. The sun was coming up, and they'd get some warmth.

Chance opened his eyes and then jumped up. "Jesus, that glow's in the south!"

Cisco scrambled out of his sleeping kit. Chance was right.

They both scrambled to the highest part of the rocks. Sure enough, just over a rise in the desert, there was a yellow glow.

Now the pair had both worked as scouts during the Indian Wars, and – in a decision they were later to supremely regret – they decided to see what was making that glow. It might be the campfire of a posse on their trail.

Chance let Cisco take the lead as the smaller and more nimble of the pair. After skulking, and then crouching, and then crawling, Cisco pulled himself up to a clump of buffalo grass and propped himself up on his elbows. He looked over the sand dune.

Chance heard Cisco suck in his breath like he had been punched in the gut.

Cisco flopped over and then rolled a few times before scrambling to his feet and heading in the opposite direction in a spray of sand.

Chance had been prone ten feet behind him. He jumped up and chased his colleague, but couldn't catch him until he stumbled over a rock.

"What the hell's got into you?" he hissed.

"Demons, demons." Cisco almost sobbed. "There's demons down there."

Chance would have thought Cisco had gone loco, but he could see the terror in his eyes.

Both men then noticed the glow behind them was growing brighter. Chance turned to look without letting go of Cisco's collar.

The glow went from yellowish to bright white, and then, in the glare, they saw some kind of craft come up out of the hollow and swoop over the dunes towards them.

Chance let go of Cisco and pulled out both his six guns. He began to shoot at whatever was coming at them.

Cisco turned and ran like a rabbit as Chance unloaded. He heard a sound like a rising wind, as whatever it was reached Chance – who let out with a loud grunt followed by a dull thud.

In a moment, whatever it was reached him, and he passed out in a white haze.

When he woke up, Chance realized he was in a pungent and dark room. He looked over towards a door. Light was coming from beneath a curtain. He sniffed the air a few times and recognized the unmistakable stench of his companion – the ever-present aroma of bacon, tobacco, and sweat. Cisco lay asleep on some kind of low platform across the room.

Chance tried to prop himself up on an elbow, but he ached all over and his muscles were unstrung. He thoughtfully scratched the yellow stubble on his chin. "I'm as weak as a kitten," he murmured to himself.

Cisco grunted.

"Cisco! Hey, Cis!" Chance hissed. "Come to!" Cisco uttered a few moans and his eyes opened.

Chance called out to him again, and Cisco turned his head.

"Are we in Hell?" asked Cisco.

"Not unless Hell's got fleas and shit," said Chance, wrinkling his nose. "I think we've been shanghaied."

"Serves us right," moaned Cisco.

"Anything beats dancing at the end of a rope," said Chance. "How do you feel?"

"Like I've been rode hard and put up wet," said Cisco. "I don't think I can move a toe in my boot."

The curtain in the doorway was pulled back. Chance winced as the sunlight fell on his face.

"I see my new friends are beginning to revive." A six-foot tall man who also happened to be six feet wide waddled into the room. He was carrying a water jug and basin in one hand, and a basket with fruit in the other. Towels were draped over one arm; the other was bare up to the elbow and displayed dark blue tattoos that would have made a cannibal proud.

He shambled over to Chance and placed the basket of fruit on a low wicker table. He placed the basin and jug by Cisco. "I know my fellow humans are still too weak to arise or eat yet, but you will soon regain your strength," he said. "I'll leave these here for now."

Chance winced at being called a human. It didn't sound right. The large man continued. "My name is Tor. I'm outside if you need anything." He turned and began to shamble off.

Chance cleared his dry throat. "Hey, hombre, what are we in for?"

Tor half-turned and knitted his brow as he thought a second before answering. "You're in for being in the wrong place at the wrong time," he said with a sly smile. He continued out and the curtain flapped behind him.

"Guess so," said Chance, looking over at Cisco.

The light was dim from beneath the curtain in the doorway by the time Chance felt strong enough to swing his legs over the edge of the platform and take a few steps.

Cisco sat against the far wall. "You okay, Chance?" he called out quietly.

"I reckon." Chance reached down and grabbed a fruit from the basket. It was a red pear-like fruit, and he devoured it in three bites.

"Damn, that's good!" He went over to where Cisco lay and drank from the pitcher.

Cisco was shifting around, so Chance helped him sit up.

Cisco shook his head to clear the cobwebs. "I wonder what happened to our bags?"

"Whoever bushwhacked us must have took them," said Chance. "I reckon we need to lay low for a while. We're lucky to be alive."

Tor came through the door, an oil lamp in hand. He smiled at the desperadoes. "Good evening, my friends. Your timing is impeccable. I was just closing up my shop."

Chance realized – by the baskets and pots and various items that lined the walls of the room – that Tor was some kind of merchant. "What kind of business are you in, mister?"

Tor smiled widely, showing a disconcerting array of peg-like teeth. "Oh, I just help outfit some of the traders who pass through."

Cisco hopped off his platform. "On the way to Nevada?" Thousands of people had been heading to the Comstock Lode.

Tor chuckled in a way that didn't reassure either man. He didn't answer, but held the curtain in the doorway aside. The delicious smell of roasting meat began to waft through. "May I invite you to dinner?" He gestured, and the two Texans walked outside.

It was obvious they were in some kind of bazaar. Flickering lights and dark shadows were scattered among a myriad of shops and stalls. Both Chance and Cisco saw meat roasting in a simple clay pit.

Tor gestured for them to sit on some rough benches. He waddled over to the fire and then brought back two wooden skewers with sizzling meat. He held them out with both hands.

Each man grabbed one and began to eat.

"No charge for the meal. These were your animals. I'm sorry they didn't survive the trip."

Cisco swallowed hard while Chance stopped chewing and spit out his mouthful. "These were our horses?"

"Yes, well, the traders wouldn't waste any care on pack animals. They died during deceleration at the end of the trip."

Chance didn't understand that, but he focused on one thing. "Trip. Trip to where?"

"To here, of course." Tor waved a skewer as he pointed skyward. The pair looked up.

45

Cisco looked up until he fell back and off his bench. Chance just stared, pop-eyed. They had no way of knowing the planet where they sat was closer to the center of the galaxy than Earth, so its sky was much fuller with stars. The spectacular tapestry of lights – along with its trio of irregularly-shaped moons – left the two Texans speechless for some time.

Cisco was still lying on his back when Chance finally spoke up. "Where are we?" he asked in a voice he hadn't used since Sunday School twenty years earlier.

Tor laid his hands on his belly in a rather self-satisfied way. "This world is called Ymilas. It's just another ball in the sky – much like Earth."

Cisco's voice came from beneath them. "We *have* been shanghaied!"

Tor staggered to his feet and looked down at the supine stage robber. "Yes, and to another world completely!" he said with a wide grin, then sat back down. "Earth is not on the official star charts any more; Terrans once sailed to the stars, but their empire fell after a great war and their society collapsed. Earth is formally off-limits – but there are brigands and traders who stop there for supplies and provisions.

"You call them angels or demons." He smiled again. "They're just people from other worlds. You came upon a group of traders extracting silicon from the sand. They needed to repair the shielding of their antimatter drive."

Chance looked at Tor with a totally puzzled expression.

"They set themselves down in a most desolate place," continued Tor, "but you still found them."

"We were on the run ourselves," said Cisco weakly as he began to pick himself up.

"That was simple enough for the traders to deduce," said Tor. "Why else would you be so far away from any settlements – and carrying such a large amount of metallic gold?"

Chance began to speak, but Tor held up a chubby hand to stop him.

"They took your gold, of course," he said. "But they felt it would be unfair to kill you after receiving such a bounty. So they sedated you and tossed both yourselves and your animals into their hold."

At the mention of the animals, Cisco – who was now back on his bench – looked over woefully towards the fire pit before looking back at Chance, who just shrugged back.

"Very well," said Chance. "Why are we here, with you?"

"The traders simply dropped you off at their next stop, which happened to be here in Ymilas, and offered you for sale to whoever happened to be interested. I was."

Both men's eyes got large. "We're slaves now?" asked Chance.

"Yes, you are." Tor rose and tapped Chance on the shoulder as he shambled over to the fire pit. "But I assure you I'm a kindly master. I'm grateful to have some human workers. That's why I bought you."

He sat back down and began to gnaw on another skewer of roast horseflesh. "As you can see, I am human. My ancestors were a people called Hebrews. They were slaves, also, but were granted their freedom. They were on their way back to their homeland when – like you – they unfortunately stumbled on some star traders in the desert and were all taken captive."

"My God, the Lost Tribes of Israel," sputtered Chance.

"Yes, exactly. It's nice to know they haven't been forgotten," said Tor.

"How do we get back home?" asked Cisco.

"You don't," said Tor. "If my people haven't made it back in over 3,000 years, you two certainly won't." He waved a hand in front of his face to indicate the subject was closed, and he rose.

Chance and Cisco looked at each other as Tor went back into the shop. Chance gave a little shrug and began to gnaw again on his skewer.

Cisco went over to the fire pit and picked up a fresh skewer. He began to nibble and looked hard at Chance.

Chance nodded. "Don't worry," he said. "I'm thinking."

Tor's accommodations for the pair were grimy but comfortable. Cisco made Chance laugh when he reminded them of the room they slept in one night over a cantina in Agua Punte.

"This is a whole lot better!" Chance agreed.

It was just after sunrise the next day when Tor showed them their duties at his shop. The Ymilan souk quickly filled with hundreds of traders representing dozens of species.

"It's a vision of hell," muttered Cisco.

"At least we're alive," said Chance.

"When do we bolt?" asked Cisco.

Chance looked at his old friend in amazement. "Bolt? To where?"

Chance nodded towards Tor. "Just do what the fat man says, keep your mouth shut and your bowels open, and we may figger something out – later."

Cisco looked around meekly. He knew Chance was right.

As it turned out, they quickly made themselves very handy around Tor's shop. The work was simple, and Tor was happy to have some human help.

He didn't have to think twice when he gave them commands. He'd had slaves before of all different species. For example, he said, he once had an assistant that was a member of an insectoid race, the Kammerer. If you asked it to pick up something, it would stand there confused until you indicated whether it was to use a limb, antenna, or tail.

Tor gradually opened up with the pair. He explained his girth was a result of growing up on a world twice the size of Earth, with the resulting gravity. He had come to Ymilas as the manager of a caravanserai for a native trade Lord – a post that, unfortunately, required he become a eunuch.

When the trade route was attacked and taken over, and his Lord killed, he escaped and found his way to the nearest crossroads – which happened to be a Ymilan city called Bardoth.

There, with the small amount of money he had carried with him, he bought the rundown shop.

All the trading in the souk was done in bullion coins. One day, while the trio were eating of midday meal – which consisted of some Terran-style wine washed down with the last of the dried horse meat – Chance noticed a trader walking through the souk shuffling shiny coins in both hands.

"I reckon," Chance said to Tor and Cisco as he looked towards the trader, "the fellow's that got our gold made quite a killing."

"Not quite as good as you would imagine," said Tor, who took a swig of the strong red wine before he continued. "Gold is certainly valuable, but it's not our most precious metal."

Cisco looked at Chance. He knew he was up to something.

Tor grunted and nodded. "There are some Earth metals that are quite valuable here. Tin is one. And Argentum is very, very valuable."

"Argentum?" asked Chance, scratching behind an ear.

"Yes, though I think where you come from, they call it silver."

Tor rose and went over to grab another piece of horse jerky from a basket on the rough wooden table. "It's an excellent conductor of electricity, plus it's very malleable."

He took a bite as he looked at Chance. "The native Ymilans also find any metal that takes a high shine very desirable. One of their religions is to worship their sun, and they feel any metal that reflects sunlight so well will bring great luck and prosperity to the bearer."

Tor smacked his hands loose of the crumbs of meat. It was time to get back to work.

That night Cisco tossed a loud "pssst!" in Chance's direction.

"Cis? What you want?" he answered in the dark.

"What was all that talk today about valuable metals?"

"When you got here, did you have any money in your trousers?"

"Heck no, I was wearing denims with no pockets. What's that got to do with anything?"

"I had a pocketful of change – a buck and seventy-five cents. I still have it."

"What are you planning to do with a buck seventy-five?"

"I think I got more than a buck seventy-five. Remember, Tor said silver is the most valuable metal on this world. I have three silver pieces – a silver dollar, half dollar and quarter dollar.

He heard Cisco grunt. "Still, what could you buy with that?"

Chance rolled over. "We'll see."

As he had said at first, Tor was a kindly master. He often gave the pair time to explore Bardoth. Humans weren't uncommon on Ymilas – a number of traders and shopkeepers were descendants of Lost Hebrews and Atlantean space colonists.

One day, when they had some extra time off, Chance took them in a direction they had never been before. Cisco didn't even ask where they were going, but just followed Chance through the jostling crowd.

After a while, the crowds thinned. They were on the outskirts of the city. Both the stall and the goods grew larger.

Chance stopped in front of a lot with a crude metal fence. Inside were a half dozen metal contraptions of all different designs and sizes.

A trader came forward, and Chance pointed to a shiny machine that was perhaps 50 feet wide. It looked like a plump discus.

Cisco looked at the machine. He had seen many strange things in the time they had been on Ymilas, but he had never seen anything like that.

Cisco saw Chance make the universally recognized gesture that said he wanted to bargain.

The Ymilan began to shout and wave his hands. Cisco could see the Ymilan wave four of his six fingers.

Chance went after it in good form – he'd picked up a lot of the Ymilan trading lingo in a half year. He held up a single digit.

Cisco smiled because it was the middle finger he was waving – a meaningless gesture on Ymilas.

After maybe five minutes of shouting and waving, the Ymilan was waving three digits. Chance was still shouting but eventually went up to two fingers.

The shouting went on for a while longer, and then suddenly the Ymilan spat in his palm and rushed over to Chance, who struck the palm with his fist.

Chance gave the Ymilan the silver dollar. The Ymilan made a gesture of thanks. Chance then handed over the half-dollar. The Ymilan gave thanks again.

Chance waved at Cisco, who been hanging back watching the proceedings.

"What the hell is going on?" Cisco asked.

"We just got us a ride home," said Chance.

"Huh?"

Chance walked over to the saucer-shaped craft and pushed on a panel. A door flipped upwards.

Chance stuck his head inside, and a moment later Cisco crowded next to him.

"This here's a kind of lifeboat, and it happens to come from Earth," said Chance. "It's left over from the great Atlantis."

"I've been snooping around, and I found out about this thing." he continued. "It was in storage and still runs, but it's only good for a one-way trip back to Earth – I guess because it's a rescue boat."

"You bought this with the money you had?"

"Hell yeah, silver's so valuable here. And there's not many people interested in a one-way trip back to a Earth." He smiled as he looked around the interior. "Except us."

"What about Tor?"

"Tor will never know. We're leaving now."

"Huh?"

"Is there anything you need to take with you?"

Cisco ran his fingers through his curly dark hair. "Guess not."

There was a braying sound, and the pair looked to see an eight-legged draft animal advancing toward the craft. A dwarf tied a rope to the saucer and began to tow it away.

"The fellow who sold me the ship is towing it to where we can launch it."

"Wait, how do we run the thing?"

"It's a rescue ship, its clockwork is designed to take you back to Earth on its own, once you set the gears spinning."

The pair trudged along. "I bought the ship with the dollar," said Chance. "And the half-dollar paid for the fuel – whatever kind of coal it burns.

Once the ship was in the middle of an empty field, the dwarf untied the rope, and walked around to the opposite side of the craft, where he punched a matter/antimatter pod into a tube.

He gave a human OK sign to the pair and left riding the eight-legged beast.

"Ready to go, pardner?"

"Chance, old bud, I'm more than ready."

Chance had scouted the saucer beforehand, so he was familiar with its interior and basic controls. The pair reclined as they snapped on all the buckles and clamps. Chance pulled a lever that closed the hatch and then showed Cisco a plunger that activated the homing device.

Once the hatch was closed, the interior smelled musty. "I hope this wagon holds together," muttered Cisco as he looked around. "If it came from Atlantis, it's pretty old."

"Cis, I don't want to grow old and die here. I want to go home – or die trying. What about you?"

Cisco thought real hard, and nodded.

"Ready?"

Cisco nodded again.

Chance pushed the red plunger.

Outside, the anti-grav buffer hummed into action. The saucer rose one hundred feet above the field before the atmospheric jets kicked in and it shot upwards at a sharp angle.

Tor was just taking a bracing swig of some late afternoon red wine, as he looked up to see the jet plume over Bardoth.

A street urchin who earned his living as a spy and informant ran and quickly told him what had transpired. Tor kicked a bench and cursed as he reached into a pouch and tossed a small coin into the bastard's dirty paw.

Chance and Cisco were clutching the armrests, unaccustomed as they were to the G's, as they rose through the atmosphere. As the FTL drive kicked on, the suspended animation system activated. Both men fell asleep as beta waves filled the cabin.

🔫

"Chance? Chance?"

Cisco was looking across to his companion.

"I'm OK." He rubbed his forehead. "I guess we've been out for a while."

After the saucer's FTL drive kicked off, a gas had entered the interior to revive them.

Chance looked over at Cisco. "I guess we're still alive. You smell horrible."

Cisco chuckled. "You don't smell like French perfume yourself."

"I hope that this thing's clockwork has been running while we were asleep," said Chance. "Let's get a look." He undid his straps and clamps and was startled as he drifted up towards the low ceiling. "Air must be pretty thin," he said. "I'm just floating around."

He grabbed the wall and dragged himself over to a small window. "Cis, come over and look at this!"

Cisco undid himself and pulled himself over to the window. Down below, a large hazy ball hung on a black background.

Cisco was stunned. "Oh, God, that must be what the Earth looks like from the heavens!"

"Yes, and it's getting bigger, so we must be heading towards it," said Chance. "This damn thing worked."

53

Neither man knew that because of the time dilation effect, it was thirty years later on the world beneath them than it had been when they left. Most of the people they had known were dead.

As the bright blue ball grew larger, they could see the continents passing below.

"I reckon if this thing can sail us in, we'll be on the ground soon," said Chance.

Cisco pointed. "Look! Down there! There's home!"

They could see the Gulf of Mexico and Texas below them.

Suddenly, a loud warning sound began coming through a speaker, and a message in a language neither man could read flashed on a panel. If they could have read it, they would have seen it said: "Automatic Reentry System Failure. Assume manual controls."

After nearly 10,000 years, something was bound to have broken down.

Cisco looked at Chance, who pushed himself back and floated to the control panel. Rows of red and blue lights were flashing.

"Dammit, this can't be good," he snarled.

Cisco's eyes grew large as flames begin to shoot around the edges of the window. They looked at each other as the interior quickly began to heat up.

"Pardner, this may be the end of the trail," said Chance.

Cisco kept his eyes on the window and looked at the turning globe below. Texas disappeared in the distance as the saucer continued its trajectory. "At least we made it home," he said quietly as the growing flames obscured the window. "We made it home."

Vasily Vasilyev was sucking some bitter tea through a sugar cube and waiting for his latkes to warm on the cast iron stove.

The sky was bright and blue this Siberian morning. His wife Nadia had stepped outside to hang a few small rugs out to air.

He was looking at her through the small panes of the kitchen window, when he saw her point upwards.

He went to the window and saw a large fireball descending from the sky. There was an enormous flash, and the fireball exploded.

Nadia ran back quickly to the cabin. Vasily grabbed her and pulled her towards the front room. The cabin shook as the concussion hit and the windows blew out. They were thrown to the floor.

After a moment, Vasily raised his head. He then stood up, brushing off his clothes. He went over to the front door, which was still banging on its hinges. He walked into the front yard and saw plumes of smoke flying upwards in the distance.

Nadia joined him on the steps. "My God, Vasily, what happened?"

"It looks like a meteor struck Tunguska."

They both heard a sound like a pebble hitting their cabin. Vasily turned and listened, as whatever had struck the cabin rolled down the steep tin roof.

He went over to where something shiny lay under the eaves. He poked at it a moment, and then blew on it as he picked it up. He fingered it gingerly as he walked back to his wife.

"What is it?"

He squinted at the shiny piece of metal and then looked back to the smoke on the horizon. "It's a silver American twenty-five cent piece," he said. "I wonder how to God it got here?"

Returning to new originals, Baen author Sarah A. Hoyt takes us next on a breathless, nonstop thrill ride of a story in which a woman narrowly survives a terrorist attack only to find herself hunted as an enemy of the state, all because she was in the wrong place, or was she?

AROUND THE BEND

Sarah A. Hoyt

When the door exploded, he landed on top of me, taking me down with him, covering me with his body. He was too large, and smelled of sweat and alcohol. I had a vague impression of a muscled male, of red hair, of fast breathing, of controlled strength. Then I realized he was taking his weight on his elbows, as the heat wave shot over us, followed by a gentle rain of ceramite fragments. He whispered, "Steady, steady."

I registered that he had a burner out and was pointing it in the direction of the exploding door.

It was a large burner, and he looked like he knew how to use it. And I realized that a lifetime of longing for adventure doesn't prepare you to face it. I wiggled to get out from under the stranger and had just started to say, "Please – " the first part of a civil plea to be let go, when my mind added up what I'd just seen.

The door of The Babel had burst inward, a flowering of fire, noise, and explosive force. There had been a sound with it, a boom and a roar. People around me screamed and dived for cover. And the large, muscular male body over me protected me from a shower of burning ceramite fragments and a pattering of pieces of door and wall and tables.

I took short breaths and coughed from the acrid smoke. To my right, someone sobbed. Before this, the most exciting thing that had happened at The Babel, a hangout for translators attached to the diplomatic corps in Peace III, was the time the automatic drink dispensers on the tables had shot mineral water clear to the ceiling.

There were sounds from the door, and screams from the patrons hiding under tables or crouching by the wall. Several men in black dimatough suits marched in.

I counted four of them, with maybe the shadow of a fifth one behind them, which was surely overkill. Dimatough battle suits, covering head to toe, are made of small scales of impenetrable material joined together so that they're flexible but impregnable. You can't kill a man in a dimatough suit unless you're very good or very lucky. The suits are also so expensive that the only people able to afford them are potentates and millionaires, and, of course, Earth's diplomatic guards.

None of these should have any interest in The Babel, and if they did, they should know they didn't need armored suits to face translators, right?

I didn't think all this very coherently. It came in a jumble of surprise and shock, and then the men were saying, "Come forward with your hands in full view. We apologize for the inconvenience. If you have done nothing, rest assured you have nothing to fear."

The man atop of me said a word. It sounded like Valhallian, and not the sort of thing they teach in school. Then he bent down and whispered in my ear. "I'm going to get out the back," and rolled off me.

People were starting to get up and walk towards the men in dimatough, hands held high.

The men still held weapons on the people. There were three men and two women whose most aggressive act ever had been to translate an adjective a little too strongly. And men in full armor were holding huge combat burners pointed at them. My stomach clenched. There was something wrong. I couldn't say what, but it was seriously wrong, whatever it was. These men had made the door explode. They'd caused unwonted damage to get in here. Why should I trust them now?

The man who'd protected me with his body was crawling fast, silently, along where the shadow was deepest, right where wall and floor met.

I followed, thanking any god that might be listening for my decision to wear black that morning. Around and around, and we came to a door. He half rose, and applied the burner to it in a way that made almost no sound and no more than a flicker of light. A look over his shoulder, as if to make sure the goons were fully occupied with the now ten people surrendering to them, and he applied his shoulder to open the door.

So I followed the tall man at a fast trot around a curving dark portion of the hallway, and then through a door he first opened partially, and then down a dark corridor to –

There was a man in front of the dark door, a barely shining silhouette against the dark, his black armor suit glistening. He said "Halt," and lifted his weapon – nothing more than a shadow in the dark – but before he could fire, my companion fired.

I'd heard that dimatough armor was impervious to all but military grade weapons, so I was surprised. The guard toppled and crashed on the floor by the time the light of the burner ray faded. My companion looked over his shoulder, as though to see if anyone had heard the crash, then stooped to grab the weapon, in a smooth motion, as he opened the door and went through it into the night.

I followed. Outside, the alley smelled of the overflowing dumpster a few paces away, and my rescuer turned halfway around and looked at me with narrowed eyes. I kept both hands in full sight, but registered that he was wearing the blue tunic and dark blue pants of a Bender, that he had the circle on the left of the breast indicating he had piloted solo, and the star in it indicating he had done so for ten years. Also that he had the sort of blunt, square features that owed nothing to beauty and yet somehow added to a pleasing – and strong – whole, and that his eyes were some light color. His very short hair was red.

I'd guess he was Valhallian, from the misbegotten colony seeded a few centuries ago by Norse fundamentalists, which – scarcity of land

and infighting and all – had never managed to progress much beyond feudalism, divided into subsistence farmers and the Lords who both protected and controlled them.

Valhalla was responsible for providing Earth with most of its Benders – which was what everyone called Schrödinger pilots, who merged with the computer to move the ships through space, and sometimes, accidentally or not, through time, instantly. A happy genetic chance. Or unhappy, for Valhalla, who routinely sold their younger sons into lethal indenture in order to keep the family fed.

When I'd come to Earth, mother had told me to stay away from Benders. And ever since I'd been on Earth, I'd learned Valhallians were the worst of Benders. If you heard a story of a brawl on the news, half of those involved would be Valhallian Benders.

Perhaps it was the fatalism that, at least to my casual acquaintance with their religion, permeated their beliefs. Perhaps it was the fact that Luf, the drug they took to allow human brain and computer to interact, usually killed them before thirty. Or perhaps there was something wrong with Benders, and Valhallian Benders most of all. But they seemed to go to hell faster than anyone else, and with more gusto, leaving behind a trail of murder, mayhem, illegitimate children, and squandered wealth.

It was trouble little Ruth Serra didn't need. Which, of course, is why I stood rooted to the spot, blinking at him.

At first, I thought he'd growled at me, and then I realized he had said, with a strong Valhallian accent, "You should go now."

I remained rooted, and the ugly-attractive features opened in an odd smile, which seemed to transform them into something devastatingly handsome. It was like most people smiled with their mouths only, but he smiled wholeheartedly.

"I see," he said. He looked around, rapidly. "If you go down that way," he pointed behind the dumpster at a narrow, smelly alley, "I don't think they'll think of it, or think to follow you. I'm going to run that way. You go on. I'll draw their attention. They'll come after me."

"They'll kill you," I said. I'd had time to process the fully armored guard defending that door.

He hesitated. It was just a moment. "It won't matter much, love," he said, very softly. The *love* sounded odd. Not like he meant it. Not like he was in love with me, but as though he were, suddenly, not a man my age, late twenties or thereabouts, but a much older man speaking to me like a young and innocent child. "Five years more or five years less. It won't make much difference. Luf will do me in anyway."

"No," I said. Mostly in reaction to his tone. "Come with me and I – "

"Will get caught for sure. I probably will, too, but there's a chance..." He frowned suddenly, and for a moment, I was afraid he was angry, but then he shook his head. "No, tell you what. Would you do something for me? Something very small?"

I nodded. He put his hand forward. For a moment there was warmth, and something small and hard was pressed into my palm. "You have a better chance of escaping. Better chance of not being noticed. If you get out of this, take that to Lenard Kavara. He'll know what to do. And now, I will go. You start down there at the same time. They'll never see you or think of you once they catch sight of me."

I started down the alley as I heard him pelt towards the main street where the entrance to The Babel was.

By the time I reached the end of the alley and turned into another alley, I could hear shouts from the street in the other direction, and the sound of burners. The Babel was isolated enough – the only establishment facing that street and the waterfront – that I didn't think anyone would hear.

Then there came a sound of an explosion that made the ground shake, and I ran faster, madly, blindly, until the network of alleys littered with refuse and dumpsters ended, and I found myself in a well-lit street where well-dressed couples strolled along the edge of a well-tended public park.

I was so tired by then that I stopped running, and leaned on the nearest building, blinking at the lights, at the couples. It took me five breaths before

I recognized the park facing me as the park of Interplanetary Harmony, three blocks from my little rented apartment.

And by the time I reached my apartment, really a largish room all of four hundred square feet, equipped with a rudimentary cooker and an even more Spartan fresher, I'd started to suspect I'd dreamed it all.

The illusion lasted until I turned the lights on, and flipped on the streaming holonews. A hologram formed of Raddy Rondel, the – I suspected simulated – news star, a blond man built as well as the Valhallian. Raddy looked sad, as he described the terrible explosion at The Babel, which had killed everyone there. The station streamed the names of the supposed dead underneath, near the groin of Raddy Rondel's tight pants. I blinked as my name appeared, and Madrasta, my world of origin.

There was only one Valhallian. His name was Glenn Braxladden. I remembered his smile in the alley, and wondered if it was true that he was dead by now. What had happened there? Had the explosion been accidental? Had it really killed everyone there? Other than Glenn, all the names appeared to be those of translators, my colleagues. Glenn was the only element that didn't fit in, the only one who might have been there for some reason other than to unwind after work. There were no names that might have belonged to those men in black armor. Their presence was not reported.

I felt something, not quite fear, something that couldn't even be articulated into words. I'd always hated the idea of conspiracies, the idea that it was somehow possible for a small group of people to control the course of history. Oh, I'd heard the normal talk about how the government of the thirty worlds, which took up most of Earth, was an evil entity. They said the space-worlds were little more than slave colonies, having to do what the mother planet said or be starved of power, of the ability to travel, of everything but the barest survival. There were even rumors about Daice, and how Earth had funded the revolution there.

I didn't buy it. I worked all day, every day, translating talk between one planet and the other, trying to get them to agree on how much to buy, what to sell, what tariffs to pay. From my vantage point, the government of the thirty worlds was not an evil entity packed with masterminds, but a lot of worlds each trying to negotiate to its advantage, while a common deliberative body, presided over, of course, by the Representative, deployed what military power was needed to keep us from space war. We'd never had one, and we'd never have one, because only Earth had Benders, only Earth had Schrödingers, and should the worlds wish to fight each other, Earth wouldn't lend them ships.

Which was why there had always been peace in space, even if some planets had been known to send terrorists to Earth.

But now –

Now I wasn't so sure. Of course, the men who'd invaded The Babel might very well be terrorists from another world. On the other hand –

On the other hand, why weren't the news stations, controlled by the government of Earth, reporting the attack yet?

Surely someone would have seen men in dimatough armor. And even if not, surely the way The Babel looked would not resemble, in any way, the explosion caused by a malfunctioning of the server mechanism? I couldn't even imagine how the server malfunctioning could cause the destruction of the whole café.

And then I realized I was still holding, pressed so tightly in my hand that it was becoming a part of it, whatever Glenn Braxladden had given me. It felt like a ring.

I opened my hand and confirmed that it was a ring, small, black, made of ceramite, the kind of prize that you can get out of any machine, in any cheap food mart all through Peace III, possibly all through Earth. It will set you back ten bits, and appeal to the very young and very broke.

A token of his esteem? I remembered the name he'd told me. Lenard Kavara. Not a female name, of course, but a Valhallian name. And the only surprising thing, given the lives most Benders lived, was not that it was a male name, but that Glenn would think it necessary to send a token of his esteem to one individual and not to a group of his nearest and dearest five hundred people, and maybe the occasional plant, say all with whom he'd been intimate in the last month.

It didn't fit. Like the feeling I'd got at that list of dead, the feeling of this was wrong. It was like being immersed in the ocean, off my native village, and feeling something move and rumble so far away that you were guessing at it, more than sensing it with any accuracy. If you were a born Madrastan and experienced enough, you got out of the way fast, because those tremors – suspected, more than felt – were the intimation of an approaching tsunami. You ran all the way to the secure tower in the middle of the village.

Now I had that same feeling of impending tsunami, but I wasn't sure there was anywhere safe. Legally, I was dead. Which meant, since they couldn't have pulled my corpse from the ruins, and identified my DNA, that someone had known I was in there. They'd known everyone who was in there. And they'd –

My mind shied away from the idea that everyone who had been there had been killed. But I was running out of any other explanation. I was also, probably, running out of time. After all, any minute now, someone would notice that my account for the holonews was still active.

No, that's crazy thinking. No one is watching, not one –

I slipped the ring on my thumb. If I was already in trouble, no one would notice a little more trouble. I punched the name Lenard Kavara into the system and waited. In seconds, I had a floating note telling me that the account had been terminated, because Schrödinger Pilot Kavara was dead.

I closed my eyes. I counted to ten. And then I moved rapidly. I didn't run. I didn't panic. Or rather, it was impossible for me to panic. I'd gone beyond panic to a sort of warbling madness, where some part of my mind was stuck saying *oh no, oh no, oh no.* But behind it, beyond it, was my rational mind, which had seen me, a girl from a fisherman's village in cursed Madrasta, all the way through the training in languages in the capital, and then all the way to training in diplomacy on Earth, and then –

Here. And no longer sure that the government I'd worked for for so long was what I'd thought it was. In fact, almost sure it wasn't.

There were some things I owned with inherent value. A golden locket my father had given me when I'd left the village. It was real gold, and gold remained rare and prized across the universe. Two hand-carved coral rings, also from my village. A dealer had offered me fifteen stellar for it not so far back. Handmade objects from the colony were rare. They had to be transported to Earth as someone's prized possession, since they counted against your weight allowance on the ship. And very few people got rid of their prized possessions. But the time might have come. Oh, the time might have come.

I put the locket in my pocket, and slipped the other rings on my fingers, around the one Glenn Braxladen had given me. I resented not having anything resembling a weapon, beyond the little knife I used for all sorts of domestic tasks. But I slipped that into my pocket, also. Then I added to it all the cash money I had – crystal gems coded with the account but with no name – the sort of money you used for vending machines that dispensed things like that ring. I didn't have much. A hundred bits and a stellar. I never kept much on hand, except for a sudden desire for a drink or something that I could only get from the machines after the human-staffed or at least human-watched establishments had closed.

Then I hesitated for a moment. If I were not being spied on and traced; if my being declared dead was an accident, then there was nothing for me to worry about. If I left my apartment like this, nothing would happen to it. Nothing would happen to me. In a day or so, when I stopped panicking, I could come back and find my place undisturbed, and point to the authorities they'd made a small mistake. I'd be reinstated among the living, and I'd go on living, right?

But if I were right... If I were right, it was possible that right now, if they suspected I hadn't died, they'd be on their way here, weapons at the ready.

I opened my front door and felt completely stupid looking both ways down the hallway. There was no one in sight. There were two grav wells on the floor, and then there were two stairways – one at each end of the building and not to be used in anything but emergencies. Then power failed to the grav wells. I was twenty floors up.

But suppose the armored toughs who'd taken out The Babble decided to come here? Which way would they come? The wells were surely too public. But how did I know there would be armored toughs? Surely to take out a woman, alone, there need be only one well-armed man. Actually, he wouldn't need armor. He wouldn't even need to be very good at his job, I thought, rather ruefully.

And then my back brain made a decision for me. I ran to the door to the stairway, and, instead of going down, I ran upward, one flight of stairs, two.

I was half up the second flight when the explosion came, rocking the building. I knew – don't ask me how, but I did – it had come from my erstwhile apartment. It was followed by cries and screams, and noises of surprise from the neighbors, but before those, lost in the after-echoes of the explosion, there was the sound of a door opening and closing almost soundlessly – the door to the stairway.

And I was moving. Walking down the stairs. I can honestly say that if there were rational thought behind it, I wasn't aware of it. There was just the idea that someone had tried to kill me, someone had destroyed my home, someone was on the stairway of my building, thinking they'd eliminated me, ready to report my demise.

It was a man, I saw as I rounded the turn in the stairway, smaller than I and pale-blond, and looking perfectly normal in street clothes – a somewhat over-tight pair of green pants, and a waist-cinched jacket in pale blue – but he moved too assuredly down those stairs. One flight, two. No one ever used those for more than a flight, and even then, most people preferred the safety of the public grav wells. But what if he was an innocent bystander? My hand dove into my pocket and gripped the knife.

And then all doubt was removed. He couldn't have heard me. He truly couldn't have heard me. And yet he did. He turned around. There was a small, dangerous-looking burner in his hand, and when he saw me, he registered both surprise and annoyance.

Not rage. Not hatred. Annoyance. Like someone confronted with yet another task to perform, when they thought their work was all done.

I ducked, instinctively, and the burner ray flew over my head. Then I was falling, rather than jumping at him, my hand outstretched, with the knife in it, a wordless scream at the back of my throat.

I'd never fought. Not for real. But in the village, in the old days, I'd learned the mock knife-fight that was the dance of peasant boys. Until mother had found out I was doing it and had forbid me. After all, I was neither a boy nor – she said – a peasant. Mind you, it would have taken a really well trained eye to discern the difference between me, the daughter of a regional export accountant, and the fisher brats grubbing on the sand. Except maybe the brats ate better.

Now, somehow, the movements of the dance came back to me. I was too close for the stranger to aim, or perhaps too fast. He tried to hit me on the side of the head with his fist clenched around the burner, but he failed as I sidestepped and ducked, and came back from a half-crouch with the knife in my hand. The blade entered his chest with surprisingly little resistance. Blood spurted out and on me, but I was grabbing the burner from his suddenly-lax hand, and running, running down the steps as fast as I could, pausing between floors for a breath, and then running again.

As I ran down, past my floor, the sounds of commotion diminished, I heard the sirens of rescue vehicles, but they were landing on the terrace of the roof, and I ran down, and down.

It was very quiet at the bottom of the building. I smelled of blood, and there was blood on my hands. I must get clean. And then, I must think what to do.

A public fresher down the block, which I unlocked with two bits, revealed to me that the blood had hit my face and my hair but had somehow managed to miss my clothes, the same black suit I'd been wearing in The Babel. Or perhaps the black hid the blood well. I used a private compartment to wash my face and hands and paid three bits to vibro my clothes in the pay-vibro. I smelled of sweat and fear, but the little fresher didn't accommodate anything like a shower. I washed as best I could with the water of the little sink. I stared at my too-pale face, my disheveled hair in the mirror above the sink and swallowed. Had I killed a man? Had I truly done something like that? It was different when you read about it in books.

But I had no time to think about it too much. I would not let myself think about it. After all, he'd tried to kill me. It seemed like rationalization. It was rationalization, but it was reason, too.

He'd tried to kill me.

I was so tired. I wanted to sleep. My feet felt like they were on fire. But I couldn't sleep. Nowhere would be safe. They'd find the remains of my would-be assassin soon, and if they didn't know, they'd suspect who I was.

Where could I go? Where had Lenard Kavara lived? Who was likely to know him? Who was likely to be able to help me? Surely the full might of dimatough-armored men, the full might of assassins, the power of Earth's government hadn't been deployed merely to get rid of one isolated man. No. Even if Glenn Braxladen was the man they wanted to destroy, there must be others in the... conspiracy?

Having made sure I was clean, I left the fresher, and watched behind me to make sure I left no footprints. If I were my pursuers, what direction would I least expect me to walk in? Why, the way I'd come. I crossed the street, but retraced my steps back, towards my building. Then I dove into an alley and navigated by memory to where I knew there was a public hollo machine. Two bits pushed into the slot bought me ten minutes' time, probably more than I needed. I brought up city directory and punched Lenard Kavara's name again. This time, I half expected it would blink up with "address unlisted" or perhaps with the death notice again. Instead, it brought up an address on the other side of the park, in a neighborhood thick with Benders.

Made sense. I couldn't erase the public hollo, of course, and I couldn't be sure they didn't have a track on Lenard Kavara's name, but the city directory wasn't a very smart system, and it was almost mechanical in its dumb simplicity.

Just in case, though, I looked for three other names in succession, none of them names of people that were in the Babble, or people in any way connected to me or, if I was lucky, to Glenn Braxladden.

And then I took to the back alleys again.

I won't describe the erratic path I took, partly because I couldn't. And I won't describe how tired I was, because back then I felt I was in a sort of sleep-walking nightmare, too tired to be awake, and still trudging on.

When I reached the park of Interplanetary Harmony, the temptation proved too strong. I walked deep into the park, and crawled under a bush. Never had a bed felt more inviting than the mulch under that bush, around a tree. I curled on it and fell asleep.

I half expected to wake up to full daylight, or perhaps to the sniffling of servos on my trail. I did neither. I woke up two hours later, cold and cramped. My feet were still on fire, my legs were still tired, but I felt less like I was walking in a dream. More in control.

I crept out of my hideout, crossed the park, and on the other side, in the warren of streets taken up with hastily built high-rises for the Benders, I traced the address of Lenard Kavara. I had the vague idea of going to the nearest place run by a human: café or bar or cluster of machines watched by a clerk, and asking about Lenard Kavara, and who his friends and contacts might be.

I might have done it, too, and likely come to grief over it.

But instead, as I walked from an alley into the street where Kavara lived, I heard someone behind me, and turned.

"You!" I think Braxladden and I said, at the same time. And then, "But you're dead," in perfect unison.

He smiled. He lowered the burner he'd been holding pointed at me, and I lowered the burner I hadn't realized I was holding on him.

"You escaped," I said.

"So did you," he said. "I thought you were gone. I thought it was gone. I heard that – I wasn't sure what name was yours. I thought – But then I heard of the explosion in the apartment of a Madrastan translator... and I thought..." He shook his head. "I thought I'd better check here, in case you'd got to Lenard, and that got him the ring, before – " He shook his head again. He was holstering his burner.

I slipped my stolen weapon into my pocket. "I guess," he said, "That Lenard really is dead?"

"I don't know," I said. "I – I don't know. I almost was. Who is after us?"

Glenn shrugged. "I'd guess the Earth government."

"But... why?"

"It would take too long to explain." The amazingly transforming grin again. "But I will. If we survive."

"We?" I said, and then, "Do you want your ring back?"

He shook his head. "No. Come. You. Come. If they find us, I fight them off, and you escape, with the ring. If you can't find anyone else to give it to, remember three taverns: the Pipe, The Sunburnst and the Manitou. One of them will still be standing hopefully. If not, then all it's gone, and the ring is useless. Or at least, it will never reach Valhalla."

"But," I asked, as he started to move with purpose. "What is the ring and where are we going?"

"I'll tell you what the ring is when we're off Earth and headed for Valhalla. If you're captured, it's best you don't know."

"But – "

"Trust me."

With people following me, trying to kill me, trusting this man might be mad, but after all, he'd saved my life, and he didn't have to.

While he took me on a circuitous route that I realized was taking us towards the field where the Schrödingers were kept, I asked, "Why did you save my life?"

He shrugged. "You were nice looking. And you looked completely harmless." Something twinkled in his eyes. "I guess you aren't, or you'd be long dead."

I don't know how long it took us to get to the Schrödinger field. There were Schrödinger ships of all sizes and shapes, from message ships, small and fleet, able to leave and enter the atmosphere of every world in record time, to large freighters, which either had to negotiate for landing rights, or would end up being emptied in orbit. For a moment it shocked me that there was no guard in sight. But why would there be? The only way to even enter the Schrödingers was to be gen coded to do so, to have your genetics inscribed as a trusted user into their locks. The exterior was impervious to any attack, being made of dimatough, which could survive the void of space.

As for a rogue Bender stealing a ship – unless he stole Luff, too, he would be locked out of the computer's mind, and no more able capable of piloting the Schodinger than of flying unassisted by flapping his arms. Technically, the Schrödingers could transport the ship and passengers, unassisted between different coordinates of space and time unassisted. But the problem was that, on their own, the computers didn't understand what the coordinates meant and were as likely to take you between here and now instantly as between here, now, and then two thousand years go. It had resulted in a lot of accidentally seeded colonies, and a lot more of missing shiploads of cargo and passengers before, two hundred years ago, the system of having the computer have a bonded pilot had been developed.

But the Benders needed Luff. And giving yourself Luff – even if it could be found outside the carefully controlled confines of space authority – without careful medical supervision was just a complex way of committing suicide.

I realized Glenn had done something to the door of a nearby Schrödinger, one of the little couriers, which had sprung open, and was climbing aboard. He offered me his hand.

"But – " I said. And then "Luff."

He grinned at me, looking conspiratorial. "Come."

I realized I was with a madman, likely to kill himself by taking Luff on his own, or worse – better? – to get us lost in the immensity of space.

Glenn closed the door after me. "Don't look so horrified," he said. "I don't think this is theft. At least, the alarms won't sound. Someone forgot to erase my gencode from the door. Or maybe they really thought they killed me. Sheer good luck."

He had already sat behind the controls and motioned me to the passenger seat as he strapped down.

I strapped down myself, shoulder-and-chest harness. He checked them with one outstretched hand before his hands danced on the controls.

"Luff," I said.

"Trust me," he said. "Orbit first."

He got us to orbit smoothly. He had, if that insignia in his uniform didn't lie, done this for ten years after all.

Once we were in orbit, the alarms started, and I said "Won't they shoot us down?"

"Not if we don't give them time," he said. "Would you give me the ring?"

I handed it to him, wondering what a little ceramite ring would do in this situation. Then I thought of all the time I'd spent running that day, of everything I'd done. Being shot out of the sky seemed a relatively clean way to go, and I regretted only that I'd never told my parents goodbye. I'd left so many years ago, in a bid to become what no one in my village had ever been – someone who helped interplanetary peace. It was all I could do not to laugh now. Particularly because it wasn't even remotely funny.

Glenn had removed a panel in the controls, and was fitting the ring carefully into place. "My aunt who is a research scientist," he said, "told me this ring would connect... I can't explain, but it would make a Schrödinger able to connect to the pilot, even if the pilot wasn't on Luff. You know Earth has kept the monopoly on travel by keeping the formula to Luff secret and killing anyone who produces it unauthorized."

"If everyone could fly, there would be interplanetary wars," I said. And then I realized what I'd said and opened my mouth to unsay it, but Glenn nodded.

"I used to think that, too. It's been a long time since I believed it. It's more, then only Earth can have interplanetary wars." Glenn paused, gave me a quick look. "My aunt's only son, my cousin Reehat, died in the Daicean revolution."

"Oh," I said.

I supposed he meant Earth really had financed that, but he only said, "Yeah, *oh*. She devoted her life to studying – Never mind." He shrugged again. "I was supposed to pass the ring on to someone who would take it aboard a freighter to Valhalla. I guess it's too late for that now. I never meant to become a Guinea pig."

"What do you mean?" I said, though I knew very well what.

He pulled down a helmet that I'd thought until then was part of the seat. It fell over his head so only the lower half of his face remained visible: the square jaw with the shadow of a red beard, the firmly set lips. The lips opened and he said, "I mean, if this doesn't work at all, and we're lucky, we'll end up a thousand years in the past, still on Earth orbit, manage to land and become one of those fabled UFOs, just before we vanish into the population of the time, to live like savages."

"Is that likely?" I asked.

"No. We're far more likely to end up a thousand years ago, in the middle of space, light years from anywhere."

And with those cheerful words, his lips sat again. His hand reached forward and touched a button, and then –

I expected something: a tremor, a spasm. But he didn't move at all, except for seeming to relax bonelessly in the pilot chair.

We... blinked. The landscape outside the windows, the lights of Earth below, flickered.

And then we were – elsewhere. For a moment, I thought we'd really gone back a thousand years, to a far less brightly lit world.

And then Glenn lifted his hand and pushed back the helmet.

He looked at the panel, he looked outside, he punched a program into the pilot, and we started flying, slowly, down from orbit.

"Did it work?" I asked.

"What?" Of course. "That," he said, "is Valhalla. Of course, you might not recognize it, because we're on the other side from the spaceport. I am trying to keep us from being spotted as anything but local traffic."

I refrained from telling him I wouldn't have recognized Valhalla from any angle, and instead, looking at him, realized from the way his face had relaxed that he was more relieved than he'd ever admitted. "It worked, then?" I asked.

He nodded. "Yes. And in Valhalla, we'll replicate it. Our people will be able to pilot Schrödingers for anyone, or for themselves. And there will be no more Luff to kill us young."

I took a deep breath. "I'm glad," I said. "I'm glad." Even though I knew this meant I was out of a job. "I'm glad the adventure had a happy ending."

He grinned as the Schrödinger glided over a land of forests and rivers. He put out his hand and touched my fingers, just the lightest touch of his warm feelings. "The adventure," he said, "is just beginning."

Next Michael S. Roberts take us into battle aboard the HDS battle cruiser Himalaya *as they encounter a dreaded sixty-year-old enemy ship known as the* Sword of Saladin, *a ship and crew right out of legends and stories but one with very real bite, they discover, as they confront her in...*

SWORD OF SALADIN

Michael S. Roberts

House Del Sol battlecruiser *Himalaya*. Somewhere out there...

"Captain on the bridge!"

"As you were. Report." Lady Eyla Melana dropped into *Himalaya*'s command chair and threw one leg casually over the armrest.

"Bogey, skipper." That was Commander Henderson, her executive officer. "Large metallic mass, warship outline, capitol ship." He checked the sensor board. "No emissions, faint thermal signature. Optic profile strongly suggests..." Henderson showed mild surprise, "...the Alliance dreadnought *Sword of Saladin*."

"Has she pinged us yet?" Eyla asked. Henderson shook his head in the negative. Eyla glanced at her yeoman. "Coffee, please. New Tahitian." Back to Henderson. "Put it on the big screen. And maintain emission control. We run silent."

"Aye, skipper, full emcon."

"Comms." Eyla looked to the communications station, Chief Miller. "Signal *Evans* and *Cossack* the same. Tight-beam wave, no leakage."

"Aye, skipper," Miller chuckled. "We hates leakage, we does. *Ernest Evans*, this is *Himalaya*..."

Eyla surveyed her bridge crew. On sensors, Henderson, taking over from a junior petty officer, probably working on her space warfare specialist pin. On weapons, Master Chief Simons, a lethal fire-controlman, recently back from instructor duty on Delta Pavonis. Shields, Warrant Officer al-Harad, already running system checks on her array. Helm, Ensign Arturo, fresh from Academy but top of his class. Communications, Chief Miller, now deep in meditation over his passive receivers after hailing the two escorting destroyers. Damage control, Senior Chief Trond, a Dobermensch, his black fur bristling as he snarled into his throatmike. Petty officers manned the secondary positions. Behind her, Command Master Chief Tira Kaulaia, ready to fix any and all problems, a brilliant Chief-of-the-Boat.

"Very well." Eyla relaxed, accepted the delicate porcelain cup, and sipped black coffee. "We listen, we watch, and we prepare for trouble."

Sword of Saladin was House Faisal, a rival House sixty years ago, a rival House still.

Minutes earlier, Eyla had been luxuriating in a tropical shower, a privilege of rank seldom enjoyed. She'd come up from the enlisted ranks and remembered. Officers had it easy.

Eyla was indulging in pleasant reminiscences, studying her extensive tattoos in the holographic rainforest's water-mirror: Pan-Pacifican style, most of them Tahitian or Samoan, some Mauri. One for sailing mastery, one for celestial navigation, an intricate textured pattern for mastery of the bone-breaking art *kapua-lua*, another for tantric adept. Then there were the modern ones: Terran shellback, for crossing Earth's equator under sail. Centauran shellback, for the same on Alpha Centaur. *Kensai*-kanji, for mastery of the Japanese *katana*, albeit on New Tahiti. And lastly, a few that were done on a whim, but accomplishments nevertheless. Grey mortarboard, for graduating Academy at age thirty-two, ten years older than the rest of the cadets. Stylized fist, memoir of a Tough Sheila bare-knuckle win in Australia. Grinning cartoon bull-head with rolling eyes, a memento for swallowing five pounds of beef in a tramside bar-and-grille in the Barony of Texas.

The most important ones of all, though, ran from the nape of her neck to the small of her back. Six infant handprints, each ringed with fine scrollwork of six names and dates. Her children.

She had just rinsed her hair when the call piped in. "Captain. Unknown contact."

Eyla reviewed her memory, recalling the *Sword of Saladin*. The greatest single loss of life in the First Elkay War, or so most presumed. She'd been surrounded and cut off from her screening vessels, savagely pounded by the alien warships. The flagship of House Faisal had fought well, crippling a dozen Elkay ships-of-the-line, but in the end she'd been severely damaged and overwhelmed. Her captain initiated hyperdrive in mid-battle, an emergency jump to get clear of the fight. Witnesses reported that the Elkay concentrated fire on her drive core just as the jump field came up; they wanted to pin her in place, prevent the jump, and kill one of the Solar Alliance's largest and most powerful warships.

She jumped.

No-one knew where, or even if the jump was completed at all. Some philosopher-engineers suggested that she was trapped between hyperspace and realspace, half-jumped, a ghost. Regardless, she was lost, nearly six decades ago, when Eyla was still in diapers.

And yet here she was.

"Weapons," Eyla addressed Simons, "I want all of her weapons targeted and locked optically. If she gets froggy, I want her slapped down hard."

"Roger that, skipper." Simons grinned. "I've got the headwork done, just waiting for your command. Recommend we open with missiles, full particle- and plasma-battery barrage while the birds are in flight."

"Agreed. Set it up, but optical targeting only." Eyla returned his grin. "My command, you paint that beast with lasers and refine the targeting solutions."

"Aye, skipper. Paint with targeting lasers on your command only."

"Very well." Eyla folded her feet beneath her, lazy-lotus style, and sipped New Tahitian Gold. Taste of home.

Home. New Tahiti. Alpha Centauri. A ring of islands in an otherwise kilometer-deep sea, remnant of an ancient asteroid strike, emerald-green in an indigo sea. Home to her House and family.

Eyla skimmed the waves on the three-meter catamaran, clipping a daredevil fourteen knots. Her shoulders and backside brushed the surface of the water, a pleasant sting-slap and tingle as she balanced the tiny boat's wind load with her body weight, its translucent sail stretched even tighter than Eyla's tendons. She was already picturing her flashy finish to the high-speed sail run, cutting towards the white beach on a starboard reach, gauging the waves' height and timing, running the little cat up onto the beach on a breaking wave. Relaxed stroll onto the sand wearing nothing but goggles and UV-resistant gel.

Waiting on the beach, she knew, would be an icy piña colada, a hammock stretched between a Terran royal palm and a Centauran feathertop, and a handsome young architect named Paul.

Eyla found her wave and turned toward shore, maintaining speed, finding her rhythm, spotting him on the beach holding two drinks aloft.

"Captain."

Eyla blinked, taste-memories of coconut-rum and architect fading. It was Henderson on the sensors. "She's ranging us, targeting lasers and fire-control radar."

"Al-Harad. Raise shields." She turned her head to Simons. "Weapons. Light her up, get a solid skin-paint, hold fire. Warm up the birds. Bring main batteries, secondaries, and point-defense to full power."

"Aye, skipper," the master chief sneer-snarled. "Fangs out."

"Shields are up, captain," from al-Harad. "Angled for optimal deflection on the main threat vector."

Eyla relaxed; al-Harad knew more about shield work than the Spartans.

The warrant officer glanced at the main display. "*Ernest Evans* and *Cossack* are shields hot as well." A second glance. "As is the bogey. A lot of gaps, though. Her shields are in bad shape."

"Very well. Simons, adjust targeting solutions for shield gaps." Eyla shifted her attention to her throat mike. "CAG. I want our Ready-one fighters out now. The rest on BARCAP ASAP." Acronyms abound, she thought: Commander Air Group, Barrier Combat Air Patrol – anachronisms, but traditional – and of course As Soon As Possible.

"Roger, skipper," Commander Kisugi's voice buzzed in her earbud. "Launching two Typhoons now-now-now, crewing the Ready-fives, scrambling all ASAP." Eyla pictured his familiar arched eyebrow as he asked, "Elkay birds for dinner?"

"Nope." She watched the main screen as two Typhoons appeared from the ventral catapults, powerful, all-purpose, space-superiority fighters. "Unknowns, used to be semi-friendlies. Do not engage unless fired upon. Primary mission is recon and forward observer."

"Roger." Kisugi clicked off. Eyla trusted him to run the fighter battle if it came.

Eyla loved the Typhoons. It had taken some serious wrangling to get into flight school, even with her status as a minor House noble. But her command master chief had mastered the ancient art of military bureaucracy, and the proper paperwork was flawlessly filled out. She chose the argument that as captain of a battlecruiser carrying four squadrons of Typhoons she should know their capabilities intimately, and that had sealed the deal. Not only flight school, but *the* flight school, the Erich Hartmann Fighter Academy in Germanaustria. The best instructors in the entire Solar Alliance.

Eyla finished fifth in her class of twenty at what used to be traditional retirement age, even managing to score a kill on Instructor Kisugi in a two-on-two dogfight. When she returned to duty as a Fleet line officer, Kisugi came with her.

"They're firing." Al-Harad made minute adjustments to the shield array. "She's weak, but two main turrets are still up. Massive railguns, but I can block most of it."

"Simons." Eyla shifted forward, steepling fingers at her chin. "Fry 'em. Helm, begin a six-degree-per-second roll to starboard, unmask our batteries in sequence."

"Six per sec delta vee, aye, skipper." Arturo brushed the large trackball, setting the battlecruiser into a slow roll. The main screen showed *Ernest Evans* and *Cossack* moving to flank the massive hulk.

"Lettin' the birds off the chain, skipper," Simons growled. "Hawks away. Copperheads away. Foxes away. Reloading caissons. Five seconds to time-on-target strike. Switching to main guns."

"Get the range, then fire for effect."

Lighting flickered and steadied. Holographic display showed a shield penetration and hull strike. Eyla flicked her eyes to Trond. "Damage control."

"Damage reports, captain." Trond's ears were perked forward in concentration, his muzzle thin-lipped. "Minor overloads on some shields, near burn-through on decks six and seven, frames eighty and eighty-one portside, but didn't penetrate, no casualties. Hull is intact."

"Hit!" Simons crowed. "First salvo very effective, her shields are down-down-down, solid hits on the two big turrets. Hawks punched six decks deep, Copperheads followed 'em right in. Foxes cooked what shields they had. Continuing broadsides, targeting secondaries."

Himalaya rolled, unmasking main and secondary energy weapons in sequence, pounding the massive old giant. The battlecruiser would have been no match for a modern dreadnought at full strength, but *Himalaya* was the latest generation of warship, and *Sword of Saladin* was past her prime. A grizzled, grey dragon nursing ancient, unhealed wounds.

Saladin sat immobile, firing obsolete missiles and very accurate – if weak now – beams of charged ions, plasma, and lasers. Even with six times the tonnage of *Himalaya,* she was outclassed. Al-Harad concentrated on her defensive displays, angling and strengthening shields to deflect or absorb the incoming fire. Shields shifted as the ship rolled, spreading the power load and preventing overheat and shutdown.

"Captain, we're being hailed – " from Miller.

"Captain, they're launching fighters – " from Kisugi.

"Captain, their volleys are pretty much done – " from Simons.

"Miller, open a visual channel. CAG, get high six fix on their birds and hound 'em. Simons, hold fire." Eyla focused on the tactical display, peripheral vision taking in the optical and laserpaint image of *Sword of Saladin.* "All right, my friend. You want to parley, let's parley. Miller, you got that channel open?"

The man in *Saladin's* command chair was ancient, a glowering, bearded grandfather. His youngest bridge officer looked to be at least eighty years old. He spoke sternly in a guttural tongue, showing only a hint of surprise in his weathered eyes.

"Miller," Eyla spoke sideways, keeping her eyes on the old man. "Get someone up here that speaks Arabic. Or Farsi."

"Beg pardon, Captain," al-Harad said quietly. "I speak both." The warrant officer was a dissident from Brunei who'd applied for asylum at the House Del Sol embassy in Indo-Malaya back in her mid-teens.

"Very well. Miller, belay my last. What did he just say, Warrant?"

"He sends greetings to the captain's concubine and asks when the captain himself will be back on the bridge."

Simons choked back a laugh, cut his eyes and a finger questioningly toward the main battery controls.

Eyla gave an infinitesimal shake of her head. Simons feigned disappointment. "Tell him *this*. That I am Lady Eyla Melana, captain of the House Del Sol battlecruiser *Himalaya*. *Tell* him that we see he is in dire need of rescue, and that we are here to render assistance to his crew, and to salvage his disabled vessel."

Al-Harad translated. The old man listened, then snarled out a short response.

"He says he is Prince-Admiral Falad of House Faisal, captain of the *Sword of Saladin*, and he does not require a woman's assistance."

"*Tell* him," Eyla's eyes hardened, "*Saladin* opened fire without warning or parley, an act of war if I wish to report it as such, and that I will claim her as a prize if necessary. Alliance Admiralty Law still applies." She waited for the exchange.

"He answers..." al-Harad looked mildly uncomfortable. "He impolitely suggests that you have intercourse with yourself."

"Tell him that when I am comfortably seated in *Saladin*'s command chair with a mug of fermented grape, I will be doing exactly that." She turned to the communication console. "Miller, as soon as she's done, cut comms. Don't wait for a response." Eyla snapped her fingers. "Well. The mystery of the *Sword of Saladin* is solved. We take her as prize."

Saladin launched a total of seven squadrons of antiquated Saracen fighter-bombers. Outnumbered almost two to one, Kisugi's four squadrons of state-of-the-art space-superiority Typhoons slashed through the formations, scattering and destroying the ancient warbirds and their equally ancient pilots. A few of them had kept their skills and reflexes, Kisugi noted, but *Saladin* might as well have pushed Japanese Zeros out of the hangar.

On board *Himalaya*, the bridge crew watched the holo-display and listened.

"Red Queen lead to Werewolf lead – send a wing in low, gut-shoot that advance element."

"Roger."

"Queen Seven, you've got one on your six – never mind. Good shooting, Palmer."

"Three bandits down, gauss overheated. Switching to missiles." Palmer replied from Cougar Eight. "Bandit down. Debris damage, clipped my starboard autocannon."

"Break off and assess."

"Roger."

"Bandit down."

"That's five! I'm an ace! I'm an ace!"

"Cool your jets, Cougar Eight. Break off and take barrier position. And calm down. Plenty here for everybody."

"Cougar Eight, Cougar Eight! You've got five – make that six – on your tail. Accelerate and break left."

"Cougar Eight is hit. Palmer! Eject!"

"She's gone. No bailout pod! Repeat, no bailout!"

"This is Cougar Lead. Waste 'em. *Himalaya*, we've lost Cougar Eight. Ensign Palmer."

Eyla pictured Ensign Savanna Palmer, Cougar Eight. Fresh from flight school, gone from rookie to ace to corpsicle within five minutes in the rolling furball. They'd raise a glass to her tonight.

"Bandit down."

"Hammer Two here, I'm skosh for ammo, breaking off."

"Bandit down."

"I'm hit. Main cannon's fried, otherwise good to go."

"Break away and provide cover as you can."

"Roger."

"Bandit down."

"I have no targets! I have no targets!"

"No targets here."

"Confirm that. *Himalaya*, you see any bad guys out here?"

"This is Henderson. Negative. Clear space."

"This is the captain. Get the damaged birds home, expend remaining missiles on anything that looks like a functioning gun battery or missile rack. Do a sweep for Palmer to be *very* sure. Then put one squadron back out as BARCAP. They may have more fighters."

🔫

Colonel Sholmir stood at rigid attention in the captain's suite, muzzle held erect and tail tightly curled at the small of his back, proper procedure for a Dobermensch Marine officer. Eyla's chief-of-the-boat and yeoman maintained military bearing behind her desk.

"We board her." Eyla studied the Chinese porcelain coffee mug in her hands. "Take prisoners whenever possible, but we need to storm the bridge and get control. Your Marines up for that?"

"Of course, Captain," Sholmir marfed, focusing on enunciation. The Dobermensch were fierce, loyal, and lethal, but their *Canis Sapiens* vocal structure had problems with AmeroEnglish. "Full battalion for the assault, second battalion in reserve."

"Very good. Have your electronics guys hack the onboard systems ASAP, get better deck plans, personnel roster, all that. If we're lucky, they're still location-chipped."

"Of course, Captain. My troops are geared and briefed already." He maintained stiff military bearing. "Permission to speak?"

"Of course." Eyla sipped her coffee.

"These men may be osteoarthritic relics, or they may have sixty-plus years of fanatical practice and training."

"Assume worst-case, Colonel. They're dangerous as hell until proven otherwise."

"My question, ma'am..." Sholmir looked briefly embarrassed, as if he'd chewed the captain's sneakers. "Will you be joining us again on this one?"

🔫

"Captain on the bridge!"

"As you were. Helm. Match our ventral fighter bay with their forward dorsal." Eyla now wore the battle-dress fatigues of flat monochrystalline-weave black, Krupp-Arisaka blaster pistol on the hip – custom trigger and fast-acquisition combat sights courtesy of Hollands Gunsmiths of London – and the *katana*, forged and folded on New Tahiti by Master Swordsmith Maria Salamanca-Hirowashi. "Match drift vectors and lock us on."

"Roger that, skipper." Arturo hazarded a sly grin. "Mounting her and putting us on top."

"Colonel Sholmir." Eyla tapped the throatmike. "Heads-up your troopers. We breach at her hangar in five minutes."

Captain Melana strode into the *Sword of Saladin's* forward hangar deck, one hand on *katana* hilt, the other swinging freely. The Marines already had it secured, less than a minute after the plasma charges breached the armored bay doors. The firefight had been brief, and Sholmir's elite Marines had rapidly overrun the token geriatric resistance. Now they swept corridor-to-corridor and compartment-to-compartment. Twenty bearded prisoners and nine corpses were lined against the empty fighter bay. Four wounded Marines were already being tended. Engineers and technicians worked to electronically intrude into the old warship's computers and communications, hacking and data-mining.

"Report." Eyla focused on the young Marine officer in charge, two meters and a hundred kilos at the least. "Mister Sailele?"

"Aye, ma'am." The huge Samoan lieutenant snapped to attention. "Our casualties are light so far, but we have three dead. Theirs are heavier, at least thirty dead. We have over a thousand prisoners, most of them locked in storage bays and staterooms. The hackers just broke into the system a few minutes ago, so we've got control of the compartment seals. We've neutralized most of the resistance by locking them in."

"At ease, Sailele." Eyla squatted. "You're too tall. Take a knee." She adjusted the sword, moving it farther back on her belt.

"Thank you, ma'am." Lieutenant Sailele removed his visored helmet, used it as a stool. When he laid his plasma carbine on the deck, Eyla noted blood on the bayonet. "We've got pockets of resistance in the engineering spaces and at the bridge – Corporal!" Sailele hailed a corporal holding a portable holo-unit, now wired into one of the hangar datapanels. "Bring up the latest deckplans." The lieutenant pointed into the two-meter hologram when it appeared. "Fighting's been heaviest here... and here. That's the bridge. The colonel's there now. About ten holdouts, including that admiral, we think." Sailele focused on Eyla's face. "Most of these guys are pushovers, but a few of them can fight pretty well. Hand-to-hand, blades for the most part. We've only run across a few with blasters and slugthrowers. Mostly bayonet and knife work. They stick to the narrow corridors and restricted spaces, too close for webguns and stun grenades. Gotta dig 'em out."

"So they still hold the bridge." Eyla reached into the hologram, spreading her fingers to expand the bridge into greater detail.

The corporal tapped a control stud; Arabic sigils became AmeroEnglish.

"Let's assume they can override our override from there. Or initiate self-destruct if they're real jerks about it."

"Aye, ma'am. They're trying. Our guys keep changing security codes on them." Sailele peered into the datascroll at the edge of the hologram. "Also, we've got access to crew roster, damage control, pretty much everything. Looks like most of the crew is dead, either battle injuries sixty years ago or old age since then. They've been doling out anagathics to the senior officers and chiefs, keeping them healthy. Looks like they converted two of the fighter bays into hydroponics, too."

"You were reading the display before the translation." Eyla studied his face. "You know Arabic?"

"Yes, ma'am. Fifth and sixth form on New Tahiti before officer school."

"Very good." She stood. "Take me to the bridge."

"He says he'll detonate the onboard atomics." Colonel Sholmir listened carefully to the gunnery sergeant translating. "Says he has a deadman switch already activated, with a hidden cut-off."

The translator, Gunny Filitov, added, "He sounds serious."

Sholmir turned and half-bowed as Eyla approached. "Captain."

"Colonel." Eyla looked over the Marines covering the heavy blast door into the bridge. "Sit-rep?"

"There are ten of them in there, Captain. They claim to have a deadman switch on the ship's remaining atomic ordinance. Our techies have eyes-on, and there's a big red button pushed in and held down by one of the men in there."

"Can you breach and get to it fast enough?"

"Yes ma'am," Sholmir growled. "Gunnery Sergeant Filitov here will take that task." Eyla nodded to Filitov, an occasional sparring partner, the *Himalaya*'s bantamweight Sambo champion, laser-fast and insanely immune to pain. "She'll secure the button before his thumb comes off of it."

Filitov was already removing her carbine and helmet, getting light.

"Very well." Eyla rolled her shoulders. "Have the hackers breach it."

The rush was expected. Two greybeards with short scimitars – cutlasses, really – charged the Marines as soon as the blast door opened. Both focused on Captain Melana as Filitov duck-rolled under them and dove into the bridge. Scimitars steady, they advanced. Eyla recognized the trained stance of expert swordsmen.

Iaijutsu. Noun. Japanese. The drawstrike: a single move to unsheathe the *katana* and execute a killing blow or sequence of blows.

Eyla's upswing caught the left-hand swordsman below the chin, halving his skull from right jawbone to left temple then arcing downswing to the right-hand scimitarman at the clavicle, cutting ribs and lung, scoring hipbone, ending ten centimeters above the deck. Eyla held the kneeling position briefly, one knee brushing the deck, blade level and motionless, as the Marines stormed past her.

When she looked up, Filitov had the button-holder's arm locked to the console, one leg hooked under the panel for leverage, the other under his chin, forcing his neck backward to the breaking point. Her wrist tendons strained as she ground the old man's thumb solidly onto the button.

The admiral held a long scimitar. He spoke. Sailele translated.

"He says he invokes House Code. Honor duel between nobles."

"So now the concubine is a worthy opponent, I see?" Eyla smiled grimly. "Tell him it's bloody well on. Clear this space!"

Two Marines had already replaced Filitov and her captive. One kept a thumb pressed on the red button while Filitov studied its glowing sigils. The Marines held the remaining bridge crew in restraining holds. Colonel Sholmir scowled, ears back in disapproval, but House Code was House Code, and Lady Melana was both a noble and a captain.

Prince-Admiral Falad looked Methuselaic, but he was fast and steady. Lady Eyla kept the *katana* in high guard as he circled, his own blade resting just off one shoulder. He struck out fast, a shoulder-level arc. Eyla caught it on the *katana* hilt, launched a lightning counterstrike at Falad's neck. Scimitar and *katana* resonated with the impact.

The gut-punch surprised Eyla, a left straight to the solar plexus. She doubled over as he raised the scimitar for a strike to the back of the neck. Eyla surged up on her toes, headbutt catching him under the chin. She dropped the *katana*, grabbing two handfuls of beard and hair, threw herself into a side-roll. Torque, technique, and leverage snapped the admiral's neck at the second and third cervical vertebrae.

"Deadman switch is a bluff, skipper." Filitov shook her head. "Roughly translated, it's the emergency auto-docking button."

"Very well." Eyla looked down at the dead Falad, then speculatively at *Saladin's* command chair, smiling. "Tell Miller to send word to the House.

Michael S. Roberts

We have raised the Jolly Roger and are taking home a prize. Then have a glass of wine brought and clear the bridge. I'd like a moment alone."

In Jennifer Campbell-Hicks' intriguing tale, Lieutenant Everett Monson finds himself perplexed and worried by an android with a strange claim – that it possesses the soul of a long-dead scientist and inventor. Could it be having a...

MALFUNCTION

Jennifer Campbell-Hicks

From his perch atop the ship's wing, Lieutenant Everett Monson singled out a wire amidst the tangle behind an access panel and examined it under the bright lights of the docking bay: 3mm gauge, red coating. Yes, this was the right one. He unhooked one end, thumbed the switch on his pencil-thin electrical prod, and inched it toward the exposed tip.

"Excuse me," a voice said. "Am I dreaming?"

Startled, Everett jerked his hand. Wire and prod sparked.

"Ow! Damn it!" He stuck his singed fingertips in his mouth and looked around the cavernous bay. The last shift had ended hours ago; he had thought he was the only one here.

An android stood below the wing. It appeared male and in its mid-twenties, although it was neither of those things. Also, it was naked. A perfectly sculpted specimen of humanity except for its neutered groin and its eyes. No manufacturer yet had managed to replicate human eyes.

What bothered Everett was that it should not have been there at all. Nine more androids, exact duplicates of this one, stood unmoving along a back wall beside barrels and crates of unloaded supplies. They had arrived with a shipment from Coelus that afternoon. Only this one had activated.

The android's eye lenses clicked and widened. It studied the huge metal doors at one end of the bay, now closed against the vacuum of space, and a series of portholes along a far wall. Visible through the windows were the curve of the space station and the blue-and-yellow surface of Coelus far below. The android then turned its attention to the small fighter ship upon which Everett crouched. Then to Everett himself. "Fascinating," it said.

"What?" Everett said, taking his fingers from his mouth. Already the tips were red and blistering.

The android's neck jerked in a mechanical spasm. "I'm sorry if I startled you. You should have a doctor look at your hand."

An apologetic machine. Funny. "Android deactivate," Everett said.

"Excuse me, but are you talking to me?"

"Android deactivate."

It chuckled. "I would enjoy the marvel of an android. But even if there were such a thing, I would not qualify as one."

"Christ," Everett muttered.

One of the other mechanics must have reprogrammed the android and suppressed its voice control. But Everett did not have time to waste on a practical joke. He was under orders to have the fighter repaired by 0600. Now, thanks to this ill-timed interruption, he had a fried wire to replace before he could continue to hunt for whatever was causing the ship to glitch.

He could ignore the android, but it would probably persist in making a nuisance of itself. Better to deal with it now.

Everett tucked the prod into his tool belt, remembering at the last moment to turn it off. Didn't want to toast his own ass. He scooted backward on the fighter's wing on hands and knees and slid down a ladder to the bay floor.

The android watched as he opened a panel in its chest to reveal the metal framing, wires, and lights of its insides.

"How fascinating. This is a remarkable dream."

"Androids don't dream." Everett opened a smaller panel inside the first, unhooked the power core, and took it out.

The android gave him a serene smile but did not shut down.

"What the hell?" Everett said. "What are you?"

It raised its eyebrows in an eerily human gesture. "An interesting question. What are any of us? A priest might say we are the soul. A psychiatrist might tell you we are the mind. A biologist would say we are molecules or DNA. Who is right? Only God knows for certain."

"Uh, right." Everett replaced the core and shut the panels. He took a communicator from his belt and punched a code.

"Yeah," answered a female voice.

"This is Lieutenant Everett Monson in Docking Bay Delta. I have a malfunctioning android in here. Could someone come take it off my hands?"

She paused. "Is it an emergency?"

"No. But it's a big annoyance."

"Both of the night-shift techs are out on calls right now. I'll send the first one who's free."

"Thanks."

He ended the call.

"You are a lieutenant?" the android asked. "That would make this a military vessel, correct?"

"Space Station Gamma, in high orbit around Coelus."

The android looked with new appreciation around the docking bay crammed with ships, both operational and not, and recently arrived supply containers. "This is the future then."

Everett snorted. "Hardly. It's 2630."

"How fascinating."

"You think a lot of things are fascinating."

The android flashed a grin of artificial white teeth. "I suppose I do. If there is one thing I have learned, it is that life is full of surprises."

"So says the android just off the assembly line."

"I have lived much longer than you."

Now Everett grinned. He had the machine dead to rights on this one. "You were manufactured six weeks ago on Coelus. It says so inside your chest panel."

"I was not. I was born eighty-one years and four months ago in Omaha, Nebraska. My name is Marcus Wolasky."

Everett ran his hands through his hair in agitation. The android had no visible power source, and now it also needed a memory wipe. He would get someone back good for this one.

"Where did you get that name?"

"My mother gave it to me."

"Christ."

"What does Christ have to do with it?"

Everett laughed. "Not a damn thing."

"Then you should not take his name in vain. My name, though – you recognized it. Your reaction gave you away."

"You got me there. *The* Marcus Wolasky was the father of spaceflight."

"I am? Quite extraordinary."

"You are not Marcus Wolasky."

"Why do you say that? Because you think I am an android? Are there not things here in the future that, despite your best efforts, you cannot explain?"

"Maybe. But this isn't one of them."

The android considered that. "Would you like to test me? Ask about my life, and I will answer."

Everett tried to remember what he had learned in school, but it was not easy. The hour was late, his brain felt fuzzy and his fingers throbbed. Besides, he had little interest in pre-space history even on a good day.

He knew the basic stuff. Wolasky had been a professor and a pacifist who protested every military action the U.S. embarked on, at least until the world's political structures fell apart after a generation of global warfare. If not for his discovery of faster-than-light travel in the late 22nd century, humans might never have gotten off old Earth. Still, no one knew about Wolasky's genius until after he was found dead in his basement workshop. When the workshop was cleaned out, his family found models, diagrams, formulas, all theorizing on spaceflight. It was a treasure trove.

But whatever Everett knew about Wolasky – and more – could be programmed into a data chip. The android probably had access to every detail of Wolasky's life, which meant the game it proposed would prove nothing.

"I don't have time for this," Everett said. "That ship won't fix itself. So if you don't mind – "

He stopped. Great. He was asking for permission from a machine now. The android had the gall to wave its consent.

Grumbling to himself, Everett headed across the bay to an adjacent storage room for a replacement wire for the one he had fried. When he came out, the android was nowhere to be seen. All was quiet. Maybe a tech had come to take it off his hands.

He climbed the ladder to the ship's wing but froze halfway up. The android had its back to him and its head poked through the access panel.

"What the hell are you doing?" Everett said.

The android did not move. "What is wrong with the ship?"

"Get out. You're not programmed for ship repair."

"I don't need programming. I'm a professor of electrical engineering, and it appears the basics haven't changed much."

"You are not Wolasky."

"I am."

"You also said you were dreaming."

"I fell asleep in my workshop before I woke up here, but I have decided this is not a dream. It is a vision, given by God to show my path." It peered over its shoulder at Everett. "If you are right that I am a malfunctioning machine, you lose nothing by letting me look. If I am right..."

"Fine." Everett threw up his hands. "I've run diagnostics, been through the whole system, and I can't find the problem. So go ahead, genius, and fix it."

The android nodded solemnly, as though it had not noticed the sarcasm in Everett's voice, and turned to the access panel. It examined the tangle of wires, then several thumb-sized receivers and transistors.

It hands twitched as it ran them over buttons, switches, and indicator lights.

"Careful," Everett said. "Don't want to touch a live wire and short-circuit the ship. Not to mention yourself."

"Shhh."

This was a waste of time. What did the android expect to accomplish without checking the diagnostic reports first?

After a few minutes, it pointed inside the panel. "This receiver is damaged."

It deftly scooted back on the wing so Everett could lean in closer. He took a flashlight from his belt and pointed it at the receiver. A hairline crack ran along its length.

"Damn. How did you see that?"

"These eyes are remarkable. I can focus on an object much more closely than I can with my own. But my own eyes have not worked properly since I was sixteen." It gave him a frank look. "Do you believe now that I am who I say I am?"

He did not. Still, Everett pitied the machine. "I think you've been programmed to believe you're Wolasky," he said. "Whether you are or not is another matter."

"I suppose that is good enough. Shall we get down? I have never liked heights."

Everett walked to a table in a corner of the bay – a round slab of synthetic wood balanced on a spare supply barrel – and the android followed. After he laid his tool belt on the table, he filled a cup with energy drink from a dispenser and sat on a crate that passed for a chair. It felt good to get off his feet.

The android also sat. "Now that your work is done, I hope you will answer some questions for me."

That seemed a pointless exercise – an hour from now, the android's memory would be wiped – but Everett did need a break. "What do you want to know?"

"When did I die?"

"Five hundred years ago, give or take. Here..."

He touched a wall, activating a holomonitor. Bay workers used the holo to track imports and exports to the station, but it also linked to the primary archives. Everett accessed the latter function now with the push of a few buttons, and the holo started flipping through photos and vidclips: Wolasky teaching a college class in his trademark tweed jacket and wire-rimmed glasses; Wolasky at a protest at the Pentagon, holding a sign that read, "No war is good war;" Wolasky seated at a table across from a congressional panel, speaking into a microphone.

The android hummed and nodded thoughtfully.

Everett stopped the slideshow on a photo of a room, dimly lit. Windows near the ceiling looked out at ground level over a yard of grass and trees. Diagrams were taped and pinned to every inch of wall space and fastened to the corners of a blackboard on which dozens of equations were scrawled in chalk. At the center of the clutter, head resting on his desk, was Wolasky as an old man. His cheek was pressed into a pile of papers, and his glasses sat askew on his nose.

"This was right after he died," Everett said.

The android sat very still. "I see." If a machine could look pale, this one did. Then it said, "How far have we spread among the stars since then? Since my death?"

Everett wiped the photo and brought up a map of the Milky Way. He pointed to a dot. "Here's the Sol system, where Earth is. This," he pointed to another dot, "is the farthest system we've colonized. And these," – two dozen dots grew brighter – "are systems where we have colonies."

"Where is Coelus, where we are now?"

Everett pointed to one of the dots farthest from Earth.

"It is what I had hoped for."

"Don't get too excited. We haven't done as well as some species have."

The android looked delighted. "Have we made contact with other intelligent life forms? Are our relations with them peaceful? Have we traded knowledge to advance our civilization and theirs?"

If only, Everett thought. "The first ones we came across, the Lacerta, almost wiped us out. That was back when we hadn't yet gotten out of our home system. They had better technology, and their attack was unprovoked."

"Lacerta? As in Latin for lizard?"

"I don't know about any Latin, but this is them."

Another swipe of buttons and Everett pulled up archival footage of the Lacerta, all scales, teeth, and claws. The stuff of children's nightmares.

"They do look hostile," the android said.

"It took twenty years of war and some damn fine soldiering to beat them. We added their technology to our own and colonized their planets."

"After them?"

"The next two, we didn't wait for an attack. Not worth the risk. We wiped them out quick."

The android stood, alarmed. "That cannot be true."

Everett remembered then that the android was programmed with pacifist sensibilities. He should have kept his mouth shut. He should have said the universe was one big happy commune. Now the android would probably march up and down the station with a picket sign, shouting about peace and love.

"The galaxy isn't a nice place," Everett said. "Competition for habitable planets is cutthroat. It gets bloody."

"It is wrong."

"The hell with right and wrong. This is about survival."

"Did it occur to you, or anyone, that some other species might have attacked the Lacerta long ago, which in turn caused them to attack you? It is a cycle of violence with one way to end it: peace."

The android sounded so righteous. Feeling a need to defend humanity, Everett cleared out the Lacerta footage and pulled up photos of humans with their heads ripped off and guts spilled out. Blood and body parts littered battlefields. Everett could almost smell the decay as he flipped through the images.

"See this? They didn't care about peace. All they cared about was planetary expansion, and we were in their way. Insects to be exterminated."

"That does not matter."

"Like hell it doesn't."

"I did not work all those years to develop my theories so humanity could slaughter other intelligent life forms. That is worse than genocide."

Everett bit back a retort and reminded himself he was not arguing with the real Marcus Wolasky. He took a sip from his cup and swished the warm liquid in his mouth before swallowing. It helped him regain some equilibrium.

"Stand on your soapbox if you want, but done is done," he said. "It's a debate for the historians now."

"Not for me."

The android straightened its shoulders, its expression one of stubborn determination.

Everett became suspicious. "What are you thinking?"

"When I am back in my workshop, I will destroy everything. No research means no spaceflight, which means no genocide."

"You're crazy."

"Many people have said so. And no offense, Lieutenant, but you cannot stop me. You are from five centuries in the future."

"Christ Almighty." Everett leaned across the table and glared at the android. "You are not from the past, and as soon as a tech shows up, you will be taken to have your memory erased." He stood and started to pace, agitated. "Why do I even bother arguing with you?"

"Because you know I am telling the truth." The android's voice was deep and low. "You are afraid you made a mistake in talking to me, and you are scared for what will happen to your present when I awake in my own time."

Everett stood with his mouth agape.

Before he could think of a coherent response, a man walked into the bay and approached their table. Everett was grateful for the diversion.

The man was older than him, with hair gone gray and skin starting to sag along his jaw line. A badge clipped to his pocket said: Paul Woods, Technical Specialist.

The man saluted. "I got a call for a broken android."

"Here you go. It needs a complete memory wipe."

"Yes, Sir." Woods turned to the android, which was leaning against the wall, arms folded. "Android deactivate."

The android smiled.

Everett sighed and tried to banish the weariness from his voice. "I already tried that."

With a chuckle and a luxurious stretch, the android said, "Do not worry. I will go peacefully." He nodded to Everett. "Thank you for taking time to speak with me, Lieutenant Monson. It has been very enlightening."

Woods and the android left, and Everett sank back onto the shipping crate. He stared into his empty cup. Did he believe Marcus Wolasky had somehow jumped through time? He supposed he did, in the same way he believed in predictions of the end of humanity on this date or that. He knew he was crap, but he could not shake the question: What if? What if it's right? What if we're all about to die?

So what if he had sat across from Marcus Wolasky, father of spaceflight, and the man who did so much to change the course of humanity would return home to destroy his research? The human race would never explore the stars. The Lacerta would wipe out every trace. No space station. No Everett. End of story.

If that were the case, Everett had taken the best course of action. A memory wipe would stop the time-traveling Wolasky from remembering anything he had learned here.

Feeling relieved, he set the cup on the table and buckled on his belt. The ship still needed repairs, and the work would occupy his mind. He did a quick inventory of his tools. Flashlight, check. Replacement wire, check. Prod...

The prod was not there.

It took Everett a moment to understand what that meant.

He sprinted for the bay doors, barreled down a hallway and went left at a junction. He had to catch them before they got to the lifts.

Everett rounded a corner to see the android press the prod to its forehead. It started to shake. Woods jumped back.

"No!" Everett yelled.

He was too late. The android's lenses popped out and rolled away. Fingers curled into useless balls. Its body shook for several seconds before it tipped forward and fell to the floor, smoke pouring from vacant eye sockets, ears, and nostrils. The air stank of smoke and charred synthetics. Everett's hand shook as he knelt and took the prod from its rigid fingers.

Behind him, Woods breathed hard. "It said it was sorry, but it couldn't have its memory erased. It needed to remember when it went home. Then it said goodbye and fried itself."

"Well, we're still here, and the space station is here, so I think its plan backfired."

Woods' voice took on a tinge of panic. "Excuse my frankness, Sir, but what the hell is going on? Their base programming forbids them from, well, from this."

Everett looked at him. "Do you believe there are things that defy logic? Things that can't be explained?"

Woods cocked his head, confused. "You mean ghosts? Demons?"

"I was thinking time travel."

"You're kidding, right?"

Everett stood and tucked the prod into his belt. Woods was right. It was nonsense. He prodded the body with his boot. The synthetic skin had melted like candle wax, revealing a mess of metal and wires. "Take this piece of junk to the compactor."

"Yes, Sir."

Everett watched as Woods grabbed the android by its feet and dragged it away. Feeling dazed, he returned to the bay and sat at the makeshift table.

The holo still displayed photos from the Lacerta war. Everett backtracked to the photo of Wolasky dead in his workshop.

In the photo, Wolasky's head was turned to the side, but part of his forehead was visible. On impulse, Everett zoomed in for a closer look. At the center of Wolasky's forehead, beneath a thatch of white hair, was a circular black mark no larger than what might result from a poke from an ink pen.

Or an electrical probe.

Everett's spine went weak. Could Wolasky have really jumped to the future and, in sending himself back, inadvertently caused his own death? He took several deep breaths. Of course not. That was a ridiculous, crazy, stupid idea.

He shut down the holo, stood on shaky legs, and walked out into the docking bay. He had a fighter to fix.

Mike Resnick's classic spacefaring scoundrel Catastrophe Baker finds himself stranded when his ship is stolen out from under him. But left behind is the culprit's ship, with whom Catastrophe Baker will soon have a close encounter of a very odd kind in...

CATASTROPHE BAKER AND THE SHIP WHO PURRED

Mike Resnick

It wasn't much of a war. It was just us humans against no more than thirty or forty little alien worlds that were feeling their oats, and after it had gone on for a few months and reached the spot in the Inner Frontier where I was hanging out at that time, I decided to do something about it before one side or the other blew up my favorite watering holes, so I hopped into my ship and soon touched down on Henry III, the third planet in the Plantagenet system, which was supposed to be one of the alien strongholds.

I hunted up the enemy encampment, which wasn't all that hard to find, walked to the middle of it, and stood there with my hands on my hips.

"My name's Baker!" I hollered. "Catastrophe Baker! And I'm here to settle this war by fighting your champion – winner take all!"

Suddenly I was instantly surrounded by armed aliens. A couple of hundred weapons were aimed at me, and finally one alien, who was wearing more medals than any of the others, stepped forward.

"Your reputation precedes you, Catastrophe Baker," he said. "But how do we know you are truly that hero?"

"If I ain't," I said, "your champion'll beat me without working up a sweat."

"True enough," said the alien. "But we are already winning the war, so your offer is meaningless."

"You ain't won nothing if I'm still standing," I told him.

"Blow his legs away," said a feminine voice.

I turned and found myself facing a beautiful young woman.

"Now that's a hell of a thing for a prisoner to suggest, ma'am," I said. "Meaning no offense."

"I'm not a prisoner."

"Well, if push comes to shove, it's an even worse thing for a turncoat to suggest."

"I'm just a businesswoman," she said. "These people need weapons. I sell weapons. We fill mutual needs." She stared at me. "What are you doing here all by yourself?"

"It goes with the heroing trade, ma'am," I answered. "I aim to take on their most fearsome fighter, wipe up the floor with him, and bring this unfortunate conflict to a close."

She stared at me for a long moment. "You really believe that, don't you?"

"Ain't nothing born, foaled, hatched, or spawned has ever been able to make me holler Uncle," I said. "I don't imagine these here alien scum got the exception."

"Why should they fight you at all?" said the woman. "They've already defeated the Navy, and you're here all by yourself. Why shouldn't they just kill you and be done with it?"

"Are you *sure* you're a woman and not just some alien look-alike?" I asked her.

"I'm a woman."

"You sure don't sound like a member of the same race. You got a name, ma'am?"

"I've got lots of names," she replied. "In my profession, it's a necessity."

"You got one you prefer to all the others?"

"Not really."

"Then, since we're on Henry III, I think I'll call you Eleanor of Provence."

"Isn't that the name of the moon?"

"You're every bit as round in the right places as the moon," I told her.

"Flattery will get you nowhere."

"I ain't flattering you, ma'am," I said. "You can't help being beautiful any more than you can help being a deceitful, backstabbing, unscrupulous traitor to the human race. But at least you're easy on the eyes."

"You still haven't answered the lady's question, Catastrophe Baker," said the alien commander. "Why shouldn't we just shoot you down in cold blood?"

"Because you don't want me to fall down," I said.

"Why not?"

I opened my tunic to show him all the explosives I had taped to my torso. "Because if I fall down, so will every alien and every structure within ten miles of me."

"Then why should we have our champion face you?" asked the commander. "If he knocks you down, the effect will be the same as if we were to shoot you right now."

"You give me your word of honor as an alien and an officer that you won't shoot me, and I'll take the bombs off before the fight," I said.

"And if we refuse, what then?"

"I ain't thought that far ahead," I admitted. "A race that's willing to take on the race of Man don't strike me as a bunch of lily-livered cowards."

"You have a remarkable way of expressing yourself," said the alien. "Even when you are complimenting us, it sounds like an insult."

"Have your champion make me apologize," I suggested, seeing a way to get the show on the road.

"You are much bigger than any of us. I don't think it would be a fair fight."

"I'm not much more'n six foot nine or ten, and I only weigh about two seventy-five," I said. "I'll tell you what. I ain't twice as big as you, but I'll take on your two best at the same time. That ought to make it a fair fight."

"It's an interesting proposition," said the alien commander. "But the stakes are unrealistic. I do not have the authority to call off the war – and when your Navy sends reinforcements, as I suspect it will, I very much doubt that you can get them to return to their base."

"Okay, you got a point," I said. "What stakes do you want to fight for?"

"We don't need money and we don't need weapons," answered the alien. "And I have no idea what else you want. So why don't *you* propose the stakes?"

"Okay," I said. "I reckon I'd better, if we're ever gonna get this thing up and running." I looked around the area, and then my eyes came back to Eleanor of Provence. "Here's my proposition. If I win, you give me the woman."

"What?" she demanded.

"Us humans got to stick together," I told her. "The closer the better."

"That's outrageous!"

"Fighting for outrageous stakes just naturally goes with being a hero, ma'am."

"Just a minute," said the alien commander. "That's what we give you if you win. What do you give us if *we* win?"

"I'll fight the rest of the war on your side," I said. "I ain't got no use for your alien scum, meaning no offense, so it'll just give me that much more incentive to win."

"But if you *do* lose, you will place yourself under my command?"

"Right," I said. "It suppose it won't be all that terrible. I *like* fighting."

"It's a deal," said the commander.

"Now wait a minute!" said Eleanor.

The alien turned to her. "I do not expect to lose this wager," he said. "But even if I do, how can I turn down the proposition? If our champions lose, then, while I will miss your wit and charm and companionship, you are, after all, merely a salesperson of dubious loyalty who can be easily replaced. But if we win, we will secure the services of the famous Catastrophe Baker." He turned to Baker. "How long will it take you to prepare?"

"As long as it takes me to unwrap these here bombs."

"We shall be ready."

They kept an eye on me while I took off all the explosives and laid them gently on the ground. When I was done, I looked around to see if my opponents had shown up yet.

They had. One was short and heavily-muscled, the other tall and lean, with the grace of a dancer.

"What are the ground rules?" asked the alien commander as the two champions approached Baker.

"What rules?" I said. "This here is a freehand fight. Hitting, kicking, biting, and gouging are all legal. So are kidney punches – always assuming you *got* kidneys."

"When is it over?"

"When only one of us is left standing."

"I agree to your rules – or lack of them," said the commander. His army moved closer, forming a circle about thirty feet in diameter around the three combatants. "Let the battle begin!"

The muscular alien charged me right away. I could have sidestepped, grabbed an arm, and twisted, but I wanted to see how he measured up to Hurricane Smith and Gravedigger Gaines – some of the other heroes I'd tussled with over the years – so I just planted my feet and took the charge against my chest and belly.

The poor little bastard bounced right off.

Now the tall one approached cautiously, dancing on his toes like a boxer. Suddenly he launched a kick at my groin. I grabbed his foot before it landed, lifted it as high as I could, and gave it a quick twist. The alien flipped in the air and landed on his back with a heavy thud.

"Come on!" I said to them. "Stop taking it so easy, and let me have your best shot!"

Both aliens charged me at once. I took a couple of blows to the face and one to the neck, then swung a roundhouse at the taller, thinner alien and floored him. I could taste a little a trickle of blood on my lip, so I licked it off, and turned to the muscular alien.

"You throw a pretty nice punch for a little feller," I said. "Now let's see how you take one."

I kind of stalked him around the circle, finally caught up with him, and gave him a medium-hard slap on the side of his head. He dropped like a ton of bricks.

Just as I was thinking the fight was already over, the taller alien leaped onto my back, biting my neck and digging his fingers into my eyes, which kind of got my temper up. I shook my head, which sent him flying through the air. I picked him up where he'd fallen, held him over my head, spun around three or four times, and hurled him as far as I could. He flew totally beyond the circle of soldiers, hit the ground with a loud thud, tried to get up, fell over, and just lay there.

When I figured no one was going to get back up, I turned to the alien commander and said, "They put up a good fight for a pair of alien heathen. Tell 'em when they wake up that they lasted about as long with me as anyone ever has."

I walked up to the woman and took her by the hand. "Come on, Queen Eleanor. Time for us to be going."

As we began walking to my ship, the alien commander called out after me. "You have forgotten your explosives, Catastrophe Baker. We are an honorable race. We will allow you to take them with you."

"You keep 'em," I said .

"You are sure?"

"Yeah," I said. "They got waterlogged back on Silverleaf VII a couple of years ago, and haven't been worth a damn ever since. You couldn't blow 'em up with a detonator."

I could tell Queen Eleanor wasn't none too happy about having been won in a fight, even though it was just what old-time heroes in armor used to do all the time. I escorted her to my ship and, just to make sure she didn't run away, I stayed on the ground while she opened the hatch and entered the airlock. And then, before I could stop her, Eleanor locked the hatch and took off, leaving me standing on the ground looking foolish as all get-out.

The aliens laughed their heads off, and for a minute there I was thinking of challenging the whole batch of 'em to a freehand fight to the death, but then I decided that it wasn't really their fault that I'd found a lemon in the garden of love, so I had 'em show me to her ship, which I figured was mine now.

It was the strangest-looking damned spaceship I'd ever laid eyes on, but I couldn't see no reason not to appropriate it just the same, so I bade all the giggling aliens good-bye, after signing twenty or thirty autographs, and climbed into the ship.

The control panel was like nothing I'd ever seen before. All the readouts were in some alien language, and the chairs and bulkheads felt kind of soft and almost lifelike. I didn't pay much attention to them, though. My main concern was trying to figure out how to activate the ship and take off.

One button on the control panel caught my eye. It was a little brighter and a little shinier than the others, and since I couldn't just stare at the panel all day and do nothing, I reached out and pushed it.

And heard a very high-pitched human squeal.

"Who's there?" I said, drawing my burner and spinning around.

"Me," said a feminine voice.

"Where are you hiding?" I demanded.

"I'm not hiding at all," said the voice. "I'm the ship."

"Are you a cyborg or an artificial intelligence?" I asked.

"Neither."

"I'm running out of guesses," I said.

"I'm a living, genetically engineered being."

"You sound female," I said.

"I am."

"Do any of these make us take off?" I asked, hitting another couple of buttons on the panel.

"Oh, my God!" she breathed.

"Did I hurt you, ma'am?"

"Do it again!"

So I pressed the buttons again, and the ship started purring just like a cat.

"You got a name, ma'am?" I said.

"Leonora," she sighed.

"Well, Leonora, ma'am," I said, "can you maybe tell me how to get the hell off Henry III before these here aliens decide to bust the truce I kind of threw on 'em when they weren't looking?"

"Just sit down," she said. "I'll take care of it."

So I sat down, and before I could strap myself into the chair, its arms grabbed me and kind of wrapped themselves around me, and then I looked at the viewscreen and saw we were already above the stratosphere.

The arms released me and kind of stroked me here and there before they went back into place, and then I got to my feet again and continued looking around.

"What's your name?" asked Leonora.

"Baker," I said. "Catastrophe Baker."

"What a romantic name!" she crooned.

"You really think so?" I said. "I always thought Hurricane Smith and Sundance Moondog grabbed up the really good names." I walked to the back of the cabin. "Where's the galley? I ain't eaten since before I landed on Henry III."

A wall slid away. "Just enter this corridor," she said, "and it's the first room on the left."

So I took a step into the corridor, and the ship shuddered a little like it was going through a minor ion storm, and I stuck my arms out against the walls to make sure I didn't fall down.

"Oh!" said Leonora. And then: "Oh! Oh! Oh!"

"I'm sorry if I've discommoded you, ma'am," I said. "I don't mean to do you no harm."

"You're not doing me any harm!" she said, and I could have sworn she was panting.

Well, I kept walking down the corridor and she kept saying "Oh!" with each step I took, and then I came to a room on the left, and I entered it, and sure enough, it was the galley, though it wasn't like any galley I'd ever seen before. There was a table and a chair right in the middle, and all kinds of incomprehensible controls and gauges along one wall.

"What would you like, Catastrophe Baker?" asked Leonora.

"Maybe a sandwich and a beer, if it's no trouble, ma'am," I said.

"No trouble at all. Do you see the glowing pink button on the wall, just to the left of the holographic readout?"

"Yeah."

"Just press it."

"Don't I have to tell it what I want?"

"Just press it!" said Leonora urgently.

So I walked over and pressed it.

"*Wow!*" purred Leonora.

"What do I do now, ma'am?" I asked.

"Now you eat."

"What I mean is, where's my food?"

"On the table," said Leonora – and sure enough, it was.

I sat down and started chewing on the sandwich.

"You're so much more considerate than my last owner," said Leonora.

"I ain't your owner, ma'am," I said. "I'm more like your borrower."

"We would make such a wonderful team!" she said. "Won't you consider it?"

"Well, sure, if you want me to keep you," I answered.

"Oh, yes!" she whispered.

"Well, as long as we're man and ship, how about heading over to Barleycorn II?" I said.

"Done."

"As simple as that?"

"Well, you *could* get us there faster by adjusting the navigational control," she said.

"How do I do that?"

A wall panel slid into the floor, revealing a whole new bunch of flashing lights and buttons and controls and such.

"Do you see that little wheel on the Q-valve?" she asked.

"Yeah."

"Turn it to the left."

"Whatever you say, ma'am."

I walked over to it and gave it a quick spin.

"Oh my oh my oh my!" she shrieked.

"Did I hurt you, ma'am?"

"No!"

"Is that it, or is there anything else I should do?"

Well, I never knew you had to fiddle with so many controls to adjust a navigational computer, but finally I must have hurt her because she told me she couldn't take any more, and I said that was okay, if we got there an hour or two later it wouldn't be no problem.

The trip took two days, and she was just the sweetest thing you'd ever want to meet or travel with. She insisted that I eat three meals a day, and we kept working on that navigational system whenever I had a chance, and then finally we touched down on Barleycorn, and suddenly, I noticed a note of concern in Leonora's voice.

"Where are you going?" she asked.

"I'm off to visit an old friend," I told her.

"Will I ever see you again?"

"Sure you will," I said. "I don't plan to spend the rest of my life on Barleycorn II."

Actually I just planned to spend one night there, renewing an old acquaintanceship with the Evening Star, a lady embezzler who doubled as an exotic dancer. I took her out to dinner, and during the course of the meal I mentioned Leonora, and nothing would do but that I took her there later in the evening so she could see the living ship for herself.

"She's certainly cute," she said as we stood in front of Leonora.

"So are you," I said, kind of gently nuzzling her neck and ear and starting to subtly remove her tunic. "And you got racier lines."

"My, you're impetuous!" she said, giggling and slapping my hand – but not so hard that I took it away.

"Could be," I replied, since I hadn't never seen my birth certificate. "But my friends call me Catastrophe."

Well, we started renewing our friendship in earnest, right there in the shadow of the ship. We kind of did a little of this and a little of that, and by the time I took her back home she decided that no woman in her right mind would ever call me Catastrophe again.

It was when I came back to the ship that the trouble started.

"I've never been so insulted in all my life!" said Leonora.

"What are you talking about?"

"The second I turn my back you seduce that ugly little tart!"

"She ain't ugly, and besides, I done it in front of your back," I said, figuring I had to speak up for the Evening Star since she wasn't there to speak up for her own self.

"And you're filthy!" continued Leonora. "Get out of those clothes and take a bath immediately!"

"You're sounding a lot more like a mother than a spaceship," I complained.

"Did I upset you?" she asked.

"Yeah, a little."

"Good!" she snapped. "Then we're even!"

Well, from that moment on, things just went from bad to worse. Every time I gave her a new location to visit, she gave me the old third degree about what woman I was planning to ravish. She wouldn't send or accept any subspace radio message that had a female at the other end. If I talked in my sleep and mentioned a lady's name, she'd wake me up and demand to know who I'd been talking about.

Finally, after three or four more days, she announced that she was taking me back to the Plantagenet system.

"What's going on?" I asked.

"I can't stand it any more!" she said. "I can't concentrate on navigation! I can't compute my fuel consumption! I can't focus on meteor swarms and ion storms!"

"You got some kind of headache?" I asked.

"I have a case of unrequited love, and it's driving me crazy!" she said. "You are my every thought, and yet I mean nothing to you."

"Sure you do," I said.

"As a woman?"

"As a spaceship."

She screamed in agony.

"I'm sorry, truly I am," I told her. "I wish I wasn't so goddamned attractive and irresistible to women, but it ain't something I can control. It just seems to go with being a practitioner of the hero trade."

She didn't say another word until we entered the atmosphere of Henry II. Then she asked in a very small voice: "Would you adjust my gyros, just once, for old time's sake?"

"Sure," I said. "Where are they?"

A couple of knobs started flashing.

"Well, I'll be damned!" I explained. "I thought you used them to home in on different radio frequencies."

I reached out and started turning the knobs.

"Mmmmmm!" said Leonora.

I spun the left-hand one.

"Ohhhhhh!" she said.

I twisted the right-hand one.

"*Oh God! Oh God! Oh God!*" she screamed. Then: "Was it good for you, too?"

We landed a couple of minutes later, and then she let me out and took off for parts unknown.

And that's the true story of The Ship Who Purred.

Brenda Cooper's Robot Girl *is one of my favorite novellas of the past decade. It made me a fan, and later, a friend of a very talented writer. Her latest, an original for us, is the tale of Lisel Mountain, a writer whose muse is music. When a singer named Holly Defiant catches her eye, Lisel discovers a startling connection to her past in...*

HOLLY DEFIANT

Brenda Cooper

Holly Defiant's voice fills the Liar's Club bar, shutting down conversations and drawing every eye to her red hair and the intense glow in her pale-blue eyes. The song's something about the devil and an asteroid farmer. Holly's hand beats rhythmically on the bohdran she cups between her breasts and her lower belly, the instrument almost a way for her to give birth. Hell, she is giving birth. She's birthing some happiness in all the students and thralls and spacers in this over-bright bar.

My foot taps to the rhythm of her hand.

Jodie sent me here. Jodie's my publicist, and the reason I'm still selling well. She said I'd like this girl.

I do. I like her a lot. The muse always comes through me near live music, has been for a hundred years now. And I have money and time to chase it, go from singer to singer. Sometimes I help them out; give them some credit or some advice. Once I had an affair with one, a gal who was stage-named Misty Moon. But I was younger then, and now I know that's not what I want. I don't want my singers to become human, I want them to stay gods and goddesses. I want to feel their songs wake the words in me so I can write a new story. It's like if I run out of singers, I'll run out of stories. I mean, everybody's got their own fetishes, right? Their own secret drives. Mine's harmless.

If we stood side by side, someone might think me and Holly Defiant are both about twenty-five. I bet she really is, maybe even younger. The half hour since I first saw her has been long enough to read the youth in the way she moves, the way she lets herself get so carried away by song she forgets to watch the audience. I watch it for her. Most of 'em are fine. There's a bouncer in the back, a big woman with no hair and a rubber stick on her belt. Good. There's two black-haired pretty-boys sitting at a table next to me. Insignia on their leather briefcase says they're cargo guild, clothes say they probably own their own ship. Look in their eyes suggests smugglers. I've been a lot of things, and one of them, a long time ago, was a cop. I don't like the way they're watching Holly. They remind me of some of the sleazes that preyed on me until I got smarter and older.

I shouldn't be letting myself get distracted. Besides, this girl is tougher than I was; she's probably smart enough not to fall for pretty faces. I turn away from them and look back at her. I'm about five tables away from the stage, close enough to feel Holly's voice and the stamp of her foot. She stops and throws her head, hair slapping her shoulders. I join the audience appreciation, fifty people clapping and stamping so the room quivers.

I can feel the connection between Holly and me. We're both entertainers, both bards in our own way. My audience is bigger, but almost never so close. I draw energy from the way she has to perform for a crowd every time, give herself to us until she's sweaty and glowing and exhausted.

I send Jodie a thank you message, and take out my journal and draw space ships and people, and write the outline for a story or three, and doodle some letters, and listen and admire. Holly Defiant sings five more songs. I notice the sweet love song the most; it draws sadness up out of my heart and I bite my bottom lip until I taste blood, faint as a whisper of ache. I drink one of the local beers, which has to be something grown in a station vat, so bitter I nurse it slow.

Holly's on the fiddle now, ripping a real bow instead of a synth one. I like her more for that; a sacrifice for her audience. A touch of showmanship.

Her head goes back and the violin points at the sky and the bow screams across the strings. She stands and throws her arms up, accepting adulation. Drinking it. After she's full, she bows low in a sweeping gesture and sets her fiddle on its wooden stand.

She comes toward me, hopping off the stage and wading between tables while people clap and reach out for her.

Maybe she's recognized me.

Just when I think she's going to take the chair opposite me, she turns the other way and plunks down in a chair next to the two black-haired spacers. My disappointment shows me how much I'd like the idea this woman might have read my work, might know me.

Her back is to me, so I can see their faces if I glance sideways, but not hers. I grimace at my next sip of bitter beer and doodle, listening. The bar's gone noisy as talk picks up in the break.

At first they're all three laughing and talking, the men congratulating her on her show, she looking appreciative and preening a bit. She doesn't know them well, but this isn't the first time she's seen them either. One of the guys says he'll come for her for dinner. He can't mean tonight; it's already almost tomorrow.

I catch a few words. They call her pretty. She asks something about money, but from her tone and the way she stands with her arms shielding her belly, I'm sure she's selling her music and not her body. I hear the word "defiance" and it catches my ear since she's Holly Defiant and not Holly Defiance. But it's hard to hear and I'm an older woman, and even with meds and mods I can't hear like a real twenty-five year old.

Her table voice is surprisingly quiet, and I have to work hard not to lean in toward her to hear her over the background din and clatter. "I have two more shows here."

The other guy says, "You can be sick."

Holly shakes her head. "Not if I want to work again."

Same guy: "You won't have to." I decide to call this one Bam 1 and the other one Bam 2. Short for "Bad Man." An old partner of mine's jargon.

Bam 2 says, "She's just giving us a trial, 'member." His voice says he's kicking the first guy under the table. I miss her answer as a big guy passes between me and the other table. Bam 2 says, "See you then," and they both get up.

She's going to get back on stage, and I *should* sit and listen.

But I get up and follow Bam 1 and Bam 2 outside instead. Maybe because I used to fall for guys like them.

Outside is a station, of course. Mixed use, so they can create economic zones. Hotels and shops and fancy houses and cheap apartments. The main drag is a big-ass tunnel full of advertising and tourist shops and last-minute-shops with stuff you might like to get between here and the next station, the next hab. Everything is open since it's all automated or tended by bots, but it's not very crowded this time of night. Half the ones I see are plain clothes or vice. And half the others are their prey, and every once in a while, a bunch of real-teens or a group of norms walks down the middle where the light is good.

Bam 1 and Bam 2 go down the sides, where it's not so light, and I see 'em going in the speed s'port tunnel. Now it's gonna cost me ten credits to follow, and I'm on a hunch at best, over a red-headed stranger with a big songbird's voice. But I'm not on a budget, so I slide through and let the counter take from me. I get on the car behind them, but they're so lost in conversation I doubt they'd see me if I sat right next to them. They look a little like twins, except Bam 1 is broader and Bam 2 is taller. They stand and sway, talking, hands tucked into the overhead straps. Backlight from the tunnel throws their shadows onto the walls.

The s'port train glides almost silent, but I still can't make out what happens in the car ahead, even though my car is over half empty and so's theirs. Even though I can't hear them, I don't like how they're looking at people like prize dogs or something.

As we pass the housing farthest from everything, a young girl gets on and walks up to the Bams. Really young. Maybe fifteen. She gets tucked under Bam 1's arm, and she wiggles her butt, and he grins at her. None of them look at me. I sit still and quiet. I watch through the window without looking directly at them. I try to look bored.

Both cars empty out as we pass through the people-places and head toward the cargo that's out in the low-grav near the spacedock. By the time we get there, it's only the Bams in the car in front of me, and a pair of quiet women in the car I'm in, both pulled inside themselves and not even looking at me or each other.

I wonder if I should get off when the Bams do. It'll be pretty conspicuous. When I chased bad guys for a living fifty years ago, I always had a partner. Now it's just me.

"This is the last stop," the train says, its voice high and sweet, but still commanding. They must have recorded all the public noise in the world with the same voice.

I should've known that – this place isn't shaped well to make s'port rings.

I shouldn't follow them. I should go home and write.

When the door opens, I get up. The two women block my way. The look on their faces say they'll kill me if I get off the car. Standing, they're bigger than me, and they're probably armed. All I've got is my journal. I step back.

As the door closes, they flow out the opening backwards, leaving me alone on the train, going the wrong way.

When I look, I see the backs of the two women, and the Bams and the girl are gone.

Even though this is the fast train, by the time I get back, Holly Defiant is gone, and a trampoline show is on, the women naked and what's left of the bar crowd watching for them to lose form and spread their legs. Not my scene. I walk to my hotel room and brood.

If I'd played this right, I would've been writing until dawn. What did I know anyway? That some young thing with a good voice was about to get in trouble? I don't even know that. Maybe the Bams are her brothers. Maybe they're harmless fans. Maybe the moon is cheese. I get up to check, looking out at Earth below me in the hotel's lobby window, but the moon isn't visible from here.

The next morning, I'm grumpy from not sleeping. I can't write a word. I don't know where Holly Defiant lives, and the privacy filters keep me from finding out, even though I look in case she's still rookie enough to publish stuff about herself. She's not. After thinking about it for a while, I look up the word "defiance."

I get dictionary definitions, an old warship from before space travel, thirty-seven books titles, five movies, and then I whisper, "Bingo." The *Defiance* is a cargo ship. Bingo. Ship contents are pretty secret (gotta protect those corporate profits), but flight plans are public. *Defiance* is leaving in two days, heading out to the work habs around Ganymede. No big deal; they need stuff and people. But why do they need a bard? They told her she didn't need to do any more shows. Tourist ships have entertainers as part of the crew; I flew on the *Circle of Spring* for a year once and let Guy M'into's voice draw three bestsellers out of me, two of which made it into the immersives. The *Circle of Spring* has big margins, heavy payers, heavy gamblers. Cargo ships travel lean.

What about the girl from last night? I dig deeper, finally recognizing her face in a news bit on a missing person. Her names Natalyi. You'd think it's hard to go missing in space, but it happens. Turns out she's seventeen. Jail bait. I'd bet money she's on the *Defiance*.

And then I know. I correlate the *Defiance*'s stops in the four major space-going ports around Earth and out at Mars's Red Station with missing persons reports. Not a big enough statistical difference to convince a judge, but it's enough for me. Even fifty-year-old skills come in handy. Whatever else *Defiance* is hauling, she's also a slaver.

There's twenty thousand people or so here. I'm not going to find Holly Defiant by accident. But I won't find her for sure if I stay in my hotel room. I always seem to have a connection to my muses that's deeper than coincidence. Not magic or anything, more like the same thing that lets lost dogs get home. Like my creativity and theirs connect up and link our subconscious for a bit. I don't look for them, but we meet up in grocery store aisles and gyms.

So I'm going to try to use that actively, see if it's my imagination.

I skip the hotel's gym, and look up the fanciest one I can find a guest pass available for. Decide it doesn't feel right. Go two levels down, find a clean, simple low-gravity gym in an old cargo space that got abandoned when the station grew past it. At least I'll get a good workout.

Low gravity means different things in different places in the hab ring. Here it's .7 – more like an assist than a real low-g gym with acrobatic and ball games. The walls aren't even padded. The place is big, so even though there's thirty or so people sweating and grunting, it doesn't feel crowded. I head for the universals. The .7g means I can do ten pull-ups in a row, and even hang for a bit at the top of each one, looking around, my arms shaking. I pull through 3500 hundred meters of rowing, and do ninety push ups. I practice low-g running on a track that runs around the whole place until sweat stings my eyes, and once I think I see her, until I get close and see the woman's eyes are green and she doesn't have Holly's spark.

I can't hang out here all day, and without food, my muscles are done in after an hour. I give up. Twenty minutes later, I'm damp from a shower and wearing a one-piece with a black tunic over it. I don't do myself up pretty.

I walk into a lunch café, and there's Holly, sitting alone at a table. She's dressed in jeans and a flowing art-shirt that's fading slowly back and forth between three different space scenes. Her red hair is pulled up and back in a ponytail. She's probably waiting for someone. I slide in across from her anyway, hold out my hand. "Hi, I'm Lisel Mountain."

Her face goes from confused to contemptuous. "The energy vampire."

I haven't been characterized that way for decades. I don't talk about my need to hear live music anymore, and singers need an audience. I keep my voice smooth. "The writer."

"The writer who wrote Misty Moon's voice away."

I'm startled. That was a long time ago. "The woman who shouldn't ever have gotten into a relationship with someone she adored so much." This wasn't going well. "Look, I need to warn you about the *Defiance*. About the guys you were talking to yesterday."

She isn't having any of it. Up close, the color of her eyes is even more striking; the summer sky in a heat wave, pale enough to look almost white. She smells faintly of honeysuckle shampoo. She stares at me, water hovering at the lower edges of her eyes and her hands clenched on the orange tabletop. "Misty Moon was my mom's best friend. You know what happened to her?"

I do. She killed herself. After I published a story about a singer committing suicide. The story wasn't about her, didn't arise out of her music. I'd forgotten her until I read her obit. Then I'd been sad, but not guilty. I hadn't meant it for her at all. "That was years later. It wasn't about me."

Holly's eyes dart toward the door. She doesn't say anything; she doesn't believe me.

"They're slavers. The men who own the *Defiance* are slavers."

Now I have her attention. Her eyes narrow and her mouth thins as her jaw tightens. I don't like her mad at me. Then her gaze shifts to someone behind me, and her whole face relaxes into a smile as she stands up. "Excuse me."

I turn to find Bam 2 – I know his name now, from my research, or at least I know the name he uses. John Johnson. He smiles broadly at her, almost intimate. The bar last night had been dark enough I hadn't seen how good he looks. Too much like a playboy to be a cargo hauler. A guy who can afford all the best mods, so his pale skin glows smooth as a baby' cheek. He carries just the right balance of fat and muscle, and his hair falls over his head in a shock of lustrous black. His eyes are still hard, a deeper blue than hers; if it weren't for the black of his hair, they might look black. He holds out his hand to me, and his grip's strong. "Hi. I don't think I know you."

I pull my hand out of his. "Lisel."

He looks me up and down. I don't mean anything to him, but he's probably a moron who doesn't read anyway. I don't look like a victim any more, and I expect he sees this, since he turns away. It dawns on me I don't want this. I call out to him, "You didn't give me your name."

He turns back. "John."

I nod and smile. "Nice to meet you."

He motions to Holly to sit down, and he slides a chair over from another table, puts it at the end. I feel like I'm not going to be able to move, like he'll block me if I lunge for the door, but I almost try it. I hate being boxed in. The look on Holly's face stops me. She's glaring at me, her eyes narrow, like I've screwed up her entire day, maybe her whole year. But he's looking at me and not her. "You a fan of Holly's?"

"Sure. She's good."

"Where do you know her from?"

How to play this? "I don't. I heard her concert last night, and when I saw her in here, I ducked in to tell her how much I liked it, and see if she's playing again." It dawns on me that what I should've done when I first saw her is offer her a record contract. I could afford it. I'd have to find a producer, but Jodie and my agent could pull that off. Maybe I will if we get out of here alive. I'd never done that before, helped produce a recording. She'd have stayed for a record contract, but no, I have to save her myself. Apparently, I haven't outgrown doing things the hard way. So now I just gaze at him, looking as placid and undisturbed as I can, trying to undo the not-a-victim I usually put out. I wish I'd put on more makeup. I try not to let him see my hands are shaking. I'm out of practice; they should be smooth as ice.

"I'm a fan of Holly's, too." He gives me a soft smile, a frog to a fly smile, and I nod at him.

"Holly's going to come over to our ship and do a concert this afternoon. Want to come?"

"Sure!" I look down at myself. "Can I go change?" Now I'm going to follow this girl onto a slave ship. That isn't in the plan. I need a minute. "I mean, you're still going to eat, right? I'll be right back."

He looks like a wolf about to let a rabbit go. Holly puts a hand on his arm and looks adoringly at him. "I'll keep you company. Lisel will be back before we're done eating."

On cue, a waitbot heads for our table.

He nods.

I try to sound like a fan girl. "I'll be right back! I'm excited."

"Okay. Don't tell anyone – it's a secret show." He puts his slimy bad man hand on my arm, and I manage not to flinch, even to pull away gracefully.

"Even better," I say, winking at Holly so he can't see. "Wait right here." And then I'm through the door and I stop for a second, shaking. I'm going to need help. Since I don't know anyone else here, I'm going to have to bring help in. The cops have probably been bribed. I know. I was one.

I best do what I said and change, so I hurry to my hotel. On the way, I message Jodie, and the conversation goes like this.

«Mppphhhh. Hi. Lisel?»

«Look, I'm about to go to a concert on a slave ship. I need your help.»

«You're kidding.»

«No.»

«What is it this time?»

«That girl. Holly Defiant. They want her so I'm going and I need backup.»

«Call the cops.»

«I want you to. Save this conversation. But the feds. I dunno about the locals. I bet they don't care.»

«Am I your slave?»

«You're my friend.»

«This Holly must be hot.»

«Not like that.» And it isn't. Except now I want to make up for Misty Moon. Whatever. I don't want Holly Defiant mad at me. «Please. Or I can't go. I need backup.»

«So she's ugly?»

«Beautiful. I'll send you a feed when I get to the hotel.»

«!of Holly Defiant?!»

I'm almost running, so it's hard to type. «Of the Defiance, the slaver ship. This isn't a story.»

«YOU REALLY ARE SERIOUS?»

«I need you.»

I cut off the conversation because I'm getting near the first last-minute-shop on the way back. I grab a handful of energy bars and some water. Crazy ideas go through my head like I should write a story about this, and maybe that will help get us free. Like there's time. I just know if I don't get back before they want to leave, they'll go. Holly's a better catch than me, and Bam 2 knows it. After I shove a bar down my belly in three bites, I get back on the horn. «Jodie?»

«Okay. I called Blake and Blade, and they'll help me out.»

Blake and Blade are two friends of ours. Blake's a guy and Blade is his girl, and they run a protection service. I had to hire them for a few years when a fan thought if I died she'd become me. She died, but not because of me. I didn't become her.

Jodie and I kept track of Blake and Blade. They're useful to know.

«Where are they?»

«New Holland Three.»

That was close. A day or so away. «Can they leave now?»

«For a fee.»

«Insurance. I want them standing by.» And still, I better hope the Bams aren't planning to just take us away. It'll take Blake and Blade a day, so I may have to stall them again. I hope Holly meant it that she has to do her performance tonight. «Tell them to leave now, say you'll send them the feeds I'm going to send you.»

«Got it, boss.»

«Friend.»

«If you say so.» But she'd be laughing if she were talking to me. I can see her pretending to be severe with her shoulders all drawn back and her chin out, and her not meaning it at all. Bless her. She's the best publicist in the business, and one of my best friends, and she's helped me solve difficult problems before.

Not this hard. I hope I'm going to get to see her again, and then I push that poison thought away.

In my hotel room, I change into something a little nicer, but comfortable. I slip on some jewelry that looks like paste but isn't and hide some that clearly isn't in the lining of my shoes. It won't survive a scan, but unless/until they admit they're slaving us, they won't be able to make an excuse for the scan. I'll just keep my shoes on. A girl needs resources. I tuck my writing gear in my pocket.

I gather up my research on the *Defiance* and missing persons, and on Natalyi, into one big file, scribble a line or two about my conclusion, and as an afterthought I add the info Josie sent me on Holly Defiant just so if anybody needs to look for us they know. When I send the packet out to Jodie, I title it, "Promotion for Today," like I title all my daily lists for Jodie, and I add a note to hurry and get info out, to let people know I'll call if I get an update. I stand and stare at the hotel room, fighting an urge to clean it up, check out, and store my luggage. It'd be safer. But leaving a mess wasn't like me; it might show the authorities I'm really a kidnap victim.

When I close the door behind me, I have to take a deep breath, and I realize I'm scared, deep scared, too scared to shake, but maybe I'll pass out. Like when I was Holly Defiant's age and I was more of a victim than she is. Maybe not more than she's about to be. That's the thought that gets my feet moving.

I fret all the way through the bright and busy tunnel, dodging foot traffic and low-g cycles. I don't need to; they're still sitting at the same orange table. Holly pays the check, and I want to scream 'stupid' at her pale blue eyes, but she's just young. I can forgive her for being young.

Bam 2 almost looks annoyed that I made it back, and Holly definitely looks annoyed that I made it back, but I roll with it, feeling like an intruder and a cop and a momma all at once, and a little bit like an old lady, even though my mods are as expensive as Bam 2's.

Holly, of course, doesn't need them yet.

If Holly remembers the word slaver, she doesn't show it. Stupid kid.

The *Defiance* is a small cylindrical cabin-section stuck on a big rounded bell of a ship. She was never meant to land anywhere but space, but she's fitted with all three standard docking mechanisms, even the old Chinese one that's been ripped out of almost all the habs. I spot a few crewbots and two crewpeople working outside the bell, handling big unmarked boxes. So does she only house a few slaves, or are the slaves cargo, or am I lost in some kind of writerly imagination game and need a cup of coffee and twenty hours sleep real bad?

Inside, we pass empty shared berths and a few private rooms. Two of the room's doors are closed. I watch for Natalyi, but I don't see any sign of her, or for that matter of anyone else. "It's pretty empty," I remark.

Bam 2 gives me a winning smile. "Everyone's on leave."

"So who's the concert for?"

He hesitates for a breath, then coughs to hide it. When he's done he says, "For you, of course." His winning smile is back. "The ship's small, but we splurged on a good entertainment deck. Some of our work's taking stuff from hab to hab in the ring, but we do some interplanetary runs, too. The six months or more between here and Jupiter is a long time."

"I imagine. Do you read much?" No, I'm not being catty.

He shrugs. "There's a library. I prefer immersives so I can work my body and mind at the same time."

My immersives would all be produced by whoever in big type with "based on the story by Lisel Mountain" in tiny print. I am willing to bet he doesn't read the fine print.

I am about to tell him I like immersives, too (who wouldn't; they make me ten times the money of a full-length novel), but he turns in a door and we follow him. He's right about the entertainment deck. Right now, soft piano music floats through the air, coming from all around me, as if a pro is playing a baby grand and a thousand tiny nano-fairies carry a thousand tiny, perfect amplifiers through the air. A small galley is tucked artfully into one corner, and an immersive footbed covers the other corner. Couches and comfy chairs are bolted down along one wall, opposite big screens, and gaming tables and chairs for two or four or six scattered around amidst a fifty-by-hundred meter space that has to be the width of the whole cylinder. This explains why the berths are so small. Crew probably only sleeps in them.

It's way too high-end for a cargo ship.

Bam 2 watches me try to take in all the details, my writer's fingers itching to take out my journal and do a 360 pix of the room to examine later.

I don't see a stage. I turn to Holly. "Where will you play?"

She chews on her bottom lip, her pale blue eyes almost white in the artificial light. She looks beaten rather than defiant. Her voice is soft and it breaks a little. "Back at the Liar's Club."

It takes me a second to process. I try bluster. "Well, that's okay. I can make your show." I turn to Bam 2, and I say, "Cool room. Thanks for showing it to me."

He says, "Stay a while."

"I'd rather not." I take a breath. "I have a meeting." I look at Holly instead of him, repeating myself louder. "I have a meeting."

She says, "This is for Misty Moon."

I shiver, the room colder by ten degrees. I'm not saving her. No one can save her. Bitch. Soul of ice bitch. I'm so, so stupid. I can smell my own fear, and I bet she can, too, but I try not to show it, make sure my voice doesn't shake. "I adored Misty. Worshipped the ground she walked on."

"She never recovered."

I'd walked out when she became so human her music didn't help me write anymore. I had learned I didn't love her. I adored her, put her on a pedestal, fell in love with the idea of her. The singer had a voice like a river. The woman cried and gossiped and watched soapshows. "I never meant her any harm."

"Words are powerful. Your words were a gun to her head. She didn't deserve them."

I swallow, my mouth dry. "How well did you really know her?"

"I lied. She was my mom."

God. I hesitate. "That means she moved on from me."

"She didn't. Not really. She went through men and women like candy."

Like she went through me, but it seems like the wrong thing to say. Misty had been good at myth. Even now, when I should, I can't quite make myself apologize. "That must be where you get your voice. From her. She had a stage-presence voice, too. She captivated audiences."

"She took your story hard. She thought it was a message from you to her."

I tap my foot. Bam 2 watches, his eyes going from one to the other of us. His curiosity must bother Holly as much as it bothers me. She jerks her head at him and he goes to stand by the door.

I adjust my opinion of who's in charge. "Look," I tell her, "When you sing, you make everyone quiet. I saw it last night. They're listening. You adjusted their mood, made them happier. You're entertaining. So am I. That's all it is. I never meant your mom – or you – harm."

Silence falls as she watches me and the piano music plays, and I hear both of us breathing and Bam 2 shifting his weight over by the door.

"Take me back," I say.

She shakes her head, and then she winks at me.

I can't explain the wink. I just take it in, deciding to think about it later. The girl's a chameleon. An actress. What did I expect? I don't want to hear Holly Defiant sing anymore, ever, anywhere.

Like Misty. Misty Moon.

Her answer is to turn and walk away. I walk after her, dogging her heels, but at the door Bam 2 lets her through and stops in front of me. He shakes his head. "Later."

Yeah, both Bams probably. I wonder if I'll be raped or sold or both. I play dumb, trying on outrage. "What are you doing? You can't keep me in here. It's against the law."

He holds his fingers to his lips. "I know."

He goes out the door, eeling through, shutting it behind him. The last glimpse I catch of him, he looks satisfied, like it makes him happy to lock people up. Makes sense, for a slaver. The music changes to something more martial, with more instruments. There's a whole horn section, now. I bet he's the one that changed it. Part of a joke. Maybe Natalyi is somewhere else, and they're playing her the latest sappy teen love songs, and she doesn't even know what bargain she's made. But I do.

The door doesn't open, of course.

I try my phone and my watch and my sos button and nothing gets through. The room's shielded. Spaceships have no windows. I need Blake and Blade pretty bad, and I'm willing to bet they can't find me here. I cruise the room to see if there's any other way to get a message out. Everything's passworded, and most of it wants a key-fob I don't have.

I sit down on the edge of a couch. I try taking my journal out and writing. I walk barefoot on the immersive pad and jump up and down and try to get its attention, my feet sinking slightly into the green surface. I think about Misty Moon in spite of my best efforts not to, and I'm mad at her and sad for her. I cry for a few minutes, the music loud in my ears, even covering some of my sobs. I bet I haven't cried for a decade.

I pace. I hate locks. If this was a smaller place I'd be screaming.

Finally, I do what writers do when there's nothing else to do. I write. Not a story, I'm not that coherent. But words and associations. I draw pictures of Blade and Blake. I even nap. As if the room knows I'm sleeping, the music quiets, finally. Sleeping isn't as hard as you'd think. After all, I spent much of last night trying to save Holly Defiant from the slavers. I draw an eye, winking. But I don't get it. I should have checked Holly's proximity to the missing and to the *Defiance*. It would be like Blade to check, maybe she will.

They can't be here yet.

I find the facilities and make dinner. At least the kitchen's stocked. I wonder who I can bribe with the jewelry. No one right now. The only people I'm sure are aboard are me and Natalyi. The only slave I'm sure is aboard is me.

I can't make sense of that. Slavers should take the unknown dreg. Not me. I have to wait for more data.

It's so late Holly's surely singing in the Liar's Bar by now.

I want a pillow and a blanket to bed down with but I can't find one. No one left any towels out either. Some hosts.

I get back up and find an electronic dartboard that works without a password and throw invisible darts until my right shoulder hurts.

The door slams open. Uniforms. Black uniforms with white piping.

The feds.

I'm so happy I jump up and down. I scream happiness at them.

They try to calm me, using shushing sounds and composed voices and easy commands. Sit down. Rest. Drink water.

I'm shaking all over again. I've had close calls before. Anybody that's over a hundred has had them. But this is today's, and I don't remember any that were worse.

Blake and Blade send me a notice that they've arrived, want to know where to meet me. I tell them where I'm staying.

Just as I finish, the hairs are high on the back of my neck – that feeling that tells you you're being watched. I look up at the door. Holly Defiant is standing in it, her red hair falling loosely around her face and shoulders and her pale blue eyes on me. She breaks out in a sloppy grin and holds up a badge.

Holly Defiant, undercover officer.

Maybe I will go watch her next concert. Damn smart bitch.

Keanan Brand brings us a brand new prequel story to the Thieves' Honor *serials which graced many an issue of* Ray Gun Revival, *detailing Captain Kristoff's first mission with his future right hand and best friend Finney as she comes up against a cocky competitor in...*

SHOOTING THE DEVIL'S EYE

a *Thieves' Honor* yarn

Keanan Brand

"Can't be done." Wyatt slammed the mug on the table, slopping beer over myriad laser-carved initials and one misspelled invitation to call Gina for a good time.

"Hide and watch." Rankin Greer stretched his arms wide, flexed, winked up at a passing barmaid. She winked back.

Kristoff laughed under his breath. *Hide the women.*

Corrigan, the ship's mechanic, drank deep, smacked his lips, and belched.

Forget the women. Hide the men.

Kristoff crossed his arms. "You might scrape through the Devil's Eye in a freighter the size of *Martina,* but you were flying empty. No cargo, no passengers."

Greer shrugged. "So?"

"*Martina* will be heavy – cargo in, cargo out. She doesn't need a hotshot. She needs a steady hand at the wheel."

The freelance pilot rubbed his belly as the barmaid set a steaming plate of stew in front of him. "Oh, I got a steady hand all right." He grinned up at her. "Two of 'em."

This joker's greasy enough to lubricate a whole ship.

Still, Greer was between jobs, and he had shot the Devil's Eye.

"There's money at the end of a successful run." Kristoff stood. "And a bonus if you don't wreck my ship."

Corrigan finished his beer. "Cap, want me to negotiate proper terms?" He pulled a wrench out of his back pocket.

"Can't afford to waste a good pilot."

"Still think we should wait for Finney." Wyatt hitched up his belt. "I ain't got a hankerin' for suicide."

The tavern doors swung open. Two men stepped in, surveyed the dim room, then moved aside, allowing a rotund man to squeeze through the opening.

Skippy the fence.

Damn.

Shouldering between two larger vessels, Finney landed the *Gaston* with nary a bump. Air sighed out from the slip, creating a vacuum that held the ship steady while docked. It could only be released by the harbor master – a measure supposed to prevent pirating, but this was Vortuna, and piracy was its stock in trade.

That was no fuel off Finney's engine. Wasn't her ship.

The all-clear sounded. She unstrapped, stood, grabbed her duffel from the locker, and exited the wheelhouse, thudding down the companionway in boots two sizes too big. Hers had been stolen at the last port.

The captain, arms folded, blocked the passage. "Was it something I said?"

"Twenty percent share. Coin, not credits." Finney held out a hand. "And a new pair of boots."

"Thirty percent, and you stay aboard for the next run."

"It's been a week, ship's time. Can't have you gettin' too fond of me."

"Too late, darlin'."

Finney adjusted her grip on the duffel straps, her other hand still extended. "This can just as easily become a fist."

The captain rubbed his bruised jaw and grinned. "See the purser on your way out."

A new bag of colonial coin weighting her bag, and the purser's leather boots on her feet, Finney strode down the gangway and onto the noisy wharf. She drew a deep breath. Dust and the odor of burnt engine oil tainted the air. A ship or two needed maintenance.

Near the end of the wharf lay another docking area, this one filled with small freighters and personal craft, quicker getaways than the *Gaston*. Among them stood the *Martina Vega*. A venerable old dame still graceful despite her years, she was the pride of Captain Helmer Kristoff, who spoke to her as to a woman, and loved her as if she were alive.

Finney understood. She'd flown the *Vega* a time or two, and blast, the ship was yar.

Gangway lowered, the *Vega* welcomed a line of folk clad in nondescript clothing – desert dwellers, perhaps, who each carried a single pack on their backs. When had the ship taken on passengers? Dangerous cargo for a pirate and a smuggler.

At the bottom of the gangway stood a tall, overweight man in a pristine apron, meaty arms crossed – Sahir the cook, standing guard – and at the top was stationed a slight man in a white lab coat, glasses pushed up onto his head. *Hm. He's new.*

The tempting fragrance of roasting meat overtook all other smells, even those of the sweating stevedores loading and unloading cargo. Finney followed her nose to a dockside tavern, tossed her duffel in a corner booth, sat, folded her arms, and propped her feet on the chair opposite. She had a bit of wait while the barmaids tended to the male customers and bypassed her table, eyes averted.

Three newcomers arrived – a large man and a couple bodyguards – and one barmaid made the mistake of glancing toward them but catching Finney's gaze instead.

"Water, beer, and whatever's cookin'."

Brows raised, the barmaid looked pointedly at Finney's dirty feet.

Finney crossed her ankles and waggled her boots. "I'll take that beer now." She smiled beneficently.

Frowning, the barmaid left. As she did, she adjusted her bosom, much as a fighter flexes his muscles. Finney laughed.

Then all hell broke loose.

A fist caught him on the ear, knocking him sideways. Kristoff stumbled into a table, righted himself, then spun around, jabbing an elbow into the bodyguard's midsection. The man grunted and hunched forward.

Corrigan's wrench descended, a flash of silvery light. The other bodyguard blocked it, and tried twisting it from the mechanic's grasp. A chair flew across the floor, catching the first guard behind the knees. He buckled – right into Kristoff's fist – then slithered to the floor.

The second guard grappled with Corrigan, slamming his hand against the wall then on a table, collapsing it and landing both men in the debris of a beer-soaked meal. Customers jumped up, cursing, throwing punches. A few of the more muscular barmaids joined the fray.

Rankin Greer continued eating, an eddy of indifference in the melee. Skippy the fence was nowhere to be seen.

Knuckles swollen, hand throbbing, Kristoff glanced around the room. Maybe Skippy had ducked behind a table.

Wyatt rose from a mass of flailing arms and legs, slapped the bloodied wrench into Kristoff's injured hand, then dove into the pile again, dragging out Corrigan and pushing through the bodies as if escaping a vortex.

Propping up the punch-drunk mechanic, who was a good foot-and-a-half taller than he, Wyatt asked, short of breath, "Skippy?"

Kristoff shook his head.

"Greer?"

The pilot had failed the interview. Kristoff could fly *Martina* himself, but with this particular cargo and the Devil's Eye –

A shot exploded, and wood splinters showered down on the combatants. They all drew back from one another, hands lifted from their sides.

Chemical smoke wisped from the barrel of the Cavanaugh Cutlass, a substantial pistol grasped in a hand too slim to lift it, let alone hold it steady. And yet the barrel did not waver.

Then it lowered, and the owner uncrossed her feet, sat upright, and rested her forearms on the table. A long, reddish-brown braid snaked over one shoulder, and the woman's green eyes surveyed the bedraggled group.

Kristoff grinned – *Finney* – and took a step toward her.

"Thought you didn't need a hotshot." Greer wiped his mouth then dropped the napkin beside his plate.

"My, my, my, if it ain't Rocket Rankin Greer," said Finney. "Still tellin' that tall tale about shooting the Eye?"

Greer leapt to his feet, knocking over the chair, and strode forward.

Kristoff stepped into his path. "Outside."

Greer shoved him aside – or tried to – but a wrench to the sternum sent him stumbling backward, into the arms of a beefy sailor with a black eye and a surly scowl.

A chuckle behind him reminded Kristoff of his reason for being in the tavern at all. "Hey, Finn," he said over his shoulder, "lookin' for work?'

"Not really."

The sailor dropped Greer, who slumped to the floor, clutching his chest and gasping.

"But I need my favorite pilot to fly my best girl through the bad part of town."

"Always the charmer." Finney stood beside him. "Feed me, and we'll talk."

"Done."

His analog radio crackled to life, signaling Sahir's frequency, and a familiar voice spoke through the static – "Good afternoon, Captain Kristoff" – but it wasn't Sahir.

Skippy was aboard the ship.

🔫

The bartender hefted a shotgun and raised her brows. Bruised customers picked up the remnants of chairs and crockery.

Finney tossed enough money on the table to cover repairs to the hole she'd shot in the pillar of rare wood from Earth, then she followed Kristoff and crew into the afternoon heat. Swinging her duffle onto one shoulder, she maintained her distance, and kept a weather-eye out for anyone suspicious.

Well, pretty much everyone in Vortuna was questionable.

She had no particular loyalty to the *Vega* crew – loyalty led to confinement, and Finney enjoyed her freedom – but she liked the ship. It was the same class as the vessel her late grandfather, Admiral Cunningham, taught her to fly. Piloting the *Martina Vega* was like talking to him again.

Stripped down and meant for short hauls between colonies, the freighter had been equipped with extra compartments concealed in the hold and elsewhere. Perhaps all those packs the desert dwellers brought aboard earlier were the illicit cargo Skippy coveted.

But why start a bar fight? Why not simply take what he wanted while the captain was ashore?

She glanced up just in time to duck out of the way of a cargo hoist depositing a crated kayak onto the dock.

More to the point, why was Kristoff talking to that greasy Rankin Greer? She shuddered. The Rocket had piloting chops, but he was better known for a recumbent skill set, one that grounded him numerous times in brigs or infirmaries.

"Hey, Finney!"

Speak of the devil.

Pallid and sweating, Greer nonetheless matched her pace. "You thinkin' of takin' my place? I don't give up easy – "

No, I expect easy *is not something you'd give up even with a fight.*

" – and I'm gonna earn that bonus."

Sure, kid.

"Kristoff likes you, but you've never even been near it."

Near what, little man? "So I've heard."

Greer frowned.

A rickshaw stood at the base of the *Vega*'s gangway. Kristoff said something to his crew. They started to skirt the ramp and go toward the back of the ship, but armed men came from hiding and surrounded them.

A gun prodded Finney's back.

She spun around, grabbed the barrel, and twisted it aside, yanking it from her attacker and slamming the heel of her hand against his chest. The man fell, wheezing.

The mouth of another gun kissed her temple. She sighed. *No good deed.*

"You robbed a bank." Seated on three folding chairs shoved together to form a bench, Skippy puffed on a cigar almost as fat as his fingers. "Prime Colonial." The fence held up the cigar, examining it. "Ballsy, but stupid."

Kristoff refused to be baited.

He and the crew stood in a loose circle, facing outward, surrounded by goons with shiny new weapons and straps of ammunition. Beside him, Finney shifted her weight. She stood with hands resting loosely on her belt, near an empty holster. Her knuckles were bruised and torn.

The only crewman missing was Alerio. The newest, he wasn't known to Skippy, and likely no one had thought to search the engine room.

"You beat the drones, but people still saw your faces. Even if they didn't, who's gonna forget the giant?" Skippy flapped a pudgy hand at Corrigan. "Or the cook."

Sahir growled deep in his throat, and one hand went to his belt, but his knife lay on top of the piled weapons.

Skippy laughed, one hand on his enormous belly. He drew on the cigar, then blew out a billowing cloud of smoke. "Law wants you bad." He flicked ashes onto the grated flooring of the hold. "We've done business a time or two. I don't want to haul you in to the constabulary. Just hand over whatever's left. I take it to the law, collect a small finder's fee, and you stay outta the brig. And maybe the law looks the other way next time I wander into, ah, shady territory."

"Sounds reasonable," said Kristoff, "until you decide to keep the loot and turn me in anyway. Or you keep it, let me go, and ruin my reputation as a reliable businessman."

"Possible. But the first law of piracy, right after 'avoid the hangman's noose,' is 'profit.' You go to the brig, I profit. You fly free, I still profit." The fence shrugged one shoulder. "Your freedom is merely a bargaining chip. Where's the loot?"

Kristoff cleared his throat, shifted his stance, knocking the heel of his boot against Wyatt's. *Pay attention, old man. Read my mind.*

"Not much left of the tech," said Kristoff. "Nothing worth your time."

"There's still money."

"Well, yeah, but what's money?" Kristoff spread his hands. "It's what dirt colonists use. It's nowhere near as shiny as a hefty tally of government credits in your account."

"Credits are so – "

"Traceable?"

" – confining." Skippy dropped the cigar stub and leaned forward, the chairs creaking under his weight. "So, give me the money, and I leave. Win-win."

Not for the families of the rebels.

Kristoff stepped forward. Two of Skippy's men blocked his way, but the fence ordered them aside. "The captain has no weapons, and we're negotiating."

Kristoff dropped to one knee and crossed his arms across the other, casual, as if hunkering down to talk to a friend. "But, y'see, Skippy, the thing is – "

He reached down as if tying the laces on his boot.

" – a man's gotta protect his good name – "

He wrapped both hands around Skippy's ankle and stood, flipping the man onto his back. The impact shuddered through Kristoff's feet and legs, and echoed through the hold.

" – as much as he protects his freedom."

Skippy flailed and wheezed, but couldn't right himself.

Behind Kristoff, the crew handled the guards. He didn't have to see the action; Wyatt's command, then grunts, curses, clangs, and thuds painted an aural picture.

The *Vega*'s engines rumbled to life. *Thank you, Alerio.*

Kristoff kicked aside the chairs and stood over Skippy. The man glared up at him in helpless anger. Kristoff rested the sole of his boot on Skippy's hand, and applied light pressure, just enough to communicate the full weight of his meaning.

"Get. Off. My. Ship."

Skippy suggested what Kristoff and his canine-bred antecedents could do with that ship.

The fence struggled to pull his hand free as Kristoff leaned forward. Corrigan and Sahir flanked him, Kristoff nodded, and they hoisted Skippy onto a flatbed dolly. One by one, trussed-up interlopers were wheeled to the gangway and kicked down the ramp.

Unbound and protesting, Greer, too, was released in similar fashion.

"We'll be keeping the weapons," Kristoff called to the writhing heap of humanity. "Finder's fee."

A shaggy-haired man with a scruffy jaw grabbed a galley chair, flipped it around, and sat facing her, arms crossed atop the chair back. He smiled, one side of his mouth tipping up.

"Go away, Kristoff." Finney tilted her head back against the wall and closed her eyes.

He chuckled. "Keep talkin' like that, a man might fall in love."

"And here I was thinkin' it was my beautiful face and perky personality."

"That, too. If I tip my head just right and squint." Kristoff cleared his throat. "So, the *Gaston*. Still running mash?"

"Only the finest in homemade illegal brews sure to make a body deaf, blind, or dead. And it's excellent paint remover." She opened her eyes and lifted her head. "Still smuggling guns?"

"Long live the rebellion." He lifted a fist and gave it a halfhearted shake. "Still not interested? Even for a short run?"

Finney sat up straight and leaned her arms on the table. Everything hurt. "Thought I'd take a little vacation. Hitch a ride to Port Henry. Relax at my favorite resort. Y'know, enjoy the fruits of my labor."

Kristoff faked a hacking, ahem-ahem cough.

She shot him a look. "You need new material."

"Precisely. So, you'll join the crew?"

Her eyes narrowed as she studied him. "Why not just fly the *Vega* yourself?"

"This run, there might be trouble."

"Always is." She stretched. "Aside from the passengers, how many guns you have now?"

"Sahir, of course. Wyatt and Corrigan are still aboard. Last week, we picked up an engineer named Alerio. He shoots a tiny little Tattersall's Special, but I wouldn't challenge him to a duel."

"Five guns."

"Yours makes six."

"Didn't say I'm takin' the job."

Kristoff leaned forward, forearms on the table, and lowered his voice. "The space we're flying, we'll shoot the Devil's Eye."

Finney's green eyes gleamed. "I'm in."

Skippy was off the trail – for now – and the freighter wasn't marked by logos or bright paint, but the *Martina Vega* wasn't nondescript to the point of invisibility. Not out here. In the space around Vortuna lurked sentinel ships, hired by men like the late Sam Quinn, infamous pirate turned respectable businessman while keeping the source of his wealth hidden.

The sentinels weren't interested in the *Vega*. However, out past the nebula, constable ships waited, looking for a reason to take any vessel doing trade – smuggling – now that Vortuna had been cast outside the colonial trade alliance. But the *Vega*'s hold was empty, her cargo elsewhere.

The crew gathered in the galley, and consumed sandwiches piled on a plate in the center of the table.

"What's your mind, cap?" Wyatt leaned on the edge of a counter, and chewed on a toothpick.

"If we're boarded, we're just innocent freighters that stopped in Vortuna for fuel on our way to the Rim to pick up colonists and their market goods for a charter trip back to Port Henry."

Corrigan grinned, contorting his unhandsome face into something even uglier. "I can be innocent."

Wyatt sucked his teeth and looked skeptical.

Sahir flipped his knife end-to-end. "I just cook."

"I, uh, might be on a wanted list." Alerio shoved his hands into the pockets of his lab coat. "Or two."

"Talk to Wyatt," said Kristoff. "Dandy forger. Make even your momma forget your name."

"So, ah, cap, now that Finney's here," ventured Corrigan, "she takin' over the laundry?"

The pilot planted her boot squarely into the mechanic's side. Corrigan grunted and bent over, clutching his ribs.

Enough said.

Finney stood with hands tucked into her back pockets, watching a chunk of flotsam float past the forward port.

The *Martina Vega* had cleared the nebula, as well as a search party from a constable freighter. The lawman had spoken pleasantly enough, but there was sharp suspicion in his glance. Occupational hazard. Still, he'd let the *Vega* go and seemed to accept Kristoff's story. That didn't keep Finney from looking over the *Vega*'s shoulder, just in case.

Her body ached with tension, and she stretched, arching her spine. *Shoulda stayed in Vortuna.* Two long hauls back-to-back. She knew better.

But she'd never shot the Eye. Any pilot who flew it in a sleek, narrow runner earned respect among his peers and free drinks at the pub. Finney had the added challenge of flying an old freighter through the narrow slit in the broken moon. If she succeeded, who'd believe her?

What if she banged up the *Vega*? Kristoff loved this boat. *What if I kill her?*

Pain shot behind Finney's eyes, and she winced.

Shoulda stayed in Vortuna.

Reflected in the glass, Kristoff ducked into the wheelhouse. He stepped between the two consoles and joined her at the forward port. "Nervous?"

"Flying a boatful of criminals past the law and through the Eye? Do it blindfolded all the time, just to keep it interesting."

He smiled.

"Why this run? Why that cargo?"

The smile disappeared. "You know the reason for the rebellion?"

"Sour grapes. Anarchy."

"The real reason. Why your grandparents joined. Why my father died."

"Freedom. Justice."

"Aye, but more."

Finney rested a hip against the pilot's console and folded her arms. "So, tell me."

He spread his feet wide, as if preparing to take a blow, and stared out at the black. "The reason for the colonies isn't exploration, mining, or establishing a base for space travel. It's experimentation."

"Say again?"

"Computers implanted behind the ear. The first truly personal computer. It was billed as unhackable, untrackable, totally safe, and it operated according to commands thought as well as spoken."

"Impressive. Why did I never learn that in school?"

"About a third of the colonists underwent the operation. Viruses were imbedded in the chips. Soon after establishing the first settlement on Prospero, some users went mad, claiming mysterious voices issued commands, turning their bodies into puppets. They either committed suicide or were confined to facilities. Others died trying to tear the computers out of their heads. Even if chips were removed or deactivated, victims rarely recovered their right minds. And then there were rumors that patients in asylums weren't being treated, but programmed to become remote-controlled soldiers."

Finney frowned, not quite believing.

"I was a bored kid, and curious. I decoded my father's encrypted files whenever he was gone."

"A little light reading?" She pinched her nose and closed her eyes, trying to push back the growing headache. "Remote-controlled soldiers. Sounds like the strange troops that burnt Andronicus Settlement."

"My father thought so."

"Andronicus lies along the Rim. Is that where we're going?" She straightened and glared at Kristoff's reflection. "You should have told me."

"Then you wouldn't have come."

"Damn right – "

"We're not going to Andronicus."

She uttered a pithy epithet.

He almost smiled. "We're going to a refugee camp inside the Eye."

"Now I know you're lying. Nothing lives there. The only life the Eye sees is when daredevils like us try to shoot it."

"Perfect place to hide, then."

"Still doesn't explain the bank heist."

Kristoff bowed his head then looked aside, as if avoiding her gaze. "The rebels are entrenched, and battle is confined to skirmishes, but the war isn't over. In trying to root out rebels, the government is harassing their families. Confiscating property, accounts." He cleared his throat. "We're righting a wrong. Returning deeds and stolen money."

She felt a lump in her throat, too, but c'mon. Who hadn't been affected by the war?

An alert blipped, and Finney looked at the telescreen. A ship bristling with antennae entered the space off the starboard bow. No signs of life.

Standing behind her, Kristoff read aloud a portion of the report scrolling up the screen: "Colonial Ship *Elsinore*, research vessel, 213 souls."

"Not anymore," said Finney. "No bodies."

"No emergency beacon, either, or marker telling us she's been abandoned on purpose. Sign of scavengers?"

"Not yet." She glanced at him. "Thinkin' of snooping around?"

"Ghost ships are notorious bad luck."

"But you don't believe in bad luck."

He stared at the screen, brows lowered in a frown of deep thought. She knew he wanted to go aboard. He couldn't help it, being a smuggler and a pirate, and an explorer who sometimes talked of heading beyond the Rim into uncharted space.

But he stepped back and shook his head. "Later. After the delivery."

"You sure? It's right there."

"No." He hesitated. "No distractions. The refugees have waited long enough."

Then he broke out that signature Kristoff grin. "See? Interesting things happen when you fly with me."

"Will you still say that if I wreck your ship?"

"Kill *Martina*, you'll owe me your life." He waggled his eyebrows.

"Only you would propose when threatened with ship-icide." Finney clamped her lips to keep from smiling, but a smile burst through nonetheless.

"Yeah" – grin widening – "I knew you liked me."

The Devil's Eye was a narrow gash, a cat's pupil, punched through the center of a pallid moon. Deep inside the chasm pulsed a red glow, the low, slow-burning flames of an old fire fueled by a deep vein of coal-like ore, remnants of a mining operation gone wrong.

Crowded into the wheelhouse, the crew watched in tense silence as Finney guided the ship toward the widest part of the tear. Bandana tied around her head, hair confined to a long thick braid down her back, hands steady on the controls, the pilot looked stone-cold calm.

Kristoff hid clenched fists behind crossed arms.

Jagged walls squeezed close, and the ship's running lights illuminated the torn rock. Shadows moved, facets glittered, fire flickered deep in the Eye, distorting the true shape of the passage.

Sweat darkened the back of Finney's shirt.

The fissure curved. Finney muttered under her breath, and guided the ship around the tight corner, but the *Vega* bumped a wall, and the crew grabbed whatever they could to keep themselves upright.

"How far?" asked Sahir.

Kristoff shrugged. "Someone'll meet us."

The fire wasn't a conflagration but low-burning flames, mostly glowing coals, with flares that cast moving light on the walls. It burned on either side of the passage and trailed up and down the walls in pulsing ropes. Toward the core of the broken moon, smoke thickened, obscuring the way. Finney slowed the *Vega* until the ship crawled just above idle.

Kristoff grabbed the radio. "Hailing Ojo del Diablo. Hailing Ojo del Diablo. This is freighter *Martina Vega* requesting assistance."

After a few moments of silence, a response crackled over the line. "Go ahead, *Martina Vega*."

"Request a guide through the smoke."

No response.

"Repeat, request a guide."

Again no response.

Either communications were down, or the refugees were skittish.

Points of light brightened within the smoke, widening as they approached.

"Runners," said Finney, reading the scans. "Armed."

"Law enforcement or military?"

"Can't tell."

Not that it mattered which. The *Vega* had no weapons. A ship with guns gained immediate attention, an encumbrance at port entries or near constable vessels. An unarmed ship, however, could easily pass cursory inspections, and with little interest from harbormasters, especially if it was a freighter so old it could have arrived with the first colonists. The *Martina Vega* neither looked like a pirate or a smuggler, nor could she defend herself like one.

"Alerio, coax as much juice as possible from the engines. Then await my command."

"Aye." The engineer disappeared through the hatchway; his running steps thundered down the passage.

"They're behind us," Finney warned.

Damn. "Corrigan, go help Al. Sahir and Wyatt, secure all hatches. You have two minutes."

"That's not enough time – "

Kristoff looked at Wyatt. "Then stop wasting it."

The men left, and Kristoff turned toward the telescreen. At least five runners fore and more aft, creeping closer.

"Why the hatches?" asked Finney.

"This could be messy. Ever play leapfrog?"

"Those runners can recover faster than the *Vega*."

"*Martina*'s still a saucy wench. She'll lead 'em a merry chase." He unclipped his radio and spoke into it. "All hands, strap in. Our pilot's gonna show off."

She shot him a startled glance.

He gripped her shoulder – *You can do this* – and again addressed the crew. "Report."

Alerio replied, "Engines'll go wide open, captain, whenever you're ready," and Wyatt added, "Me and Sahir in the hold. All hatches secure."

Just as hampered by the smoke but fleeter than *Martina*, the runners were within a few hundred yards. The Eye confined them to tight formation, stacked rather than abreast.

A shot screamed past *Martina*'s port bow, and Finney flinched.

"Just a warning," Kristoff assured her. "We still have time."

Skippy's face appeared on the telescreen, smiling, chomping on an unlit cigar. "Well, now. There you are." He moved his screen to reveal his pilot. Greer.

Kristoff turned off the screen and, reaching over to the co-pilot console, cut external communications. The refugee settlement of Ojo del Diablo might try to make contact, but he doubted it. Not with runners infesting the Eye.

A second shot blazed along portside, stem to stern.

Time to dance.

Finney slowed the ship to full stop, spun the wheel directing the engines, and radioed the engine room: "Prepare for vertical. On my mark."

The *Vega* needed to leap high enough to clear the runners ahead, but not so high that she'd impale on the rocks overhead. These old First Colony freighters had been designed with uncertain terrain in mind: a ship could land or ascend without needing wide clearance for an angled descent or a forward takeoff.

Kristoff dropped into the other chair and buckled in just as a third shot skimmed starboard.

The engines raced.

"Mark!" Finney pulled back on the stick, and the freighter jumped like a frog afire. The *Vega* cleared the stack of runners, Finney spun the wheel again, repositioning the engines, and the ship raced forward into the smoke.

Dear God and gearshifts, let there not be a ship hiding there. It was more a nebulous thought than a complete prayer. Her hands were too busy at the controls, and her focus narrowed to seeing a way through the murk.

A black shadow loomed.

"Wall!" Kristoff shouted, bracing himself.

She dropped the ship straight down. The sudden change in direction strained the straps as her body tried to remain in one position while the seat fell away; for a few sickening moments, she felt weightless.

Two pursuers didn't correct course in time, and crashed against the rock wall, exploding, the fireballs displayed on the telescreen. A third runner skimmed along the face and tumbled out of control, scraping the upper aft skin of the *Vega* with a piercing screech that echoed through the ship.

The smoke thinned. The Eye continued through a passage just below the *Vega*. Finney guided the freighter into the cut and exhaled in relief. In the distance lay the ragged edge of the Eye and black space.

Her hands trembled, and sweat sopped her clothes.

"Well," said Kristoff with a shaky smile, "that was a pleasant walk in the park."

"Too bad it's not over. They can still catch us."

"True." He fiddled with controls on the co-pilot console. "And we may have missed our contact. At the risk of tipping off Skippy – " He held the ship's radio to his mouth. "Hailing Ojo del Diablo. Hailing Ojo del Diablo."

The response this time was immediate: "All clear ahead. Follow our lead."

A small, odd-shaped vessel appeared at the tunnel mouth. It appeared to be pieced together from runners of varying provenance, and by no means spaceworthy. Still, it hovered until the *Vega* approached, then it bobbed to the side and down, out of sight.

Finney cleared the Eye then dropped the ship below the moon, into its shadow. The patchwork runner stopped, waited for the *Vega*, then rose, disappearing into the underside of the moon. Finney glanced at Kristoff, who nodded – "Carry on" – and she followed the runner up into a deep well lit by torches. A massive black slab of metal closed behind the *Vega*. Near the top of the well glowed a broad light, revealing a landing deck and another door that slid open as the two vessels approached.

A woman with salt-and-pepper hair appeared on the telescreen, and her voice crackled over the radio. "My son brings trouble in his wake."

Kristoff chuckled. "Better than a bouquet of rock roses."

Wrung out, Finney landed the ship, released the controls, leaned back in her chair, and let her arms flop on the armrests.

"Young lady," said the elegant voice, "are you all right? I apologize for my son. He's never been one for the niceties."

"Aye, ma'am, but he gives the best gifts."

Mrs. Kristoff looked puzzled.

Finney straightened, and ran a hand over her hair, pulling wet strands out of her face. "Bragging rights. I took a freighter through the Eye."

"Ah." The woman smiled. "You are Fiona Grace."

Finney shot a narrow glance at Kristoff, who, shrugging, looked wide-eyed and innocent.

"Yes, well, welcome to the Devil's Eye, Miss Grace."

She reported to the hold, expecting to help haul reacquired funds down to the refugees.

Instead, weary and battered, the cargo crawled out of secret compartments and impossible spaces. The desert dwellers with their sand-colored clothing filed past Kristoff and nodded their thanks before descending the gangway. Their packs sagged as if weighted by more than simple supplies, and emitted a slithery, clanking sound whenever they shifted.

Of course. The money from the bank job.

And not desert dwellers, but refugees, families of the rebels, original owners of the coin.

His mother stepped away from Kristoff and clasped Finney's arm. The women strolled among the stone-built structures comprising a tidy village. Beyond the houses glowed a glass structure filled with tubes, lights, and hanging plants. The main cavern gave way to tributaries, smaller tunnels leading deeper into the broken moon.

Why was his mother living here? The family was wealthy, influential. Kristoff leaving the military and turning freighter with sketchy dealings had been a disappointment, surely, but had the family fallen to the point of being outcasts?

The woman smiled. "You have questions."

Aye, but they were rude. Finney asked instead, "Why is everyone piling their money together? It was wrongfully seized. It's why they're here. You'd think they'd want to start over."

"They've already started over. And we have no need of money here," said Mrs. Kristoff. "It will be set aside, awaiting necessity. Perhaps we can acquire a fleet of kayaks, perhaps larger runners, even a mining vessel."

Finney looked around. "It's certainly a *quiet* life." She tried to sound neutral, but there was a doubting edge to her words.

Mrs. Kristoff chuckled. "You are very like him."

"Pardon?"

"He has approached you many times to join his crew."

Finney nodded.

"Strange, don't you think, that a man would sublimate his pride and keep asking a question that has been rejected so many times?"

"I thought it was pride kept bringing him back."

The pair walked in silence, wandering nearer the glass structure. They stopped in its glow, staring up at the green silhouettes inside. Mrs. Kristoff spoke once more. "You are free to go where you will. There is nothing to anchor you. The families of Kristoff, Grace, and Cunningham are gone. Our efforts to right the wrongs and end the war were in vain." She turned toward the village. "Although not the freedom I sought with my husband and our son, here is life and hope."

What does she mean? Stay here? Join the rebellion?

Mrs. Kristoff clasped Finney's hand, patted it, and said nothing more.

Skippy and his fleet of runners still lurked near the Eye, but even if he succeeded in boarding the *Vega*, he'd find as much as he had the first time: nothing.

Kristoff stopped at the wheelhouse hatchway. "Your job's done. You took her through the Eye. I'll take her to Port Henry."

Finney spun the chair to face him. "Got any fancy plans to outmaneuver Skippy?"

"As soon as his little patrol passes, we'll scoot out behind 'em and head for open space."

"So, run like hell and pray he's blind?"

"Pretty much."

She smiled. "He probably hasn't paid much attention to that ghost ship out there."

Kristoff just looked at her, not certain how to take that remark.

"Way I figure it" – she leaned forward – "the *Elsinore*, being a research vessel with space for collecting specimens and carrying equipment, is plenty big enough to hide the *Vega* in her cargo bay. We can man the *Elsinore*, give us time to scavenge."

Us? He stepped inside the wheelhouse.

She turned toward the console. "I like the *Vega*. Reminds me of flying with Grandfather."

"So." He looked at her reflection in the forward port. "You're just using me for my ship."

She shrugged. "Don't know when I'll catch another ride out here on the Rim."

Yeah, good point.

"But I'm only staying aboard as long as it's interesting."

Fair enough.

He grabbed the radio – "All hands, strap in. This is gonna be fast, rough, and ugly" – and dropped into the seat beside Finney.

First ghost ship to starboard, then straight on 'til morning.

When Jake Ekhunder arrives late for his first day at Time Corp., he gets a curious reaction as his supervisor and coworkers hail him at their "king." What follows is his discovery of the truth and a mysterious plot surrounding his life of which he never knew in Alice M. Roelke's...

LAST, FULL MEASURE

A. M. Roelke

A locker door slammed shut, jolting Jace back to the present. Or rather, the future.

"First day at the Time Corps, eh?" said the door-slammer, his strange-sounding words translated by Jace's tiny ear device. "Well, pleased to meet you. I'm Fillmore, 2310, Vega." The black-suited man extended a hand.

Jace shook it. He wished he wore something more official-looking than jeans and a jacket. "I'm Jace Ekunder, 2000, Earth."

"Come on, kid. The speech is in five."

Jace followed Fillmore down the blue plexi-steel corridor, dodging T.C. agents of various positions and periods. He passed a long, curved window and caught a dizzying glance of the outdoors. He paused by the window. The T.C. building stretched hundreds of floors below. Outside, skyscrapers blanketed everything in sight except a pale hint of sky. 5500s Earth!

He blinked and glanced around the empty corridor. *I'm late! And on my first day.* He dashed down the hall and into the auditorium. It sprawled as big as a football stadium and was packed to its seams. The speaker, tiny and forlorn-looking at its middle, had already begun. His voice sounded much closer, translating in Jace's ear as he looked around for a seat.

"...know you are joining one of the most prestigious, most secret organizations in all of history."

One of the security guards moved towards Jace. Jace intensified his search. The last thing he wanted was more trouble. A young woman with caramel hair motioned to the seat beside her. Jace smiled in gratitude and hurried over.

As he leaned forward to sit, the ring hanging from a string around his neck fell forward. The girl's gaze riveted on it. "My king!" she gasped, falling to her knees.

So much for no trouble. Jace drew back, blinking. "Hey, c'mon, I'm no king."

A man tapped the bowing girl's shoulder. "Pharez, what do you think you're – " Then he spotted Jace's pendant. "Sire!" He also knelt. Now others stared at Jace. Too many others. Even the speaker frowned in his direction.

Jace fingered the heavy blue ring he always kept on a string around his neck. Why were people staring at it?

"You know the rules." A voice behind him caused Jace to turn. The security guard! The stocky man caught one glimpse of Jace's ring, and paled. "I apologize, sire!" He fell to one knee and formed a fist over his heart. "I am your loyal subject. Whoever you are."

"But I'm nobody! Please, get up." Jace glanced around. The people who weren't staring at him with rapt faces glared at him or whispered to one another behind their hands.

Far below, the speaker cleared his throat. "Young man, would you come here?" His face burning, Jace walked down. It took a long time.

The speaker, a jowly man with commanding red hair, frowned at Jace. "Name and date," he snapped.

"Jace Ekhunder, the year 2000."

The man's eyes focused on Jace's pendant, and he snapped his fingers. "Give me the ring."

"It's just a – personal effect, sir." Jace's fingers fumbled. The speaker waited pointedly until he handed it over. Jace watched the man, whom he now remembered was Warren Sky, one of the highest T.C. superagents. Superagent Sky turned Jace's ring in his hands, examining the bluish metal and odd, deeply cut symbols.

Superagent Sky looked up. "Where did you find this?"

"I've had it all my life. My adoptive parents found it with me."

Sky stared at him with hard green eyes. "Follow me." He turned and started out of the auditorium.

Murmurs rose to a crescendo. Jace kept his gaze down and wished he could disappear.

Superagent Sky paused outside and spoke into his lapel. "Tref, Melg, and Parol, meet me in my quarters." He strode down halls until he reached a door with "Superagent Sky" etched on its front.

Jace followed him in. Soft green walls surrounded him. The apartment was gigantic, at least five times the size Jace's home had been – before he'd been picked to join T.C....

That seemed so long ago. He hadn't even known about the Time Corps then.

No one did, unless chosen. T.C. involvement, and the T.C. itself, had to be kept completely secret. After their orientation and training, agents returned to the same day they'd left, as they did after every mission and conference.

T.C. picked people from many different times, since it was easier to have many agents fixed in various times than it was to spend years training agents to go anywhere. There were, of course, exceptions – superagents who could go to any time-place. But most agents lived their whole lives nearly normally, performing only a few missions within their timelines.

Superagent Sky ran his hand along a panel and dim lights turned bright. He turned to Jace. "Do you know what this is?" He held up the ring. It shone in his hand like metallic blue ice.

"It's just a ring. Can I have it back?"

Sky ignored Jace's words and looked past him to the door. It slid open, and three men entered wearing dark suits.

When the second one glimpsed Jace and the ring, he gasped. He slipped slowly to one knee, and clasped a fist over his heart. "Sire!"

Jace felt funny looking down at the balding man's salt-and-pepper hair. He turned to Sky. "Please tell him I'm not a king."

"But you are."

Jace blinked. "What?"

Superagent Sky glared at the kneeling man. "Melg, get up!"

"What do you mean?" Jace's head buzzed.

Sky turned to him. "It's simple. You have the ring of Re'he'galia. The ring – not to mention Re'he'galia – won't be around for more than a thousand years. Obviously, time has been disrupted. Now the question is *when* do you belong?" The superagent paced to the opposite wall, ripped the string free and dropped Jace's ring into a slit in the wall.

Jace jerked forward. "What are you – "

Sky ignored him. Modulated beeps sounded from the wall. A screen emerged and Sky peered at it. "Strange," he murmured. "This ring is as old as Re'he'galia itself." He pulled it from a lower slot and regarded it, then Jace curiously. "Who picked your first name?"

"I think my birth parents did," said Jace. "It was on a bib found with me."

Sky turned to the man who had bowed. "Melg, was there ever a King Jace in Re'he'galia?"

Melg cleared his throat. "No sir. But there was a Prince Jace. Re'he'galia was destroyed while he was still an infant."

"Destroyed?" Jace had never even heard of Re'he'galia before, and now he found out it had been destroyed?

"Yes, sire." Melg addressed Jace. "We tried everything to stop its demise. We failed." He dropped his gaze.

"What – what happened?" asked Jace.

Melg glanced at Sky, who nodded.

"Many a year from now," began Melg, "during the soft green days of Re'he'galia, in the reign of His Royal Highness King Selvano Shanandon the Fourteenth – "

"Get on with it, would you?" snapped Sky.

"There was a powerful man, Ensard Sejamsin Jelgors – " Melg caught a glare from Sky. "Anyway, he wanted to rule Re'he'galia. Though he was powerful, he knew no one would follow him unless he got rid of beloved King Selvano. He waited until the new year, when the king gave his annual speech. Jelgors's mercenaries, posing as terrorists from the rival country Stellring, assassinated the king. Jelgors stepped into the gap, promising revenge on the Stellrings. He started a war, rallying Re'he'galia behind him and hoping for conquest. Instead, he got several thousand tons of Stellring's new biological weaponry. There was no defense. In a matter of days, all of Re'he'galia lay dead. It was the end of a good and beautiful nation. The end of an era."

Sky spoke. "Now we find out someone interfered with the timeline by 'rescuing' the boy and the ring, and depositing them in a different time, leading to a great many problems and opportunities for abuse. The ring has already caused trouble. It's too dangerous a symbol to be allowed out of its time. We'll have to destroy it. And, of course, we'll have to prevent the infant from being 'rescued.'"

"And let me die instead?" said Jace.

"It was an illegal, unapproved interference with time." Sky deigned to glance at him. "The consequences could be disastrous."

"Could be? You're going to kill me for a 'could be?!'" Jace leaned forward, clenching his fists and glaring.

"Not kill," said Sky. "Simply stop the interference with time." He drew out his superagent's time orb, a fancier version of the one regular agents used. The semicircular handheld device had no lock; superagents could go to any time and place. "If you'll excuse me," said Sky to the other superagents, looking past Jace as though he already didn't exist.

Jace shook his head to clear the shock. "No!" He leaped forward and wrenched at the ring in Sky's hand.

The superagent's face contorted in fury. He drew back an arm and sent a punch sailing into Jace's jaw.

Stumbling back, Jace clung to the ring, but his grip slipped. "I want it back. It's mine."

"You're nothing, just an anomaly." Sky twisted Jace's hand, his smile grim.

Another superagent tackled Jace from behind. Jace squeezed his eyes shut and hung on.

Then a punch hit Sky. He reeled, and dropped his orb. It skittered across the floor. The ring popped from his fingers.

Jace stumbled backwards with it and landed hard on his rear end. He looked up to see Melg fighting the other superagents.

"Hurry sire!" Melg called, just before a fist hit him.

Jace scrambled to his feet and started for the door. He glimpsed Sky's orb and stooped to grab it. Straightening, he saw Melg hit the floor, his eyes closed.

Sky, his nose bleeding, rose grimly and started towards Jace, reaching for his gun belt. "Stop, thief," he said in an ironic monotone, and pulled his gun.

No! Not like this. Jace wrenched one of the orb's dials, then slammed down the prominent orange button.

Nothing happened.

Sky's shadow fell over him. In a panic, Jace looked down. Of course! He yanked loose the safety on the orb's back and slapped the button again. Around him, the superagents disappeared and darkness descended just as Sky's finger found the trigger.

Jace stood in the same now empty and dimly-lit room. He let out a ragged sigh and sank to the floor, his head pounding, and he felt a warm trickle from his mouth. He opened his hand and saw sharp imprints in his palm – the symbols from his ring. He gave the ring a quick kiss and slid it into his pocket.

A mumble sounded from the next room. Jace twitched. He eased forward and peered through the door.

There, asleep, lay Superagent Sky, his mouth open, one arm hanging down from his bed. Jace glanced down at the orb. The date read 4-3-5509. Two days ago.

Jace's head spun. He leaned back against a soft wall and slid to the ground. He needed time to think.

Of course, with the time orb, he had all the time in the world. Or did he? If a superagent went to Re'he'galia and stopped Jace from being rescued, he could suddenly cease to exist, no matter what he did now.

It was possible he'd live on anyway, an anomaly, a hiccup in time. But Jace was a little fuzzy on the theory. He certainly didn't want to test it.

I'll have to go back, er, forward, and make sure they don't interfere with the person who rescues me, he decided.

While I'm there, I should try to save Re'he'galia; if I'm really one of its royalty. Silently, he laughed at himself. If superagents hadn't succeeded, how could he? But he ought to try. Besides, he had always wanted to meet his birth parents.

Wait a minute. His plan had already hit a snag. He didn't know Re'he'galia's location. Without it, he could do nothing.

Maybe Sky had something that would help, such as a place-coordinate. Jace stood up to look around.

The main room lay nearly bare around him. He glanced at the green floor where the fight would later be held then moved past. The room branched on either side into other rooms, the bedroom on the left. Jace turned to the right.

This room held a huge desk brimming with electronic equipment and books. Jace couldn't decipher most of the book titles. Some looked almost medieval, while others looked strangely futuristic. He realized with disheartening clarity that he wouldn't be able to read a place-coordinate directory even if he found one. The language translator simply didn't work on written words.

He sighed and slumped against the desk. "Oh, Re'he'galia, where are you?" he murmured.

"Re'he'galia is a large country on the planet Gensen IV," said a precise, computerized voice. Jace's eyebrows jerked up.

In the next room, the superagent grumbled in his sleep. "...never do that again, do you hear?" He sounded like he was dressing someone down in his dreams. Jace waited until Sky fell silent, then leaned forward and whispered, "What are its coordinates? Please answer quietly."

"Name a city," said the voice politely, with lower volume.

"Um, the capital."

"The coordinates of Rhengston are 2934.28223."

With shaking fingers, Jace punched the numbers into the time orb, then had the computer repeat them. He nodded, and whispered, "When is the last king assassinated?"

"January 1, 6969," replied the computer.

"Thank you." Jace spun the dials until the date on the time orb read 1-1-6969. With a last, long look around, he squared his shoulders, drew a breath, and pressed the button.

꙰

Bright sunlight shone through his closed eyelids. Shouting and the press of bodies told Jace he was in a crowd. He opened his eyes to a dazzling assault of colorful, blurry objects. He blinked and slowly, his eyes adjusted to the light. A ceiling of bright stained glass stretched overhead almost too high to see. People milled around the huge, echoey building in clothing with colors so bright Jace's eyes hurt.

Backing away from the throng, he bumped into a man in a purple-and-yellow dotted suit. "Excuse me," he mumbled. The translator made his words come out strange to his own ears.

"I saw you appear," the man growled. With the small buzz from his translator, Jace understood the words. "You think you can push me out just because you've got some high tech device?" The glaring man shouldered forward.

"Uh, sorry." Jace backed away.

"Where'd you get that device, anyway?" The stranger motioned to the time orb. "You're not allowed to have anything like that in here. Don't you know there's a security watch?"

"Uh, it's nothing." Jace shoved the orb into his pocket, turned, and pushed through the crowd, trying to keep his head down.

Most of the people made way easily, many while offering new year greetings. A few people gave Jace puzzled stares, but he hurried past. His subdued denim certainly didn't allow him to blend in here; he'd have to be quick.

He reached a wall of blue and green tiles and paused to look around. Up ahead stood a stage-like platform, covered with guards. Most people stood facing that way expectantly. Jace glanced back and saw the grumpy man elbowing his way through the crowd after him.

Uh oh. Jace pushed along the wall, hoping to escape and, at the same time, wondering why it was necessary. Did the man really think Jace was a security risk? It didn't matter what he thought; right now Jace couldn't afford any trouble.

Jace reached the stage's wall, and a small door at its edge. It was the same color as the wall and barely visible. He looked back. The man moved nearer, trapping him in the corner. Beginning to feel desperate, Jace tried the door. It didn't open.

Then he noticed something. Where the keyhole should be lay a familiar mark. Involuntarily, Jace glanced down at his hand. It bore the same round mark, with now-fading symbols from his ring. Glancing back at the approaching man, Jace dug the ring from his pocket. He pressed it into the indentation.

A perfect fit! The door opened with a click. He stepped inside, drew the door shut after him, and heard the click again.

A tall bookcase obscured most of his view. What he could see of the new room looked small and plain after the riotous crowded place. Strange words floated to Jace's ears. His translator immediately interpreted them.

"...I beg of you, don't go out there!"

Jace peered around the bookcase. A man wearing a golden crown and a red cape, his back to the bookcase, stood before a kneeling man. Nearby, a beautiful woman in a shimmering, silver gown held an infant. The infant wore blue baby clothes – and a bib with letters written in an 'olde' style print. The letters spelled "Jace."

Jace's heart thumped loud in his chest. His fingers tightened on the bookcase.

The kneeling man still spoke. "Please sire! I – I've seen what happens in the future. As soon as you go out there, you'll be assassinated! *Please don't do it!*"

The king turned slightly, and Jace glimpsed his profile. The king looked so much like Jace that they could have been brothers. Or father and son. Then Jace saw the kneeling man's face. He was a younger version of Melg.

"If what you say is true..." began the king. Then he shook his head. "No. I cannot abandon the kingdom for a superstition. Who could make it past our security?"

They continued speaking, but their words slid past Jace, as he leaned against the door, thinking.

Finally, he straightened, stepped around the bookcase, and cleared his throat. The king whirled and whipped out a decorative-looking gun. The woman and Melg gaped at Jace. The infant just gurgled, and the king pointed his gun. "What treachery is this?"

"Don't be frightened, your highness." Jace raised his hands into the air. "I'm also a time-traveler, one who happens to look like you. Don't worry. I'm a loyal subject with no wish to usurp your throne. But if you permit me, I may be able to help. You can lend me your clothing and let me take your place. If anyone attempts assassination, you'll still be safe."

The king watched him, a frown puckering his brow. Then he slid his gun into its holster, and nodded. "You are a true son of Re'he'galia. Very well. I shall give you the royal outfit to wear, and hook up something so that I can dictate my speech. I'll have to cut it short, of course." The king strode from the room, looking preoccupied.

The queen stepped nearer. "Thank you," she murmured. "You are a good man." She smiled at Jace, and joggled the baby Jace in her arms. "What is your name?"

Jace's eyes flicked to the baby. He smiled sadly. "My name isn't important."

Melg drew Jace aside. "Who are you?" he whispered.

"Just a friend."

"You're not a robot, are you? We tried that already, it didn't work. It couldn't fool the assassins' weaponry. And the king refused to let us use clones on moral grounds."

"I'm not a clone," said Jace. "Just a regular person." He moved past Melg and sat on a footstool, drew his knees up to his chest and squeezed his eyes shut, to wait, trying to still the pounding of his heart.

It seemed only moments later that Jace stood ready, wearing heavy royal robes and electronic equipment. He waited by the door to the main stage. The king opened it for him with his ring, then turned and gave Jace's hand a brisk shake. "Thank you, young man. And good luck."

You too, father, thought Jace.

He stood on the stage's threshold, dragonflies in his stomach. From the corner of his eye, he glimpsed the bright red hair of Superagent Sky across the stage. Waiting. Somewhere, assassins also waited. Would this work? It was the end for Jace, whatever happened. He took a deep breath.

A half-remembered line from history lessons flitted through Jace's mind. "...Those who gave the last, full measure of devotion."

For Re'he'galia, thought Jace, and stepped out.

Prince Jace of Re'he'galia leaned back and propped his feet on a picnic table. Royal gardens stretched away from the pavilion, and below him, the water in the fish pond sparkled deliciously. Perhaps he would sneak a swim later. At twenty summers old, he was nearly a man, with many stately duties to occupy his time, and he relished the rare pleasure of a day free of duty.

Footsteps sounded nearby. Jace twisted around to see his father descending the path, wearing a simple robe, no crown. With a sigh, the king seated himself beside Jace and clapped his son on the back. For a moment they just sat there, too full from the glorious sunrise to talk.

Then the king spoke. "It is a bright day for Re'he'galia, is it not?"

When starship captain Sharla and her crew are sucked into one of the very aurorae they were trying to avoid, they make a startling discovery about their nature that could change everything in Paula R. Stiles'...

SPIDER ON A SIDEWALK

Paula R. Stiles

Sharla met the remains of her crew in a bar near the City's rim. It wasn't that there were any fewer of them than the last time they'd all made a business run, just that they were all three in a lot rougher shape than before. "I'm making the run on the Torpha Space. Any of you guys up for it?"

Gobhat, Sharla's pilot, snorted into his smoldering Emerald Spume. "Yeah, right. Maybe I'll go play under the sewers while I'm at it." Esquey City being situated in midair, "under the sewers" meant being suspended five miles above the surface of Coris 9.

Next to him, Tktk, Sharla's Asken navigator, clicked enthusiastically in agreement. Whatever it was drinking, it was doing so out of what looked like a giant cricket's head with roving eyes.

"Nice touch," Sharla said, indicating the cricket's head. "Is that real?"

TkTk made a noise that sounded remarkably like a rasberry. It had been around humans enough to know what the sound meant, and to pick up a fair bit of English, so that had to be derisive. Nobody knew much about what TkTk was saying whenever it wasn't tapping data into the ship's translator. Gobhat, who didn't like small talk, would always say that was just as well. Nobody really knew how TkTk felt about the lack of communication, but TkTk had never complained – at least not so that anybody understood it.

Morvin, Sharla's obsessive-compulsive engineer, who had a tendency to wear technicolor coveralls to bars, pushed doubtfully at the globe containing Gobhat's Emerald Spume. Then she waved her hand into the ionizer candle in the center of the table to sterilize it. "Are you aware that stuff's on fire? I don't think carbonized hallucinogens are a good thing to drink."

"They're not hallucinogenic once you carbonize 'em," Gobhat said wisely, or as wisely as he could after three such drinks.

"Come on, guys." Sharla snapped her fingers to get their attention. "Work with me here."

"We're trying," Morvin said. "But since you just said something completely insane, we decided to wait until you got your senses back."

Tktk went off into a long rattle sound that must have been laughter. Even Gobhat snickered.

"Ha. Very funny. I mean it, guys. I've got an idea about that section of space and I think we could take the Torpha Prize when we get back." The Torpha Prize had been up for decades, for anyone who could figure out a safe passage through Torpha Space. The prize was huge, and so far, unwinnable.

"If we get back," Gobhat said with a drooling smirk.

Sharla laid it out for them. "We have no money and we are wanted for non-payment of bribes – I mean, taxes, of course – on three planets in three separate solar systems. If we do not come up with our docking fees soon, we will either be evicted from this planet or have our ship impounded. We would be grounded, and we might well end up in debtor's prison then. I don't think any of us would like either option. I have an idea that can get us out of debt and get our names in the history books at the same time. What's so bad about that?"

"Have you ever seen a ship after it gets back from Torpha Space?" Morvin said. "If it gets back from Torpha Space?" She crushed her empty, disposable glass in her hand as a graphic example. It disappeared with a snap, a crinkle, and a puff of sparkly smoke. "I've heard of binary stars there where the gas giant gets sucked down superfast by its white dwarf companion. The process speeds up for no reason, like somebody drinking up all that plasma gas through a straw."

Tktk chose that moment to slurp the last of its cricket puree. Morvin flashed the Asken a frown.

"If you're caught anywhere near a system in overdrive like that, you go down with the giant. Then there are those ships that get tossed lightyears off course and can take months or years to get back – when they survive the tossing. And there are others that get caught in the middle of a deep space aurora when it blows up out of nowhere like a planetary storm and end up..." She waved her hands in the remains of the sparkly smoke.

"Crushed like a bug on a sidewalk," Gobhat added.

Tktk chittered and thwacked him upside the head with one of its chitin legs.

"Ow! Hey! I didn't mean you!" Gobhat yelped, grabbing his head more in reflex than from any likely pain after what he'd been drinking. "I'm just saying – those aurorae are nasty. They're not just electromagnetic interference, like an aurora in a planetary atmosphere. You let them hit you unawares, you end up dead – all your instrumentation fried, no navigation, no communications, no life support, nothing."

"And that's if you survive those gravitational vector force shears I've heard about," Morvin added with bloodthirsty relish. "One million Newtons going one way and, in the next second, going at a ninety degree angle to the first vector or in the opposite direction. It's crew puree then, my friends, even if your ship doesn't rip apart from the stress."

Sharla couldn't say that she was surprised by their lack of enthusiasm. After all, they had made very good points. On the other hand, the planetary portmaster had made some even better points, particularly before Sharla had talked him out of having his minions toss her off the edge of the City. She and her crew were poor. They needed to pay their port fees or leave – now.

Sharla smacked her hand down on the table to get their attention back. "Guys, guys, listen to me, okay? I hear what you're saying, but I've got a plan."

Two pairs of Human and a multifaceted pair of Asken eyes stared back at her across the table with deep and (if she was honest) well-earned mistrust. "Oooooer," Morvin said. "She's got a plan, boys. I don't like the sound of that."

Sharla decided to call them on their cynicism. Otherwise, they could keep her begging for hours. They'd done it before. "Guys, I'm not gonna haggle with you here. It's a simple request. Tell me 'yes' and we'll go or 'no' and I'll look for another crew."

The Human eyes narrowed and the Asken eyes turned a disconcerting shade of crimson.

"Come on. What have you got to lose?"

Nothing, as it turned out. By the next day, they were refueled, resupplied, and ready to go. Sharla thought she could hear the Port air controllers barely holding back the tears of hilarity when she told them her flight plan as per regulations before the ship exited the planet's atmosphere. But they kept it together until she signed off, at least – except for that last snort and peal before the channel clicked off.

"They know we're buggered," Morvin said sourly.

"Just get down there and check on the engines before we get to the Space; there's a good girl," Sharla said, ignoring the glare that Morvin shot her way and turning her attention to the communications panel that was the Captain's big toy and tool. She clicked up the board and started connecting it to the translator.

"You screw things up like that time we tried to smuggle binary gems to Earth and I'll make you clean up the dust," was Morvin's parting shot before she disappeared below.

"We're gonna be crushed like bugs," Gobhat said, adding insult to injury.

"Not if we're a spider," Sharla retorted.

"Huh?" Gobhat gave her a blank look.

"Spiders. Earth arthropods. Predators. Got eight legs. Fond of crossing walkways, but paranoid about vibrations of approaching heavy animals – you know, like us. Fortunately, they're very, very quick and can usually get out of the way. Like us. I hope."

"Okay..." Gobhat shrugged that off, probably because he had no idea what she was talking about. "You want me to find an aurora to coast?" he said as they cleared the planet's gravity well and keyed up the tachyon drive. The edges of Torpha Space started only a quarter of a lightyear away from the Coris system, though no one there had ever felt any effects of it in recorded history. On the other hand, humans had only colonized Coris 9 two hundred years before. Nobody had ever figured out how such a dangerous patch of space nearly half a lightyear wide and twenty lightyears long could occur in a star cluster with so much traffic and so many inhabitable systems. How could life have grown up in that kind of area?

"No, I want you to map out all recent aurora activity and avoid it wherever possible." Sharla had her head stuck in the communications console to avoid seeing Gobhat's incredulous look and getting her ears blasted by Tktk's skeptical clicks. "I'm raising the tachyon intranet for the nearest monitoring stations on the outside of the Space and sending you the telemetry now."

"Are you kidding?" Gobhat said, the incredulous look still in place (unfortunately) when Sharla pulled her head out from under the console.

Tktk also greeted her with that blast. So much for avoidance.

"How the hell are we gonna predict their behavior if we try to stay away from them all?"

"If we stay away from them all, we may not have to," Sharla said. "I hope," she added as Gobhat's face remained skeptical. "Gobhat, have you ever heard of anybody actually benefiting from trying to ride an aurora through the Space?"

Gobhat fingered his chin. "Well, sure, it's not exactly safe, but if you're riding one aurora, it'll pull you through faster, and you're not likely to run into another one, or another ship."

Sharla raised one eyebrow. "Except for that time when those two battle cruisers from Jabrat 4 collided while riding two aurorae going in opposite directions."

"That was over thirty years ago," Gobhat said.

"Yeah, but it does happen." Sharla made a final connection. "That's it. It's coming over now."

"Yeah, yeah..." Gobhat called up the information on his own console, pushing buttons and clicking levers. Buttons and levers were a lot more reliable than fancier stuff in the high-radiation environment of space. "Let me see what I can do by mapping the relative luminosity. Each aurora tends to have a pattern of increasing and decreasing in visibility as it crosses the Space."

"Have fun," Sharla said. She stuck her head back under the console. She could still hear Gobhat well enough, though her own voice echoed inside the console whenever she answered.

"What are you doing in there now?" he said.

"I'm rewiring the communications console to the translator computer we've got wired into the navigational banks for TkTk to use so that I can send a universal message."

Gobhat hooted and Tktk whistled in laughter. "Good luck with that! Hope you've got something real simple in mind to say or you'll end up insulting somebody somewhere."

"Don't worry." Sharla finished stripping a wire and started wrapping it around another one. "It is."

"So, what is it?" Gobhat never could resist the call of curiosity.

"Well, as I said, it's pretty simple: 'Please don't step on me.'"

"'Please don't step on me'? What the hell does that mean? Who are you trying to contact?"

"Anybody who's out there." Sharla finished the adjustments and pulled out. "I thought we might catch a ride."

"From what?" Gobhat said, frowning.

"From someone intelligent. Or oblivious enough not to brush us off. Either one works."

As Sharla slid the console panel back in place, Morvin came up through the hatchway and closed it behind her. Engineering would quickly get too hot in infrared and higher frequencies for anything living.

Morvin wiped off her hands with the ionizing pad she always carried with her, then floated over to her station and buckled herself in. "I miss planetary gravity," she groused. "Freefall sucks chunks. We there yet?"

"In about fifteen minutes," Gobhat said. He leaned over toward Morvin's station. "Sharla just put out a signal saying 'Don't step on me' in TkTk's translator."

"'Please don't step on me,'" Sharla corrected him, knowing it wouldn't help.

Morvin rolled her eyes. "Oh, yeah. We're screwed."

Sharla decided not to fight any battles she couldn't win. "Gobhat, you and TkTk got that map set up yet?"

"Working on it," Gobhat said over TkTk's affirmative clicks.

"Hurry up. I'd like it before we get there, not five seconds before we get smacked with an aurora."

"Sharla wants us to avoid the aurorae, not ride them," Gobhat told Morvin.

"Thanks for including me in that decision," Morvin told Sharla, looking disgusted.

Sharla chuckled. "Didn't see any reason to tell you when Gobhat was doing such a good job already."

"Sharla thinks we're some kind of Earth bug," Gobhat expanded helpfully.

Morvin snickered at that. "How long have you been hatching this nefarious plan, anyway?" she asked Sharla.

"The two months since we last went out. That's why I've been in bars all over the planet. I've been buying drinks for every loser with a story about the Space. That's when I noticed the pattern."

"What pattern?" Morvin said.

"She's got the map," Gobhat said. TkTk clicked and flashed up the map on the screen in the middle of their stations that Sharla had sent from her station. It showed the Space in white, with the stars black and the aurorae as red rivulets across the Space.

Sharla pointed them out. "See how they look like trails? That's what I noticed first. The traffic of the aurorae is concentrated into certain paths."

Morvin leaned over to have a better squint at the map. "Except here, here and here," she said, indicating three spots instead of a continuous line. "They just reappear and disappear, genius."

"I know. Like footprints. You notice that?"

Morvin squinted at her. "Living beings leave footprints on ground. You're not trying to say that aurorae are living, are you?"

"You're trying to argue that they're sentient," Gobhat broke in. "Or that they're left by something sentient. That's why you want to broadcast a general signal."

"They're too big to be alive – or sentient," Morvin said, shaking her head. "Some of these aurorae are over two tenths of a lightyear wide. That's big!"

Sharla shrugged. "Who knows what's too big and too small for – "

TkTk started chittering loudly.

"I think that's TkTk's way of saying we're coming into Torpha Space now," Gobhat broke in. "Oh, and if you were hoping to avoid the aurorae, there's one coming our way right now."

"Crap!" Sharla pulled herself back into her seat and tightened the straps. She fumbled at her earpiece and stuck it in her ear. So much for finding out more than five seconds beforehand. Out of the corner of her eye, she saw Morvin revving up her console. "Can we avoid it?"

"I don't think so," Gobhat said, hauling up the joystick he used for his crazier evasive maneuvers. "I'm trying to turn us around. It's gonna take a little... dammit! It's switched direction and it's heading our way."

"See if you can just skim it."

"'Skim it'?! You want me to 'skim it'? Now?" Gobhat was yanking on the joystick before it was even in place "Why didn't you say that when it was easy to do it?"

"I've got the engines up but I can't push them any harder," Morvin said. "We can't turn on a dime after dropping out of tachyon drive. Too much momentum."

Gobhat swore. A lot. "We're going right into the middle of it. I can't – "

It was like being a handful of beans picked up in a can and shaken – hard. Sharla tried to sink into the chair under her straps and let it protect her from being thrown around. But she still banged her wrist against her console before pulling her arms in. She yelped.

"We're trapped right in the middle of it!" Gobhat was shouting. "I can't get us out. Every time I try to go someplace, it pushes me back."

This was what she'd had in mind, even if she was regretting it now. "Don't push!" Sharla yelled back. "Morvin, turn off our engines!"

"What?!" Morvin yelled back. But Sharla could hear through the rattling and shaking that Morvin had already obeyed, probably because the engines had redlined. Morvin knew a lost cause when she saw one and wouldn't waste time arguing while Rome burned.

As the engines died, the shaking died with it. It got quiet – too quiet. "Status, everybody?" Sharla said as she checked her communications console.

"We'll still have engines, if we live long enough to use them," Morvin said.

"We're still moving at a hell of a clip," Gobhat added.

TkTk was chittering continuously, but not tapping anything into its console since there was nowhere to navigate.

"The aurora's got us, but it's just carrying us along," Gobhat said over TkTk. He gave Sharla a tight, stressed look. "You still broadcasting your message?"

"Yep," Sharla said. It hadn't been a foregone conclusion that communications would survive, but they usually did well beyond even life support. They were built that way. Once you lost communications and couldn't put out a distress call, life support wasn't much good, anyway. It only prolonged the inevitable.

"You get an answer back?" Morvin asked her.

Sharla glanced down at her console. "Nope. But considering that the aurora, even if it is a creature, or its trail, is one that makes TkTk look like my brother, I'm not surprised. No offense, TkTk."

TkTk responded with a chitter that Sharla figured from previous experience meant, "None taken."

"Let's hang on and see what happens."

"Not like we can do much else," Morvin said. "And I just bit my tongue."

"The aurora's starting to dissipate," Gobhat said. "I think we're – oh, crap! There's another aurora coming our way in the opposite direction."

"Any objects in its wake?" Sharla said. She'd been dreading this. The itsy-bitsy spider went up the water spout... oh, we are so gonna get squashed.

"No, but if they collide, the shear stresses will rip up us apart." Gobhat was clinging to the useless joystick for dear life. "It still won't let me – wait, ours is turning. Yeah, it's turning!"

Yes! A sign of intelligence. Just what she'd been hoping for. "What about the other one?"

"That one's turning, too. They're avoiding each other. Hell, Sharla, I think you could be right."

"Yeah, but it's not proof." The last thing she wanted to do was risk their necks all over again, but they really needed that reward.

Gobhat scoffed. "Screw proof! I'll be happy if we get out of this one alive. We're almost across the Space, and in a third of the time it would take us normally. Damned if the aurora didn't carry us all the way – and that's not the direction it was going originally. The other one's history, now. Gone its own merry way. This one's dissipating... I got control again." He laughed, sounding breathless. Sharla knew the feeling. She glanced at Morvin, who reached over and slapped her shoulder.

"We made it!" Morvin said, grinning. Then she sanitized her hand out of sheer habit.

"Get us over the limit and back into normal space," Sharla said to Gobhat and TkTk. As she did, her earpiece crackled. Her jaw dropped open, and then she scrambled to make sure the record button was on.

Gobhat was sighing in relief as the engines revved up. "We're back online," Morvin said, sounding happier than she had been over the past ten minutes. Hard to believe that was all it had taken.

"We're back in normal space, too," Gobhat said. "It just released us, whatever it was." He grinned. "Nice 'landing', too. Did you feel a jolt? I didn't feel any jolt."

"Guys," Sharla said, breaking in on their chatter. "I've got a reply to my message."

All three of them stared at her in astonishment. "Seriously?" Morvin said. "What's it say?"

Sharla put the message out on the intercom. The flat, computerized tones of the translator rattled through the air. First, it was Sharla's "Please don't step on me" message and then:

"I won't. Hope you enjoyed the ride. Good luck."

Our next original story comes from Former SFWA President and 2008 Nebula Award nominee Robin Wayne Bailey, known for his bestselling Dragonkin *series as well as his* Frost *novels and stories, amongst others. But pulp space opera is one of his passions, and here he gives us a new classic tale in which a Galaxy Knight seeks to protect the spaceways and become...*

KING OF THE GALAXY KNIGHTS

Robin Wayne Bailey

The distress call lit up Jan's console and jangled through the cybernetic jacks that linked him to every part of his ship. He winced with unexpected pain as the alarm stabbed straight into his brain, awakening him prematurely from scheduled phase-sleep.

"Kill the alarm," he ordered. The ship's computer instantly obeyed, but the lights on the console continued to flash. Sometimes, the ship could be so literal. Switching off the phase-sleep beam that shone down from overhead, he rose from the command chair and stretched.

"Location and view," he said.

The computer answered in his head, its mechanical voice softly feminine, always calm and reassuring. "Star sector 2416." Except for the console, the ship seemed to disappear around him. The bulkheads and deck, even his chair, faded away, leaving him standing in the infinite gulf of space. The holographic effect never ceased to startle him; he caught his breath as he gazed upon a wild ocean of stars and nebulae. "Quadrant Epsilon," the computer continued, "near the *Catharik* system on the edge of the Orion arm. We are still on our assigned patrol course."

"Can you identify the nature of the distress call?"

"Negative," the computer answered.

Jan King leaned on the console and touched a control that dimmed its lighting. With a wave of his hand, a round screen opened. He stared for a long moment, frowning. The distress call originated from void space, the empty and unexplored area between the Orion arm and the Sagittarius arm of the galaxy where no ships ever journeyed.

Still, he was a Galaxy Knight. His job was to patrol the space ways, to keep the peace in a war-torn universe struggling to recover, and to deal with emergencies where he found them. He was a police officer, an ambassador, a messenger, and when needed, a one-man rescue team.

"Chair," he said, and the command chair appeared behind him. He took his seat and shut off the holographic view. The bulkheads and deck reappeared as he calculated the number of jumps and the time it would take to reach the distress call's location. "Send a hyper-response," he told the computer. "Standard response message with identifiers."

"Here we come to save the day?" the computer answered.

Jan King frowned again. "Nobody likes a smart-mouthed starship."

The computer pouted. "Where's your sense of humor?"

Jan removed the cybernetic link from his temples so that he could think in private. He had never been in void space, nor did he know anyone who had. He found the idea vaguely unsettling, like jumping into uncharted water with no land in sight. Yet, someone was in distress, and *jumping* was the right word. Three long jumps, in fact.

Replacing the cybernetic jacks, he felt the ship around him once more like an intimate extension of his body. "View," he said again, but this time he opened only the forward bulkhead. He wanted to see what was coming.

"Hi ho, hi ho," the computer sang. "It's off to work we go."

Jan King stared straight ahead toward the shimmering edge of the Orion arm and the black expanse beyond. "Remind me to reprogram you," he muttered as the ship initiated the first jump.

Strings of spatio-temporal equations flashed through his consciousness. Multi-dimensional geometries overlaid the numbers. Beyond the forward bulkhead, the holographic view turned stark white. With an unblinking gaze, he continued to stare ahead until the whiteness resolved into a star field again, but with new systems, clusters and nebulae. The equations faded from his mind, and he rubbed his temples around the cybernetic links.

The ship's engines rested briefly, then began the build-up for the next jump. Jan King braced himself. The second jump lasted longer than the first. The numbers and equations, usually a gentle stream of images, burned swaths across his brain. He understood little of such mathematics, but the visions were an unavoidable effect of merging his mind with the computer and the ship. Beyond the forward bulkhead, the universe again turned white.

And once again, as the ship emerged from the jump, the star field resolved into new stellar patterns. A rare red double-star shimmered in the upper corner of his holographic View, and in the lower right corner, at a far distance, a strange new phenomenon that impossibly looked like a black hole trinary. Jan made sure that all the ship's recorders were functioning, but he barely had time to appreciate the spare grandeur that confronted him before the engines began to build for the third jump.

"Where are we?" he said quickly to the computer. Speech was not really necessary, but habits were hard to break.

"At the very edge of the Orion arm," the computer answered. "We are charting new space, and you are going where no one has gone before."

"Someone sent that distress call," he reminded the computer as he crossed his arms over his chest and furrowed his brow. He wondered who was out there and why they were so far off the civilized space lanes. The back of his neck began to itch as he anticipated trouble.

The ship jumped. Again, the universe turned white. Equations consumed him, seared his mind like fire until he thought his eyes would smolder and bake in their sockets. He lost any separate sense of himself, all human awareness. Jan King became his ship, a creature of metal and drive and power hurtling through the unknown.

He was not sure how long the jump lasted. The physics eluded him. But when the ship emerged into normal space, he experienced a mental whiplash that made him cry out in pain. He ripped away the cybernetic links at his temples and dropped them. Sweating, heart hammering, gripping the arms of his command chair with all his strength, he fought to re-orient himself.

It didn't help that he saw no star field at all on the holographic View. Lifting his aching head, senses still spinning, he stared into the black emptiness of Void-space.

It helped even less that the console lights began flashing in wild sequences or that an ear-splitting alarm rang throughout the bridge. Through it all, the computer spoke in its usual reassuring tones. "Detecting multiple vessels in the vicinity," it said.

The ship rocked suddenly. Jan felt a violent impact and lurched sideways in his command chair.

"We are under attack," the computer informed him. "Battle shields are coming online at full strength."

Jan snarled as he scooped up his temple links and pressed them back into place. Headache or not, he needed the devices. "Turn off that damned noise!" he ordered. "Then give me a full three-sixty degree View! What have we jumped into?"

The bulkheads and deck flooring all disappeared, leaving only Jan, his chair, and the colorful console seemingly adrift in open space. As Jan leaned forward, an array of flat buttons magically appeared on the arms of the chair right at his fingertips. He snarled again at what he saw.

Nearby, three Stinger warships fired dazzling and deadly beams at a fourth smaller ship, whose shields shimmered and burned like fire as the beams were repelled. Quantum impulse missiles, launched from the Stingers, exploded around the smaller ship, as well, and the vessel shivered.

"I believe the attack was not meant for us," the computer said. "We caught a deflection."

Jan King clenched a fist. Every place mankind ventured, with every step taken into a new unknown, he started a fight. Violence clung to humanity like bad body odor. *We never learn,* he thought to himself. *There really was no intelligent life in the universe.* He hated that he had become so cynical.

"Hail all vessels," he instructed. "Warn them to cease hostilities at once."

He continued to watch the action. The Stinger warships ignored his hails. Two of them continued firing on the fourth vessel. The third Stinger turned directly toward him and began accelerating. Jan King raised an eyebrow. Nobody dared to attack a Galaxy Knight. No ships anywhere were better armed.

Yet, the Stinger kept coming. Its gun began to blaze.

Jan felt the impact to his shields. He touched a button on the arm of his chair. "Firing a warning shot," he said aloud. A brilliant blue beam lanced outward and brushed the Stinger's outermost shielding. Light crackled and flared, but the Stinger continued to advance. It fired again, and Jan felt his engines scream.

"Now that is interesting," the computer said softly. "The Stinger weapon is something new. Its energy concentration is beyond all meaningful scales." The computer seemed to hesitate, and when it spoke again, Jan King heard something unusual in its mechanical voice – fear. "It could destroy us."

Jan felt his shields weakening as the Stinger fired on him again. He accelerated his ship, taking it off the line of fire, but the Stinger surprised him as its next beam actually *curved* to follow! Jan leaped to his feet. "What the hell?"

The Stinger continued to accelerate, as if it intended not only to blow him out of space, but ram him broadside. Jan stabbed flat buttons on his chair, launching batteries of quantum missiles and EMP bombs, firing all cutter beams and disruptors.

The Stinger's shields deflected everything.

Jan King watched in dumbfounded amazement as some corner of his brain calculated the odds of making an unconfigured jump. Those odds weren't good.

"So long, it's been nice to know you," the computer sang.

Without warning, another beam of scintillant energy, golden in color and blue at the edges flashed across the void. It struck the advancing Stinger warship, sliced through its shields with scissile ease, and carved the craft in half from bow to stern. Debris blasted in all directions.

"Where did that come from?" Jan King demanded.

The computer made a noise not unlike swallowing. "From the smaller ship," it answered. "Apparently, size does not matter."

Jan swore he would reprogram the computer at first opportunity, but now he gave his attention to the smaller ship. He didn't recognize it from any known registry. It fired the golden beam again. Another Stinger spilled its guts to the ether. The remaining warship turned tail and ran as fast as it could.

Jan felt a tingling through his links. Someone was hailing him. He sat back down in his chair. The buttons melted away under his fingers, and the deck and bulkheads restored themselves. He looked at the round monitor on the console where a woman's face gazed back at him.

"Commander King, my gallant knight," she said. "Thank you for the timely rescue."

"I'm pretty sure that it was you who rescued me," he answered as he studied her razor-sharp features, the short, spiky cut of her blond hair, her blue eyes. He found her startlingly attractive. "And you obviously have me at a name disadvantage."

"Forgive me," she answered. "I am Diana van Vogt, and before you say it, allow me: yes, I am the mad scientist's daughter."

The mad scientist's beautiful daughter, he thought to himself with a carefully concealed grin. Then, he recognized the name, and his eyebrows shot up toward his hairline. "Doctor Edward van Vogt? He's your father?"

Edward van Vogt was the most notorious war criminal on the books. The Galaxy Knights, along with scores of other military and para-military police forces, had been searching for him for decades. Both a genius and a monster, people called him *The Weaponeer.* His weapon shops had churned out terrible machines of destruction and, at the height of the great galactic war, van Vogt had been personally responsible for the deaths of billions.

"It's not my fault," Diana van Vogt said defensively. "And don't even think about trying to take me in. You'll never get to my father through me."

"What are you doing out here?" Jan King demanded. "Why were the Stingers attacking you?"

"They were my father's ships," she answered, pausing to let that sink in. "I brought you out here, Commander King, to help me stop a war, a war that could ignite all the old conflicts again." Her face hardened as she gazed directly through the monitor. "A war my father is about to start."

Jan felt a cold chill. The ships of the Galaxy Knights were the most powerful and formidable vessels ever built. The mere presence of a Galaxy Knight in any sector pretty much guaranteed peace. Yet, his arsenal and tactics had proven completely ineffective against the Stinger with its new beam weapons and obviously advanced shielding.

"Why?" Jan said, his brow creasing as he realized the implication.

"Why else, but for profit?" Diana van Vogt answered. "The weapon shops are open again."

Almost unconsciously, he reached out through his links to assess the damage to his ship. All he found was some minor bruising to the hull and a couple of burned out shield generators. With a thought, he initiated automatic repairs. The rest of his mind raced. *Doctor van Vogt, the weaponeer. Edward van Vogt, the butcher.* His was a name that still caused fear in a hundred star systems.

Jan's face turned stony as he thought back and remembered the giant *Gnark* bombs falling on the cities of Sesterak, his home world when he was still a boy. He remembered his dead parents and his years as an orphan. Those bombs had come from Edward van Vogt's weapon shops.

Those memories and experiences had led him to the Galaxy Knights. In a very real sense, Edward van Vogt had made Jan King who he was.

"I guess we'd better talk," he said. "Draw closer on my port bow. Open an airlock, and I'll take a sled to you."

Diana van Vogt agreed and disappeared from the monitor. Jan stared at the blank screen for a long moment, then waved a hand over the console to diminish the garish panel lights and waited in near darkness as Diana's strange ship reconnoitered with his. She performed the necessary navigations with admirable precision.

"I am programmed to warn you when there is a high probability of treachery and deceit," the computer said. "In addition, I read tension and conflict in your body language. Your judgment may be clouded."

"Thank you, Mother," Jan responded as he switched off the three-sixty holographic view. The deck and bulkheads reappeared, leaving him with an unfamiliar feeling of claustrophobia. "You have the bridge."

A few minutes later, wearing a lightweight, brief-exposure spacesuit, Jan exited his ship on a gray metal platform, his gloved hands gripping a pair of upright maneuvering sticks, his boots magnetically locked in place. With balletic grace, he guided the sled across the distance, studying Diana van Vogt's ship as he approached. Its configuration was completely unknown to him. The craft appeared almost featureless as it gleamed like a silver dart against the Void.

A small blue dot, a homing beacon, began to pulse on the inside of his helmet's face-plate. It guided him to an airlock large enough to admit his sled. He floated inside and set down gently as the airlock door closed behind him. He removed his helmet and tucked it under one arm as a hatch opened.

Diana van Vogt stood silhouetted by the corridor light behind her. "Welcome aboard, Commander," she said. "We have a lot to discuss, and not much time, I'm afraid. However, there are drinks in my ready room."

She turned, and Jan King followed her through a twisting maze of corridors and hallways with unmarked hatches and doors everywhere. It was all holographic trickery designed to confuse or mislead him. He dragged his finger along a bulkhead, and it rippled ever so slightly like water, confirming his realization. In the back of his mind, he heard his computer's final warning about deceit.

He stopped in his tracks, refusing to go farther. "You said you trusted me," he said. "So why the camouflage?"

Turning toward him, she put on a quizzical look, as if genuinely surprised. Then she tapped a small device strapped to her right wrist. The corridors straightened and the unmarked hatches disappeared. "It's an old habit." Her apology sounded sincere. "I'm afraid the concealment and subterfuge are second nature with me. My father raised me that way and kept me hidden for years. I've actually found some benefit in it, but I see that I've alarmed you."

"I'm not alarmed," he answered. "Just cautious."

When they reached Diana's ready room, she pushed open the hatch and led him inside. The chamber was a teseract or a good holographic illusion of one. The rest of her ship reminded him of an ant colony or a beehive, but this single room was expansive. "There are things and places on this ship that I haven't let anyone else see," she explained as she approached a blank wall. She snapped her fingers softly and the wall disappeared. Jan King found himself staring once more into the Void. Diana tapped the cybernetic link at her left temple. "But my entire vessel is now open to you."

A flood of information poured through his cybernetic link and into his mind. Suddenly, he knew every detail of her craft – its corridors and holds, its astonishing armament and power sources, every last secret of its construction.

He grabbed his temple links, tore them away and stared at them with wide eyes. No one was supposed to be able to access his links in such a manner. "How did you do that?"

She barely smiled. "My father is not the only genius in the family. My links piggy-backed onto yours and gave you access to my computer. You can now command this ship as well as your own. Consider it a gesture of trust to make up for my earlier clumsiness." She turned away again and pointed into the Void. "But to business. As I said, we've little time. You saw what my father's Stinger warships can do. Imagine an armada of such vessels. And the bendable wave-ray you witnessed is only one of his new inventions. Look!"

She continued to point into the holographic Void. Jan King moved closer, but he saw nothing except the blackness of space. "There's nothing there," he said.

"That's what my father wants you to think," she answered. "Let me show you what your eyes can't see." She snapped her fingers again. Space seemed to ripple and shift, and where before there had only been darkness, a small lonely star burned with a single blue planet to keep it company.

At first, Jan thought it a holographic trick, but as he studied Diana's face, he changed his mind. "Tell me what I'm seeing," he said.

Diana folded her arms across her chest, and her mouth drew into a thin line of controlled anger. "My father has cloaked this entire sun and its planet. Even if some ship ventured out this far, they would not find this star. He has installed the same cloaking technology on his Stinger ships. When he attacks, nobody will see him coming."

"Why weren't the Stingers cloaked when they attacked you?" Jan asked.

Diana turned and looked at him with cold eyes as blue as the planet behind her. "I told you, he's not the only genius. I've developed the means to jam his cloaking tech." She snapped her fingers a third time. The View shut down, and the bulkheads returned to normal. "Even when I was a child, I knew the evil my father did. He tried to keep me hidden way, but I heard the stories, and realized that I was the daughter of a monster. Eventually, I masterminded my own escape from his weapon shops, and since then I've devoted my life to thwarting his schemes."

He thought for a long moment, "I'll take that drink now," he said. "Old world brandy if it's available."

Diana went to a sideboard and entered a code on a flat keypad. A moment later, two glasses with sparkling amber liquid materialized beside the keypad. While her attention was diverted, Jan used his links to verify everything she had told him by accessing her own computer which, he grinned to discover, she called *Alfie*.

"So where do I come into this?" he asked as he accepted the drink she handed him. "You said you *lured* me out here, so you had me in mind specifically."

"I've come to realize I can no longer do everything on my own, Commander King." She touched her glass to his and waved him toward a couple of chairs. "I know your record. I know everything about the Galaxy Knights. You're not only a brave lawman, you're untouched by the corruption that's just beginning to spread through your organization."

It didn't surprise him that a woman of her talents had hacked into his files, but her allegation about the Knights disturbed him, because he had suspected the same thing for some time.

"That, too, is more of my father's work," she informed him. "His tentacles are everywhere, and nothing is beyond his reach, not even the vaunted Galaxy Knights. When he wants someone to turn their back, he generally finds a way to make them turn their back, be that money or blackmail or the promise of power." She crossed her legs and regarded him as she sipped her brandy. "But your record and background suggests that you're different. You may actually be incorruptible, and that's why the Knights keep you patrolling the farthest reaches away from the centers of command." She paused, scrutinizing him with an unflinching gaze, weighing his reaction. "You also have almost as much reason as I do to hate my father."

"I don't hate him," Jan answered too quickly. He took a drink from his glass and reflected on the destruction of *Sesterak*. Maybe he did hate Doctor Edward van Vogt after all. "But if he intends to start new wars, I'll do what I can to stop him. The peace is too fragile, and many of the old animosities still linger."

"That's what I wanted to hear," Diana van Vogt said. Rising, she set her glass back on the sideboard. I've already given you command authority of my ship, Jan King. Now I'm going to put an amazing weapon in your hand. I do it, because I need help and, because after all this time, I need someone to trust."

She led him from the ready room. This time, the corridors were straight and predictable with no attempt to confuse. Only a few steps away, they entered a hold. It had been converted into a laboratory and workshop.

In the center of the workshop, stood a Mark Twelve Sagan-class battle suit. He walked respectfully around it and gave a low whistle. "I've never worn one of these," he admitted.

"Nobody has ever worn one of these," Diana shot back. "It only looks like a Mark Twelve, but I've designed at least ten generations of new technology into this suit. Most of the design is mine, but I stole some of the tech from my father. It possesses the wave-ray and the cloaking technology. It's completely self-contained for all environments, even the open vacuum of space." She rapped the suit with her knuckles. The metal alloy can withstand the heat of atmospheric entry, and it's five times as fast as an actual Sagan suit."

Jan nodded. As he walked around the suit, he began to appreciate the modifications and changes. "What powers it?" he asked with a hand on his chin.

For the first time, Diana van Vogt actually smiled. "That's the beauty of it," she answered with pride. "This suit collects cosmic radiation and transduces that into raw power. It does the same with any energy source. Whatever an enemy throws at it only makes it stronger, faster, and more powerful. The only downside is that all that energy must be released or the suit will overload with catastrophic effect." Her smile vanished, and her face turned hard again. "Make no mistake, Commander King, this suit is built for destruction."

She touched the device on her wrist. The back of the battle suit opened in response and Jan studied the sleekly simple interior and the in-board computer, the mounts for hands and arms and legs. His heart hammered.

"What do you expect me to destroy?" he asked, his throat dry.

"The blue world I just showed you," she answered without hesitation. "Not literally, of course, but everything on it, every structure and every building. That planet is home to my father's new weapon shops. His armada is either on it or in orbit around it. I want you to destroy it, Commander. Destroy everything." She clenched her fists as she turned away from him and toward the suit, "I couldn't live with myself if I let him spark another war."

He thought about what she was asking of him, the lives he would inevitably be taking. He weighed that against all the lives that would be lost in another galactic conflagration. Wordlessly, he began stripping out of his space suit. If he was going to go, he might as well go now.

"Just as I did before, I've remotely reprogrammed your links so you can command the battle suit. The moment you step aboard, its computer will provide you with all the necessary skills and information. You need only think about what you want the suit to do."

Naked but for his briefs and flexible boots, Jan King mounted the battle suit. It seemed to mold around him to fit him like a glove as it sealed itself. His cybernetic links immediately made contact with the suit, and he jerked his head back sharply as its computer force-fed streams of data and schematics into his brain.

"Oh, my God!" Jan King wasn't a religious man, but he gasped in awe as he realized the battle suit's full potential. He looked through the suit's helmet with augmented vision to where Diana van Vogt stood, and he felt an intense sympathy for her. What hurt and anger had driven her to create such a weapon and turn it against her father?

He strained for a feeble moment of levity. "This Mark One van Vogt battle suit is now online," he said.

"Try Mark Twenty." Her voice came back to him over his links. "I've never put much faith in prototypes. Good luck, Commander."

He took one more look at Diana van Vogt as she backed out of the hold. She represented beauty, mystery, and intelligence all in one package. He hoped he would get the chance to know her better. Behind him, the laboratory's bulkhead slid open. Simultaneously, repressor rays activated from above, insuring that every tool and instrument and scrap of paper remained in place as the air rushed out.

Numbers flashed across his brain – launch codes and operational sequences. His suit began to collect, store, and convert cosmic rays into usable energy. With a mere thought, he triggered the suit's propulsion systems and soared into the Void.

For a moment, he experienced a stark fear. The Void was so vast and deep, and he felt so small. An inexplicable wave of loneliness swept over him. Yet, those feelings diminished as he focused on his mission and raced through space like a comet toward a cloaked world that only his computer could see.

"It can be a little overwhelming at first." Diana's voice came through his links. She seemed to know what he was thinking and feeling. "But you're not alone. Focus on the warships in orbit first. They're the most immediate threat."

Beautiful, mysterious, intelligent – and controlling. He grinned inside his helmet.

More numbers flickered through his consciousness. He found the sensation disconcerting, but tolerable. The equations pinpointed the orbital positions of five Stinger warships. The nearest lay directly in his path. He powered up his suit's arsenal and programmed a minimal alteration to his trajectory that would take him beneath the ship's belly.

Yet, as he flashed beneath the warship's immense hull, he hesitated to strike. It seemed cowardly. To attack without warning violated his personal code of honor and against everything it meant to be a Galaxy Knight. "Hail all ships," he instructed his suit's computer. A Stinger warship operated with a barebones crew of ten. He had no idea how many other soldiers or technicians might also be aboard. "Advise them to abandon ship immediately."

Reversing course, he turned toward the ship again, hoping against hope to witness the rapid launch of lifeboats. Instead, a wide-beam cutter ray burned across space. Back-tracking his message, the ray engulfed him. Black space became a rainbow maelstrom of violent radiation. Jan King's battle suit practically purred as it absorbed the energy.

It was all the provocation he needed. "For *Sesterak* and a thousand other worlds," he said aloud as he extended his arms toward the Stinger and unleashed a wave-ray blast. Grim-jawed, he admitted it to himself – he had been dying to try the weapon. The cobalt beam stabbed into the warship's heart, and with a gesture, he ripped the vessel open. The ease of it startled him, and the shockwave from the explosion of its massive engines hurled him backward.

Diana van Vogt spoke over the links. "Well done, Commander. I sensed some reticence, however. A troublesome moral code, perhaps. Try to think of this as a war to prevent a greater war."

Where had he heard that before?

He charged toward the next Stinger, which was already turning toward him with full shields burning. He wondered how it could see him, and then realized that the suit's cloak was deactivated. He tried to reactivate it and failed. "What's happened to cloaking?" he demanded of the computer.

"Miss van Vogt has remotely shut it down," the computer answered. "She thinks it will motivate you."

With cold rage, he glanced across space to where his ship and Diana's floated side by side like two bright stars. "Tell Miss van Vogt that she can..."

He didn't finish the sentence. The second Stinger fired an extended beam blast. His suit crackled as it absorbed the energy. This time, a tiny colored gauge appeared in the lower corner of his helmet's faceplate, and he watched his power levels climb from green into yellow, but well below red.

"Send the warning to abandon ship," Jan said to his computer. When the computer hesitated, he shouted. He knew Diana van Vogt was listening, too. "Send the warning! Either I command this battle suit or you can have it back!"

The computer sent the warning. The Stinger replied by firing a second shot. Again, he watched his power levels shoot up almost into the red zone. He had to return fire or risk an overload. He raced across the warship's bow, brushing its shields, and his power levels shot up again. Reflexively, he extended one hand. A blue globe of radiance grew around his fingers, then lanced outward, ripping through the vessel's shielding and blowing a gaping hole in its port side. It wasn't a fatal blow, but enough, he hoped, to make the crew abandon ship.

Instead, the ship fired a third time. A beam of incredible force shot over his head, missing him. It curved back again, missing him yet again. They knew he was out here, but now he wondered just how clearly they could really see him. On the next pass, the beam found him. His power levels shot into the red.

Jan King screamed, whether from fear or frustration or anger, he wasn't sure. He had no choice now and returned fire with both hands. Twin beams struck the Stinger at stern and amidships, carving it into thirds. When the engines exploded this time, he was ready and blasted his way through debris until his power levels dropped into the green zone.

Without warning, a third Stinger exploded behind him. Jan turned as a second Sagan-class battle suit flashed by. It didn't surprise him that Diana van Vogt had made a battle suit for herself, but his eyes widened as he realized her destination and target.

Like a veil melting away, the hidden planet wavered into view with its bright yellow sun perched on its northern horizon. The sight took his breath away.

Diana spoke in an icy voice. "The orbiting Stingers maintained the cloak," she said. "When we destroyed enough of them, the cloak collapsed."

"Where are you going?" he shouted, but she didn't respond. He already knew the answer.

Two Stingers still remained. One of them turned toward him while the other broke orbit and headed toward Void space. He wanted nothing more than to follow Diana van Vogt down to the surface and prevent her from doing what he knew she meant to do, but he thought of what might happen if either of the Stingers got away.

Then, the voice of his ship's computer spoke through the links. "You are not alone, Jan King. We are with you."

With no real choice, Jan prepared to meet the oncoming warship. "We?" he said. "Who is *we*? You're a good ship, but you're not strong enough to take on these Stingers."

Yet another voice spoke in his head. "But I am." It was *Alfie*, the computer on Diana's ship. Jan risked a glance into deep space and watched as his ship and Diana's changed course and accelerated toward the escaping Stinger.

With unexpected allies, Jan made short work of the oncoming vessel, rupturing its belly with a sweeping wave-ray blast. He didn't wait for the explosion of the engines. Reprogramming his trajectory, he chased after Diana van Vogt.

He gave her solemn credit for efficiency. Even as he dove through space, he spied an irregular series of explosions on the planet's surface, and as he plunged through the atmosphere, fire and smoke rose up to meet him. He scanned the landscape, finding ruin, rubble, and devastation – all that remained of the weapon shops of Doctor van Vogt.

Through the smoke and fire, he saw survivors and bodies, too – a lot of bodies. Finally, he found Diana, encased in the cool metal of her battle suit, standing in the scorched and flattened wreckage of a once-sprawling shipyard. A single, blackened wall loomed unsteadily behind her, and waves of heat-shimmer rippled around her shoulders as she looked down upon a solitary corpse, whose aged face was contorted by disbelief and terror.

"My father," she whispered, her voice flat and emotionless. "Now it's over."

But Jan King, standing beside her, looked around and wondered if it would ever really be over.

In Rob Mancebo's action packed tale, Massy McKinney and her fellow slaves stage a revolt, determined to at last escape and free themselves from their loquar masters...

THE SLAVERS OF RUHN

Rob Mancebo

Massy McKinney barely managed to duck the loquar's swinging fist. She knew she'd been lucky. As big as the creature was, the blow could've staved her head in. She stumbled for the sanctuary of the slave wagon, but she wasn't fast enough to avoid the loquar's follow-up kick. It struck before she was completely out of range, sending her sprawling onto the dirt of the road. She was still young and strong enough to roll with the impact, but the pain jarred her into calling out a desperate lie.

"I just wanted a drink of water!" she yelled blindly as she tried to untangle her yellow sun dress from her legs and scrub the dust out of her eyes.

"No escape!" the beast warned her in its rumbling voice, then picked her up in a powerful grip and pitched her toward the slave wagon.

Massy bounced when she hit the ground but managed to scrabble to her feet before she was abused further. She staggered toward the bleary image of the slave wagon and felt Moody and Cyane's frantic grip as they helped her climb back aboard.

She wiped the sandy dust out of her eyes in time to see the blocky, noseless face of the loquar as it leaned over the wagon after her. Exactly like every other loquar, it was a ten foot tall, leathery-skinned giant with hands the size of frying pans.

"No escape!" the creature warned again, forming the unfamiliar words carefully. "I beat." It took her head in one crude hand and gave a squeeze that threatened to crush her skull.

She tried to scream but the pain was too much and the edges of the world were dimming around her before the slaver released her again to drop into the wagon bed.

The loquar vented a plethora of alien curses as it tromped away.

"Well," Massy said to the other girls while trying to cough out all the dust she'd swallowed, "we know that won't work."

"I warned you you couldn't make it to the trees," Moody Reynolds chided. "The loquar are too fast."

"Well, what do you expect us to do?" Massy demanded. "Just sit in this wagon until we're sold and taken off-planet? It'll be a little late to try and escape then, won't it?"

"She's right," Cyane Dubois came to her defense. "We've got to do something before we're sold."

"And that means soon," Massy told them. "When they captured us I heard them say something about 'three days travel', and it's been two already. We're out of range of any security patrols, and Ellis radar station is blocked by these mountains. We're getting into the sort of wild country a ship could land in without detection."

"You speak loquar?" Moody asked with her blue eyes opened wide under her shading bonnet.

"A little," Massy admitted. "But for heaven's sake don't let on. We don't want to give away any advantage we might have."

"But what can we do?" Cyane whined. "They're so big! And they're armed."

"Yes, but there are only two of them." Massy reminded the girl. "And they want us, more-or-less, undamaged. We're no good to them dead or broken up."

The girls lapsed into a guarded silence as one of their captors came to the wagon and gave a tug at the harness of the draft oxen.

The wagon rolled along, with one loquar leading the oxen and the other striding behind to make sure the girls didn't try and drop off the back.

For the thousandth time, Massy considered their captors. The stony-faced loquar were not native to Ruhn any more than humans were. They generally stayed in their small clans in the southwest, raising cattle upon the rich grasslands. Humans and loquar frequently traded, but didn't live near each other.

Ruhn was a world of endless land and few people. Plenty of room for all. Too much room for most people. On Ruhn, most of the population, human and loquar, were involved in ranching or farming of some type. Working hours were long, and in a harsh world of few settlements, there wasn't much time for romance. The girls had been traveling to an annual match-making festival when the slavers had jumped them and dragged them off.

Slaving was a recent crime-wave on Ruhn. Obviously someone had decided that raising crops, cattle, and horses was more work than kidnapping. It was rumored that somehow girls were being taken and shipped off-planet. Being so far out on the galactic frontier, there were no patrolling constabulary ships to put a halt to the foul trade.

"We've got to try something – anything!" Massy encouraged when she was sure the loquar couldn't possibly hear.

"There is one thing," Moody suggested slowly.

"What?" Cyane whispered.

"The odds are two-to-three," Moody said with a fatalistic shrug. "We each run in a different direction. We have to gamble that they can only run-down two – one of us will get away."

They were all quiet for a long time. Massy thought she saw Moody wipe away a terrified tear, but the girl never made a sound.

"We'll try it tonight," Massy whispered. "Just at dusk."

"Whoever gets away has to inform the authorities which of the loquar did it," Moody said grimly. "They need to be ID'd and hunted down."

"How are we supposed to tell which ones did it?" Cyane said with a snort. "We can't tell one from another anymore than they can tell us apart. They're as alike as peas in a pod!"

"They've got some sort of recognition factors," Massy said. "We just don't understand each other well enough to tell."

"Which means, if we don't catch them in the act," Cyane said, "we can't prove who they are. A fat lot of good it will be to report them after the fact."

"We'll do what we can do," Massy told them. "We can't do anything unless one of us can get away."

"This evening then," Moody agreed. "Just before dark. By the time they catch two of us, there won't be enough light to track down the third."

That evening their captors stopped in a wide clearing. The girls were given food of some bland, unidentifiable type, and a cup of water. They ate carefully, always with one eye on the sun setting behind the mountains.

Each of them had already chosen a direction of travel. Each girl had removed and pocketed her sunbonnet. They waited until the last direct rays of the setting sun dipped behind a mountaintop, and the loquar were together setting up a polished alloy tube in the center of the clearing.

"That's a signal beacon," Moody told them quietly. "They're calling for a ship."

"Then let's get out of here," Massy whispered. "Luck to us all."

Without another word the girls bounded over the wagon box and scattered. They were as quiet as they could be, and Massy found it was several running steps before she heard an inhuman growl of recognition.

"Stop!" a voice bellowed. "No escape! No escape!" The order was punctuated by the evil thrum of a loquar handgun.

That only spurred Massy to greater exertion though. She knew it was probably an idle threat. And if it wasn't, if she were really shot, that was better than the despicable life of a slave-whore in some seedy brothel.

THE SLAVERS OF RUHN

Her dress hiked up, her long legs stretched out in a sprinter's stride to carry her straight down the road until she cut hard into the trees. The local conifers weren't so thick that she couldn't pass through at full speed. She must've run a mile before she thought it might be safe to slow down. In all that time, she'd heard no sound of pursuit. She could only guess that the slavers had chased the other girls.

She jogged through the darkening woods almost blindly following a game trail, until she saw the soft flickering of a campfire. As she approached, she called out breathlessly and was thankful to hear a human reply, "C'mon in."

Before she ever registered who she was talking to, she shouted, "Loquar slavers!" The words seemed to tumble out of her mouth between gasps. "They took three of us. There's a clearing about a mile back. They were signaling for a ship!"

The startled man who greeted her was a mountain hunter. A small, wiry fellow, he had long, shaggy hair, but was clean shaven and dressed in faded homespun and flannel. At her warning, he scooped up a Kalashnikov rifle and kicked dirt over his small campfire. "Slavers here?" he repeated. "Calling a ship?"

"Yes!" she wondered if the man was an idiot. Couldn't he understand? "They may be right behind me! They were calling a ship to pick us up – "

He suddenly bounded forward and clamped a hand over her mouth to silence her.

Massy's first impulse was to fight. She began to struggle against his grip, but he shushed her and she realized that he wasn't attacking her. She rolled her eyes to where he was looking.

The stark light of Tsolan, Ruhn's first moon, revealed the shambling shadow of a loquar coming up one of the many forest paths. Its large head dipped frequently as it carefully scanned the trail. The loquar obviously *could* track at night. The girl's whole escape plan had failed.

She nodded when it seemed that he was protecting her, but his hand didn't release her mouth. Instead, he dropped his rifle and clamped a muscular arm around her neck. Massy struggled against him but it was useless; he had her in some sort of martial arts restraint. It wasn't until the shadowy forest faded around her that she realized she'd been betrayed.

Massy awoke in the cold darkness. Fingers of pale moonlight were filtering through the forest branches around her. The dim woods were quiet except for the chirping of Ruhn's great, green frogs.

She felt an odd breeze as she sat up and realized that she was stripped to her skimpy underwear and rudely wrapped in a blanket. What had happened to her? Where were her clothes? She remembered the hunter, the loquar coming, and then – nothing. The man had put her in a 'sleeper hold' to render her unconscious. But then he had just left her there? And without her clothes? As she moved, Massy felt something cold and hard against her leg. It was the man's rifle. Why ever had he put her out, but then left her with a rifle?

Massy stood and wrapped the blanket around herself, pinning it together with several sticks from the forest litter. She hit the latch and pulled the rifle's magazine. There wasn't enough light to see clearly, but it was easy enough to tell it was full by its weight. She loaded the weapon and snapped on the safety.

She didn't know what had happened to the man or to her clothes, but she had a loaded rifle and she knew where the slavers were.

Massy's lip curled defiantly in the moonlight and she headed back down the trail toward the slavers camp. She was going to do her best to see that no more girls would be kidnapped.

Her heart beat in her throat as she crept back to the open glade. Every shadow might've held one of the hulking loquar. She crept along with the rifle up and her finger ready upon the safety.

She was nearing the area she and her fellow captives had tried to make their escape, when an explosion rocked the forest. She flinched as a tall, billowing fireball ripped up into the night sky.

She snapped off the rifle's safety and placed her finger firmly along the trigger guard, ready. Then she trotted forward to see what had happened.

The conifers thinned out as she approached the site of the explosion. Through their thinning mass, she recognized the shimmering blue flames of pectral rocket fuel.

She heard a warning crashing of brush and thundering of approaching feet just before a loquar stumbled out of some bushes in front of her. Its pale skin shone a leprous white in the moonlight and its blunt face was disfigured by night shadows. Her first impulse was to shoot it, but was it one of the pair who had kidnapped her? She couldn't tell, and murder was still murder on Ruhn.

When it saw her standing there, the creature identified itself by yanking its sidearm and leveling it in her direction. Their shots sounded together, and she kept on pulling the trigger until she'd put a half-a-dozen .30 caliber rounds into the massive creature's chest.

It took two stumbling steps toward her, then crumpled in a lifeless heap. Only then did she allow her focus to break as she looked up to see a tree branch burning beside her ear.

She banged the glowing branch with the rifle stock to snuff the tendrils of flame and cursed the loquar as she stomped on the sparks that fell. What sort of an idiot used a thermal gun in a forest?

Massy kicked over the body keeping her rifle trained and ready as she did. Once she was certain it was dead, she took up the fallen pistol. It was a Timurian made arm, obviously an expensive import weapon from one of the industrial worlds. Not the sort of thing anyone would find out on the ragged edge of the galactic frontier where daily use arms were ancient, surplus Kalashnikovs and archaic Mausers.

She pushed forward with a weapon ready in each hand. When she came out into the glade, she found Moody and Cyane simply standing by the cart that had so recently been their prison. There was a grounded spaceship burning merrily in the center of the glade, and someone standing by the harnessed oxen who was wearing her dusty yellow sun dress.

"What? You!" she exclaimed when she recognized the hunter she'd met in the woods.

"Ma'am," he said with a wave of his hand.

"What are you doing in my clothes?" she demanded.

"Oh, I was just giving them slavers a sort of a surprise."

"He was wonderful!" Cyane gushed. "He shot the loquar and blew up their ship! Oh, you should've seen it!"

"I couldn't very well watch when I was unconscious and naked, could I?"

"Sorry about that, Ma'am," the hunter apologized. "There just wasn't much time for planning."

"Time for planning?" Massy raised the rifle muzzle to the stars and snapped on the safety. It seemed that all the trouble was over for the moment. Only an explanation was lacking.

"No, Ma'am," the man assured her. "It's like this," he turned to Moody and snapped, "Quick, take off all your clothes!"

Moody scowled and held her collar closed self-consciously. "What ever are you talking about?" she demanded.

"See?" He waved a dismissing hand. "A natural reaction. Some things take planning and explaining to organize between people. We just didn't have the time."

"He dressed up like you and let them capture him," Moody told Massy. "The loquar didn't know the difference, what with your bonnet on and in the dark. When they dragged us into the ship, he let loose on them. He was a regular terror. Shot a couple and overloaded one of their engines to destroy the ship. I only saw one of them get away."

"I got that one in the woods," Massy assured them. She looked the disguised man up and down before commenting, "But you say he got those local boys, *and* the ones in the ship, too?"

"It was no trick, catching the small fry," the man told her. "Getting into a position to destroy their transport ship to put the whole crew out of business, that was the tricky part."

"And here I thought you were a little slow on the uptake," Massy admitted.

"No. Ma'am, I just haven't met up with a woman in these hills all these last eight months. You sort of took me by surprise."

"Do this sort of thing often, do you?" she asked.

"I blew a few ships during the war, Ma'am," he admitted. "I'm a little out of practice, but – "

"No, I mean, stealing and wearing women's clothing!" she snapped.

"Why – er – no."

"Good. It's best you don't make a habit of it," she told him. "In a land short on fellers, it riles a girl to see a man go to waste. Besides, I'd get real tired of explaining such behavior to friends and family."

"Huh?"

"I mean, I just won't have a man who won't wear his own britches, that's all. Call it a personal preference."

"Have a man – ?"

"Well, you're out here alone. You're not wearing a ring. You're not married nor engaged, are you?" Massy demanded.

"I am not," the man admitted.

"Then I'm throwing in my bid," she tossed the Kalashnikov to Moody. "I am Massy McKinney. I'm twenty-five years old, I have a horse ranch on the upper blue river, and I'm pleased to meet you." She took ahold of his shoulders and kissed him, a bit awkwardly, but long and hard. The man didn't reply, but he didn't push her away either.

"Well, that's a start," she said quietly. "I'll tell you, I raise the prettiest horseflesh you've ever beheld. But that country is rough, and I've had some trouble with rustlers. They killed my husband George last year, poor soul. I'm not what you call a needful woman, but I like havin' a man's company. I need a man I can depend on not to buckle when times get rough. So, what do you say?"

In reply, the man took her carefully in his arms, swept her back off-balance, and kissed her.

When he untangled himself from her lips, she didn't pull away, but kept her arms wrapped about his neck. He nuzzled her ear and whispered, "Can't remember that I've ever buckled in my life."

"Things are getting better and better all the time," she murmured as she looked into his dark eyes.

"Well we've got a long trip back to talk things over," he told her while easing her back to her feet and letting go of her waist.

She slid her hand down his sturdy bicep and took his arm. Arm in arm they walked toward the wagon.

"There's just two things I'm going to ask of you," Massy said as they walked. "First, whatever is your name?"

"Pete," he replied. "Peter Brown."

"A good name, Pete," she acknowledged. "A simple name; I like that."

"What's the second thing?"

She stopped and tapped him on the chest with the loquar's thermal blaster and said seriously, "Will you get yourself out of my best dress before I'm tempted to shoot you?"

For a change of pace, we move on with a tale in which aliens visitors interact with life on Earth, releasing a neo-virus which causes strange color changes in one of Earth's larger mammals. Jenny Schwartz mixes humor and culture clash in...

CAN GIRAFFES CHANGE THEIR SPOTS?

Jenny Schwartz

Giraffes were the perfect hosts. They occupied one continent and had outposts in zoos around the globe.

Zod finished tinkering with the delta chromosome of the neo-virus and laid down his crawtech.

"All done," Zod leaned back on four tentacles with a grunt of satisfaction. "We can release this over Earth and pick up the results on our way back from Sola-Vma3."

"Fine," Aiin sharpened a gold tipped tentacle. It was the data that interested her; not the method of collecting it. "Spin the neo-virus and let's get going."

Zod winked at his partner, the glare of one orange eye dimming a moment before blazing anew. "To hear is to obey."

Zod dropped the giraffe-modified neo-virus into the exo-vortex cone, and cut the cone loose from the spaceship.

"Bye-bye, baby," yawned Aiin. She stretched a long aqua tentacle to the control board and tapped "burst." The spaceship vanished from the solar system.

Within the tumbling exo-vortex cone, the virus multiplied. The cone penetrated the Earth's heated outer atmosphere and then, in the gentler stratosphere, dissolved. Released, the viral bodies dispersed and floated down to earth. Some even landed on giraffes.

🔫

Conrad Bilkem Sr., Congressman for a deluded State, had an agile brain which he usually drove only along certain well-defined tracks, but he could recognise a crisis when he saw one. Giraffes turning blue with orange splotches was a crackadoodle of a crisis.

"Who knows where it will end?" cried Conrad, pounding his desk and spilling his coffee. "What if humans start to change color? How will we distinguish between races?" Worst of all, what if he turned a minority color?

Conrad shuddered, spilling the rest of his coffee, and faced the necessity for urgent unpleasant action. He phoned his wife's brother.

Jackson Forbes was tall and lanky, his bony face gentled by wide brown eyes heavily rimmed with long lashes. When he took off his glasses, the eminent scientist had the endearingly defenceless look of a baby giraffe.

Most people regarded Jackson as a pedantic successful scientist, one who had an in with the establishment. Conrad, however, knew better. He saw Jackson as a lily-livered, doom and gloom, environmentalist panic merchant.

"If Jackson had his way," Conrad often told his wife, "industry would be stifled and the economy would die. We'd all starve in rags while monkeys and butterflies multiply." This was gross calumny since Jackson, as a rich man's son, had inherited both a large industrial stock portfolio and economic sense, but Conrad's wife had long since ceased to argue with him. She practiced therapeutic voodoo instead.

Now, however, the unthinkable had happened: Faced with rainbow giraffes and the potential social catastrophe of rainbow humans, Conrad had found a use for his brother-in-law's scientific credentials.

"Jackson, we need to know what's causing giraffes to change color, and we need to know fast."

The President backed up Conrad's demand, and Jackson went to work. He had substantial funding and confidence in his own abilities, but weeks followed days and stretched into months, and Jackson was no forwarder. His lovely brown eyes were blood shot, and if he heard Conrad's bullying demands one more time he would punch that fat cat in his fat gut. At which point, Jackson faced the reality of his own frustrated failure and decided to call in his own expert. He sent a team of marines to track her through the Congo and bring her back.

Henrietta Illich was an Aleut from Alaska, and the world's foremost giraffe expert. At the age of seven, on a trip to the zoo, an enormously leggy giraffe had eaten her straw hat, and Henrietta had fallen in love. Short, dark-haired and indestructible, Henrietta had learned all there was to know about giraffes.

Jackson had tangled with her once over the desertification of Africa which was decreasing her beloved giraffes' habitat. Where Jackson was willing to compromise over strategies to deal with global warming, Henrietta showed no mercy. When she learned of Jackson's industrial stock portfolio, he really feared he'd collect a black eye; but fortunately, Henrietta was too short to deliver.

"What's Henri doing in the Congo?" Jackson demanded fretfully of his pet rat, Fido. He – Jackson, not the rat – knew the answer: Henrietta was in pursuit of a dream. If the Congo hid pygmy elephants, why not pygmy giraffes?

"Here I am," Henrietta burst into Jackson's office. Fido scuttled onto the desk to greet her, and Henrietta spared him a quick ear scratch. "I've read all the papers you sent along with the marines. I can think of a couple of things you've missed."

That didn't surprise Jackson, but he did venture a small protest. "Aren't you jet-lagged?"

"No." And the stepped-up campaign to understand the changes in giraffes began.

🔫

"The phlan on *sta4 is growing well," said Aiin, two tentacles flicking expertly through the data cubes. "The Xi, *sta4's dominant sentient species, are cooperating nicely."

Zod wrung two tentacles together with the pleased gesture of a Phog who has seen his investment return dividends. "If this new planet, Earth, proves as suitable a farm as *sta4, we'll be vacuuming it in. Lots and lots of lovely phlan. Lots and lots of lovely money."

"It depends on the humans," said Aiin sharply, less inclined by nature to count her phlan before it ectoplasmed.

"Ha!" said Zod. "Earth's a dandy planet, perfectly suited to humans. What could they have to war about?"

Jackson and Henrietta were nose to nose despite their nearly foot difference in height. Jackson loomed over Henrietta, and she glared up at him.

"I tested for all this while you were playing in the Congo. Food, trace nutrients, changes in weather patterns, radiation levels, fungi, bacteria, pollution. Nothing! Now, you've wasted all this time re-testing and still nothing!"

Henrietta's eyes narrowed to slits. Her voice grated. "Don't make this my fault. Of course I wouldn't trust your data."

Jackson straightened to his full height and tried to pull out his hair. Words failed him.

Henrietta's glare faltered. "I didn't mean it quite that way. I just meant that you operate so far inside the establishment that someone could easily have falsified your data. I mean, look at your brother-in-law."

Jackson's rage dropped a level, too. "I prefer not to." Not that Jackson had much choice since Conrad had taken to invading the lab. Jackson sighed. "What's left to check?"

"I'll run the blood tests again," said Henrietta. She was calm now, and hitched herself up onto Jack's desk, where she sat kicking thoughtfully at his chair. Jackson, himself, prowled his office, while Fido squeaked in a corner. "The change has to be cellular," continued Henrietta. "The good thing," and her face split with a fond smile, "is that the giraffes don't seem bothered in the least by their color change."

✦

"Zod!" shrieked Aiin.

"Oh my wobbly eels," Zod felt faint.

They stared through the view screen at Earth.

"The neo-virus is meant to leave the host unchanged," said Aiin. She pointed an accusing tentacle. "Those giraffes have changed color."

Zod changed color, too. The Phlan Harvesters' Board had very clear, rigorously enforced rules of non-interference. The neo-virus was the allowed means of measuring phlan levels, but it was explicitly designed not to interfere with its host. His tinkering with it had been a bad idea.

Aiin was equally worried. She waved her tentacles wildly. "Quick. Suck up the virus. Maybe the creatures will change back. Maybe no one will notice."

"Some hope," said Zod, but he activated the vacuum, and the little spaceship quartered the Earth, sucking vigorously for seventy two hours.

While Aiin occupied herself with converting the phlan data coming in from the neo-virus into data cubes, Zod maintained a mournful watch for Phlan Harvesters' Board scouts, and a desperate watch for signs of the giraffes returning to their pre-virus state.

"Bother," Aiin threw the data cubes against the wall of the spaceship. "Phlan levels are low on Earth. Lower per sentient capita than Rixx. It must be all the energy humans waste balancing on two legs; that and the fact that they're cunning."

Zod stared mournfully through the view screen at Earth. "We had such high hopes of Earth. Humans must be very hard to satisfy."

Aiin snorted through her snorkel and it turned a distressed red. "Now all we need is to be caught altering Earth's poxy ecosystem by the Board's scouts, and we'll lose our phlan licence and our ship, all for nothing. Those wretched giraffes had better recover now that they're free of the neo-virus."

205

"They are," said Zod in an awestruck voice. He tapped the view screen excitedly with two tentacles. "Look. 'Alleluia' and cut the cake."

Aiin was equally pleased. "Then let's get the Hades out of here." The spaceship whined as she upped power to the engine preparatory to a swift shedding of this annoying solar system.

"Uh, Aiin," Zod really wished he hadn't looked back at Earth, and in particular, at those two tiresome humans, Jackson and Henrietta.

Conrad slammed open Jackson's office door. Henrietta, looking up from her happy viewing of live giraffe footage, decided to follow him in and see the show.

"You've fixed it," boomed Conrad. He could bask now in the scientific glory of his brother-in-law. "The giraffes are back to their original color. So, how did you do it? A new drug? Laser treatment?" Conrad sat and crossed his legs, gripping one ankle happily.

"Actually," Jackson cleared his throat. "We're not responsible. The giraffes changed back by themselves."

Conrad's bonhomie vanished. "You mean those damn fool animals could change color again?"

"Yes."

"Well, hell." Conrad stormed out of the office.

"I guess that means the end of our funding," said Henrietta.

Jackson slumped in his chair. He looked green. But then, Henrietta shrugged, she felt green, too. Conrad had that effect on sensitive people.

Henrietta made the effort and dismissed Conrad from her mind. She pulled a folded printout from her pocket and dropped it on the desk in front of Jackson. "Look at this."

He unfolded the paper slowly. "A virus?" Jackson hazarded. Hope dawned in his eyes. "The giraffes have a virus?"

Henrietta shook her head. "I can't find any evidence beyond this image; even the original slide from which this was taken doesn't show the virus anymore."

Jackson groaned. He looked up at Henrietta. "Let's go home."

"Pardon?"

"My house. I'll cook you dinner. Let's just get out of here."

"You're on," said Henrietta.

Jackson's home was an old sprawling house with a wide front porch set some distance from its neighbors.

"Oh, no," hovering above Jackson's house, Zod groaned. He knotted two tentacles so tightly that they turned orange. "The neo-virus has gone rogue. Now we'll have to call in the scouts."

"Ahem," an image shimmered onto the view screen.

Zod groaned again, longer and louder. They were caught.

A scout from the Phlan Harvesters' Board circled their ship. It would have to be the sternest of them all, Mod.

"Prepare to meet the humans," said Mod, and the view screen went black.

"Maybe we can outfly him," said Zod. In his desperation, Zod forgot the furto-charger fitted to scout ships. Aiin didn't. She tapped the landing button.

Zod whimpered. He maintained a litany of foreboding as he and Aiin exited the spaceship, were gathered up by Mod, and tumbled towards the house where the two humans stood on the porch and watched them coming.

"Did you put anything in the coffee, Jackson?" asked Henrietta, staring at the approaching visitors.

"No," Jackson goggled at the aliens. "Perhaps I should have."

A snort of irrepressible laughter escaped from Henrietta. She edged nearer the warm humanity of Jackson, and he responded by wrapping an arm around her and hauling her even closer.

The three alien creatures tumbled towards them, looking for all the world like giant pompoms composed of retractable tentacles. The largest of the three was a sage green, easily visible in the starlight. It rolled along just behind the smallest of the trio which glowed a strong turquoise blue. The third alien was a bright unmissable yellow, like neon. As they came closer, it was possible to distinguish from among the tentacles five eyes on each, similar to snails' stalk eyes. Each pompom had a snorkel, wider at the base than the surrounding tentacles, which scented the air. Presumably somewhere in the mass of tentacles was a mouth.

The mid-sized alien rolled to a stop just short of the veranda. "Greetings. I am Mod and this is Aiin," a wave at the smallest alien, "and Zod, and thank goodness for the xeno-translator that makes this conversation possible."

"Thank goodness, indeed," returned Jackson with suspicious politeness. Henrietta felt him shake with hidden laughter. Really, these pompoms were ridiculous.

Mod continued his burbling introductions, explanations and reassurances. He re-introduced Zod and Aiin as phlan harvesters.

Jackson was captivated by the notion of phlan. Mod went over it for him one more time.

"Phlan is a high demand drug with us Phogs. It serves as both an individual mood booster and a crowd control agent. All sentient carbon-based creatures produce phlan when they're happy. That's because all carbon brains think via electrical impulses. When sentient, the electrical impulses are stronger, or more frequent, either way, in happy brain states this electricity is strong enough for the energy to radiate from the creature. This energy is what we call phlan. Most sentient beings use it, without being aware of doing so, to regulate their emotions. So people who want to be happy, go to where other people are happy. Hence the euphoria of a good party.

"However, only us Phogs learned to do this consciously, and then we worked on how to collect the energy. The important factor was to find planets where the dominant sentient species was sufficiently happy that excess phlan pools developed in its atmosphere. Locating and harvesting these pools is the phlan farming from which Zod and Aiin make their living.

"Their first step is to measure the amount and distribution of phlan on a planet. They do this by releasing an inert virus to reproduce within a host species and later sucking it back up. They then read out the amount and nature of phlan stored in the virus bodies. Unfortunately, this time on Earth, the virus went rogue."

"Ha!" Henrietta suddenly saw the light. "Hence the giraffes' color change."

"That was only a superficial alteration," said Mod. "There's more."

Zod winced.

"When Zod sucked up the virus, you and Jackson were taking blood samples from a giraffe. The virus, sucked out of the giraffe, was loose in the atmosphere and entered you and Jackson. That's when it went rogue. It established itself in your unused DNA storehouse, the only way it couldn't be sucked up.

"Let me get this straight," said Henrietta in a dangerous voice. "You're saying that a new primitive virus has colonised some of the junk DNA in our human genome?"

"It's not possible," said Jackson, unwinding his arm from around Henrietta and giving her a little push – as if that might make her see sense.

"Possible, impossible," Zod waved his tentacles wildly. "It happened."

Mod ignored them both and concentrated on Henrietta.

"I'm afraid it's a little more complicated than that. Humans have a small discredited branch of microbiology which holds that an ancient virus can re-emerge from DNA."

"Ah," Aiin snuffled her satisfaction.

Mod waggled his tentacles gravely. "A virus does not think. It is not consciously purposeful, but it will try to live, to reproduce and survive via any medium it can. Survival, you must understand, is the continuation of the genetic material which the virus contains. Sometimes the virus survives and copies itself within the bloodstream; more rarely, it co-opts its host's DNA."

"I made it possible," Zod's tentacles quivered alarmingly. "Me, with my tinkering." Aiin gave him a surreptitious pinch to behave himself.

"The virus," continued Mod, "was originally lifted from a segment of our Phog genome. It is the portion responsible for our sensitivity to phlan. Since that DNA segment is now in you both, you have Recognised Mutant Status under Phog law. That means we at the Phlan Harvesters' Board have a responsibility to work with you to 'grow' phlan on Earth."

"Sensitivity to phlan," muttered Henrietta. If, and it was a big if, the virus segment had the same effect for humans as it did in Phogs, then... "Of course. Conrad would dissipate all phlan in an area. That's why Jackson turned green."

"Green," repeated Aiin, interested. She tapped and tangled her tentacles in swift calculation. "So in moderate phlan you'd flush red, and high phlan areas, purple."

"Green. Purple." Jackson sounded winded.

"What about the giraffes?" asked Henrietta, annoyed that the Phogs had risked them by introducing the not so inert virus.

"Forget the giraffes," said Jackson. He was starting to think through what an increase of phlan could mean for humanity.

Henrietta narrowed her eyes at Jackson, but she, too, could see the benefits of phlan growth for people and the planet. Greater cooperation as a result of improved emotional well being would lead to better decision making, leading to improved environmental controls and, most importantly, a better global environment for giraffes.

"Can other people be given the rogue virus?" asked Henrietta cautiously.

"No. A rogue virus is too dangerous. We destroyed it," said Mod. His yellow color tinted an indescribably sly orange. "You'll just have to pass on the mutation the old fashioned way – through your children."

Children! Henrietta grasped the arm of the porch swing. Her biological clock had never ticked, let alone sounded an alarm. Giraffes, she had long ago decided, were much more satisfactory than toddling monsters.

Mod continued blithely. "Of course, the probability of passing on the appropriate piece of DNA is increased if you have children together."

"Oh dear," Henrietta sat on the swing chair. Jackson looked interested.

"We're very sorry about the trouble we've caused," said Zod tentatively.

"Not to worry," said Jackson cheerfully. "There could be advantages." A glare from Henrietta hurried him on. "Planned phlan growth will help us save our planet and ourselves." It might even redeem Conrad.

"So all's well that ends well," said Aiin, determinedly upbeat and with one eye swivelled to assess Mod's reaction.

"Ahem, all is well for the humans."

Henrietta snorted that that was a matter of opinion. Jackson pushed his luck and sat beside her on the porch swing. Their hips nudged companionably. Henrietta looked at Jackson's gentle brown eyes behind his glasses.

"We share the child minding," she said, just before Jackson kissed her.

The Phogs retreated tactfully to the scout's ship.

Mod wrung two tentacles together in a pleased gesture. "That went well."

"What?" said Zod and Aiin together.

"It's the obvious next step in phlan harvesting," said Mod. "Mutants grow the phlan and sell it. You'll have to spend a few weeks tutoring them and roughing out the strategy for phlan growth."

It took a couple of seconds for the implications to register with Zod, then he roared. "You slimy sea urchin devil. You set us up."

"A little tinkering with the virus we sold you," admitted Mod with becoming modesty. He waggled a cautionary tentacle. "Now, don't do anything rash. You don't want to jeopardise your monopoly contract for Earth, do you?"

Another semi-regular at Ray Gun Revival *was Milo James Fowler's Captain Quasar, a bravado, larger-than-life, pulp-esque hero whose comical adventures take him into all sorts of challenging situations. Including this one where he faces unexpected resistance to his solution...*

CAPTAIN QUASAR AND THE INSURMOUNTABLE BARRIER OF SPACE JUNK

Milo James Fowler

"They say you can never go home again." Bartholomew Quasar leaned back in his deluxe-model captain's chair as the star cruiser raced toward Earth. "But I tend to disagree."

"Humph." Hank, the very hairy, four-armed helmsman of the *Effervescent Magnitude*, seldom replied in more than a monosyllable. A cross between a large sloth and an orangutan in appearance, he sat hunched over his console in front of a massive viewscreen mounted on the fore wall. Somehow, despite the captain's frequent interruptions, Hank managed to remain focused on the task at hand: maintaining the ship's trajectory while dodging flurries of perilous meteorites and asteroids intent on taking the ship apart.

"How long has it been? Twenty years?" Quasar gazed into the unfathomable depths of star-punctured black. He narrowed his eyes, strumming his clean-shaven chin. "But taking into consideration our near-lightspeed travel, centuries could have passed while we were out gallivanting around the universe."

"They did," Hank muttered. "Two hundred thirty-four years, nine months, six weeks – "

"Please round up." Quasar emerged from his reverie.

"Two hundred thirty-five years have passed since you exited Earth space."

"Imagine that." Quasar failed to blink. "Yet I don't feel a day over thirty!"

Hank's posterior and superior hands traveled across the display panel as if they had minds of their own, tapping in coordinates and compensating for Saturn's gravitational pull. "There's nothing left on that rock. Why return?"

"Home is where the heart is, Hank ol' buddy." Quasar rose to approach the screen with long strides, thick muscled arms folded across his taut-uniformed chest. "I'm afraid I left my heart in Earth orbit."

"Humph," Hank reiterated.

"Only earthborn natives can appreciate the gorgeous blue of the oceans from space, how the planet gleams like topaz from black velvet, a brilliant oasis in the void." Quasar found himself waxing poetic, and he rather liked it. "Favored by the gods of old, lone fount of humanity in all its splendor – "

"Laid to waste centuries ago."

Quasar glared at his hairy helmsman. But Hank was right. Earth had been abandoned in droves after the global fallout and nuclear winters. When Quasar first left the planet, as a fresh-faced space cadet during the Great Expansion, his North American continent had yet to become a smoldering ash heap. Deep space colonization was in its earliest stages back then, as other planets capable of supporting human life were discovered. Little had Earth leaders realized how crucial it would be for off-world options to be made available to the future masses.

But no matter what he found waiting for him, Captain Quasar was brimming to overflowing with nostalgia. Mere thoughts of Earth always had that effect on him. "How much longer?"

"This solar system is crowded with space debris." As if on cue, a miniscule meteorite bumped into the port side, sheering off a section of the hull despite the electromagnetic shielding. Hank winced at the ship's violent shudder. "We have to take it slow."

"I know it's a little out of our way – " Quasar conceded.

"Just half a light-year."

" – but we'll be sure to visit your home planet next. What's it called again? Carpeteria?"

Hank merely growled, twin throats giving the noise an oddly harmonic quality.

It was another hour or so before Earth came into view – unlike anything the captain could have expected. There was so much flotsam and jetsam orbiting the planet that, despite enlarging the image on the viewscreen, Quasar could not see even a centimeter of the giant blue jewel itself amidst all the wreckage.

"Orbital junkyard," Hank observed.

"How'd it get like this?"

Hank shrugged his superior set of shoulders. "Earth's always been messy."

"I beg your pardon!"

The helmsman swiveled to face his commanding officer. "Your people have dumped crap into space as long as they could ignite rockets."

"Open a channel. I want to speak to whoever's in charge down there." No world president could ever have allowed such a disgrace to befall the Earth.

"Captain, there will unlikely be any sort of infrastructure to support inter-space communication."

Quasar glared at him, and the very hairy helmsman complied.

"People of Earth, this is the *Effervescent Magnitude*. We will soon be entering your space. Please respond." Nothing. The captain cleared his throat. "People of Earth, this is Captain Bartholomew Quasar." He paused, eyes stinging with emotion as the floating debris came into sharper focus, a barrier so dense even sunlight couldn't penetrate it. "Please answer me."

"It's a wasteland down there, Captain."

Quasar was tempted to agree. But then a ray of hope pierced his heart as a flurry of static whined on the comm.

"Hello?" came an uncertain voice.

Quasar released a whoop. "Hello! You're there! Well, of course you are. To whom am I speaking?"

More static. "Uh, Bill."

"Bill? A pleasure to make your acquaintance! What is your designation?"

"Uh..."

The fellow seemed to need a little coaxing. "I am Captain Bartholomew Quasar of the *Effervescent Magnitude*. And you are?"

"The janitor."

Hank pointed to the display panel where a single life sign blinked on a map of the North American continent. There were no other readings anywhere else on the globe. Quasar suffered a sudden sinking feeling.

"What do your duties entail – as janitor?"

"Waste disposal. I get rid of all the crap."

Quasar nodded, though he did not fully understand. There was no one left down there to clean after. "And where does it go?"

"Up."

The captain's hands tightened into fists, one of which he pounded against the mute button. "That moron is responsible for this mess!" His eyes narrowed to slits. "But we've arrived just in time." He nodded to himself. "Hank, discharge all weapons."

"Captain?"

"You heard me. We're going to blow that junk to smithereens. Now fire!"

Hank did as commanded. Every laser beam, plasma torpedo, and depth charge from the ship's arsenal hurtled toward the debris to explode on impact, spreading like wildfire as incendiary plasma tends to do, dissolving the Earth's trash shield as if it was a piece of paper set aflame, revealing the reflected glare of the sun in a violent yet glorious outburst.

"Let there be light!" Captain Quasar roared as the brilliant blue orb he remembered returned in full effect.

At the same instant, life signs appeared across Hank's display panel, thousands upon thousands of them at all points of the globe.

"Captain?" Hank gestured.

"You see? It's no post-apocalyptic wasteland! It's a thing of beauty, and life is thriving down there!" Quasar almost jumped for joy. "We have liberated them!"

"Uh, hello?" Bill's voice returned through static.

"You're free, my man, free! You and all your friends!"

"You've destroyed the sun barrier."

"Guilty as charged!" Quasar laughed. "If that's what you called that orbiting sea of space crap!"

"You really shouldn't have done that."

"Oh?" Quasar swallowed his chuckles. Bill's tone sounded just a bit on the grave side. "Why is that?"

"It was shielding us from the sun. The annihilation bots left by Emperor Zhan are solar-powered."

Quasar frowned. Annihilation bots? Emperor Zhan? Hank pointed to the blinking life signs which weren't really life signs at all but rather heat signatures: machines powering up.

"They were tasked with destroying the Western Conglomerate, but I come from a long line of Janitors, left behind after the Great Exodus to pack the sun-shield with fresh junk – pretty much anything I can launch into orbit. I've done a good job of blocking the sunlight for some time now. Until today, that is."

"So you're saying – "

"The whole planet's gonna blow."

Hank's four hands were already flying across the nav console, plotting a new course out of Earth space. Captain Quasar's sinking feeling began to rebound; he was about to be sick in a major way.

"There must be something we can do."

Hank nodded. "Run."

"We can't let the Earth be destroyed!"

"Too late," said Bill.

Quasar cursed. "How were we supposed to know about solar-powered annihilation bots? And who the hell is Emperor Zhan?"

"He was head of the whole Eastern Conglomerate. How long have you been away?"

"Two hundred thirty-five years," Hank replied.

Static. "Oh."

"We won't leave you to die, and we won't let those robots have their way." Quasar's eyes darted from the console to the viewscreen. "We're here for a reason – to save the day!"

"Don't you worry about me," said Bill. "I've already programmed my jettison pod. But maybe you could hook onto me with a tractor beam once I'm up there?"

Quasar ended the transmission. "Take us in, Hank." He returned to his chair and buckled up, activating the ship-wide intercom. "Attention all hands. Things are about to get a little dicey."

Hank swiveled to face his commanding officer. "Captain?"

Quasar pointed at the viewscreen. "Enter the atmosphere. We've got some bots to smash."

"With what?"

The sinking feeling returned as Quasar remembered they had already exhausted their entire weapons complement against the sun barrier. "Is the tractor beam still functional?"

Hank nodded with a puzzled look on his very hairy face.

"Take us in, then!" The Captain raised a fist.

Hank did as commanded, and the *Effervescent Magnitude* plowed into the Earth's atmosphere, breaking through massive cloud banks to pass over the gutted moonscape of a continent ravaged by nuclear war. Across the crater-pocked surface, scores of giant robots a hundred meters high lumbered to and fro bearing signs of carbon scoring, evidence that they had seen serious battle. Directing high-powered, shoulder-mounted laser cannons at the ground, they scorched through the Earth's crust, blasting it to pieces with chunks of the planet flying upward around them in all directions.

But as the star cruiser approached, the annihilation bots lost their focus on the task at hand – destroying the planet one continent at a time, by all appearances – and whirled around to face the *Magnitude*. A barrage of laser-fire hit the ship head-on, instantly sapping the electromagnetic shield and blasting straight through to the exposed hull.

"Captain!" Hank caterwauled over the shrieking alarms as his console and everything else on the bridge quaked and rattled, and the ship itself moaned like a whale giving birth.

"Hold course!" Quasar's fingers danced across the console on each armrest of his chair, activating the ship's tractor beam.

All of a sudden the alarms fell silent as two, then four, then half a dozen of the annihilation bots stopped firing and floated upward from the ground, rotating awkwardly in midair and unable to compensate for the abrupt lack of equilibrium, their central processors perplexed by the unexpected weightlessness. But their confusion didn't last long. They reactivated the laser cannons in a matter of moments – but only succeeded in blowing each other to pieces with explosions of jittery electric light and plumes of black smoke. Captain Quasar let out a victorious whoop as their dismembered pieces rained down to punch into the earth.

"Six down, sixty thousand to go," muttered Hank.

Quasar glared at him. He would not be swayed by the helmsman's negativity.

The ship crossed kilometers of ash-covered earth and the charred, mangled skeletons of major city skyscrapers. As each giant robot with evil intent came into view, the captain sucked it up with the tractor beam and whipped it around in mid-air, employing its laser cannons against the other bad bots in brilliant streaks of sizzling white. In no more than an hour's time, he had destroyed nearly a hundred of the awful automatons, leaving a trail of smoldering ruins in the ship's wake.

"We can't take much more of this," Hank reported as a new batch of bots appeared and opened fire upon the creaking, swaying *Magnitude* before Quasar had time to activate the tractor beam. "The next barrage will end us."

Quasar grimaced, clenching the controls with white knuckles as he pulled the robots higher into the air only to thrash them back to the ground in a jumbled heap of broken, sparking metal. "How many enemies lie ahead?"

Hank blinked at the display. "Too many to count."

Quasar was quicker this time as a dozen more bots lumbered into view, and they too were left behind in crumpled, smoking piles of junk discarded across the cratered earth. "Why didn't we pack an EMP or something?"

Hank shrugged.

"Get that janitor back on the line." Quasar grimaced, punching at the consoles in a heroic effort to destroy yet another batch of ill-intending bots.

"I'm still here," Bill said.

"Can you see what we're doing?" Quasar shouted.

"Yeah, I figured that was you."

"Care to lend us a hand?"

"Don't see how I could help."

"Have you an EMP or a few?"

"Nope."

"Then what *do* you have, man? How'd you send all that junk into space?"

"Uh-rockets."

Quasar ended the transmission. "Hank, take us to Bill."

Moments later, after scouring the surrounding countryside of every annihilation bot in sight, the *Effervescent Magnitude* – looking much the worse for wear – arrived at what appeared to be the remains of a military command center, half-buried in the earth under dunes of charcoal-colored ash.

"He's in there," Hank gestured, reopening the comm channel.

"Bill, we're going to need your rockets." Quasar licked his lips, glancing at the display where thousands of heat signatures remained, heralding the Earth's imminent demise. "How many do you have?"

No response.

"Captain," Hank pointed at the viewscreen, their window to the world, as a projectile launched itself from the command center to pierce the sky and beyond, leaving a thick tail of smoke.

"The escape pod," Quasar muttered. "He's left us to fend for ourselves."

Then something very unexpected happened: missile silos creaked open in the scarred earth, iron hatches yawning as rockets poked their noses upward like weasels sniffing the air after a long internment.

"Are you thinking what I'm thinking?" Quasar grinned.

"Humph," replied Hank.

In a matter of minutes, the captain had utilized the tractor beam to haul each of the missiles into the cargo bays of the *Effervescent Magnitude* where his engineers and best weapons tech officers immediately went to work modifying, transporting, and loading the rockets into the ship's empty torpedo tubes.

"Captain," said Hank. "Before Bill left, he triggered silos across the continent – "

"How many rockets are we looking at?" Captain Quasar glanced up from his console.

"Hundreds – and all viable, as long as the bots don't get to them first."

Quasar grinned. "Let's not keep them waiting. We've got a planet to rescue."

Hank couldn't help asking: "For who?"

Captain Quasar glared at his very hairy helmsman for the fourth time in half as many hours. "It's the principle of the thing!"

It took some doing, but the crew of the *Magnitude* were up to the challenge, and between the captain's hand at the tractor beam and the retrofitting of the rockets as makeshift torpedoes, they managed to get the job done, wiping the Earth clean of every annihilation bot they encountered. Granted, hundreds of the robots succeeded in breaking apart a continent or two and sinking the pieces into the sea, but the oceans of the world ultimately aided in the machines' demise, drowning them with elaborate sparks and fizzles as they drifted out of sight.

Thanks to the undying devotion of Captain Quasar and company, the dastardly plans of one Emperor Zhan – whoever he was – were thwarted with extreme prejudice, and the Earth was ultimately saved.

Limping back into orbit with major blast damage and exhaust venting from every pore like a death shroud, the *Effervescent Magnitude* encountered the escape pod of Bill the Janitor, which Quasar promptly tractor-beamed into a cargo hold.

"We did it," the captain said with pride, escorting a disheveled, grizzled, and stinky fellow from his cramped quarters to gaze out a wide portside window at the Earth's glory. "We saved the planet!"

Bill nodded, twitching as he dragged his feet in a stiff, awkward gait. "Looks that way."

Quasar couldn't understand the man's less-than-enthusiastic demeanor. "We've done it! The bots are destroyed!"

"Yeah." Bill sniffed and ran a stained sleeve across his bulbous nose, glancing out through transparent plasticon at the Earth. "Guess I'm out of a job."

"You're failing to see the big picture here – "

"No, I get it. You're the hero. You saved the day." Bill shrugged. "So now what? You got some plan to keep the Sea Nukembers at bay?"

"Sea-*what*?"

"It'll take a while for the sunlight to reach them in the ocean, but Emperor Zhan dumped a bunch down there. They make those annihilation bots look like kids' stuff. Instead of lasers, they're each armed with multiple megaton warheads. And they're solar-powered, too – but, ironically, not very Earth-friendly."

"Gah!" Quasar threw up his hands. "What did this Zhan fellow have against our planet?"

Bill offered another shrug. "He always said if he couldn't have it, then nobody would."

Captain Quasar clenched his jaw until the muscle twitched. "The ultimate villain."

"Uh – he's been dead for a while now – "

"Nevertheless," the captain retorted, "there appears to be only one way to foil him."

The remains of those sixty thousand annihilation bots would make a good start. As well as anything else the crew of the *Effervescent Magnitude* could locate down on the surface, suck up with the tractor beam, and drag out into space before the sun's light was able to pierce the ocean depths.

Quasar jabbed the wall-mounted intercom. "Hank."

"Yes, Captain?"

"Looks like we've got a new sun barrier to build."

Shaun Farrell is the founder and former cohost of the Adventures In Scifi Publishing Podcast, *and has thus spent hours interviewing and learning from the top people in the business. In his own story, young saboteurs struggle to break free of the control of the mysterious NET which runs their society in...*

CONVERSION

Shaun Farrell

"They're here, aren't they? Aren't they? Hush. I already know. I can feel them. The music, the music!" Flapper stumbled away, leaving Gen to huddle over his hand held computer interface. Flapper's right hand shook uncontrollably, like it always did, his arm tucked into his side.

"Yes," Gen replied, feeling nauseous. He rubbed his leathery face. "They're here."

Flapper danced, left shoulder tilted to the floor, right leg kicking sideways. To Gen, the youth looked like the Hunchback of Notre Dame, except uglier.

"I knew it!" Flapper exclaimed. "Maybe my nans are working again! I can hear the network. The voices." He fell to the floor, lifting his arms in exaltation, drinking the wireless energy beaming around him. Then he stopped and looked at Gen in concern. "Are they going to kill you?"

Gen grunted. He saved his work on the computer and resisted the temptation to throw it against the wall. For twenty years he had sought a way to infiltrate NET, to break their seemingly impenetrable control. But their firewalls were too advanced, and, by now, they were so complex he hardly understood what he was looking at. There was always a backdoor, and he better find it in the next few hours or he'd be converted himself.

Unless he forced NET to kill him. Which suited him just fine. Better than conversion.

"Are they going to kill you, Gen? Are they?" Flapper stood at Gen's side now, eyes strangely focused and sincere. They had grown to like each other over the years. Weird.

"They'll try," Gen said, softly.

"What will you do?"

Gen sighed and turned back to his computer. Captain Tuck should just about be ready with his traps. Gen would have to finish his work from within the underground facility.

"I'm going to kill them back."

"How about you give us some of those guns," Dixon said.

Tuck looked over his shoulder at the ex-criminal. No, Tuck reminded himself, still a criminal. Just beyond the short reach of the law. For now.

"Is that a joke?" Tuck asked. His low voice was faint but managed to carry inside the vast underground chamber. He had just finished setting the primary trap for the NET soldiers. This was the most logical entry point into the warehouse, and he had rigged it with enough explosives to demolish a small house.

He gazed over Dixon's shoulder. Lynda huddled against the wall, shushing her baby girl. The baby cried softly, as if she understood the need for stealth but couldn't control her fear.

"When have you known me to joke, Captain America?" Dixon asked. His ivory skin gleamed under a thick layer of sweat and grease. Green eyes peered out from shaggy eyebrows with feline malice. The eyebrows looked huge under his bald head.

Dixon swaggered a few steps forward. "Come on, you can't hold them off by yourself."

Tuck aimed a pistol at Dixon's face. "Why don't you stay where you are? No one touches my guns."

Dixon hesitated, then slapped his thighs with clenched fists. "Why the hell not? If something happens to you the rest of us are screwed!"

"Not my problem. I need them." Tuck had five guns on him altogether. Two pistols on either leg, a spitfire – a gun so small he could barely hold it – wrapped around his ankle, and two L-20 rifles strapped to his back. They fired a pea-sized round capable of splitting a man in two.

Dixon started to stay something else, but threw his arms up in disgust. "Fine." He turned, muttering under his breath. "Come all the way to this damn planet just to have those NET bastards chase me down anyway. Now, Captain Superman here – will you shut that kid up!"

Lynda hugged her daughter even more tightly to her breast. "She's scared. She knows something bad is happening, and you're not helping!"

"Whatever." Dixon spat on the floor as he walked away.

Chloe, Lynda's daughter, continued to cry.

"They're here, they're here!" Flapper announced as he and Gen rejoined the others.

"What about the virus?" Lynda asked Gen.

The ex-computer expert shook his head, his hand still punching commands into his small computer. He remembered when this stuff used to be easy. That seemed like another lifetime.

"Oh, sure," Dixon said, leaning against the wall. "You're smart enough to help create the little bastards, but you can't stop them. Figures."

"I had nothing to do with nanotech," Gen growled, a warning in his voice.

Dixon responded to perceived challenges like a rabid dog inhaling bloody meat. He pushed off from the wall with the heel of his foot, muscles in his thick arms twitching. "I think you're lying," he whispered with a smile. "I think you helped NET infest the nations of earth, but when they turned on you, you ran away like the little coward you are. You booked passage on a ship and fled as far as you could. And here you are, one of the last clean humans in the universe, facing your own creation."

Gen's face turned a deep shade of red. Blue veins throbbed in his temples.

"That's enough," Tuck said. "We need to get deeper underground. Their troop landers will be here any minute. We need to – "

"Son of a – " Gen swung at Dixon, but the bigger, stronger man easily blocked it. He returned the blow, splitting Gen's cheek open with callused knuckles.

The world blacked out for a minute, and when Gen came to he saw Tuck pointing a gun at Dixon's head, both men yelling obscenities. Flapper jumped around like a monkey, grabbing his head with both hands, screaming that he could no longer hear the music. The buzz was gone. (Of course, Gen knew Flapper hadn't heard it before. The nans in the boy's body were completely dead, making it impossible for him to interface their network.) Chloe screamed at the top of her baby lungs, and Lynda wept, begging Tuck and Dixon to be quiet.

Humanity's last children, Gen thought. The final non-trans, and perhaps the last pure vestiges of Earth's greatest species.

They didn't stand a chance.

Besides storing food and supplies for the three hundred colonists, which only accounted for a few, relatively small rooms, the underground structure processed the water gathered from Columbus' moon. Columbus itself was practically desert. The snowy poles could provide them with water, but the snow was so full of toxins that the energy to purify it outweighed the expenditure needed to travel to the moon and back.

Ice mining in a vacuum was dangerous, but Dixon didn't mind. This was freedom, even if the elements threatened to kill you at any given moment. He had been here for two years, and while he couldn't say he had made any true friends, he had found peace.

Until now.

He finished packing the duffle bags with food stuffs. Tempted to take the food and hide on his own just to spite Captain America for ordering him around, Dixon grumbled as he rejoined the group. This food would keep them full for at least two months. With luck, NET wouldn't be able to locate them deep within the warehouse. NET would wait around for awhile, but after sixty days of silence they'd classify Columbus as neutralized and move on, leaving the desert world to burn in its sun forever.

At least that's what they hoped. He knew better. NET was relentless. Tuck knew better, as well, or he wouldn't waste his time setting traps.

While Dixon cleaned out the food closet, Tuck, Gen and Flapper had vandalized everything in sight. All the spacecraft were gone, and while other colonists had fled for the dunes and caves, Tuck wanted to give the appearance that all of them had escaped. But not before wrecking the place. It was consistent with human behavior, Tuck had said. When humans couldn't have something, they would rather destroy it than allow enemies to utilize that resource.

Whatever. Dixon thought the Commando Extraordinaire just wanted to shoot something.

"Did you get the food?" Gen asked.

"What do you think?" Dixon replied, dropping the bags on the floor.

"Pick those up," Tuck ordered. "We're done here. Time to get deeper underground."

A thud echoed from above. They all looked at the ceiling, hearts racing. Tuck cocked one of his L-20s, aimed it upward.

Silence.

"They couldn't have landed already, could they?" Lynda asked. Chloe, for the moment, had fallen asleep in her arms. The little girl's fingers gripped a lock of Lynda's hair.

"Impossible," Gen muttered. He pulled his computer from his pocket and switched on the screen. Accessing the facility's security systems, he brought up a view from the rooftop cameras.

A metallic cylinder glided across the roof on matching, polymer legs, its round body swiveling from side to side. Gen recognized it, though the design had changed drastically over the last few years. It looked alive. And it looked hungry.

"It's a transponder," Gen said. "They're going to infect our system with nans."

"Can't they do that from space?" Lynda asked.

"I made sure the firewall was up," Gen said. "I didn't realize they could land these things on a planet now. We only have a minute or two before all the computers are out of our control."

"Oh, well that's just – " Dixon began.

Gen cut him off. "Luckily, none of the doors or lights down here are automated. It's as old fashioned as can be. We did that on purpose, just in case."

"Just in case?" Dixon sneered. Then his voice deepened into a growl. "You've known this day was coming all along."

"I suspected," Gen admitted. "But things have changed so much, I'm not sure that any precautions can help. If I can just get through their firewall..."

"Come on," Tuck said. "Let's get moving. I think our window is even shorter."

Gen shut off the image and disconnected his computer from the colony network. His unit would continue to function uninfected. For now.

As they jogged toward a staircase, he glanced at Flapper and wondered if the boy would cause a bigger problem then he was worth. He was acting much calmer than usual.

Gen would keep an eye on him.

Lynda tripped as she scurried down the dimly lit passageway and nearly fell on her baby. She managed to twist into the wall and keep her balance. Nobody else noticed. She was the last in a fleeing procession venturing down dark passages as most of the lights were non-functional. The rest of her group was too focused on their impending destruction to care if she couldn't keep up.

An explosion rocked the facility. Tuck's trap. NET was coming for them.

Chloe stirred, awakened by the stumble. She sighed and blinked tired eyes.

"Hi, baby girl," Lynda whispered. She tried to keep her heart rate down. Chloe was quite susceptible to her mother's emotions, and a fussy baby was the last thing they needed.

Two years had passed since Lynda fled Earth. NET had nearly converted every nation on the globe. She had heard rumors that doctors were injecting newborns at birth. Not even wiping them off first. The nanotech engineered transhuman era had truly begun, and Lynda wanted no part of it.

It was sin. It was evil. She wouldn't allow those beasts to steal her baby's soul.

Finding a ship to take her away hadn't been easy. Booking off-world passage required years of sifting through yellow tape, acquiring insurance, submitting to dozens of medical exams. And what did the doctors do in those exams?

"Not you, baby girl," Lynda said, kissing Chloe on the head. Chloe smiled, still groggy.

A tear spilled down Lynda's cheek at the sight. They would never take her baby. They would never destroy what made her so special. When the time came, Lynda knew what she had to do.

They finally stopped at a cross-section of halls, taking refuge in an abandoned storage room to rest. The water aqueducts spanned the ceiling and floors above them. Several feet of concrete and millions of gallons of water would make it very difficult to locate them with sensors.

Of course, Tuck thought, that also makes it a likely hiding place. If I were them, I'd look here first.

But that was fine with Tuck. He was tired of running. He was tired of hearing how superior a man became with nans pumping his blood. Most of all, he was tired of missing his wife.

"Only takes one bullet to kill a NET. Doesn't sound so advanced to me."

"What?" Gen asked.

"Nothin."

A single light bulb hung from the center of the storage room, spilling dim light that didn't reach the far corners. Storage crates made of mesh plastic were stacked near the north wall. Dust covered the floor. Grains of sand had slowly filtered through a crack in the roof.

Tuck kicked at the dirt, enjoying the smell. It made him feel alive. He marched across the room to the door.

Activating the laser sight on the old L-20, he gazed down the narrow scope into the dark hall. He could kill their troops from here. He had the advantage as long as he didn't run out of bullets. But the bodies would pile very high before that happened.

Very high, indeed.

"What's his problem?" Dixon asked. He crouched next to Gen against the back wall.

Flapper danced in a circle directly under the light bulb. He tapped his forehead with a knuckle and murmured under his breath.

Lynda sang to Chloe somewhere in the darkness.

Gen looked at Flapper. "He used to be NET. The nans caught some kind of virus and screwed him up before they winked out. I've been... studying him, hoping to learn how his firewall failed."

"Not him," Dixon said. He pointed at Tuck. "Him. Marine Boy."

"Oh." Gen blushed. He was grateful for the darkness. "He was an

American soldier. Some terrorists caught him and tortured him for years. Locked him up in a closet for weeks at time, so he was practically bathing in his own wastes. By the time he was released, most of the U.S. was pro-nan. His wife had been injected and was an important asset to NET. We all know what NET programming does to a personality."

"Yeah. Wipes it dry."

Gen looked at his computer and continued to punch in commands.

"Must be nice to have dirt on everyone," Dixon muttered.

"That was my job. Know who's coming, who's going. Keep people safe."

Dixon just snorted.

"Nanotechnology isn't the real problem," Gen said, trying to sound casual.

Dixon nearly growled. "Could have fooled me."

"It's the programming," Gen insisted. "It's NET, the single most corrupt institution the planet has ever known, hiding behind a fake religion to justify its actions." Gen realized he was nearly yelling.

Dixon grabbed Gen by the collar and pulled him off the ground. The computer slipped from Gen's grasp, rattled on the floor.

"You should probably shut your mouth, old man, and get back to work," Dixon spit out between clenched teeth.

Gen gasped, embarrassed at being manhandled with such ease. "I'm not old!"

Dixon stopped, blinked. His eyes widened, and he seemed to really see Gen for the first time. Very slowly, he set Gen down.

"Just do your thing." Dixon spun and stormed out of the room. He bumped Tuck on the way, ignored the Captain's protests.

"What was that all about?" Lynda asked.

Gen shook his head.

"Music, music, music, music." Flapper rocked on the floor, knees tucked up against his chest.

Gen watched, wishing he could help the young man. He still didn't understand why Flapper had been warped so badly. It was more than nan-failure, Gen was sure of that. But what?

He turned back to his computer, studying the data. Flapper was a goner, just like the rest of them.

"Do you hear that?" Lynda asked. Chloe stirred in her mother's arms.

"No," Gen said. "What?"

"Footsteps from above," Tuck replied. He stared down the hallway over the scope of his gun, relaxed and still. "They'll be here in a few minutes."

Dixon suddenly rushed back into the room from the hall, chest heaving. "NET! They're here."

"We can hear them," Tuck said. He rose, casually turning the L-20 toward Dixon. "So, Dixs, where have you been?"

Dixon paused in the middle of wiping sweat from his forehead. "What are you talking about? I've been sitting out there thinking about my death, that's where I've been."

Tuck cocked his head. "Really, because I've been right by this door, just waiting for something to shoot at. I didn't see you in the hall."

"It was dark! What, are you Nocturnal Boy, too?" He paused, looked at the gun. "Why don't you put that down before you piss me off?"

Lynda stepped out of the darkness and joined Flapper, who had gone still under the light bulb. "What are you saying, Tuck?" she asked.

"Doesn't anyone else find it interesting that the moment we hear the troops coming, Dixon reappears after being gone an hour?"

"Hold on a sec, Tuck," Gen said. "Dixon hates NET as much as any of us. He – "

Tuck smiled. "Oh, I know he hates NET with a passion. That's the only reason I've let him live. But you know what I think? I think there's something he hates even worse than NET or nans or being displaced on this rock."

Dixon fumed. His hands, balled into fists, pushed into his thighs so hard his legs were going numb. "All right," Dixon yelled. "Let's hear it!"

"Keep your voice down!" Lynda said.

"Why?" Dixon said. "If he's right, they already know where we are. Besides – ah, did you hear that? They're getting closer. They're right on top of us! Any second now, they'll rush around that corner and fill our heads with little machines that will make our brains shrivel up and shut off, and then you know what happens! You know what happens THEN?"

Tuck cocked the rifle, brought it up to his shoulder. "Shut your mouth."

"Why should I?" Dixon said. "You don't trust anyone. Either you kill me, or they do. Either way, I'm dead."

"Tuck," Gen started.

"Shut up, Gen. Get back to work."

"Yes, work on the music, the music," Flapper said. "You are close to the music."

They all paused, the tension in the room coming to a sudden halt.

"I am?" Gen asked. "How can you..." his voice trailed off. He held up his computer and pressed a command.

Flapper's back arched. His eyes rolled back into his head. Then he shook it off and started rocking on the floor.

"What was that?" Tuck asked.

"The nans, the ones inside of him, must still be alive somehow. They reacted to my transmission. I think – " Gen turned away, hands typing rapidly.

"I think you can put the piece down now, soldier boy," Dixon said.

"How about I keep it where it is, just for fun?"

Synchronized footsteps filled the hallway. In the midst of their argument, they hadn't heard the NET soldiers. Tuck and Dixon looked down the hall in unison, their eyes widening.

A dozen soldiers stood out there, with more in the stairwell behind them, no doubt.

"I knew it," Tuck whispered, face twisting into a scowl. "You betrayed us!"

Tuck began to re-aim the L-20 at Dixon. Simultaneously, Dixon jutted forward and reached for Tuck's leg. With his other hand, he deflected the rifle toward the ceiling.

Tuck tried to sidestep, but Dixon was too fast. In that moment, Tuck realized his feelings of control had been an illusion. Dixon could have done this whenever he wanted.

Before Tuck could regain his bearings, Dixon had relieved the Captain of a pistol and darted down the hallway.

"He's joining NET!" Tuck yelled, scrambling for the door.

Then gunshots echoed around him. And screams. Dixon's screams. He was charging the enemy soldiers, gun spitting fire, lungs releasing the last breath of a man embracing his fate.

"No," Tuck whispered. "It can't be."

The troops responded in unison, their minds joined through NET, as they unleashed hell into the hallway. Dixon was chopped to pieces, but he continued forward anyway, as if the sheer force of his hatred could hold his flesh together. His gun fired again and again.

Two men collapsed under the barrage of his attack, but that was all Dixon could manage. He fell, dead before he hit the floor.

"Dixon!" Tuck's throat was instantly dry, adrenaline zapping his mouth of moisture, replacing it with salt. He screamed and took aim with his L-20. Barely able to control the gun with his shaky arms, he leaned around the doorframe and fired.

NET responded with typical effectiveness, aiming their fire at Tuck's side of the door. With nans guiding their eyes and fingers, the NET soldiers demonstrated considerable skill. Tuck continually turned back into the room, the metal doorframe disintegrating around him. At one point, he dove across the entry to the other side. Miraculously, only one enemy projectile grazed his leg.

Once the shooting began, Gen, Flapper, and Lynda ran to the opposite

234

side of the room. Debris and bullets rattled all over the place, but they found somewhat suitable shelter in the far corner behind the empty storage crates.

Flapper yelled and tried to run into the hall. He wanted to rejoin his brothers, and he slapped at Gen when the older man held him back.

"They don't want you anymore," Gen screamed, feeling the futility of the situation overtake him. He should let Flapper run into the sea of bullets. He would die instantly, but at least he would die believing NET had come for him.

"I know, I know," Flapper returned, still struggling.

A growl of agony slipped from Tuck's lips. They could hear him clearly over the constant barrage. He must be hit. Gen looked around the crates. Sure enough, Tuck huddled against the wall, trying to tie off a bleeding arm. His shooting arm.

Time was up.

Flapper saw it, too. "Here," he said. Without waiting for Gen's approval, he snatched the computer from Gen's grasp.

Gen lunged for it like he would a lifeline at sea. That interface was his last connection with humanity, his last reminder of what he once was, and his only hope to have a life ever again.

Flapper punched Gen in the face with surprising strength. They stared into each other's eyes, the sound of violence deafening around them.

"We're the only friends you have!" Gen yelled, betrayal turning to anger. Yes, he had initially brought Flapper to Columbus because he wanted to study him, but things had changed since then. They were the closest remnants of family either would ever know. Or so Gen had believed.

"I know," Flapper replied, his face still, his right arm steady, his eyes confident. Gen froze. He had never seen Flapper like this. He looked NET. His eyes seemed to flicker silver, as if swarming with nans.

"I can hear the music, Gen. It sounds sick."

Gen shook his head. "That's impossible. The nans inside you are dead!"

Flapper turned to Lynda. "I'm sorry about your baby."

Without giving an explanation, he turned to the computer and began to type one handed. He moved with unnatural speed, as if he was intimately familiar with the interface.

"Hey!" Gen reached for the computer.

Flapper kicked him.

Chloe screamed, and Lynda hugged the child so tight the baby couldn't breathe.

Tuck's war-cry began again, his rifle spitting death into the darkness.

Flapper handed the computer back to Gen. His right hand seemed to shrivel, then shake, and he hid it against his side. Bending at the waist, his knees began flexing.

"Push initiate!" Flapper said.

"What did you do?" Gen asked. He didn't recognize the code filling the screen.

"Push it!" Tears began streaming down Flapper's face. Mucus leaked from his nose.

Knowing he had no other option, Gen pushed the button and transmitted Flapper's program.

The world suddenly turned silent. Tuck fired a few more rounds before he realized the enemy was no longer firing back. Flapper went rigid as steel, his face placid. He fell backward into the mesh crates, spilled them across the floor.

"What the hell?" Tuck muttered.

Realization dawned in Gen's mind, and he rushed to join the Captain at the door. The NET soldiers had collapsed just as Flapper had.

"What happened?" Tuck asked.

Gen looked at his computer. Flapper had jacked the interface into NET's network. He studied the signals coming from the nans. He could still detect an energy signature, but it was faint.

"He reformatted them," Gen whispered.

"What?" Tuck asked, now on his feet. Sweat and blood covered his body. He had been hit several times.

"Flapper. He must have remembered some kind of... access code, or something. He reformatted them. Amazing!"

"What does that mean?" Tuck asked.

"I haven't the faintest idea."

"No! NO!"

Then Gen realized how deep the silence in the room had truly been. Chloe was no longer crying. He rushed back around the crates, Tuck stumbling after him.

Lynda had placed Chloe on the ground. Her hands hovered over the child, shaking.

"Lynda?" Gen asked.

"She's dead. My baby girl is dead!" Sobs racked her as she lay down next to her child.

Gen knelt, put his hand on Chloe's chest. There was a gentle heartbeat there. Life still held on. Flapper must have known. That was why he apologized.

It took several minutes for Gen to calm Lynda enough to talk with her. "She's not dead," he finally said. "She was NET. The nans have reset."

He wiped wetness from her face.

"How is that p-possible?" she finally asked. "She wasn't b-born on Earth."

"I don't know. But somehow NET infected her."

"I don't mean to break up our moment of rest," Tuck said, "but eventually they'll wake up, right? If they're just reformatting – "

"Then once the basic programs initialize, they should wake, yes," Gen said.

Tuck pointed at Gen's computer. "What's the range on that thing? Did it reach their spaceship?"

Gen considered it. "Probably."

He swallowed, clearly in pain. "Alright, pick up your kid. Gen, grab twitchy."

"His name is Flapper," Gen protested.

"Whatever," Tuck said. "Come on, we'll take the landing shuttle to the ship, blow the rest of them out an airlock, pick up the colonists in the desert, and get the hell out of here." He limped for the door.

"Where will we go?" Lynda asked, gently scooping Chloe into her arms.

"Don't ask me," Tuck replied, vanishing out the door.

Gen put the computer in his pants pocket. Flapper didn't even weigh a hundred pounds, and Gen lifted him with fair ease. He wondered what the boy would be like when he woke. Would he be his old self or a NET agent? And what about Chloe? She must have been infected in the womb, yet she acted like any normal child.

What was NET up to?

Dixon's blood covered the floor in the hall, his body in pieces. He had given himself for the group. Gen wished he had known the man better, had tried to understand what had happened to him. It was too late for that. It was too late for a lot of things. But maybe they could start over someplace else.

He walked past the sleeping soldiers. They stared at him, and he imagined that he could see programs coming online through their vacant eyes.

Realizing he was falling behind, he rushed to catch up with the others.

A.C. Crispin was recently awarded the Grand Master award by the International Society of Media Tie-In Writers for her work on properties such as Star Trek, Star Wars, V *and* Pirates Of The Carribean, *but her story for us was excerpted from her own original space opera series* StarBridge. *A chapter from the first novel in that series, with brand new material added for framing, gives us this fascinating first encounter story...*

TWILIGHT WORLD

a Starbridge story

A.C. Crispin

Mahree Burroughs crouched on the ill-fitting seat designed for non-human crew members, her eyes never leaving the chrono that was counting down how long she had to live.

Despite her studies, she couldn't yet read the Simiu written language fluently, but numbers were easy. The chrono was silent as the numbers counted down the alien time-units. Mahree did a rough computation in her head and realized that they had just a little under a Terran day to live. About twenty-three hours until the three inhabitants of the little courier ship they'd dubbed *Rosinante* used up the last of the oxygen in the ship's air supply. Less than a day's worth of breathable air. She fought back panic, twisting her long, dark braid in her hands until it hurt, then forcing herself to breathe slowly through her nose, then out through her mouth.

Breathing was such a simple, basic act, she thought. People hardly ever even thought about it. *Until the air runs out.* Then the need for air, just simple air, overwhelmed everything. In a day, the two humans and one Simiu aboard *Rosinante* would be dead. Mahree Burroughs, her Simiu friend Dhurrrkk', and Rob Gable, the ship's physician from the trading vessel *Désirée*... all of them, dead. Unless, of course the alarm they'd rigged on the ship's sensors sounded, alerting them that they'd found a world with a breathable oxygen atmosphere.

Some rescue mission, Mahree thought bitterly. *Here we are, trying to bring about a peaceful solution between our peoples, only to die out here when our air runs out.*

Sixteen-year-old Mahree and her young Simiu friend, Dhurrrkk', out of all the human crew of the trading ship *Désirée* and the Simiu world of Hurrreeah, were the only two of their respective species who had learned to actually speak each other's language. The trading ship crew and the authorities of Hurrreeah had relied on computer translations to communicate – translations that had led to a tragic misunderstanding between the two peoples. Now the two species stood poised on the brink of violence, possibly outright war.

Mahree and Dhurrrkk' had decided that they couldn't let that happen. Dhurrrkk' had confided in Mahree that there was an interstellar organization of all the Known Worlds that might be able to help. The headquarters of the Cooperative League of Systems was located on a giant space station near the bright star Mizar. Dhurrrkk' was a pilot. Together, they'd stolen this ship, and set off for Shassiszss. Only one thing had gone wrong with their escape. Rob Gable had come upon them just as they were about to leave, and Mahree had to bring him along – at gunpoint.

Yeah, not only do I get myself and Dhurrrkk' killed on this escapade, she thought, *I've condemned Rob to die, too.*

The alien numbers continued to count down, measuring out the Simiu equivalent of seconds, minutes, and hours.

Mahree tried not to think about what it would be like at the end. Gasping for oxygen, lungs straining, eyes bulging, their faces suffusing with blood as their 02-starved tissues died. Would it hurt before they passed out? Would they feel as though they were strangling, or being choked? Or would the three of them just quietly pass out? Who would go first?

Death by asphyxiation didn't sound very appealing. *And all we were trying to do was help... who could have anticipated that human effluvia and exhalations would kill the oxygen-producing plants in the hydroponics lab?*

At first, everything had gone well. Once Mahree and Dhurrrkk' had explained their mission, Rob had thrown himself into the rescue effort, and the two humans had spent days growing accustomed to eating Simiu food, living under the slightly heavier Simiu gravity, sleeping on Simiu bedding, and, most challenging of all, utilizing Simiu plumbing. But then, about ten days out from Hurrreeah, Dhurrrkk' had come to them, visibly upset. His usually bright violet eyes were dimmed, his forehead crest of fur drooped, and his mane was ragged, as if he'd been clawing at it with his long, tough nails. "There is trouble, my friends," he said, in his harshly accented English. "An emergency in the hydroponics lab. Come see for yourselves."

Rob and Mahree had scrambled up from the Simiu sleeping pads, and followed their four-footed friend into the bowels of the little courier ship. One glance at the plants in the hydroponics lab had shown them sickly, drooping vegetation, obviously dying. Nearly all of the species were affected. "I have checked everything repeatedly," Dhurrrkk' told them, sitting back on his haunches rather like a Terran baboon. "Nothing has changed in the ship's environment except for your presence. The plant life is dying because it has been exposed to human exhalations and effluvia. At this rate we will not have sufficient oxygen in our air to reach Shassiszss."

The three of them had stared at each other in shock. At first, Mahree had thought it must be some kind of nightmare, but the danger was real, and there seemed to be no solution.

The chrono continued its inexorable countdown.

"Mahree," came a human voice from behind her. Mahree started, then turned to see Rob Gable, short and dark-haired, his good-looking features lined with concern. "Are you still staring at that thing? Come and get some sleep. You'll use less air that way, and staring at that chrono would drive anyone round the bend."

"I don't want to waste my last day sleeping," she protested.

"I can't think of a better strategy," he pointed out. "Maybe you'll have good dreams."

"I doubt it. Last time I slept I had nightmares."

"Well, give it a try. It really will help to conserve our remaining air."

She frowned, but let herself be persuaded. She *was* tired... her eyes were heavy and sore. Following Rob into the cabin they'd converted for human use, she lay down beside him, taking some comfort in his nearness. Her heavy eyes gradually closed and her breathing became regular...

Dhurrrkk' wailed, clutching his chest as it heaved, seeking air – but there was none. Mahree's face was contorted and purple as she, too, shrilled a high, keening scream. Both of them tumbled to the deck, thrashing convulsively, their mouths opening and closing, emitting that never-ending shrieking wail –

Rob jerked awake, carrying that last hideous dream-image before his eyes so vividly that it took him a moment to realize that it was, indeed, only a nightmare. And still the wailing shrilled that insistent, nerve-wracking shriek of – *of Dhurrrkk's alarm!*

Rob sat up, eyes wide. "Whatthe*hell?*"

Mahree was staring at him, eyes wide with incredulous hope.

Minutes later, the alarm silenced, the three travelers stared dubiously at the data on the screens. Mahree was able to translate the information for Rob, whose frown deepened as she continued. "That rinky-dink little thing?" he exclaimed, eyeing the red dwarf occupying the middle of *Rosinante*'s main viewscreen. "Good grief, it's only 170,000 kilometers in diameter – barely bigger than Jupiter!"

"It's the only system we've found," Mahree reminded him, "so be nice."

Dhurrrkk' nodded. "It is indeed very small," he admitted.

Mahree translated from the screen data. "It's got two planets – one a frozen hunk not even big enough to be spherical, the other about six-tenths the size of Earth. That's the one with the atmosphere. It orbits the star at a distance of about four million kilometers, and it's tidally locked, so it always keeps the same face toward its sun. Its year is a whopping four and a half days."

"But there are definite readings of oxygen in its atmosphere," Dhurrrkk' pointed out. "Not as high oxygen content as we could have wished, perhaps, but at this point, we have no alternative. We will need to find and harvest whatever plants are emitting that oxygen."

Mahree nodded. "Let's set her down, then go find us some air."

Mahree stood in the control room hatch, wearing her spacesuit, her helmet tucked under her arm. She listened intently as Rob and Dhurrrkk' completed the atmospheric analysis of the chill little worldlet where *Rosinante* now rested.

"That's all very well and good," she broke in, interrupting their jargon-laden exchange impatiently after a few minutes, "but what's the bottom line? Can we *breathe* out there?"

Rob scowled at his link, considering. "Doubtful," he concluded. "At least, not for more than a minute or so. Nothing in the air can *hurt* us to breathe it, but the overall oxy level is like being on top of a high mountain, Earthside. The slightest exertion, and we'd pass out in short order."

"Could we breathe it while we're resting? Sit down and take off our helmets to conserve our breathing packs?"

"*You* might – and I stress *might* – be able to, for a short time, because you were raised on Jolie, which has a lower oxygen content than Earth or Hurrreeah, but I wouldn't risk either Dhurrrkk' or me trying it."

Mahree bit her lip. "What about the plants?" she said.

Rob shook his head, obviously bewildered. "I just don't know," he said. "It's an extremely peculiar situation out there. Certain locations have significantly higher concentrations of O_2 than others – but there's no consistent correlation between those oxy concentrations and the patches we identified as vegetation during our low-level sweep. Sometimes they coincide, sometimes they don't. We're not too far from one of the higher concentrations of oxygen, so we'll just have to take a look."

"How can there be higher concentrations of oxygen? Doesn't the gas dissipate into the atmosphere?"

"Sure – some. But this place has fixed tides, hardly any weather. The temperature is a constant four degrees, just above freezing, and that doesn't vary, because there's no night. So there's no wind to move the atmosphere around. And oxygen is a comparatively heavy gas, so that when it's emitted under these circumstances, it tends to stay in one place, at least for a while." He glanced at his watch. "We'd better get going. Air's awasting."

Within minutes, the three explorers were ready. The doctor carried a sensing device to help them locate and analyze the local vegetation in their search for the oxygen concentrations.

"The gravity is low," he warned Mahree as Dhurrrkk' began cycling the air out of the airlock into storage, where it could be reused. "About half a gee. Be careful."

"Does Dhurrrkk' know that?" she asked. The two humans could talk to each other, but there had been no time to adjust their suit radios to the Simiu wavelength. They could communicate sketchily by touching helmets and shouting, but that form of conversation had obvious limits.

"Yeah, he knows."

The outer doors split apart, then opened wide. Mahree stepped cautiously down the ramp, watching her footing, because the ramp was steep, and her feet had an alarming tendency to slip in the low gravity – gravity which felt doubly light, because she'd spent days now living at one and a half gee.

Finally she was standing safely on solid ground, free to look around. Mahree caught her breath with excitement, thrilled despite their desperate situation to actually be standing on an alien world. *I'm the first human to ever tread here*, she realized. *One giant step, and all that stuff.*

Slowly, searching for any patches of the vegetation that had so puzzled Rob, she rotated 360 degrees, staring avidly.

It was a bleak vista that met her eyes – cold, yet washed everywhere with a hellish scarlet illumination from the red dwarf overhead. The ground beneath her feet was hard, black-brown rock, with a thin, damp layer of dark grayish brown soil overlaying it. A dank red mist lay close along the ground, pooling deeper in any depressions. Mahree could see for a long way in most directions, because the ground, though rock-strewn and broken, was relatively flat.

She lifted her face to the sun, and her faceplate's polarizing ability automatically cut in – but the protection was hardly necessary. The light level was dim, about that of a cloudy twilight. *Dhurrrkk's going to be nearly blind,* she realized, and said as much to Rob.

"We'll have to keep him right with us," he agreed. "Will you *look* at that sun!"

"I'm looking," she said, awed. "It doesn't look small from here, does it?"

Overhead, the unnamed red dwarf dominated the cloudless sky, appearing five times the diameter of Sol or Jolie's sun. As it flamed dully in the deep purply red sky, it appeared almost close enough to touch; Mahree and Rob could clearly make out solar prominences lashing outward from its disk.

"It probably flares every so often," Mahree said, remembering one of Professor Morrissey's astronomy lectures. "Let's hope it doesn't decide to belch out a heavy concentration of x-rays while we're here."

"Let's hope it doesn't," Rob agreed fervently.

After a minute, Dhurrrkk' touched her arm, and Mahree came out of her reverie with a start. "We'd better go," she said. "We can't waste air just standing here gawking."

The three set off across the rocky ground, Rob in the lead, Dhurrrkk' and Mahree close behind him. Once the girl caught the toe of her boot on one of the multitudes of small, jagged outcrops and stumbled badly, but her fall was slow enough that she was able to catch herself on her hands.

"Easy," Rob said, pulling her up one-handed in the light gravity. "One of these volcanic ridges could rip your suit. You okay?"

"Fine," she said, trying not to gasp with reaction to her near disaster. "You'd think walking in gravity this low would be easy, but it's not; the ground's so broken."

The explorers halted when they reached the little lake they'd charted during the flyby. Crimson mist obscured its surface, reflecting the light of the red sun.

"How deep is that water? Any vegetation down there?" Mahree asked Rob, stepping cautiously onto the dark rocks of the "shore."

He examined his scanning device. "Not very deep. About two meters in the middle. And yes, there's plant life down there."

"Is it giving off oxygen?"

"Yes, but we can't use these plants, because the Simiu hydroponics lab, unlike *Désirée's*, is set up for land-based vegetation. The tanks are way too shallow. Not to mention that I can't envision any way of hauling enough of this water aboard to support a significant amount of plant life. Even at one-half gee, water's *heavy.*"

They walked on, frequently having to detour around patches of the mist that were thick enough to obscure their footing, and skirting an occasional head-high upthrust of the black rock.

Finally, they reached the closest large patch of vegetation. The alien plants filled an entire shallow "basin" in the rocky surface, and were clumped together so closely they resembled thick moss. Each plant stood only a few centimeters above the soil that nourished its roots. The moss-plants were a dull, dark green in color, with tiny, fleshy-thick "leaves."

His boots hidden by a knee-high patch of mist, Rob bent over to carefully scan the plants. After a moment, he shook his head. "No O_2?" Mahree asked numbly.

"Some, but not enough. These plants photosynthesize, but..." he trailed off, then burst out, "they *can't* be the source of those higher O_2 levels I was reading!"

"How many of these moss-plants would we need to keep us going?"

"Half an acre of them," Rob said disgustedly. "Forget it."

Dhurrrkk' tugged on Mahree's arm, and she leaned over to touch helmets. After conveying the bad news, she straightened. "Okay, where's that higher O_2 concentration you mentioned, Rob?"

He consulted the instrument and pointed. "Thataway."

"Let's get going."

They trudged toward the area he had indicated. Mahree checked the homing grid displayed just above eye level in her helmet, and discovered that they were now well over a straight-line kilometer away from *Rosinante*. The strangely close horizon made estimating distances by eye difficult. She cast a swift, nervous glance at the gauge showing the status of her breathing pack. *Just about two hours left. The walking's so difficult that I'm using more air than I realized.*

The thought made her want to stride faster, but she forced herself to move deliberately, fighting off the sensation of a cold hand slowly tightening around her throat. *Fear uses up oxygen,* she told herself sternly. *Calm down.*

A few minutes later, as though he had read her thoughts, Rob said, "How's your air holding out?"

"One hundred and sixteen minutes," she said. "How about yours?"

"One hundred and eight," he said. "As we predicted, I'm burning my O_2 supply faster than you are."

"That means that Dhurrrkk' has a little more than ninety minutes left," Mahree calculated, her mouth going dry. "The Simiu breathing packs hold less than ours do, and Simiu lungs require more oxygen than human lungs. And we can't share our air with him, because our packs won't fit his suit couplings!"

"I know," Rob agreed bleakly. "Nearly half his air's gone. Maybe we ought to tell him to go back to the ship and wait for us there, while we continue searching."

Mahree shook her head. "Dhurrrkk' won't do it. We'd just be wasting time and air trying to convince him. He'd regard leaving us out here as being cowardly and dishonorable. I know that without even asking."

"Well, then, we'll just have to allow enough air for all of us to make it back to *Rosinante*."

She licked her lips, trying unsuccessfully to moisten them. "What for, Rob?" Resisting the urge to slam her gloved hand against the nearest rock in frustration, she managed to keep her voice calm. "What's the point of that? We'd just be postponing the inevitable for a few hours. I'd rather spend our last minutes out here *trying*, than lying around the ship watching those final seconds tick by. I don't think I have enough courage to face that. Do you?"

Rob did not reply.

A few minutes later he abruptly halted, announcing, "Right in front of us are the O2 coordinates I pinpointed earlier."

Both of them hurried forward, then Mahree let out a low cry of disappointment. There was nothing to see.

Nothing.

Nothing but the bare, upthrust ridges of blackish rock, small, tumbled boulders, pebbles that lay nearly buried in a comparatively deep layer of the soil, and a growth of the fleshy-leaved moss-plants. The ubiquitous mist drifted as their feet displaced it, eddying away from them, then settled again.

Rob's voice filled her helmet, harsh with dismay. "But... but these are the right coordinates; I *swear* I didn't make a mistake! This is crazy! These are the same plants as before, but there aren't nearly enough of them to cause the O2 concentration I measured just a couple of hours ago!"

"Is the oxygen level any higher, here?"

He consulted the instrument again. "The overall oxygen level is a little higher, but it's dropped considerably from what I saw earlier. I just don't understand it!"

Mahree felt sick with defeat. She bent over, staring intently at the ground. "These plants look funny," she observed, after a moment. "They're shinier than the ones we saw earlier, though they appear to be the same species."

"You're right," he said. "That's odd."

She walked slowly around, peering down at all the plants in the area. "They're all the same," she reported. "Could there be some kind of natural process going on that causes the change from dull to shiny, producing oxygen as it does so?"

Rob shook his head dubiously. "Maybe. That makes as much sense as anything on this crazy planet. But I don't see any agent that could be the cause of such a change. No other vegetation, nothing. It's also possible that these plants represent a different variety of the basic species. You know, like long- and short-stemmed roses – one type is naturally shiny, and the other is naturally dull."

"I've never seen a rose, except on a holo-vid," Mahree reminded him. *And it looks like I'm never going to see one now.* Resolutely, she squelched that train of thought. "Look, Rob, we have to discover one of those patches that's still emitting O2 so we can find out where the oxygen readings are coming from. I think we should search this entire area. Maybe your coordinates were just a little off?"

"Not a chance," he replied grimly. "I checked those readings four times, and then Dhurrrkk' verified them after me. But we might as well do as you suggest – there's nothing else we can do, except keep trying."

Mahree leaned over to touch her helmet to Dhurrrkk's, and explained what had happened. The Simiu nodded silently.

"I'll go first from now on. You watch the scanner, Rob," she said, beckoning them to follow her. Trying to choose the clearest path, she increased her pace until she was traveling at the fastest walk possible, given the broken ground.

The three explorers began circling around the area Rob's coordinates had indicated, searching for any sign of the mysterious higher-oxygen pockets. Dhurrrkk' gamely followed the two humans' lead, but Mahree knew that her Simiu friend was nearly blind in the dim light, and thus would be of little help.

Ninety minutes of air left, she noted, reading from her gauge, and had to clench her jaw against panic.

They kept going as the minutes slipped by, Mahree in the forefront, picking the smoothest path possible, Rob behind her, scarcely taking his eyes off his sensing device, and Dhurrrkk' bringing up the rear.

Eighty-two minutes.

Grimly, Mahree fought the urge to glance constantly at her air gauge; avoiding obstacles on the rocky ground required all her concentration. But every so often, she just *had* to look up.

Seventy-one minutes.

Rob's breathing sounded harsh in her ears. Mahree thought of what it would be like to have to helplessly listen to that sound falter and cease, and fought the desire to ask him how much air he had left. *You're better off not knowing,* she thought. *Keep your mind on your job.*

Fifty-four minutes.

Now there was no question of trying to head back for *Rosinante* and the few hours of air remaining aboard the ship. *Rob's taken me at my word,* she realized, grimly. *We're going to keep going until we drop in our tracks.*

She swallowed as she realized that Dhurrrkk' had little more than a half hour of air remaining. *Exactly how many minutes?* she wondered, mentally comparing the ratio, but losing track of the numbers in her growing panic. She tried to fight the fear, but it was like a live creature writhing inside her, gnawing at her mind, until she wanted to shriek and run away.

Calm, calm. You have to stay calm! Dhurrrkk's life may depend on you not losing your head! Breathe slowly... slowly. In... out... in... out... Gradually, her fear ebbed; she was able to control her breathing.

Seconds later, Mahree turned a corner around a low outcrop of rock, then halted so abruptly that Rob bumped into her. "Look! What are those things?"

"Damned if I know," he said, staring.

The ground before them was covered with the moss-plants, but lying among them, obscuring them in patches, were five large, thick, phosphorescent shapes. They shone white-violet in the red dimness and were roughly rectangular.

Each faintly glowing growth was a meter or so long by three-quarters of a meter wide. They were entirely featureless. The moment she saw them, Mahree found herself irresistibly reminded of a fuzzy white baby blanket her brother Steven had dragged around with him until it fell apart – these things were exactly the same size and shape, and even their edges were ragged, just like Steven's security blanket.

She turned eagerly to regard Rob as he scanned the patch. "Have we found the O2 emitters?" she asked.

He shook his head, and even in the vacuum suit she could see his shoulders sag. "Negative," he said, in a voice that betrayed the fact that he'd experienced a flash of hope, too. "The oxy level's a little higher here, true enough, just like in the shiny-leaved place, but these things aren't emitting anything. I scan no photosynthesizing capability at all – which fits. Look at their color."

Mahree walked out into the midst of the moss-plants, wisps of red mist swirling around her boots. Feeling a strange reluctance to get too near any of them, she placed her boots with exaggerated care. "Are they plants?"

"No. More like fungi." Rob checked his readings again. "Actually, they share some kinship with lichens, too. They must derive nourishment from the moss-plants as they decay."

Mahree glanced at her air gauge and squared her shoulders. *Forty-nine minutes.* "We'd better keep going," she said.

Rob raised his hand to halt her. "Wait. I want Dhurrrkk' to stay here. This place is easily recognizable, and I've got its coordinates. You and I can circle around and wind up back here in fifteen or twenty minutes. Tell him to lie down and conserve his air. That'll increase his time by five minutes or so. Otherwise, he doesn't have a prayer."

"He'll never agree, Rob!"

"Try, dammit!" he insisted. "Tell him that if he insists on accompanying us until he drops, we'll just end up using the last of our air carrying him."

"That's a good point," she admitted. Kneeling beside the Simiu, Mahree touched her helmet to his, repeating Rob's plea.

The Simiu looked uncertain. Then, slowly, he nodded and deliberately lay down in the midst of the plants, also being careful not to touch any of the phosphorescent growths.

Surprised, because she hadn't expected him to give in so easily, Mahree peered down into Dhurrrkk's helmet, trying to make out his features in the dim light. *He looks kind of funny,* she thought, worried. *Abstracted. Glassy-eyed. Could the Simiu equivalent of hypoxia be hitting him already? Or is he praying or something like that?*

Once more, she touched helmets. "Dhurrrkk', are you okay?"

"I feel fine, FriendMahree," the alien said remotely, as though he was listening to her with only part of his mind. "I promise that I will wait for you here."

As he followed Mahree away from the recumbent Simiu, Robert Gable couldn't resist a last glance back at the alien. *He's got about twenty-five minutes to live,* he thought, *give or take five minutes. And I've got twenty-eight minutes and forty seconds.*

"How you fixed for air?" he asked Mahree.

"Forty-five minutes and thirty seconds. You?"

"I'm okay," he replied. "Thirty-nine minutes here."

Her voice was puzzled and suspicious in his radio. "But before, you were *eight* minutes less than me," she said. "You *gained* a couple of minutes?"

"It takes a lot more effort to lead out here than to follow," he said, using his most reasonable tone. "You're burning O2 much faster now that you're going first."

She started to say something else, but Rob snapped, "Watch out! You nearly snagged your leg on that rock!"

"I did not!" She increased her pace a bit, and Rob struggled to match it without stumbling. "I hope Dhurrrkk' is okay," she muttered. "He looked sort of odd."

"If there's something wrong with him, there's not a damned thing either of us can do about it," Rob pointed out. "The only chance any of us has now is for us to locate the source of the oxygen emissions – pronto."

"And if we do?"

"Then you can take off your helmet, lie down, and wait there, while I use the last air in both our breathing packs to carry Dhurrrkk' back to the ship. Then he can take off and pilot *Rosinante* closer to the oxygen emissions source, and I'll come back and get you – then we'll both collect the plants."

"Why do I have to be the one that stays, while you go rescue Dhurrrkk'? Why not the other way around?" Mahree demanded irritably.

"Because you need less O2 to breathe, and I'm stronger than you are," Rob replied calmly, forcing himself not to glance at his air gauge. "Dhurrrkk's no lightweight, even at a half gee."

"Oh. But how will you come back to get me if you use up the last of our breathing packs carrying Dhurrrkk' back to the ship?"

"I've got a two-hour supply of pure oxygen in the oxy pack in my medical kit. I can use it to recharge two breathing packs. Pure oxygen will last us longer than standard airmix. That'll give us each slightly more than an hour's worth of air."

"Oh," Mahree said again. After a moment, she asked hesitantly, "Rob do you really think that plan will work?"

"No," the doctor said tightly. "I don't think it has a snowball's chance in hell of really working. But if you can think of anything better, I'm all ears."

Mahree had no response. Rob was relieved, because his powers of invention were drying up. He glanced at his air gauge. *Twenty-one minutes.*

Knowing full well that he would use up his air faster than Mahree, the doctor had decided before they left *Rosinante* that their only hope might lie in keeping her going as long as possible. So he had surreptitiously disabled the emergency broadcast unit in his suit. Otherwise, as his breathing pack ran out, she would have been warned as to his status. *Worrying about me running out of air would only make her use her own supply faster,* he thought, repressing a twinge of guilt. *But if by some miracle we both survive this, she's going to be pissed.*

Struggling to keep up the swift pace Mahree set, while checking the sensing device he carried, Rob had little time to note his surroundings. He knew from the location grid in his helmet that Mahree was leading them in a wide circle, gradually taking them back to the spot where Dhurrrkk' waited.

A flat, computer-generated voice suddenly spoke inside the doctor's helmet. "Automatic reminder to the occupant of this suit. You have fifteen minutes of air remaining. Fifteen minutes of air."

Fifteen minutes to live. I feel like Dorothy when the witch turns over that big hourglass. Fifteen minutes...

Rob found himself remembering how he'd arrived at this moment. Memories of his parents, his sisters, of medical school, and the Lotis Plague flicked through his mind like flat, grainy mages from one of his antique black-and-white films. He grinned wryly as he followed Mahree, careful to keep glancing at his sensing device every few seconds. *So it's true, what they say – your life does flash before your eyes...*

"Automatic reminder to the occupant of this suit. You have ten minutes of air remaining. Ten minutes of air. You are advised to change breathing packs within the next five minutes."

Rob listened to Mahree's breathing over the radio, remembering the first day they'd met, the nearly instantaneous rapport between them; only she, of all the people aboard *Désirée*, had matched his own eagerness for making the First Contact – not because doing so would make them famous or rich, but because she, too, had an abiding belief that contact with extraterrestrial beings would be a good thing for the human race.

And then his own belief had wavered and nearly toppled... along with Raoul's and the rest of the human crew – and, to hear Dhurrrkk' tell it, the Simiu had lost faith, too. Only Mahree and Dhurrrkk' had managed to retain their belief in each other's continuing goodwill. Was that because they were so young that they hadn't had as much opportunity to have their hopes and ideals trampled?

"Rob, how much air do you have left?"

The doctor sneaked a glance at his readout. *Seven minutes.* "Seventeen minutes," he lied glibly. *There's nothing she can do about it,* he rationalized, repressing a stab of guilt for lying to her, *and worrying will just make her use air even faster. Our only chance is for Mahree to stay on her feet and locate those oxygen concentrations.* "How about you?" he asked.

"Twenty-seven minutes," she replied. "How far are we from Dhurrrkk'? He must be almost out of air by now."

"We're close," Rob said, checking the location grid. "Here, you carry this." *So I won't drop it or damage it when I fall.*

She took the instrument without question, and they pressed on. Rob watched her stride forward, forcing herself onward, though he knew she must be at least as tired as he was. *Not one complaint,* he thought. *Not even the suggestion of a whimper. I wonder if she'd concede that this counts as courage...*

The doctor experienced a sudden rush of affection for Mahree; they'd grown to know each other so well during this strange odyssey. Comrades, friends in some ways, Rob mused, Mahree had become one of the closest friends he'd ever had. *Too bad I won't get to see her all grown up; she'd have been something, I'd bet.*

"Automatic reminder to the occupant of this suit. You have five minutes of air remaining. Five minutes of air. If breathing pack is not replaced within four minutes, hypoxia will commence."

Oh, shut up, he thought irritably. *There's not a goddamned thing I can do about it.* Acting on a sudden impulse, he twisted his head around and deliberately tongued the two manual controls that would shut off his suit readouts. The air gauge and location grid went dark. *There, that's better.*

Rob found himself thinking back over his relationships with women. He'd had liaisons with several while he'd been in school (and was proud that, after the affairs had ended, he'd remained friends with all of them) — but he'd never been *in love*.

If there's anything I regret, Rob thought, pushing himself after Mahree with dogged persistence, and realizing with a sinking feeling that he was beginning to gasp a little, and not from exertion, *it's that I never felt that way about...*

"There he is!" Mahree cried, as they caught sight of the moss-plant hollow and the phosphorescent growths. Dhurrrkk' lay sprawled among them, hands clutching his helmet.

"Is he breathing?" Rob asked, coming to a halt on the edge of the hollow. His voice sounded strange in his own ears, tinny and far away. *But I'm not far away; I'm right here,* he thought fuzzily. He tried to move forward, staggered a little, then recovered by bracing himself on a low outcrop of rock. He let himself slide down until he was sitting atop it. All his limbs felt pleasantly heavy, and his mind was beginning to float.

Like drifting off to sleep after a few beers, he realized detachedly. Somewhere a portion of his brain was shrieking "apoxia!" but the word meant nothing. His head nodded, and his eyelids began to close.

"He's still alive!" Mahree's voice reached him, and Rob had to think hard to remember whom she was talking about. "But he's barely breathing!"

He forced his eyes open, saw Mahree crouched on the ground beside Dhurrrkk'. *I should get up,* he thought. *Go help...*

But his body would not obey him. Black spots danced before his eyes, and he closed them again because they were making him so terribly dizzy.

"*Rob!*" screamed a voice over his radio. The doctor opened his eyes again as he felt himself being shaken violently. He saw Mahree bent over him, her own eyes wide and terrified behind the faceplate of her helmet.

"Rob, how much air do you have left? Don't lie to me this time, goddammit!"

He tried to tell her that he had turned off his readouts, that it was okay, it didn't hurt, but his tongue moved sluggishly, and no sound emerged. All the black spots coalesced suddenly into an all-encompassing darkness that swooped toward him like a live creature, enfolding him past all struggle.

With a sigh, Rob gave in and let it carry him away.

🖛

"Oh, God!" Mahree sobbed, catching her companion as he tumbled over bonelessly. "God, help me! Somebody please, please help me, someone – anyone!"

How much air does he have left?

She lowered Rob onto the moss-plants, beside Dhurrrkk', then turned him half over so she could read his breathing pack's outside gauge, located on his right hip.

The first thing she saw was the flash of the red "Low Oxygen Level – Condition Critical" reading on the indicator as it pulsed steadily in the dimness, then before her eyes it changed.

ZERO O2, it read, in double-size letters. HYPOXIA IMMINENT – CHANGE PACK IMMEDIATELY.

Reflexively, then, Mahree looked up at her own display. *Eighteen minutes.* Eighteen long minutes...

I cannot sit here for eighteen minutes and watch them die, Mahree realized, feeling a calm that went beyond despair. *No way.*

Moving as quickly and surely as if she'd rehearsed the procedure hundreds of times, she detached Rob's used breathing pack in a matter of moments, and just as quickly replaced it with her own. *I'm sorry, Rob,* she thought, hearing the sounds of his gasping breaths ease as his oxygen-starved lungs took in the new air. *This is a rotten thing to do to you, love, but I just don't have the courage to let you go first. If we're both lucky, you won't even wake up.*

Then she sat back between the two prone figures, and, picking up Rob's gloved hand, held it in her lap between her own two. *I've got maybe ninety seconds' worth of air left in my suit,* she thought, still calm. *How should I spend them?*

Her early religious training argued that she ought to pray, but the only prayer Mahree could remember at the moment was the one with the line about, "If I should die before I wake."

Talk about stating the obvious, she thought, with grim amusement. *No, I guess praying is out.*

As she sat there, waiting, Mahree found that she was fighting a growing urge to take off her helmet.

It's the hypoxia, she thought dazedly. *It must be. The first thing to go is judgment.*

A conviction that, if she would just remove her helmet, everything would be all right filled her mind. Mahree glanced around, seeing the phosphorescent growths gleaming weirdly in the sanguine light. *What's happening to me? My mind feels as though it's not mine anymore!* By now she was panting, suffocating, her lungs laboring as they strained frantically to gasp in the last vestiges of oxygen her suit air contained.

Darkness crouched on the edges of her vision, an expanding, hungry darkness without end. But the darkness would go away if she would just get rid of her helmet.

Mahree blinked, dazed, and realized that, without being aware of her actions, she'd released the fastenings of her helmet, and now had both hands on its sides, preparatory to twisting it, then lifting it free of her shoulders. The urge to remove it was a driving imperative within her now, a command that she had no strength left to fight.

What am I doing? she wondered frantically as she twisted, breaking the helmet's seal. She was in agony now, her lungs stabbing fire as they rebelled against the surfeit of carbon dioxide. *Oxygen!* something deep within her mind was insisting. *There will be oxygen! Take the helmet off!*

With a final, lung-tearing gasp, Mahree tore her helmet free, dropping it onto the moss-plants beside her. Cold, moist atmosphere smote her sweaty face like a blow. As blackness flowed across her vision, she inhaled deeply...

Slowly, the blackness began to recede.

Moments later, Mahree realized that she was crouched on hands and knees between Rob and Dhurrrkk', her head hanging down, and that she was *breathing*.

Oxygen! she thought, hardly able to believe this wasn't some dying hallucination. *Something here is emitting oxygen!*

A strong sense of affirmation filled her, affirmation mixed with concern. Mahree hastily groped for the fastenings of Dhurrrkk's helmet. Her gloved fingers couldn't grasp the alien shapes, and, with a sob of impatience, she unsealed her gloves, ripping them off. She fumbled again at the Simiu's helmet, and found, to her astonishment, that the seals had already been released. But the helmet was stuck; she had to use all her strength and leverage to twist it free. Finally it gave.

Seconds later, she had rolled the Simiu onto his back. She could not tell whether he was breathing, or whether his heart was still beating.

"Dhurrrkk'!" she yelled, then slapped his face.

When he did not respond, Mahree hastily scuttled around him until she was kneeling facing his feet, then she grasped his chin and pulled the alien's head toward her, tilting it back. His jaw opened, and she peered into his mouth to check the location of his tongue. It was hard to tell in the dimness, but she *thought* she now had a clear airway.

Cupping both hands hard around his muzzle to seal his mouth shut, Mahree inhaled a deep breath of the blessedly oxygenated air, then she bent, placed her own mouth tightly over his nostrils, and blew as hard as she could.

First, she gave him four quick, hard breaths to deliver an initial jolt of oxygen; then she tried to settle into a regular rhythm. Mahree *thought* she felt the sense of resistance that meant she'd achieved a proper airway and seal, but she couldn't be sure.

Darkness gathered again at the fringes of her vision as she continued to suck in air, then blow it hard into the unmoving alien's nostrils.

Come on, Dhurrrkk', she thought, *I'll pass out if I keep this up much longer, so come on!*

As Mahree dizzily raised her head for the next gulp of air, she started and barely prevented herself from recoiling violently. A hand-span away from Dhurrrkk's head lay a spectrally glowing, faintly pulsing mass.

My God, it's the baby blanket! It moved!

She missed half a beat, then resolutely inhaled again and blew. Her dizziness returned, but as she snatched a quick gasp for her own lungs, it abated. *That fungus has to be what's giving off the oxygen,* she thought, with sudden certainty. *And right now it's giving off extra oxygen, as if it knows how much I really need it! But that would mean that it's –*

Beneath her fingers, Dhurrrkk's muzzle twitched. *Right! That's it!* she cheered him on, drawing in another lungful of oxygen-rich air. She blew again, and this time when she turned toward the blanket to gulp air, she unmistakably felt a faint tickle of warm exhalation against her cheek.

Another breath. This time she *saw* his exhaled breath steam in the cold, damp air. Another breath... and yet another...

Dhurrrkk' abruptly gasped, twitched, then gasped again. *He's breathing!*

Mahree hovered, ready to resume the artificial respiration if necessary, but the Simiu no longer needed her help. Soon Dhurrrkk's violet eyes opened and focused on her.

"Do not try to move, FriendDhurrrkk'. You passed out, but now that we have air, you will be fine," Mahree managed to say, though her abused throat rebelled more than usual at the Simiu syllables. "Just lie still, please. I must check on Rob."

She turned around to regard the doctor, then glanced at the breathing pack's external gauge. *Fourteen minutes.* She shook her head and looked again. *Fourteen minutes? I don't believe it! All that, and it's only been four minutes?*

Hastily, she pulled off his helmet, then disconnected the airflow from the breathing pack to conserve the remainder. Rob did not stir. Mahree pulled up an eyelid, then touched her fingers to the pulse in his throat. *He's okay... just out cold.*

She smiled as an idea occurred to her, then, after making sure Dhurrrkk' wasn't watching, she bent over and kissed her unconscious companion lingeringly on the mouth. "Call it my fee for saving your ass, you oh-so-noble bastard," she muttered, remembering how he'd lied to her about how much air he had left.

Then, grasping his limp form beneath the arms, she dragged him over the moss-plants until he, too, was lying with his face close to the phosphorescent growth. "Here, Blanket," she gasped, "you can give *him* some oxygen, too. Please."

Then she sat down, gazing wonderingly at the fungus-creature. Their savior.

When Rob scanned them earlier, they weren't emitting any oxygen. But when we were in danger of dying, they – or this one at least – started to emit it. And, just when I was getting ready to pass out, the creature moved closer, and gave off additional oxygen. That has to mean that –

Mahree wiped cold sweat off her forehead, then licked her lips nervously. *That's impossible! This is a fungus, one of the simplest forms of life around! Don't be crazy, Mahree!*

She bent over, peering closely at the faintly shining growth. It was completely featureless, except for millions of short, threadlike cilia on its top-side. She lay down on her side amid the moss-plants, then squinted up at the fungus's underside. *It moved; it must have. How the hell can it move?*

The blanket's bottom side was covered with tiny appendages nearly the length of her little finger. They moved constantly, rippling over the moss-plants like minuscule tentacles. "So *that's* how you get around," Mahree muttered.

Scrambling back up to hands and knees, she cautiously inched closer to the phosphorescent creature, until her nose was only a hand-span away. "Hi, Blanket," she said, feeling ridiculous – *I'm talking to a fungus? I must have cleared my jets!* – "My name is Mahree Burroughs. I really appreciate your helping us out just now. We desperately needed that oxygen. I hope you folks don't suddenly stop emitting it." She shook her head. "I don't know why I'm talking. You don't have ears, so you can't possibly hear or understand me, can you?"

Slowly, the edge of the phosphorescent growth lifted clear of the moss-plants, extending itself toward her face.

Mahree couldn't help it – she let out a startled yelp and jerked back. Her heart slammed in her chest. Biting her lip savagely, she steadied her breathing, forcing herself to inhale and exhale lightly and evenly. There wasn't sufficient oxygen in the hollow to sustain her if she hyperventilated.

Maybe it was just exhibiting some kind of involuntary reflex in response to movement? she thought, watching the baby blanket settle back down onto the moss-plants.

Slowly, she leaned forward again. "If you can understand me, Blanket, *don't* move. Stay still, okay?"

Mahree moved so close that her nose nearly brushed the blanket's side, but the phosphorescence did not stir.

"Ohhh-kay," she muttered. "If you can understand me, Blanket, please move *now*."

The edge of the creature rippled, then rose until it was a full hand-span above the moss-plants.

"Holy shit," Mahree gulped. "I was right. You're *sentient*."

Again the sense of affirmation filled her mind.

"And telepathic, right? You can make what you're thinking and feeling go from your 'mind' – or whatever equivalent you've got – into mine?"

Affirmation.

A human groan interrupted her "conversation." Mahree turned to see that Dhurrrkk' was sitting up, holding Rob's hands, and that the doctor was stirring. "Excuse me a moment, please, Blanket," she said. "I must check on my friend. I will return."

Affirmation.

Mahree hastily crawled over to put a hand on Dhurrrkk's shoulder. "FriendDhurrrkk'," she said. "How do you feel?"

The Simiu put a hand on his forehead. "There is pain here," he said. "But otherwise I am fine."

"Just promise me you'll take it easy for a while. You were pretty far gone."

"I promise, FriendMahree." The Simiu's violet eyes were full of emotion. Slowly, minus his customary ease and grace, he reached over to grasp her hand. "You gave me your own breath, so that I could live," he said, switching to her own language. "I will be forever grateful, my friend. We are honor-bound, you and I. For as long as I may live, your honor and your life will be as important to me as my own."

"Dhurrrkk'..." Mahree tried to think of something to say, but words failed her. Instead, she gripped his six-fingered hand hard, nodding.

He motioned to Rob. "Honored HealerGable is awakening." Mahree hastily turned around, to find the doctor lying there with his eyes open. "Hi," she said softly, bending over him. "How are you feeling?"

"I'm breathing," he whispered, his eyes filled with profound bewilderment. "Why am I still alive?"

"Because we've found the source of the oxygen emissions, Rob," she told him. "And a lot more besides."

"Huh? You located one of the O2 sources?"

"Yes," she said, seeing that he was still weak and disoriented. The rest of her news could wait.

He put out a hand. "Are you sure you're really here?" he mumbled, uncertainly. "I'm not hallucinating?"

For answer, Mahree took his gloved hand, unsealed it, pulled off the covering, then grasped his bare fingers tightly. "I'm really here," she said. "Feel."

"Feels good," he mumbled, smiling. "Squeeze tight." After a moment, he shakily sat up, then looked at the Simiu. "Honored Dhurrrkk', I'm glad to see that you're all right."

The alien made the formal greeting gesture of his people. "Honored Healer Gable," he said in English, with a twinkle, "I'm pleased to observe the same about you."

The doctor shook his head, confusion filling his eyes. "But I don't understand how we got here – wherever we are. I was out of air. I must've passed out." He glanced down at his side.

"*Waitaminit!* This says I've got twelve minutes left on this pack." He looked back up, glaring at Mahree. "You switched breathing packs, didn't you? Gave me the last of your air?"

"It was the least I could do, after you lied to me," she said acerbically. "One dirty trick deserves another." She returned his glare with interest. "And if you dare to tell me that it was for my own good, you're going to find yourself stretched out on these damned moss-plants again."

"I knew you'd be pissed," he mumbled, obviously deeply touched by his discovery of the switched breathing pack. "But I didn't figure I'd live to hear about it. Forgive me?"

Rob sounded so uncharacteristically meek that Mahree had to laugh. "Let's call it even."

The doctor glanced around him, and his eyes widened as he recognized their location. "Hey, this is the same place as we left Dhurrrkk'." He scratched his head. "Now, let me get this straight. We came back here to get Dhurrrkk', only this time there was oxygen in this hollow? But how?"

"Thank *them*," Mahree said, pointing to the blanket-creatures. "They're the things that have been emitting the O_2."

"*Them?* The fungi?" He blinked. "That's impossible. Crazy. They can't even photosynthesize."

"You *ain't seen* crazy, yet. Brace yourself, Rob. They're *sentient*. We've just made a First Contact."

He stared at her in silence, no expression on his face. "Sentient," he repeated, finally.

"They *are*," Mahree insisted. "They knew we needed oxygen, so they convinced me to take off my helmet, so I could breathe. And when I'd taken it off, this one" – she pointed to the closest blanket-creature – "crawled over just so it could give me extra O_2 when I was giving Dhurrrkk' artificial respiration."

He hesitated. "Uhhhhh... that's hard to believe," he said, finally, using a carefully neutral tone. "Are you *sure*?"

"Honored Mahree is correct," Dhurrrkk' interjected, in English. "Before I lost my awareness of my surroundings, I was conscious of something contacting my mind, something that touched and questioned with intelligent purpose. It instructed me to take off my helmet, but I was unable to comply."

"That's because it was stuck," she told him.

Rob stared at both of them. Then he looked down at the blanket. "You're telling me this *thing* is sentient," he said, in a this-can't-be-happening-to-me tone of voice. "*This* thing" – he pointed – "this phosphorescent patch of fungus?"

"It's not a *thing*, it's a *person*, Rob. Mind your manners," Mahree admonished. "Watch, I'll prove it."

Turning back to "her" blanket, Mahree ran through the same demonstration that she had earlier. Finally, she said to the being, "This is my friend, Robert Gable – Rob, as he's called. This is what he looks like." She glanced at the doctor's face. "And this is my friend Honored Dhurrrkk'." She looked at the Simiu. "Now, if you don't mind, Blanket, I'd like you to move over and stop in front of Rob, so he'll know for sure that you can understand me."

With surprising speed, the alien creature crawled unhesitatingly over to Rob, stopped, then raised one edge into the air and waved at him.

The doctor paled as he stared at the being, eyes wide, then suddenly he bent forward until his forehead rested on the moss-plants before him.

"Good grief, Rob," Mahree exclaimed, "you don't have to *pray* to it! Just say 'hello'!"

He drew several long breaths. "I'm not praying, you idiot," he said crossly in a muffled voice. "If I hadn't gotten my head down, I would've fainted. Give me a break, sweetheart. It's been a long, hard day."

After a minute Rob sat back up, his color much improved. "I'll be damned," he whispered softly, eyeing the fungus-being. He cleared his throat. "How do you do, uh, Blanket? It's a real pleasure."

Mahree concentrated, and received a clear sense of inquiry. "It's telepathic – or something – " she said. "Right now, it wants to know about us. How we got here."

"It is asking me the same thing," Dhurrrkk' said.

Trying to be as clear and simple as she could, Mahree thought slowly, deliberately, of how they had come to this world, aboard *Rosinante*, and why. She tried to make her images of the ship as vivid as possible, knowing instinctively that the creature before her could have no concept of technology or artificial constructions.

Finally, she turned to Dhurrrkk'. "Did you tell it?"

"Yes," he said. "As clearly as I could. Communication with the being is growing easier for me, the more I do it."

Mahree felt a prickle of envy. "It's still pretty hard for me," she admitted.

Rob was watching them. "I can feel it now, too," he said. "A sense of inquiry, and curiosity, right?" When they nodded, he continued, "But it's sure nothing like what Great-Aunt Louise used to do. She spoke in words, except they were silent."

"Maybe Blanket can learn words, eventually," Mahree said. "At first it just communicated faint impressions. Now they're getting stronger."

"It would like to help us," Dhurrrkk' announced suddenly.

"It already *has* helped us," Rob said. "Though I have to admit that it might have been kinder if it hadn't interfered when we passed out. Spending the rest of my life here in this hollow, while we slowly die of thirst, isn't a very appealing prospect."

Dhurrrkk' said. "It is giving me images, now. It thinks it knows a way."

Mahree felt an absurd sense of abandonment as she realized that "her" blanket was now communicating most effectively with the Simiu. *Don't be stupid,* she thought sternly. *It obviously has discovered that a Simiu brain is easier for it to reach.*

She and Rob waited as the Simiu sat there, an abstracted expression on his face. Finally, he raised his violet eyes to theirs. "I have learned something about these beings. Each of these creatures is very, very old,

266

and each is intelligent. Normally, they are not interested in much outside of pursuing their own obscure musings, mental games, and philosophical reflections. However, the one that Mahree calls 'Blanket' is different. For one thing, it is younger – perhaps only a million or so of my years old."

Mahree and Rob gasped sharply. "A *million* years old?" she repeated, and the Simiu nodded soberly.

"Blanket is far more interested in external stimuli and events than its companions. It is intrigued by the notion of our ship, and traveling through space. It likes us. It does not want us to perish, and it is willing to help us safely reach our destination. If we would like it to, Blanket has volunteered to join us aboard *Rosinante*, and provide us with oxygen. In return, we must promise to bring it back here, when it asks to be returned to its own world."

"Can it give off that much oxygen?" Rob said skeptically, after he'd spent a moment assimilating the Simiu's words. "Doesn't it need its oxygen for itself?"

"No, the blankets themselves require very little oxygen. It is a by-product they produce during digestion. It has no part in their breathing process."

They fart oxygen? Mahree thought, wildly, and giggled shrilly before she could stop herself. Rob reached over to put a steadying hand on her shoulder.

"We will need to provide Blanket with native rock and moss-plants, sufficient to allow it ample nourishment for the duration of our journey," Dhurrrkk' concluded.

"Well, if it tells us how much it needs, we'll be happy to do that," Rob said. "But there's just one thing. How the hell do we get out of this hollow, and back to *Rosinante*?"

"Blanket has asked its companions to assist, and they have agreed. They think their companion foolish for wishing to depart this world in order to aid us," the Simiu paused, then continued, as he evidently received additional information, "but none of them wish to see us perish. As long as they can remain here, the others are willing to help us reach the ship."

"How do they propose to help us?"

"You will see. Please remain still. They mean no harm." Rob started as two more of the creatures stirred, then began moving across the moss-plants toward them.

Mahree's "Blanket" began crawling back toward her. She felt a moment of pleased satisfaction that it had evidently elected to return to her instead of staying with Dhurrrkk', then the creature moved past her, out of her line of sight unless she turned her head. *What is it going to do?*

Mahree swallowed hard as she both heard and felt something brush against the material of her vacuum suit, then the front collar of the suit was pressed against her throat as something heavy begin pulling itself up her back. She clenched her fists, squeezing her eyes shut, as Blanket slowly inched its way up. *It's saving your life,* she thought, repeatedly. *That's not a fungus crawling up your body, it's a person. A good, kind person. It's saving your life...*

Finally, the creature lay over her shoulders and down her back like a phosphorescent cape. At the extreme edge of her peripheral vision, she caught movement, then two glowing narrow "fingers" appeared as Blanket extruded two corners across her cheeks.

Mahree shivered, forcing herself to sit quietly. She closed her eyes as she felt the cold, admittedly damp substance of the alien being creep across her skin, until both pseudopods met, linking together across her upper lip.

She opened her eyes to find Rob staring down at the phosphorescent mass moving toward him. The doctor was chalky pale and runnels of sweat coursed down his face. He was trembling violently.

"Rob!" she said sharply. "*Rob!*"

Slowly, he looked up. "Don't pull a Simon Viorst on us, Rob! They're helping us; just keep telling yourself that."

The doctor took several deep breaths, then finally nodded. A touch of color reappeared in his lips. "Okay. Don't worry about me, honey. I'm okay now."

He sat still as the phosphorescent mass crept slowly up his back. "I just wish," he said, and the control he was exerting over himself was palpable, "that I hadn't watched that nineties version of *The Puppet Masters* so *many* times. Remind me to show it to you if we ever get home."

Mahree drew a deep breath of relief, then picked up her helmet and gloves. "Everybody ready?" she said, standing. She discovered that, even with her head above the level of the hollow, she was breathing easily – the O2 level was no thinner than what she'd experienced camping in the mountains on Jolie.

"Ready," Dhurrrkk' said, handing Rob his helmet to carry. His blanket-creature was draped over his neck and back like a second, glowing mane.

"Ready," Rob said. "Let's rock."

"Rock?" echoed Dhurrrkk', as the three blanket-caped explorers picked their way out of the moss-plant hollow. "We must gather a number of rocks, true, along with harvesting plants, but don't you believe, FriendRob, that we would be better served to do that closer to our ship? Rocks are heavy to carry."

"Uh... yeah," Rob said, giving Mahree a wink, and speaking with some difficulty because of the pseudopods linked across his upper lip, "you're right, FriendDhurrrkk'. Rocks *are* heavy."

In Mike Resnick's second tale for us, Catastrophe Baker returns, this time to face an ancient concubine who is revived when he enters Royal ground in...

CATASTROPHE BAKER IN THE HALL OF THE NEPTUNIAN KINGS

Mike Resnick

I know there's people who swear there ain't no Neptunian Kings, but I'm in a position to know better, because I been there.

It happened maybe four years ago. I'd just left Oom Paul, the little diamond-mining world out by Antares, and I'd heard tell that Fort Knox wasn't radioactive any longer, and that all you had to do was just waltz in and carry out as many gold bars as you wanted, and there was nothing there to stop you except maybe thirty or forty guards, and they were mostly little ones at that.

But my navigational computer and I got to telling dirty jokes to one another, and playing poker, and otherwise amusing ourselves to combat the boredom of the long voyage, and damned if we didn't combat it so well that the computer forgot to pay attention to where we were, and all of a sudden we were orbiting Neptune rather than Earth.

Problem is, I didn't know it until we landed, and the ship told me I'd better put on a spacesuit and helmet. It struck me as kind of a strange request, but I just figured we'd touched down near a toxic waste dump. It wasn't until I stepped out of the ship that I realized that the landscape didn't bear a lot of resemblance to all the holos I'd seen of Earth.

I was about to climb back in and give the computer a piece of my mind when I saw a huge building off in the distance. It had all kinds of strange angles, and stained-glass windows with colors I hadn't never seen before, all of which roused my curiosity, so I decided to take a closer look at it.

I headed on over to it, and found myself facing a door that must have been seventy feet high. I pushed against it, but it was latched or bolted from the inside and it didn't give an inch. This just made me more interested to see what was on the inside, so I walked around the whole of the building, which must have been about half a mile on each side, looking for a way in.

When I couldn't find none – there were maybe ten other doors, all of them locked – I decided to climb up the side of the building and ease myself in through one of the windows.

Well, let me tell you, that was a lot easier said than done. Oh, the building was easy enough to climb, because it was covered with weird carvings and strange-looking gargoyles, so I had no trouble getting handholds and footholds – but when I reached the window, which was maybe forty feet above the ground, I discovered that it was locked, too, and strong as I am, I couldn't kick it in.

I considered melting it with my burner, but I wasn't exactly sure what the atmospheric make-up of Neptune was, and I figured that if it happened to have a high concentration of oxygen, like maybe 80% or so, I could set the whole planet on fire just by pulling the trigger.

So I kept climbing, and after another hour, I reached the roof, which was about three hundred feet above the ground, and started walking along it, looking for vents or chimneys I could slide down. Sure enough, I found one smack-dab in the middle of the roof. Problem was, it went straight down, and I figured the fall could kill or cripple me, so I looked further, and finally found a hatch leading to the interior of the building. I decided it had been used by the guys who built the place, or maybe the one who had to keep the roof clean – but whoever used it were as big as the guys who walked through the doorways, because each step was maybe fifteen feet down from the last one.

I hung down from the top step by one arm, then let go and dropped maybe six feet to the next one, and climbed down the whole staircase like that.

271

Mike Resnick

When I got to the bottom, I found myself in a pitch-black chamber. I turned on my helmet's spotlight, found a door, and pushed against it – and this one gave way. I stepped out into a huge room, filled with two dozen ornate chairs, each capable of holding a being that was maybe seventy feet high.

Then I heard a voice in my ear: "You can breathe the air in here now."

I spun around and whipped out my pistol.

"Who said that?" I demanded.

"Me," came the answer. "Your suit. I have analyzed the air, and it is breathable."

"Thanks."

"It's just damned lucky you didn't break that window," said the suit.

I figured I could spend the rest of the day standing there arguing with it, or I could climb out of it and start exploring, so I did the latter.

Then I started at one end of the hall, and began walking past all the chairs, and I decided that each of them was a throne, and had probably been retired when the king who sat on it had died or lit out for greener pastures.

Now, truth to tell, I didn't have no serious interest in Neptunian Kings, but I didn't have nothing against maybe finding some palace jewels, so I set out to see if there were any around for the taking.

The hall was mostly empty except for the chairs and some weird-looking tapestries hanging on the walls, but then I stumbled onto an anteroom just behind Throne Number Nine – and what should I find but an absolutely gorgeous naked lady standing there staring at me.

"Good morning, ma'am," I said. "I'm Catastrophe Baker, at your service."

She didn't say a word or move a muscle, and I figured I'd kind of startled her into immobility.

"Dressed in kind of a hurry this morning, didn't you?" I said, trying to break the ice with a little friendly conversation.

She still didn't answer, so I walked a little closer to see if maybe she was a statue.

272

I couldn't see her breathing, and her eyes seemed fixed on some spot in the Hall of the Neptunian Kings, but she sure looked like a flesh-and-blood lady to me, rather than an imitation.

Then I realized that I had to be mistaken, because she was maybe a foot smaller than me, whereas anyone who lived in this place seemed like they couldn't go much less than fifty feet at the shoulder or the withers, whichever came first.

It was a shame, because in a long lifetime of looking at beautiful naked ladies, I hadn't never seen one more beautiful than this one.

I was going to leave and go back to looking for jewels and other marketable trinkets, but first I walked over to more closely admire the artist's handiwork. Even from two feet away you couldn't tell that she wasn't a real flesh-and-blood woman. Her skin was as smooth as could be, and I reached out to touch it, just to see if it was marble or stone or some artificial fabric – and damned if it didn't feel just like a real woman's skin.

I wondered just how realistic all the details were, so I kind of got to feeling her here and there and the next place – and when I laid my hand on the next place, she gave out a shriek that would have woke the dead and slapped my face.

"I thought you were a statue!" I said, startled.

"I was," she answered in the most melodic voice. "I apologize for hitting you. It was an instinctive reaction."

"You got some mighty powerful instincts there, ma'am," I said.

"Actually, I owe you my gratitude. I've been frozen in that position for the past fifteen millennia." She shuddered, which produced an eye-popping effect. "I could have been there forever if it hadn't been for you."

"Suppose you tell me what's going on, ma'am," I said, trying to grasp it all.

"I was King Thoraster's favorite concubine, and when he thought I might have lost my heart to one of the palace guards, he had his technicians put me in stasis. There was only one way to release me in case he should change his mind at a later date, but he never thought any casual observer would be so gross and uncouth as to touch me *there*."

"How did he manage to freeze you for fifteen thousand years?" I asked.

She began explaining it to me, but as far as I'm concerned any sufficiently advanced technology is indistinguishable from doubletalk, so I just kind of tuned her out after a couple of minutes and settled for admiring what old King Thoraster had been wasteful enough to freeze.

"And that's how he did it," she concluded.

"Just how big was he?" I asked.

"The same size as all the others," she replied, looking puzzled by my question.

"Then, pardon an indelicate inquiry, but how – ?"

"Ah! I see!" she said. "Let's go into the Hall of the Kings, where the ceiling is a little higher."

I followed her, until we were standing right in the middle of the hall.

"Now I want you to do me one last favor," she said.

"If it's within my power to do, ma'am," I said, "you've but to ask."

Suddenly she turned the prettiest shade of red. "It's very embarrassing," she said. "I think I'd prefer to whisper it to you."

"I'm all ears," I said.

She leaned over and began whispering.

"You want me to do *what*?" I asked aloud.

She turned an even brighter red and repeated it.

"Are you sure, ma'am?" I said. "I don't believe there can be five planets in the galaxy where doing that won't get us both thrown into the hoosegow." Then I paused. "Still, it sounds pretty interesting now that I come to think about it."

"Please!" she said.

So I did it – and then, right in the middle, when things were getting both interesting and complicated, she pushed me back.

"Get away!" she whispered.

"What's the matter?" I asked. "Did I do it wrong?"

"You were doing it perfectly!" she said, blushing furiously. "Now get back!"

274

So I got back, and none too soon, because suddenly she started growing right before my eyes, and a minute later she was mighty close to sixty feet tall, give or take a couple of inches.

"Thank you, Catastrophe Baker!" she said. "Thoraster's scientists made that the only way I could ever regain my true size. They never dreamed that I'd find anyone twisted enough to help me!" She smiled down on me. "I shall never forget you!"

"But we ain't finished!" I protested.

"It's no longer possible," she said. "I must find out if any of my race still survives, and you must don your suit and return to your ship."

"I ain't in no hurry," I said.

"Yes you are," she corrected me. "The mechanism that controls the Hall of the Kings sensed your metabolic needs and created a breathable atmosphere for you, but now that I am alive again, it will soon revert to the atmosphere that exists outside the building."

"This is a hell of a way to leave someone who did you such an enormous favor," I said unhappily.

She looked at me thoughtfully for a moment. "Yes, I suppose it is," she said, and scooped me up in one of her giant hands.

Decorum forbids me from telling you what she did next. Besides, there's worlds where I could get twenty years to life just for describing it.

When we were done, I put on my spacesuit and went back to the ship and took off. It was only after I'd left Sol far behind me that I remembered I hadn't finished looking for the jewels. I considered turning around and going back for them, but then I figured that I'd experienced the most precious jewel of all, so I just kept going, and never did return to the Hall of the Neptunian Kings.

T.M. Hunter

Our third Ray Gun Revival *regular is T.M. Hunter's Aston West, who in this tale finds himself confronted by authorities after he raids an abandoned freighter and takes her cargo, only to discover the authority ship's crew might know more about what happened to the freighter and her crew than expected in...*

EVER DARK

an Aston West Tale

T.M. Hunter

Space is a glamorous place, at least so spaceship salesmen and travel agents would have you believe. In reality, journeys through the darkness bore one to near-death and usually get exciting when you least expect it.

Or want it to.

My ship's computer broke the silence with her female voice. "We're in range."

"Full stop."

On my forward viewscreen, a background of dismal black was sprinkled with tiny pinpoints of light. A shiny metal sphere hovered a couple of kilpars ahead, its sole purpose to span information throughout the darkness. Identical devices were placed around the galaxy, marked on every space chart one could buy. Even in the dark regions of the galaxy, we still needed to communicate with one other.

I leaned back and folded my hands behind my head. "Hack in, Jeanie."

"Already done."

I smiled. It was cheaper than paying for a login subscription.

"Retrieve. Start with the newest."

"Three new messages. First from Tabor Yurick."

276

I was tempted to skip his message, but there was always a slim chance he might say something useful. Tabor's ragged voice carried over the internal speakers.

"West? You're still alive? I thought you'd have stumbled across the wrong end of a blast rifle by now."

I rolled my eyes as he continued.

"Not a lot of takers around here for low-value cargo. Bring me something I can sell or don't bother."

It didn't matter what people were buying, as my four cargo bays were all empty. "Delete."

"Second message, from an unknown sender."

I sat up. "Pause and explain."

"It appears the sender's identity has been masked."

Rather odd, but intriguing. "Continue."

A quiet voice mumbled, to the point I could barely make it out. "Mr. West, I received your name from a mutual acquaintance and would like to hire you for a cargo run. If you're interested, proceed to Mahs system spacedock."

I was.

The message continued. "We'll find you."

"Save for later."

"Last message, from..."

A white flash filled every spot on my viewscreen and disrupted the beacon's signal. A vessel appeared a few kilpars on the other side of the beacon.

I cursed and shielded my eyes too late. "Jeanie, report."

"An Ursulan freighter just dropped out of hyperspeed."

I blinked, then squinted at the viewscreen as spots danced before my eyes. Six exhaust nozzles at the back of the vessel lay dormant against the starfield while the mammoth ship raced along on its own momentum.

The hairs on the back of my neck rose. Cargo freighters didn't make unscheduled stops, especially in the middle of nowhere.

"Freighter's status?"

A few moments passed as Jeanie gathered information from the freighter's computer. "Original destination was the Triton system. The ship is out of fuel."

"Triton? I'd say the crew is having navigation problems. We're not on any shipping route to Triton."

"The crew does not have a navigation problem."

"How's that?"

"I find no life signs to indicate a crew."

Her statement made me pause, though some of my best scavenging efforts had been from crewless ships.

She continued. "They are transmitting on the emergency channel."

I had to take a golden opportunity for what it was, and quickly.

"Move to intercept."

I watched the squashed hexagon of a ship as our aft thrusters fired and we closed the distance. Every usable amount of space on the hull was covered with a cargo bay door, five rows down the length and eight bays around the perimeter. A large spherical dome rested on top of the freighter at its front end. A pair of docking stations waited for us, one on each side.

"So, any idea what happened to the crew?"

"There is evidence of video logs, but they can only be accessed from the Captain's quarters."

There was a more pressing issue at stake anyway.

"What's the cargo?"

Jeanie paused a little longer than she probably should have. "According to the manifest, all of the bays are filled with containers of platinum ore."

I let out a laugh of excitement. "Can you drop the bays remotely?"

Again, she paused. "Negative."

If not for the fact she was a machine programmed to obey, I would have thought she had just sabotaged my efforts.

"Guess I'll have to do it myself." I shook my head and sighed. "Take us in."

I stood and made my way to the back as we adjusted course toward the port docking station.

The air inside the Ursulan freighter was stale when I stepped out of the airlock. I licked my lips, then looked up and down a narrow corridor with bland tan walls and floorboards. The stench of burnt flesh lingered in the air.

I pulled my Mark II blaster out of its holster, then gripped the handle of the stubby weapon. My palm was moist as I switched it over to a three-shot burst. I raised my other hand and spoke into the cuff transmitter. "Jeanie, I'm going to need directions." I'd only seen Ursulan freighters from the outside before.

"Are you still at the airlock?"

"Yes."

"Go left down a small corridor and the bridge should be around the corner, the first hatch on your right."

"Thanks."

I stepped down the hall and the hairs in my nose curled. As I turned the corner, a pile of light gray ash lay on the floor along the left wall. A handheld energy weapon rested next to the debris.

Disintegrator cannon fire was one of the more horrific ways to die and not something a decent person would wish on even their worst enemy. Out of paranoia, I lifted my wrist. "Jeanie, let me know if you see anything inside or outside the freighter."

"Acknowledged."

A hatch in the right wall split apart as I approached. Three more piles of ash lay at various spots around the rectangular bridge. Only one energy weapon was nearby, which told me someone had disintegrated unarmed victims.

I shuddered.

The console stations around the bridge were all functional, so it didn't take long to find the cargo bay controls at the aft end of the room.

Fortunately for me, they weren't locked down, so I ejected the first four bays and lifted my transmitter.

"Jeanie, pull those containers in."

"Acknowledged."

I heard the far-off clunk as Jeanie broke free from the docking station.

With time to kill, my curiosity arose and I walked toward a small door half-open in the corner. A golden plaque lay at chest level and marked the room as Captain's quarters.

I pushed the door aside and saw a grey-haired head atop a wooden desk. The attached body was slumped forward in the matching chair. He had a loose grip on a small energy weapon, same as the others I'd seen. I snuck a glance at his left temple where a scorch mark was etched into his leathery skin.

Sad to say, it wasn't the first dead body I'd ever seen, and wouldn't be the last. The same could be said for a being who took his own life. Sometimes the darkness of death was preferable to the alternative.

I lifted my sleeve. "How's it going out there?"

"One container retrieved. I am bringing the second into the ship."

"Let me know as soon as you have the last one."

"Acknowledged."

I ventured behind him and looked at a small monitor sitting on the corner of his desk. A menu of available log videos showed on the thin screen, so I reached over and tapped the most recent entry.

The dead captain's face appeared on the screen, with his attention on the camera embedded in the upper edge of the monitor. Pounding echoed in the background of the recording. "This will be my last entry."

A cold chill ran up my spine.

"We were ambushed. The rest of the crew, massacred."

The energy weapon in his hand shifted.

"Our computer is back to minimum operation, and she has been programmed to engage the hyperspeed engines as soon as she's able. The ship won't stop until the fuel tanks run dry. Hopefully these scumbags will be stranded on this ship until they're caught."

My guess, they discovered his plan and abandoned ship. It would have been hard giving up forty bays of platinum ore. But all that wealth wouldn't have helped any if they had no way to take the ship anywhere.

Bad for them, good for me.

Tears fell in crooked lines down his face. "They say a captain must go down with his ship. But I have seen the horror that goes with disintegrator cannons and there is a reason civilized societies outlaw them. I won't become another victim."

He raised the weapon to his temple and I flinched as he emptied the discharge chamber. His eyes went wide just after the bright flash, then rolled up into his head before he fell forward.

Death, destruction – I'd seen so much out here in this vast wasteland. You never really got used to it as much as you became better armed to deal with the emotional baggage. My normal weapon of choice was a bottle of alcohol, but I'd have to wait until I got back to my ship to pull that trigger.

Jeanie's voice echoed. "All cargo containers have been retrieved."

"Meet me back where you dropped me off."

"Acknowledged."

I stepped back around the desk and glanced at the piles of ash on my way through the bridge. If there was one major reason why I stayed in the scavenging business, this was it. I couldn't attack innocent people, especially if it meant they'd suffer in the process. I steered away from more direct forms of piracy for a reason.

Jeanie's frantic voice returned as I walked down the main corridor. "Aston, three AP-2s have appeared on long-range sensors."

Patrol ships. They weren't out for a stroll.

I ran for the port docking station. "Mask the cargo. I'll be right there."

"Acknowledged."

I jumped into my chair as we broke free from the docking station and moved away.

"Incoming message."

I breathed deep and settled myself. "Put it through."

The left half of my viewscreen switched to a man with light skin and jet black curls, who stood tall in a dark blue uniform. Two crewmen in similar uniforms sat at segregated consoles in front of him, both with their heads down.

"Commander Jameson of the Triton Security Service."

"Aston West. How can I help you, Commander?"

He snarled. "You can start with what you're doing to this freighter."

"I was accessing a communications beacon, when it dropped out of hyperspeed."

"An automatic emergency beacon was activated on the freighter. We decided to check it out." He curled one corner of his mouth to make a point.

"It's out of fuel."

He turned to one of his crew. "Get a fuel transport out here on the double."

I moved my hand up to the console on my left and gently shut off the audio portion of the transmission. I moved my other hand up and mimicked a cough.

"Jeanie, where are the other ships?"

"Docking with the freighter."

Another mock cough. "On the viewscreen."

I brought the audio back as Jameson noticed I was muted. "Sorry. Must have something caught in my throat."

On the other half of the viewscreen, I watched the two ships move closer to the freighter. Their bulbous front end tapered to a single engine at the back, all on top of triangular delta wings.

He folded his arms across his chest. "We noticed you were docked to the freighter."

"My ship's computer informed me there was no crew aboard. I wanted to see for myself."

Was it really lying if you just omitted facts? Little things, like the fact I'd dumped four bays of precious cargo in the process.

"And did you find anything?"

"Looks like they were massacred in an ambush."

"Of which I'm sure you're completely innocent."

I snorted. "I don't have the firepower to stop that freighter."

"So you had help."

"They weren't ambushed here. Check the last video log, in the Captain's quarters."

"We will."

One of the crew interrupted a short while later as he turned back to the Commander. "They're in. Looks like everyone's dead."

"Have them check the log."

"I can tell you what they'll find. The captain killed himself rather than get disintegrated."

Jameson passed between the consoles and approached his viewscreen with another snarl. "You'll understand if I don't just take your word for it."

"Suit yourself."

A few moments passed before the crewman jumped in again. "They've checked the log. It's just like he said."

I smirked. "You're welcome."

"They say there are four bays of ore missing."

Oops.

The Commander sneered. "Know anything about that?"

I paused a moment to collect my thoughts. Jeanie had the cargo masked, so there would be no evidence for them to connect me to the missing ore. Unless, of course, they boarded my ship.

"Nope, not a thing."

From the raised eyebrow, I could tell he knew I was lying.

I shrugged. "Scan my hold if you don't believe me."

"I have a better idea. How about we come over and look for ourselves?"

I muted the audio and faked another cough. "Jeanie set a course for Iopeia. Get ready to jump to hyperspeed."

"Acknowledged."

I rejoined the conversation. "Sorry about that. Guess I must be catching something."

"Prepare to be boarded."

I was a moment away from making the jump before an idea clicked in my mind. I held back a smile.

"Not to be a stickler for the rules, Commander, but aren't you a bit out of your jurisdiction?"

He frowned. "You're trying to get out of this on a technicality?"

His ship closed on my position.

"If you'd like, we could have the local authorities settle this."

I watched for a sign of his next move behind the frown on his face. Time was running out, and a hyperspeed jump was looking more and more viable with every moment.

Jameson glared at me. "Get out of here before I blast your ship apart."

"Glad we could come to an understanding, Commander." I smiled as he turned and walked back to his chair.

All's well that ends well, even if I had no idea whether the local authorities would make matters worse or not. With victory now in hand, I nearly terminated the transmission when I caught sight of a disintegrator cannon tucked away on the floor beside his chair. There was no mistaking the long-barreled heavy weapon.

Every nerve ending in my body fired off at the same time.

I tried to keep my mind off the obvious. "If you don't mind, Commander, I have one last communication to send out, then I'll be out of your hair."

"Make it quick."

The conversation was terminated and the full viewscreen displayed the freighter and two patrol ships already docked on either side of the spherical dome. Jameson's ship moved toward the freighter.

"Take us back to the beacon, Jeanie."

I reached down beside my chair as we turned. I pulled a bottle of Vladirian liquor out of the pocket. A large dose of the pale yellow liquid was just the thing to take the edge off.

I didn't really need to make this transmission. Tabor didn't really care if he had advance notice of my arrival. Time was what I was after, to process what I'd just seen.

My ship wasn't capable of taking on three patrol ships, and it looked like this group of sadists was going to get away with mass murder. I felt sorry for the crew. They'd likely trusted these lawmen, and had given their lives in exchange.

Jeanie caught my attention. "We're in range."

I sighed and sent out a useless message. "Message to Tabor Yurick. I have some high-value merchandise. See you soon. End message."

"Message packaged."

I took another drink. "Send it."

"Done."

"Course still laid in for Iopeia?"

"Yes."

I watched Jameson's vessel as it drew closer to the two patrol ships docked with the freighter. Anger burned inside me, an intense hatred for murderers who'd taken an innocent crew's life for their own greed. I took another drink.

"Jeanie, are you still inside the freighter's computer system?"

"Yes."

"Does it have a self-destruct system?"

"Yes."

I guzzled the liquor one more time, then placed the nearly empty bottle back in its pocket. "Set it."

"Any specific amount of time?"

I watched as Jameson's patrol ship skimmed the upper surface of the freighter.

I didn't plan to let them have a chance to get out like the first time. "Just blow it now."

The Ursulan freighter burst apart in a sequence of huge fiery explosions. Each firestorm collapsed just moments after it escaped the outer hull, but not before the destructive blasts took out all three patrol ships.

As debris scattered, I smiled with the knowledge that justice had been dispensed, almost in the way the freighter's captain had wanted.

Sometimes the darkness of death was preferable to the alternative.

"Hyperspeed."

In Michael Merriam's action-packed tale, our last Ray Gun Revival *highlight, two rebels develop interesting rapport with their hostages as they wait to transfer them to safer holding and find themselves clashing over their captives' destiny in...*

NOR TO THE STRONG

Michael Merriam

Becker pulled the small box of cards from his trouser pocket and settled at the kitchen table. "Shall we?"

I pulled a wobbly chair up next to him. We had nothing else to do, we four. Nothing except wait. "Of course."

"I haven't got the credits, I lost all of mine last night," Knowles said.

"I'll spot you," Becker told her.

"Thanks," said Knowles. "You know I'm good for it. I'll pay you back when we get to Earth."

I looked over at Montry. I thought it might be some time before either Becker or Knowles returned to Earth. The two Earthers might find themselves in our care on Gawain for months yet.

Montry passed back a grim smile. He was thinking the same as I. He looked at Becker.

"Two," Becker said, setting his bet.

Montry's blue eyes narrowed. He was a new recruit; young, energetic, and not happy with guard detail. Montry would rather be out fighting. He wanted desperately to go to battle with the troops Earth had sent to keep its colonies in line. I remembered being like Montry, before three years of useless warfare ate at my soul and a trip-wire explosive took half of my right foot. Guard duty suited me fine these days.

"Two?" said Knowles. "Two's hardly any bet at all. You'd think a religious man would have more faith. Surely if you ask your God, he'll provide you winning cards."

Knowles' voice was high and came through her nose. I'd been told that she was an accountant or something, not even a combatant, but a civilian who had been at the wrong place at the wrong time. Becker was her escort.

"Wouldn't you think that, Becker?" Knowles continued.

Becker shrugged as Knowles tossed in two chips and glared at Montry. Knowles hated religion, and Montry was a card carrying Catholic, loyal to the Pope in hiding somewhere in the Outer Colonies.

Montry frowned at her. "It doesn't work that way. Free will and all."

"What does free will have to do with anything? Couldn't your mighty God conjure up a winning hand for you?"

"Two and one," I said, trying to head off the impending argument. Every night Knowles picked one topic and tried to push Montry's buttons.

Becker looked at his cards. He mixed them around in his large hands, and tossed in four credit chips, raising the pot.

"Four, now there's a real bet, don't you think?" Knowles sneered at Montry, her little brown eyes gleaming from behind her glasses.

Montry tossed his cards onto the table, face down. Knowles started to open her mouth, but closed it at a look from Becker. That was the way it usually played out. If Knowles was feeling nasty, Becker would silence her with a look, his deep blue eyes glaring from under shaggy black brows, telling the frumpy little woman that she was about to go too far.

"In," I said, tossing another chip into the middle of the table.

"It was my bet!" Knowles said, giving me an angry look, her small hands working her cards nervously.

"Then bet."

Knowles scowled and tossed in her cards.

"Draw or reveal?" Becker said to me.

"Reveal."

Becker laid down his cards. I tried not to swear.

He took the pile of credit chips from the center of the table. "Sorry, Ferg."

I shook my head and took the cards from Becker, placing them in the randomizer.

Knowles opened her mouth, about to make another go at Montry, but the sound of the randomizer burping out the cards stopped her. I dealt the next hand.

Widow Somogyi shook me awake. "Someone is coming," she said in a low whisper.

I stood and yawned. I picked up the rifle next to my chair and limped out the door into the yard, where the Widow's two old hounds glared up the dusty lane past Becker chopping wood under Montry's careful guard. That was Becker. Captive or not, he liked being helpful.

I did not recognize two of the men coming up the lane, but the third one, the one leading them, was a small, nervous man named Ramirez, our contact with the local rebellion cell. He glanced at Becker, then at the trees, I supposed searching for an ambush by Earth forces. As if the army of the mother planet cared one way or another about us out here in the remote countryside.

"Fergus, are the prisoners secure?" he said without preamble. That was Ramirez: all cold business. I did not like Ramirez, but I did not need to like him.

"Yes."

"Good. Good. You and Montry have them ready to be moved. I'll be by tonight with some men."

"Where are you taking them?"

"That's none of your concern," he said, his face pinched and closed. "Just blindfold them and bring them down to the river at sundown. I'll be taking charge of them from there. You and Montry will be given a new assignment in a few days."

Ramirez looked around again, then reached into his jacket and handed me a small bag. "Give this to Mrs. Somogyi for her troubles, and tell her we will be borrowing some tools from her husband's shed, but plan to return them in the morning."

He placed the bag in my hand and turned away before I could respond, abruptly ending our conversation.

I watched as one of the men walked toward Widow Somogyi's tool shed while Ramirez and the other man started back up the lane. The man eventually trotted after them, carrying two shovels and a pickaxe.

"What was that all about?" Montry asked in a low voice as he and Becker followed me back into the cottage.

I dropped the bag on the kitchen table, where Widow Somogyi sat, sipping coffee. She opened it, and a handful of credits fell out. Becker grabbed three chipped ceramic cups and poured coffee, setting a cup in front of me.

"We're to turn Becker and Knowles over to Ramirez tonight," I told Montry. "He wants us to meet him by the river at sundown." I looked up to see Becker's reaction, but his expression did not change.

"I see," was all Montry said.

"We're supposed to get new assignments. Maybe yours will be something combat."

After breakfast, Widow Somogyi left for the little village a few miles away, her bag of credits in hand. I cleaned the dishes, washing and drying them. Montry and I decided to let Becker tell Knowles about the plan to move them to a new location.

That afternoon Knowles and Montry fought over politics.

"I'm not saying I'm for the war, mind you. I just think what's Earth's is Earth's," Knowles said. "Who sends supplies to your world? Who makes sure you're safe? Earth, that's who."

"Who takes half of everything we have? Earth, that's who," Montry countered. "And who do we need protecting from?"

"Raiders," came the instant reply, Knowles trotting out the old argument. Raiders were the generic name for the alien race Earth had encountered in this region of space. They could not compete with Earth militarily, so they contented themselves with attacking remote outposts and fleeing before the local patrols could intervene.

"There hasn't been a raider in this sector of space in over twenty years. We're not a border world anymore," said Montry.

"You're an Earth colony, subject to Earth rule," Knowles replied, her anger starting to rise.

"But we've got no say," Montry snarled back, his jaw clenching. "We don't even get a vote in the assembly."

Knowles frowned. "You're colonists, not citizens. That's the charter. That's the way it always has been. If you're not a citizen, you can't vote. Isn't that right, Becker?"

"True," Becker answered from where he sat repairing a broken lamp.

"That doesn't make it right," I whispered, reloading the rifle I had finished cleaning.

Knowles turned her dark little eyes on me. "And planting a bomb in a government official's home is?"

"Would Earth listen to us otherwise?"

"They're not legitimate military targets," Knowles spat back. "I suppose you can sleep fine at night knowing your people blew up some lieutenant-governor's defenseless children?"

I glared. "I suppose you can sleep fine at night knowing someone's child starved to death because of Earth's oppressive taxes?"

"It's not my fault you colonists don't use your resources properly."

I opened my mouth to retort, than closed it and shrugged. "It's obvious we aren't going to agree."

"So you're going to give up? Just like that?" Knowles pressed.

"That's enough," Becker said softly.

Knowles sighed. "I need some air," she said, looking at me and Montry. "Which one of you is going to make sure I don't flee?"

"I'll go," Montry said, standing up from his chair.

I watched them walk out the door and into the growing dusk. "I hope they both come back alive."

Becker snorted and pushed the switch on the lamp. It lit. "They'll be fine," he said.

I gave him a look. "Why haven't you run for it? You seem resourceful enough; you'd probably get away if you tried."

"I can't leave Knowles behind. I'm supposed to keep her safe." Becker looked up at me and smiled. "I could try to take her and run, but she wouldn't make it very far, and that mouth of hers would get us caught again." He reached for a book on the table next to him and opened it. "No, I'll wait until your people make a trade for us," he said, looking down at the pages.

I nodded in understanding. Earth and the rebels traded prisoners all the time.

Two hours later, I wondered if perhaps I should make sure Montry and Knowles *were* still alive. Becker was still reading by the light of the recently repaired lamp, so I started for the door to search for them, when they stumbled inside. Knowles' clothes were in disarray, and they were both covered in a light film of sweat. Knowles ignored me as she headed for the stairs up to her room. I looked at Montry. He shrugged and followed her.

I settled into a chair by the front door to keep watch, listening to Becker chuckle softly from where he sat pretending to read.

When Montry placed the blindfold over her eyes, Knowles launched into a tirade about the mistreatment of prisoners, and how there were certain codes of conduct civilized combatants were supposed to follow. Montry pointed out that she was not even a combatant, but an accountant, and anyway, everyone knew how poorly Earth's forces treated their prisoners. Compared to that, Montry said, she had been living in the lap of luxury during her imprisonment. Knowles snarled that the rebellious colonists did not deserve to be treated like prisoners of war, but like the common criminals they were.

Through it all, Becker held his tongue, his flat expression never changing.

We trudged toward the river in silence, except for Knowles occasionally grumbling about the blindfold. She allowed herself to be led along the overgrown path by Montry, who guided her with a soft voice and gentle hand while lighting our way. Becker kept a firm grip on my left elbow as I led him down the lantern-lit path. He had not spoken after I'd placed the blindfold over his eyes. I carried my rifle slung over my right shoulder, away from Becker. As we neared the river, the smell of dank vegetation, stagnant water, and fresh-turned earth filled my nose.

"What's all this?" I heard Montry say ahead of me.

I stepped into the small clearing at the end of the path. Ramirez stood in front of a freshly dug pit with two lanterns suspended on poles over it. He held a pistol at his side. The two men I had seen with him earlier in the day leaned on shovels, both covered in sweat and breathing heavily from exertion. Their rifles were propped against a tree a few feet behind them.

I realized what the fresh dug pit was: a grave. "What's going on?" I asked Ramirez.

Ramirez took Knowles by the arm and pulled her away from Montry. He walked her to the foot of the open grave and stepped behind her.

"What are you doing?" Montry said, starting to move toward Ramirez. "I thought we ransomed or traded our prisoners?"

Ramirez pointed his pistol at Montry. "Earth forces leveled Columbia City. They killed everyone: men, women, children, all of them. Six thousand people wiped out because the mayor couldn't tell them who the local rebel leaders were. We're to kill all of our prisoners in retaliation."

Knowles started to whimper and shake.

"I didn't sign up to be a murderer," said Montry.

"This is a war; people kill each other," Ramirez snapped. "*They* murdered *six thousand people*."

"So we're to act just like them?" I asked softly.

"Those are my orders," Ramirez said.

"You're not really going to shoot me, are you?" Knowles said in a shaky voice. "I'm not even a soldier. I've never killed anyone." She started to cry. "Montry, you're not going to let him kill me, are you? I thought we were friends, I thought – "

Ramirez turned and fired his pistol into her back. The shot echoed across the nearby river. For a moment, Knowles stood still, then she toppled into the grave.

I looked at Ramirez. He was pale and shaking, his breath coming hard and heavy. Over his shoulder, I saw Montry fall to his knees and throw up. Ramirez pointed his pistol at me. "Bring the next one," he said in a shaky voice. I hesitated, and Ramirez cocked the hammer back on the pistol. "Now."

I walked Becker to the foot of the grave. "I'm sorry about this," I said, as if somehow that would make everything better. "I didn't know. I thought you were to be traded for prisoners from our side."

"Just do me a favor," Becker said.

"Sure."

"Take this blindfold off me."

I reached up and untied the blindfold while Ramirez held his pistol on us, his hand shaking so badly I thought he might accidentally fire. I could hear Montry being sick.

"There are some papers in my jacket pocket," Becker said, his voice calm and even. "My daughter lives on Perseus; her address is on one of the letters. Could you send them to her and make sure she knows what happened?"

I reached inside his jacket and withdrew the small pouch of papers. "I promise."

"Here now, hurry up," Ramirez whispered.

I heard a low moan and looked into the lantern-lit grave. Knowles, her blood soaking into the moist earth underneath her, was still alive. She clawed at the ground, making gurgling, wheezing noises.

I turned to Ramirez. "For God's sake, do something. Just – finish her."

Ramirez stared down at Knowles, his face shocked. He looked up at me as she gave a strangled cry. Behind him, I saw Montry stand and stumble back up the path toward Widow Somogyi's cottage.

I unslung my rifle and fired a round into her back. She stilled and quieted.

I looked up. Before I could stop him, Ramirez pointed his pistol at the back of Becker's head and fired. The roar of the discharge made my ears ring, and the force of the bullet flung Becker into the grave on top of Knowles.

Ramirez holstered his pistol. "Well, that nastiness is done. I – "

I turned, aimed my rifle at Ramirez, and squeezed the trigger. The bullet hit Ramirez in the chest. He flew from his feet and landed on his back. I pointed the rifle at the other two men. Both held up their hands. I kept them covered as I threw their rifles and Ramirez's pistol into the hole. I made them drop Ramirez into the grave and forced them to fill it, then I told them to leave. They disappeared into the night.

I ran back to Widow Somogyi's cottage, stumping along on my lame foot, stumbling and falling several times in the dark.

I found Montry in the living room. He was kneeling and holding his rosary beads, his mouth moving silently.

Widow Somogyi knelt next to him, her eyes closed. She opened them as I entered the room. "What happened out there Fergus? What have you done?" Her voice was filled with accusation.

I dropped the rifle on the floor and walked past her, into the room I shared with Montry. I packed my clothes, placing Becker's papers in my bag and, unable to face Montry, the widow, or even myself, slipped out the back door into the darkness.

In the first of three originals which wind up our journey together, Peter J. Wacks puts a whole new spin and meaning to the term space opera as a conductor and his orchestra relive a famous battle for their audience through a musical score in the aptly titled...

SPACE OPERA

Peter J. Wacks

Wilhelm tapped one of the conductor's batons against the side of his stand, glancing at the audience with his posterior eyestalks, while his anterior orbs faced the orchestra. A full auditorium tonight. The pressure of thousands of eyes watching behind him, eagerly awaiting the performance, sent a pleasant shiver down his notochord. The auditorium hushed, silence spreading on bated breath. Tonight's Tri-Galactic Philharmonic, the introduction to his favorite operatic saga, would be brilliant, would be beautiful, would be everything expected of a master conductor, and more.

He gazed at his orchestra. Every player was ready to fulfill their role, every instrument ready to produce music unequaled anywhere in the galaxy. The lights dimmed. Wilhelm once again tapped the batons held in his upper arms on the edges of the stand. Everyone awaited his command. He closed his eyes, savoring the moment. He lived in the perfect silence, the harmony in silence...

His hand moved upward, unfolding the story...

The overture's first notes breached the quiet – a butterfly emerging from the cocoon. The opening bars – heavy with cello, percussion, and bass – reverberated through the audience, who all watched from the inky blackness of the auditorium; a thousand eyes that glittered in the darkness like stars in the night sky. On Wilhelm's cue, the brass launched in, like massive warships landing their jump drives around a planet.

Admiral Tal studied the screens on the bridge of the command ship *Valkyrie*, ignoring the brash music of the proximity jump klaxons. His entire fleet appeared, a perfect unspooling of their drive cores, surrounding the dark side of the planet below. Eighteen ships, each one the size of a city, assumed a hemispherical formation above the planet's surface. He scanned the bridge's monitors, eyes intent while his mind boiled in the pre-battle chaos.

This battle was not his preferred command. With all the dangers of the universe, to be fighting other humans seemed ludicrous. But these people had started a civil war over not wanting to join galactic society, and that was a threat to the whole human race. His colony could have been cured by an Accolian Serum, but these people, the colony of New Oceana, had voted against it, then declared war on Earth, choosing instead to be barred from galactic trade, expansion, and culture. That was when he had come back from retirement to fight for Earth. His fingers tightened into a fist.

"Ready!" he commanded his X.O. "Prep all fleet fighters for launch."

The tactical monitors flashed green, and Tal yelled at the artillery officer. "Artillery, prep the Planet Busters! We're late! The colony may have already launched their defenses. Hustle!"

Lower ranked officers scurried about the bridge, quietly prepping the ship's attack systems.

Tal watched the tactical command screen carefully. A klaxon, indicating that the ship's planet buster energy weapons were ready to deploy, sounded, before being counterpointed by a new, shrill alert siren. There was a tempo underlying all of the alerts sounding on the bridge, a crescendo which would climax with the gentle squeeze of the first trigger pulled. Planetary defenses had been ready for the fleet's jump, and scans indicated a counter attack launch was imminent.

"Ready defensive measures. Bring up shields, now! All ships." he commanded. "Fire Planet Busters, on my mark..." He watched the reactor core meters until the weapons were about to overload, then shouted, "MARK!"

At that command, all of the Earth's galactic class battleships fired the massive energy bombs. Each one had a guided reactor at its core, capable of corrective targeting once in the atmosphere.

Bursts of golden-green energy, surrounding the targeting cores, arced from the Earth's fleet, silently pulsing through space towards the planet below. They would slow when impacting the atmosphere, but, despite the lack of speed, they could ravage continents and win a battle by themselves.

Wilhelm pointed at the brass section as his baton kept the battle's tempo, and they dropped an octave, giving the piece depth, enfolding the remaining movement's higher ranges.

The Planet Busters hit the outer atmosphere, ribbons of energy flashing deep crimson as they struck the planet's gaseous shell. Fighters swarmed silently up from the surface, dodging the actinic helixes of light spiraling downwards toward the planet. Countless tiny dots flared into life across the globe below, growing in size, reddening as they shot up through the atmosphere. First a score, then hundreds, then thousands burst through the upper mesosphere into space. The pitch of the battle was about to change.

Wilhelm gestured rapidly with his lower pair of hands, signaling the woodwinds and strings to enter the symphony. Dum Dah Da-ah... The engines of a thousand fighters joined the music on wings of breath and vibration. With another motion of his lower hands he launched the deeper woodwinds; all while keeping the two tempos steady with his batons: his right for Earth, and his left for the colony of New Oceana.

Admiral Tal watched the red lights crowd the edges of his command displays. Every Klaxon on the bridge screamed shrilly; Tal had to shout to be heard over the cacophony of off key alarms. "Tactical, launch all fighters! Engineering, get my orbital shields in position! Command, I need eyes on planetary defenses. Go, go, go!"

The massive battleships disgorged swarms of fighters, squadron upon squadron moving to intercept their colonial counterparts. Planet and fleet made their next moves simultaneously. A salvo of blue pulses, as formidable in power as the descending Planet Busters, raced from the surface to attacking fleet.

As these deadly energies approached their targets, massive sections of each battleship detached from their parent vessels. The orbitals – little more than maneuverable armor plates – drifted a safe distance away from their parent ships before positioning themselves via rocket jets between the fleet and the surface weapons.

Wilhelm snapped his upper wrists to the side now that the orbitals were in place, then gently lowered his batons. The orchestra responded, its volume dropping to a teasing susurrus. Wilhelm cued his first chair violin. She was a Sylaxian, a tripedal, tentacled race masterfully adept with stringed instruments. Standing proudly, she launched into a complex solo that sounded like multiple violins playing in unison, though it was only her instrument soaring in flight over the hushed orchestra – a single, focused voice in the battle.

Major Thomasson, a virtuoso of flight, adjusted the yaw and roll of his fighter, diving to intercept the incoming colonial fighters. His squadron followed in perfect formation behind him, a dance of thirty-two ships eager to engage as they began their descent from orbit. The leading enemy squadron was almost close enough to break out of the refrain and crescendo into violence.

He glanced at the sensor array. "Break into wings now, my devils! Wings one and two flank sun side, three go moon, and four, play sniper. Mark!"

A brief burst of static resolved into voices over his com.

"Wing one, acknowledged."

"Wing two, gotcha, bossman."

"Wing three, headed out! Good luck, boys!"

"Wing four, one shot, one kill; we've got your back."

Thomasson grinned, sizing up the oncoming horde. Earth's fighter corps was outnumbered at least two to one, but that didn't concern him. His squadron was one of the best, and the fleet had devised a plan for dealing with just this contingency.

"Launching cover, choose your targets on three. One. Two – " He pulled the trigger, firing all forty of his fighter's SPARCs. The SPARCs, Spatial Atmosphere-less Reactive Combustible missiles, blasted away from his ship and streamed towards the enemy.

" – Three." He laughed.

"Nice. I hate you sometimes, Major." That was from Wing Two.

"Engaging missiles now, hope you all have your target." Thomasson did a quick visual double-check, confirming that enemy fighters had all maneuvered clear of the incoming SPARCs. They had. He thumbed the trigger guard, flipping it up, and hit the 'munitions destruct' button next to the trigger. His timing was perfectly matched with the rest of the squadron leaders.

With the SPARCs launched, Wilhelm signaled the cymbals and snare drums. Rapid pulses of percussion saturated the tonal landscape created by the violin, filling out the solo like a monsoon flood as the beats and crashes grew in volume.

SPARC missiles exploded. Loaded with alloy powders, they created a glittery silvery screen between the battle fleet and the closing planetary forces. The planet's entire hemisphere sparkled in the darkness, blanketed in shining silver already beginning to dissipate. Thomasson had only seconds. Sensor screens on both sides went black, unable to penetrate the metallic cloud, but Earth's invasion forces fired weapons nonetheless, using specially coded predictive algorithms to track their invisible foes through the screen. Bursts of light peppered the silence of space as colonial fighters perished by the thousands.

"Yeahhhhhh boyyyyyyy!" Major Thomasson screamed in jubilation as his fighter ripped through the dust cloud, revealing the mass destruction they had wreaked. "Enemy forces seventy percent destroyed. Go get 'em!" Around the planet, two hundred other squadron commanders echoed his sentiment. Voice after voice cheered as the alloy smokescreen dissipated.

Wilhelm blinked back a tear from his eye, the triumph in death of this part of the piece spoke to his compassion, a private missive to the conductor. Furiously signaling, all four batons wove through the air, and the entire orchestra to launch into life. The music swelled, each section fully rejoining the movement, until the whole battle was once more being played.

Massive shockwaves shook the fleet's ships as the planetary weapons impacted, and half a dozen Earth battleships erupted like miniature suns. The planetary defense weapons had finally scored hits, tearing through all the orbitals and wiping out a third of the command ships. In the blink of an eye, six hundred thousand lives were lost.

Admiral Tal watched amidst the shouting and klaxons, a bastion of silence amid the pandemonium, hiding his shaking hands. He had just lost friends, colleagues, Earthmen. He was a good, seasoned commander, however, and wouldn't surrender to his fear or to the overwhelming loss. He straightened his shoulders, ignoring the devastation, the cacophony and the bridge chaos. "Update..." he commanded tersely.

His X.O. scanned the tactical summary screens. "Enemy fighter force at nineteen percent. We're at ninety-six percent. Orbitals are gone, though, and six battleships destroyed. It should be over soon, sir. We have twenty seconds until Planet Busters hit. Surface is powering up round two, but they'll need at least thirty seconds, sir."

Tal grunted. "Focus on supporting our fighters."

"Yes, sir. Tactical – small and medium weapons ready, target planet-side. Engage cookie cutters and synchronize with fighter trajectory computers. Fire all weapons!"

The twelve remaining battleships glowed yellow and orange as hundreds of ballistic and energy weapons charged to life and fired. Light streaked across the starfield like fireflies dancing to unheard music on a cloudy night.

Wilhelm flattened the baton in his upper left hand, ordering all of the high-toned instruments into silence. Bass notes shook the very auditorium, ominous, dark, and overpowering.

Hundreds of cubic miles of shrapnel and floating wreckage were laced with swarming fighters and radiant weapons fire. A massive energy wave ripped through the entire floating field of deadly flotsam, sending ships and shrapnel alike spinning.

Another of Earth's battleships was now wreckage. Weapons rotated as the remaining Earth forces repositioned. A juggernaut class ship, four times the size of Earth's most formidable battleship, had been hidden by the colonists behind the planet's one small moon. Now it made its move.

All eleven remaining battleships opened fire, every instrument being used, every trigger pulled, lighting up the juggernaut till it was brighter than the moon behind it. Yet still it continued to fire. And with each apocalyptic burst from its positron lances, a battleship would explode.

Tal cursed silently as one of Earth's battleships, the *Archimedes*, vanished in the telltale green spark-burst of a jump spooling. The *Valkyrie* and the *Imperius* poured the last of their formidable magazine stores into the girded colossus, but it was futile, the juggernaut was too heavily armored. Earth's triumphal march had turned into a dirge of desperation. Tal knew they had lost.

Wilhelm jerked all four of his arms to a stop, then signaled the deepest basses and percussions. A lone cello's poignant note of despair cut through the melancholy ambiance.

Green Saint Elmo's Fire erupted from the juggernaut's main weapon battery, the plasma danced outward along the ship's once impregnable armor. *Archimedes'* aft became briefly visible as the Earth battleship unspooled from its micro jump into the juggernaut's heart. The resulting explosion shattered the unstoppable juggernaut, the noble *Archimedes*, and also fractured the small moon, wresting it from orbit.

Chunks of moon drifted towards the plant below, a lunar apocalypse of fragmented death. Meteors formed, arcing through the battle's flotsam and reducing it to dust as the moon fell towards the planet. A single chunk, about one third of the moon's original mass, ponderously wobbled, gently drifting away towards the deeper portions of the solar system. Golden light changed to red on the surface below as the Planet Busters finally struck, destroying tectonic plates and reducing the colony to rubble across the globe.

Wilhelm signaled the Theremins and bass drums. Jarring, otherworldly sounds crashed into the symphony, rising and fading like a pulse.

Tal watched, unbelieving, horrified, as fragments of the moon struck the devastated planet below. Volcanoes erupted as magnitude nine and ten earthquakes shook the planet's landmasses, firestorms blazed across the planet's face, consuming everything. Lightning swarmed and danced thickly through the atmosphere, a maelstrom of pure annihilation. The planet was dead, uninhabitable, an epithet declaring 'Humanity Warred Here'.

Wilhelm gently nudged the orchestra to segue with a steady harmony, changing the tone and feel of the piece to the aftermath of the despair.

The battle was done. The colony, part of the dissenting voice in humanity's unified government, had been crushed. But it was only the first, and war had now been declared. The remaining fighters jetted around the battlefield, collecting survivors. It didn't matter whether those collected were Earth fleet or Colonial. After the devastation this encounter had wrought, every human life was worth saving.

Wilhelm meticulously silenced each section of the orchestra, leaving only a lone bass drum beating to the rhythm of a human heart, and a solitary violin to speak quietly to the audience.

Admiral Tal, alone in his ready room, splashed water on his face. The cold shock wouldn't ease the grief in his red-rimmed eyes, nor wash away the still falling tears. "What have we done?" he softly asked his reflection. "What have we done?!" His reflection refused to respond, and only watched him wrestle silently with his guilt.

Then violin and drum fell still. The house lights rose.

Wilhelm wiped his own tears away as the audience broke into thunderous applause. He turned to face the standing ovation, motioning for his musicians to stand also. Together they bowed.

He let it continue for about thirty seconds before tapping his batons together over his head, a signal for quiet. The audience retook their seats.

Wilhelm cleared his throat. "Thank you ladies and gentlemen. This concludes the overture to the opera *Humanity; a struggle against inner nature to join the galactic parliament.* There will now be a thirty minute interlude before the curtains rise on Act One, in which three years later, now promoted Ambassador Tal struggles to find the qualities which will redeem humanity by joining the Monks of Compassion on the planet Korge. Please avail yourselves of the refreshments in the lobby and stretch your limbs."

Multi-Hugo Award winning author Allen M. Steele's novels include the Coyote *trilogy and his latest, a Heinlein-esque YA space opera novel titled* Apollo's Outcasts *from PYR. For us, he spins the tale of men sent to rescue a heiress from kidnappers who uncover a surprising scenario that leads to asking and answering questions they never expected in...*

THE HEIRESS OF AIR

Allen M. Steele

"Tell me about the job."

Red couldn't see the one who spoke to him. The voice came from the other side of the cone of light surrounding the chair in which he sat; it wasn't unfriendly, but neither was it particularly kind. Two men stood behind him, menacingly silent. They might be told to offer him lunch or drag him to the nearest airlock; it all depended on how he answered the questions of the unseen figure seated just out of sight.

"I think you know that already." Red started to casually cross his legs, then decided against it; he didn't want to come off as insolent. "I mean... not to be obtuse about such things, but if you don't, then why am I here?"

"You were caught taking something that doesn't belong to you."

"Well, no. Not exactly." Red tried not to smile. "We were taking back something that belongs to someone else. Besides, she doesn't belong to anyone, not even her father. And you didn't catch me... I'm here of my own free will." He quietly hoped that hadn't been a mistake.

A moment of silence. "All true," the man on the other side of the lights admitted. "Which makes the situation even more interesting. If you could have avoided us, then why have you...?"

"I want to try to work things out." This time Red smiled. "It's not smart to get on your bad side. Everyone knows that. And if the Crew had known you had anything to do with this, we wouldn't have taken the job in the first place."

A quiet laugh. For an instant, Red caught a glimpse of a face white as comet ice, eyes the color of the Martian sky. Then the face retreated back into the darkness. "No, I'm not someone to be trifled with, Captain McGee. And that brings us back to my original question. The job..."

"The job was to find Cozy and bring her home. That simple. Her father hired us. Finding her wasn't a problem. But getting her back – " Red let out his breath " – well, I guess that's why I'm here, isn't it?"

It only made sense that the men who'd kidnapped Cosette Trudeau would head for Ceres. There were few other places they could have gone once they'd left the Moon. Cislunar traffic control hadn't reported any vessels on an earthbound trajectory during the time-frame in which the abduction occurred that matched witness descriptions of the one that had lifted off from the Trudeau family's private estate outside Descartes City. Mars was currently at opposition on the other side of the Sun from Earth; Jupiter was too far away, and no one but the mad and the desperate go to Venus. Ceres was in conjunction, though, making it conveniently accessible for a deep-space craft fleeing for the outer system, and as the largest port between Mars and Jupiter, Ceres Station was the jump-off point for the rest of the belt.

So it made sense that the kidnappers would dock at Ceres Station, wait for its orbit to take it within distance of their ultimate destination – wherever that may be – then make the final sprint to whatever rockhound hideaway was awaiting them.

Unless, of course, Antoine Trudeau decided to pay the one million lox ransom the kidnappers had demanded in the laser transmission received by the Lunar Air Company twenty-four hours after three heavily-armed men took the girl from her crater home. By then, *père* Trudeau had already made that very decision. His people got in touch with the Crew and told Red McGee that he was willing to pay an identical sum to have his daughter brought back to him, plus expenses.

"I wonder why he didn't just pay the ransom," the voice behind the lights said. "It would have been easier."

"But he'd lose face that way, wouldn't he?" Red replied. "Money's not a problem for someone like that, but reputation... well, that's another matter, isn't it? If it got out that one of the wealthiest men in the system could be horned out of a million lox by a bunch of lowlifes..." He shrugged. "So, of course, he'd rather hire someone to retrieve his little girl."

"Of course. Go on. You figured out they were headed for Ceres..."

And wasted no time getting there. In fact, *Wormtown Sally* reached Ceres Station just hours after its traffic control center reported the arrival of a light-cargo freighter christened the *Olympus Dreamer*. Full thrust at 1-g had seen to that. Indeed, *Sally* could have even overtaken the *Dreamer* if Red had known for sure that it was the ship they were chasing, but it wasn't until a friendly source at Ceres Traffic informed him that the freighter's crew hadn't left their vessel but instead were still inside that Red was certain – reasonably certain, at least – that the *Dreamer* was the right ship. And besides, rendezvousing and docking with another spacecraft is nearly impossible when both ships are under thrust.

So *Wormtown Sally* – itself another converted freighter, albeit with upgraded gas-core nuclear engines and plasma-beam cannons concealed within its forward hull – quietly approached Ceres and, with the cooperation of the friendly trafco guy ("who received a nice finder's fee for his tip," Red added), slid into berth adjacent to the *Dreamer*. And even before the massive outer doors closed behind *Sally*, the Crew was getting ready to earn its pay.

There were four men in the Crew: Red, Raphael Coto, Jack Dog Jones, and Breaker. Tough guys. Hardasses. Red, Raphael, and Jack Dog were Pax Astra Royal Navy vets, while no one knew any more about Breaker's background than they did his real name. They suited up in the airlock ready-room – body armor fitted with holo projectors, straps stuffed with tear gas and stun grenades – and then they loaded their flechette rifles, cycled through the portside hatch, and quietly went down the ladder.

Wormtown Sally and *Olympus Dreamer* lay side by side upon their retractable berths within Ceres's cavernous spaceport. The docking tunnels had been repressurized after the ships came in. Dock workers and 'bots unloaded cargo and performed routine maintenance on other vessels berthed in adjacent tunnels, but no one was in sight near the two ships.

Peering through the narrow access tunnel leading from *Sally*'s berth to *Dreamer*'s, the four men studied the other ship. A ladder had been lowered from the port side, and fuel lines had been connected to the tank cluster, but the hatches remained shut. The lights were on in the command deck windows and side portholes, yet no one could be seen through them. No signs of exterior weapons; no sentries. If the people aboard were waiting it out, they weren't taking any precautions.

"I guess they thought playing possum was enough," Red said. "That was the first clue we had that we were dealing with amateurs."

They had cutting tools, but Red decided that there was an easier way to get aboard. He removed his armor and all his weapons except for a flechette pistol, which he stuck in his belt just above his butt. Then he rolled up his shirt sleeves, took a pad from a trouser pocket, and sauntered through the tunnel to the *Dreamer*. While the rest of the Crew watched, he went up the ladder and pounded a fist against the airlock hatch until it slid open a few inches and a wary face peered out at him.

"A kid... it was just a kid." Red grinned and shook his head, still not quite believing what he was seeing. "I mean, I was expecting another pro, but this guy looked like he'd just learned how to shave. And totally gullible, too. He completely bought it when I told him I was with port authority and there to perform a routine inspection."

"That's all it took to get him to open the hatch?"

"Yup, that's it. And as soon as he did..."

If a flechette pistol a few inches from his face wasn't enough to frighten the kid, then the sight of the Crew as they charged from the tunnel must have scared the crap out of him. Red's team had been having fun with the holo projectors ever since they acquired them for covert work; the images they'd chosen for this job were scanned from stuff they'd found in old movies. So Jack Dog looked like a blue-skinned Plutonian from *The Man from Planet X*, Raphael was a claw-handed alien with a protruding brain from *This Island Earth*, and Breaker was the amphibious monster from *Creature from the Black Lagoon*. He was still staring at them with gape-mouthed astonishment as they charged up the ladder, and probably would have surrendered without a fight even if Breaker hadn't decked him with one punch. The kid bounced off the airlock wall and slid to the floor. The rest was easy.

Ridiculously, stupidly easy. The Crew made their way through the *Dreamer*, rifles raised as they checked one compartment after another. There were three more crew members aboard, and all three were taken by surprise, one at a time. Apparently none of them had anticipated anything like this; they weren't armed, and the guy they found in the head with his pants around his ankles even went down on his knees to beg Jack Dog for his life. It was just pathetic; Jack Dog didn't even bother to hit him, just told him to pull his pants up and stop blubbering.

The *Dreamer*'s captain was having coffee in the rec room with Cosette when the Crew found them. Red expected to find the heiress locked in a stateroom, bound and gagged, possibly ravished, doubtless terrified. Instead, it was if this was an afternoon tea rudely interrupted. She wore a white silk dress that clung to her in a very fetching matter, silver-streaked raven hair flowing halfway down her back, and she looked very much like a young lady who'd have Cozy as her nickname.

Her reaction surprised everyone. They dropped their squeezebulbs as soon as the Crew came through the door, but while the captain immediately held up his hands, Cozy whipped out a taser hidden in a calf holster beneath her dress. She dropped Jack Dog and was about to take down Red as well before he lobbed a stun grenade into the room. Breaker and Raphael dragged Jack Dog from the room – the taser charge had shorted out his projector, making him appear human again – while Red disarmed the girl. Then he waited until she, the captain, and Jack Dog regained their senses.

The captain's name was Morton, Cyril Morton, and he'd alternated between apoplexy and apology: outraged that his ship had been invaded and his crew beaten up – except for the kid in the toilet, who deserved nothing but contempt – but also embarrassed that he'd been caught so easily. Jack Dog put him down on the floor and held a gun to the back of his head while Raphael and Breaker took the girl and – against her will, protesting angrily every step of the way – hustled her out of the *Dreamer* and back to *Sally*.

Red wanted an explanation for all this. By then it had become obvious that, if this was really a kidnapping, it was the lamest in history. But the Crew couldn't afford to stick around; Ceres port authority might get wind of what had happened, and Red didn't want to have to talk his way out of a situation he didn't quite understand himself. Besides, the only person he could count on to for the truth about this alleged abduction was its alleged victim: Cosette Trudeau, the heiress to the Lunar Air fortune.

So he went forward to *Dreamer's* bridge and used a fire extinguisher to batter the instrument panels into junk, thereby making certain Morton wouldn't give them any trouble on the way out. Then he and Jack Dog hurried back to *Sally*, and within minutes, they'd disembarked from Ceres and were headed back out into space.

"And that brings me to you," he said to the man seated behind the lights.

"And so it does," replied Mister Chicago.

Pasquale Chicago stood up from his chair and strolled across the darkened room to where Red McGee sat. Red could see him clearly once he stepped into the light: tall and thin, with the white skin and long platinum hair of an albino.

"As I recall," Mister Chicago went on, "you said she'd told you that I'd kidnapped her. Correct?"

"That's right, yes."

Mister Chicago nodded as he reached into a breast pocket of his black tunic and pulled out a cigar. Red shook his head when it was offered to him, and Mister Chicago clipped the cigar with a tiny gold guillotine and let one of his men light it for him. He took his time, knowing it was his to waste.

"I did not," he said at last, exhaling smoke that became blue haze drifting upward into the light. "Fact is, I barely even know *Ma'moiselle* Trudeau. I've had some dealings with her father in the past, yes, but the last time I saw her, she was barely this tall." His left hand lifted slightly, to the height of his waist. "And abducting her would be... shall we say, bad for business?"

Red nodded. Mister Chicago was known throughout the system as an underworld kingpin, a criminal mastermind who'd managed to become virtually untouchable. It wasn't even certain that Pasquale Chicago was his real name. Rumor had it that he'd once been a senior government official in the Pax Astra treasury before fleeing with a considerable fortune for the outer solar system, where he'd established a permanent residence on the asteroid 4442 Garcia. His organization, the Zodiac, had a hand in every smuggling and black market operation between Venus and Jupiter, but Red had never heard of him kidnapping heiresses for ransom.

"That's what I thought," he said. "To be honest, this sort of thing is beneath you."

A wry smile. "It is... and thank you for giving me the benefit of the doubt." Mister Chicago took a luxurious pull from his cigar. "And even if I had, I wouldn't have used men as amateurish as those you describe."

"We didn't think so either, but..." Red hesitated. "Well, we had to make sure you weren't involved. That's why I sent a message requesting a parlay, and you..."

"Invited you to my home. I prefer to discuss such weighty issues face to face, but nonetheless, I appreciate your taking the effort to travel all this way."

Red was beginning to relax a little, yet he remained on his guard. While *Wormtown Sally* was docked with 4442 Garcia, he and the Crew were at Mister Chicago's mercy, present hospitality notwithstanding. "Only wanted to make certain that we weren't going to have any misunderstandings."

"We don't, but..." Mister Chicago blew a delicate smoke ring at the ceiling. "Nonetheless, we still have an issue that needs to be addressed. Why did she pretend to be abducted, if that is indeed what appears to be the case? And why did she claim that I was responsible?"

Before Red could respond, he turned away, lifting a hand to his face to gently prod his right cheekbone and murmur something under his breath. A subcutaneous comlink connected him to someone outside the room. "Perhaps we should ask dear Cosette herself," he said, turning to Red again.

A few moments went by, then a door silently slid open and two figures were briefly silhouetted against the light from the corridor outside. The door shut once more and Cosette Trudeau was escorted into the luminescent circle by another one of Mister Chicago's henchmen. She wore the standard-issue ship's jumpsuit instead of the silk outfit she'd been wearing on Ceres, but she still looked delectable, if nervous.

"Pasquale..." she began.

"Mister Chicago." His pale eyes seemed to darken as they settled upon her. "It's been many years since we met, Cozy, and I'm afraid you've taken advantage of our brief acquaintance. You have much to explain, my dear."

Her slim shoulders fell and she quickly looked away. "I'm sorry," she said quietly, and the arrogance she'd shown Red aboard *Wormtown Sally* seemed to dissipate. "I thought that if... if I managed to make my way out here, you'd... I hoped you'd want me, that's all."

Red stared at Cosette, not quite believing what he'd just heard. Until now, he'd been impressed with her. Smart enough to fake her own kidnapping, courageous enough to take on four armed men with only a taser, wily enough to try pinning everything on the most successful crime lord in space... and why? A foolish crush on a man she'd met once as a little girl?

"It doesn't make sense," he murmured. "I'm not buying it."

"Neither am I." Mister Chicago dropped his cigar – it fell slowly in 4442 Garcia's low gravity, and one of his minions swooped in to snatch it before it hit the floor – and stepped closer, looking her straight in the eye. "Cozy, my sweet, you're not that stupid. Please don't pretend to be. What were you really trying to do?"

Cosette looked up at him again and slowly let out her breath. "All right, okay," she said, no longer contrite and innocent. "I'll admit it... I was just trying to get away from Papa." Her lovely mouth ticked upward a bit. "And make a little money off him, too."

"Ah. I think I begin to understand." Crossing his arms, Mister Chicago regarded her dispassionately. "You staged your own abduction in hopes that I'd willingly accept the blame for it, provided that your father paid the ransom. And what did you expect me to do? Split the money with you?"

A shrug. "I was thinking fifty-fifty."

"Half a million lox?" Mister Chicago closed his eyes, shook his head. "Do you realize how little a half-million lox means to me? Besides the fact that I'd make an enemy of your father, who supplies me with oxygen along with just about everyone else in the system."

Cosette pouted. "It was only a thought."

"Who were those guys who nabbed you... pretended to nab you, that is?" Red leaned back in his chair. "I'm surprised they were able to get past the bodyguards... you do have bodyguards, I assume."

"I do, but I gave them the night off. And Papa was in Tycho City on business, so I had the house to myself. Except for the servants, and I knew they wouldn't do anything." Cosette hesitated. "The one Breaker punched out in the airlock was a boy I was going with. The other two were his friends. The three of them hired Captain Morton." She looked at Mister

Chicago again. "I hope you're not going to hold anything against them. They were only doing what I asked them to do."

"If your friends can get home on their own, I'll leave them alone. Morton will be informed by the Zodiac that his Ceres docking privileges have been revoked. You've never had much difficulty getting men to do what you want them to, have you?"

A sly grin. "Not really, no." The grin became coy smile as she inched a little closer. "Are you sure you're not interested in having me, Pasquale? I'd be quite... grateful."

Mister Chicago lay a gentle hand on her shoulder, pushed her back to where she'd been standing. "*Ma'moiselle*, I have plenty of girls and boys to amuse me already. And I'm not in the practice of taking in urchins."

The smile vanished and her shoulders sagged again. "Great. Just excellent. Guess that means I'm going to be dragged home."

"What's so bad about that?" Red was genuinely curious. "You've got it pretty well, so far as I can tell. A private lunar estate, more money than you know what to do with, boyfriends who'd crawl across Venus to make you happy..."

"Yeah, right." Her eyes flashed in anger. "Do you realize how boring all that is? I can't go anywhere without Papa's bodyguards, and the places I do go are the same stupid places where the same stupid rich people hang out." She sighed, looked at Mister Chicago again. "You want to know the truth? I didn't particularly want you, either... I just wanted what I thought you be able to offer me. A life that wasn't so goddamn dull."

Mister Chicago didn't say anything for a moment. Tapping a finger against his lips, he regarded her thoughtfully. "Let me ask you something," he said after a moment. "Captain McGee tells me you took out one of his men with one shot."

"Yes, I did." She glanced at Red. "I told Jack Dog I'm sorry, but I'm not sure he's forgiven me."

"He has... he's just embarrassed you got the better of him, that's all." Red caught a sidelong look from Mister Chicago. "Come to think of it, though... where did you learn to shoot like that?

"One of Papa's bodyguards trained me. Not that it was Papa's idea, but... as I said, things get dull, and learning how to use a gun is more interesting than fixing my hair again."

"I see. What else did he teach you?"

"Flechette and particle-beam rifles. Hand-to-hand combat. Basic assault and escape tactics." She smiled. "Men like to do things for me."

"Fascinating." Mister Chicago turned to Red. "I think I have an idea."

"And so do I," Red replied.

Feet propped up on the main console, coffee mug nestled in his lap, Red McGee sat in *Wormtown Sally*'s bridge. Through the bow windows, he saw a lone figure in a moonsuit step through of the Trudeau estate's main airlock and, carrying a shoulder bag, begin walking across the landing pad.

"Prime the engines, Raphael," he said. "I think we're about ready to go."

Raphael Coto grinned as he leaned forward in the co-pilot's seat and began flipping switches. Red pulled out his pad and ran a finger across its screen. He smiled when he saw the Crew's current balance at the Pax Royal Bank. Just as he'd expected, $l1,000,000$ had been transferred to their account from the Lunar Air Company. Antoine Trudeau had met his obligations, just as the Crew had met theirs.

Nonetheless, he wasn't *quite* getting everything that he wanted.

A low hum was passing through the hull as Red got up from his seat and left the bridge. His steps took him down a ladder to *Sally*'s airlock. He arrived just it was cycling through. Jack Dog and Breaker were already there; they waited patiently in the ready room as the inner hatch opened and the person who'd left the crater home stepped through.

Cosette Trudeau had already removed her helmet. She dropped her bag on the deck, took a moment to shake out her hair, then pushed her helmet into the rack and began peeling off her suit. "Hi, guys. Thanks for waiting."

"No problem." Red traded a look with Jack Dog and Breaker. Jack Dog was openly admiring the slinky way she was discarding her suit – no one else could make getting rid of pressure gear look so sexy – while Breaker leaned against a bulkhead, arms crossed, studiously unimpressed. "Any difficulties on your end?"

"Not really. Papa's grateful you got me back from those evil men, but he's also pissed that I'm leaving." An indifferent shrug. "What's he going to do? He's been telling me that I needed to find something to do besides hang around here, so..."

"Joining us probably wasn't what he was expecting."

"Life's full of little surprises." Cozy racked the suit, reached for a pair of stikshoes. "So... do we have another job yet?"

"There's always another job." Jack Dog offered her a hand in putting on the adhesive-soled shoes, and seemed mildly perturbed when she wouldn't let him. "Of course, you'll need get a holo projector. It's one of those kind of..."

"Way ahead of you." Bending down, Cozy unzipped her bag, felt around inside, then produced a projector. "Got one already. Bought it for Halloween last year."

"Yeah, okay, but you still pick a disguise."

Standing up, Cosette ran her fingers across its control menu. "I sort of had one in mind." She grinned. "Ever seen a movie called *Alien*?"

Before anyone could answer, she activated the projector. Red and Jack Dog stepped back in horror, and Breaker nearly bolted through the door.

"Like it?" Cozy asked.

"You're going to fit right in," Red said.

As we close our journey together, David Farland returns to his Golden Queen *novel universe with the tale of Orick, a bear who always wanted to be a priest, and how he stumbles his way into becoming...*

SAINT ORICK

David Farland

"Och, hold it right there!" someone said in a reedy voice. Orick the black bear stopped dead, and squinted, willing his eyes to adjust to the gloom. The only light came from the ancient world gate behind him, a decrepit arch that sported more than its share of cobwebs. As the gate's magenta glow dimmed, the speaker said in a thick brogue, "This world is interdicted! That means: get, your, arse, off our planet!"

Orick could still feel the cold rush that came with walking between worlds, as if some atoms in his stomach had frozen while whisking between the stars.

Before him stood a man who shone dimly, wavering as if he were made of fog. He was small, with thick lamb-chop sideburns. He wore tan breeches and a green vest over a white shirt, and held a meerschaum pipe, a bit of smoke wafting from it. He wasn't human, of course. In his youth, Orick had thought such creatures were wights, but now he knew the truth: they were plasmatic life forms, fields of energy.

Just my luck, Orick thought. *I had to land at night, when the artefs are out.*

He chose his next words carefully. Over the years, thousands of folks on Tihrglas had been absconded by artefs – folks who poked around in forbidden lore, or voiced strange philosophies. Once the artefs dragged someone off, kicking and screaming, the body was never found.

"Actually," Orick objected, "this world isn't interdicted. The colony was founded with a *restricted* status, so it *can* have visitors. Children may come to visit their parents."

The artef frowned, peered at the ground and scratched his head. "That law must be 8,000 years old? I'm sure we fixed that loophole."

Orick was on thin ice. He couldn't visit without the artef's permission.

"Not according to the Republic's records," Orick countered. He mustered courage and said firmly, "Now, give me the road."

The artef stood, dumbfounded, and time seemed to stop, along with Orick's heart.

Overhead, pines brooded, twisted limbs casting black shadows against a night sky bursting with stars. In the distance, frogs croaked beside some limpid forest pool, while moon moths fluttered. The scent here always made Orick feel ancient, as if he had been aging in these woods for thousands of years. The loam of the forest in Coille Sidhe smelled of wild mushrooms and the tang of moldy pine needles, along with the bitter reek of mouse musk. In fact, he could hear mice now, rustling among the detritus, prodding through pine needles for grubs.

The world gate behind Orick strobed like lightning. Tallea burst through.

Orick was suddenly aware of a cobweb tickling his snout, so he licked at it.

Tallea must have gauged the situation instantly. "This pudgy bloke giving you trouble?" she asked.

Orick said, "Naw. He's an artef, sort of a lawman on this world." He introduced Tallea. "This is my wife. She was a lawman on *her* world."

"A plasmoid!" Tallea said as she studied the creature. "Pretty old-school."

The artef scowled. "A lawman? She's a bear!" He drew a thoughtful breath on his pipe. Its smoke gave no scent. Like the man himself, it was merely an energy field, little more than a recording taken from the mind of a man who had died thousands of years before "Two bears," he said, "talking bears, visiting from off-world? What kind of shenanigans would the likes of you be pulling? You wouldn't be carrying any illegal tech, would you? Rayguns? Robots? World demolishers – that sort of thing?"

Orick guffawed, "Do I look like I'm hiding something in my pockets?" He had nothing more than the pelt on his back. Tallea held the key to the world gate in her teeth. She set it down.

The gate was dimming steadily. It was ancient, covered in bas reliefs that could not be seen in the darkness then splotched with lichens in grays and greens. Broken cobwebs hung from its arch in ragged curtains.

"You can't come through," the artef decided. "We don't allow that kind of thing." He stepped forward dangerously.

"Och," Orick said, adopting his thickest brogue, in a mournful tone. "It was only my dear mother I was hoping to see. I'm worried she might be homeless, wintering in a hollow log, filled with slugs and wet, rotting leaves. I wanted to make sure she's taken care of proper, as a good son should. Surely you have a mother, don't you?"

The artef gazed emotionlessly, "Not in a long time." He concluded. "I'm not sure if you're a wise bear, or just a wise ass. But I'll give you the road – for now. I'll have to take this up with the Eldritch Council."

Something in the way that the artef puffed his chest suggested that he was a High Councilor himself, and that unnerved Orick.

The artef warned, "You know our laws. This is a simple world. No tech. We'd outlaw the wheel, but folks keep reinventing it. You'll keep your yaps shut. You'll not talk of worlds beyond this, or anything that will give folks queer notions. I'll not be having you tell your mother – "

"I know," Orick said. "I'll tell her that I've been wandering in 'far places.'" After having visited twenty-six separate worlds, it was close enough to the truth.

The artef nodded, then cocked his head and warned. "I'll be sure that you do."

Orick had come with more in mind than just seeing his mother. He and his wife had been together for four years now, raised two sets of cubs.

But he sometimes felt there was a gap between them, as if he and Tallea didn't quite understand each other. Perhaps by getting to know his world, they might draw closer.

Sunrise brought a bright dawn, with bands of rose-colored clouds on the horizon and a glorious sun that shone more golden than most. In the forest, nuthatches bounded from bough to bough in the vine maples while woodpeckers went to work tapping at the tall pines overhead. The bears padded down the hills to a dirt road, and gamboled along as the day began.

It was late summer, and blackberries were ripe on the vines, so Orick and Tallea stopped at a thicket beside a stream to forage for sweet, heavy berries. Orick had eaten berries on several worlds, but none tasted as good as these.

After dozens of mouthfuls, Tallea's stomach grumbled. "Uh, oh," she said. "Do these things give you the runs?"

"An unfortunate side-effect of having only berries for breakfast." Down in the grass, Orick spotted a pair of large slugs as yellow as buttercups. "Here, have a little protein. He snapped one up, took the other in his teeth, and then dropped it at Tallea's feet. Tallea sniffed at it with a crinkled snout.

"Banana slug, for dessert," Orick urged.

She studied his face, questioning, then bobbed her head and gripped it in her teeth. She chewed it a few times, gulped. "That's a surprise," she said. She ruffled her lower lip thoughtfully then snuffled through the brush, searching for another. Tallea had been human once, before she'd downloaded her memories into the body of a bear, so she'd never dined on slug until now.

"If you see a big brown one," Orick suggested, "try it. The best ones are down among the sweet clover. They're all juicy fat, no muscle."

Tallea grinned appreciatively. "And no bones to choke on. It's a good thing that the humans don't know how tasty they are."

"Och, to be sure," Orick said, "Tis a high treat. I got my friend Gallen to try one once, but he didn't care for it. Maybe because he over-cooked it."

Orick wished that the salmon were running in the streams. He'd show her a feast, then.

However, nature suddenly called, and he realized that he had to poop. He strolled behind a large fern and squatted.

"I have a saying," he said. "Leave every world better than you find it. Of course," he grunted, "with this world, there's not much that we can do to improve it." He finished then scratched the dirt with his back paws in order to cover the offending pile. He pronounced a blessing on his dung in mock solemnity. "You have been carried from far worlds at great price. May you make this planet even more fertile than it has been. Yea, may a veritable Garden of Eden spring from – "

A twig snapped. Orick glanced into the shadows of the woods. A shimmering green light flitted in the deep shadows, followed by one in blue. They disappeared into the pines.

Artefs. At least two. Orick's heart surged. Hackles rose on the back of his neck.

"Don't stare," Tallea whispered. "They've been following us all night."

No good will come of this, Orick realized.

It wasn't him that he was worried about. It was Tallea. She was as fierce a warrior as he had ever known, but no one had escaped the artefs. He didn't know if they could be killed. He knew that they hid from the sun, for it emitted radio waves that could stun and confuse them.

Orick whispered, "What are they, exactly?"

"Stabilized energy fields," Tallea explained. "Like robots, made from energy... The physics is far beyond anything I can understand."

He said hopefully, "They can't follow us much longer. They can't endure the sun, so they'll go underground."

"They're tricky," Tallea warned. "Stay spry."

Long before they arrived at the village of Clere, Orick heard the welcome sounds of it. The distant laughter of children rang through the trees, along with the thunk of a peasant chopping wood, and the squeals of pigs.

As they came into the village proper, Tallea chuckled in delight. It was dressed for celebration.

Like all human villages on this world, Clere had a quaint charm. It was situated among a grove of "house trees," plants genetically engineered to grow with fat hollow trunks down low and leafy branches above. As the trees grew, parts of the exterior trunk would thin and the bark would attenuate, so that rooms and doorways and windows would form almost at random.

The doors were all painted in intense colors – canary and violet and titanium white – while the windows had flower boxes beneath them filled with honeysuckle, begonias and giant colorful daisies.

But it wasn't the homes that held the eye – it was the decorations. The trees had been festooned with streamers of cardinal with silver trim and hung with giant paper lanterns in a riot of hues. The house trees were in bloom, with golden flowers as large as plates.

"Why, it's Saint Paddy's Day!" Orick exclaimed. That would mean feasting and games during the day and drunken revelry at night.

He inhaled deeply, relishing the scent of wood smoke, and horse manure, and brown bread baking at Mahoney's Inn.

After four years, it felt good to be home. He loved the sight of a goat cart pulling a load of turnips, and a black banty rooster racing around the streets, chasing the dun-colored hens. He loved the rope swing down by the river, and the lush vegetable gardens between the houses.

Most of all, he loved the sight of children playing. A gaggle raced about with sticks in hand, wiggling them down in the grass. They were playing, "Drive out the snakes." There were no serpents on Tihrglas, so none of the children had ever seen one, but they each had a long limb, thinner than a broomstick, and on the end was a short piece of string. Feather boas were tied to this, each dyed in bright colors, in order to create fanciful snakes in crimsons and gold, or blacks and midnight blues. Each snake had an elongated forked tongue, while buttons were sewn on for eyes.

They were evil-looking things, for the Good Book said that serpents were subtle and dishonest creatures, servants of the devil.

Orick had been sorely disappointed to find snakes on other worlds and learn that they weren't much more than scale-covered worms.

And so the children waved their sticks near the ground, making their feathered serpents wriggle about, uttering threats and trying to scare others

"What's a Saint Paddy's Day?" Tallea asked. On her world, she'd learned nothing of God or saints. Orick put up with her heathen ways.

"A feast day," Orick said. He'd researched Saint Paddy on other worlds, and legends all varied, but he told it now as he had learned it here in his youth. "Saint Paddy was the greatest of all saints, one of Jesus' apostles, sort of his right-hand man. He was kidnapped in his youth, and carried to an island. He was such a righteous warrior, the cherubim gave him a flaming sword, and he converted entire nations. Then, he drove all of the snakes from the Tihrglas, and when they reached the sea, he walked all the way across the ocean until he got home."

Tallea raised her brow, incredulous as ever, but wisely held her tongue. Suddenly, a fiddle struck up in the distance.

"Sounds like the party has begun," Orick said.

On the far side of the town, at the "party green," the grass had been mowed short, and a feast was in the making. Tables were loaded with cut watermelons and green Saint Paddy cakes, while whole lambs were roasting over spits.

It was a glorious celebration indeed. Most of the revelers were human, though a couple of other bears had caught wind of the feast and dropped by. As always, the "bear-folks" were welcome.

Orick didn't give his real name. In the past four years, he had matured – grown large and into his prime. No one seemed to recognize him, so he went by the name of Guy, and his disguise was complete. It is said that to humans, all bears look alike. In this case, it seemed to be true.

The day was spent amid sporting events.

Young folks swam in the river that morning, racing to the far side and back, and then the boys engaged in boxing matches while still in their bathing suits. There was tree climbing for children, and games of "find Paddy's candy," where toddlers searched for treats and toys in the chapel.

While the young ones sported, the townsfolk spent most of their time in gossip. Eventually the topic turned to Gallen O'Day and the strange happenings here four years earlier, when the trolls came to town and killed the local priest. But it was old news.

"Such a lot of hullabaloo," said Father McGinty. "I heard about it at the seminary. I would sure love to see a troll, now."

A young woman ventured, "Had you been here, I'm sure that you'd have been able to cast the demons out of town." She was all teeth and smiles, and it seemed obvious that she was fond of the priest.

Some people get itches that can never be scratched.

Orick considered, *If I had stayed here and studied for the priesthood, that could be me wearing the frock.* A part of him mourned for the simple life that he had lost.

By lunch, folks were dining on lamb basted in plums and mint sauce, roasted corn fresh from the gardens, cucumber salads, the inn's buckwheat rolls, bread pudding, and other delectable fare – all of it decreed by tradition older than time.

The afternoon was spent in gossip, sleeping under the trees, and listening to a war of the bands. There were harpers galore, along with lutists and bagpipe players and fiddlers and men banging on huge war drums.

Tallea encouraged Orick to sing a song himself, and in his rich baritone he took the open stage, stood, and recalled a song he'd once heard on the world of Rothmore.

To Orick, it summed up his battles against the Dronon Empire,

insectoids that had plagued the galaxy. It told of the war he'd helped
Gallen win, and of the peace that eluded him.

> *The day is done, the battle o'er.*
> *Peace is won forever more.*
>
> *A bit like heaven, a bit like hell.*
> *We fought well, men died well.*
>
> *My brother's gone, but I remain.*
> *To take his glory, in secret shame.*
>
> *The day is done the war is o'er,*
> *And I'll know peace, never more.*

Near the end of the song, Orick choked up. The lutist and the piper
trailed off for the last line, and let Orick sing A Cappella.

The audience fell silent, and many were in tears.

Later, the judges announced the winner of the battle of the bands:
Orick. The award consisted of a badge, which the mayor pinned to Orick's
chest, along with a sizeable cash pot. Orick had no use for money. "Give
it to the church," he told them. "I'm sure that Father McGinty will find a
good use for it."

After that, a crowd gathered as folks came to clap Orick on the back.
He stood, beaming, and became a bit tongue-tied. He introduced Tallea as
his "bride," and there was more clapping on the back, mixed with cheers
and "Congratulations." Somehow, everyone assumed that they were
newlyweds, and Orick didn't dare correct them.

The mayor, a short man who wore a maroon coat with tails, bustled
up with gifts: a loaf of rye bread, a bottle of wine, and a pregnant tabby cat,
fat with kittens.

When Orick stood and held the cat up in one paw for everyone to
see, she mewed plaintively indeed, as if she feared that Orick would
eat her.

Much to Orick's surprise, folks in the crowd introduced themselves and suggested that Orick and Tallea move to Clere. There was a fine old house tree to spare on the edge of town, and they were welcome to it.

Orick found himself overwhelmed by such shows of generosity. In all of his travels, on all of the worlds he had visited, he'd never felt such hospitality. He glanced over at Tallea, and saw sadness in her eyes.

She knew that they couldn't stay.

That evening there was more food and dancing. Sean Mahoney stopped by from the inn and offered Orick and Tallea his "bridal suite" for the night.

Yet Orick was eager to be on his way. When bears grow old, they often go blind with age. He wanted his mother to see Tallea, to share a little of the joy that she'd given him. Orick had been his mother's only cub, and he needed to tell her that she had grandchildren, to let her know that her life had not... been fruitless.

So he looked to Tallea, and she said softly, affecting the local brogue, "Can we stay... just for one night?"

He could tell by her tone that she was falling in love with the town of Clere.

Orick accepted the kind offer.

After the dinner feasting, as the sun fell low in a windless sky, and the heavens purpled and first stars began shining, the townsfolk lit the colored lanterns under the trees, and they spent the night in slow dances. The gentle music lured the weary children asleep, and people filed off until few were left in the field.

As they swayed to the music, Tallea whispered into Orick's ear, "You were right. It's a lot like heaven."

"Aye, that it is," Orick agreed.

"Why the cat?" she wondered.

"It's tradition," he said. "Every house needs a cat, to keep down the mice. And a pregnant cat – well, she gives you plenty of mousers."

Tallea laughed softly. "This whole planet smells... mousey. Saint Paddy did you no favors, when he drove off your snakes."

"Really?" Orick wondered. "You mean snakes eat mice?"

"Aye, they're good at that. A snake can wriggle down into their burrows, root them out."

They finished the dance, and headed toward the inn. It was built in an ancient house tree, hoary with age, and had grown a remarkable seven bedrooms in the upper story. The lower common room had a nice stone hearth, and a bar that held dozens of patrons.

The party still seemed to be in full swing as they neared the inn, which had silver streamers hanging in its branches, along with enormous paper lanterns like worlds of blue and gold.

Orick glanced to the edge of the green, and saw a pair of dark lumps hopping through the shadows toward the inn: rats.

He sniffed. Tallea was right. There was the bitter tang of mouse musk in the air. He'd always thought of it as the "smell of home," but realized now just how infested this place was.

Suddenly, a lone fellow stepped from the shadows, the hood of his robe pulled low over his eyes. As he drew his sword, he said in a rough voice, "Stand and deliver!"

Tihrglas was lousy with highwaymen. The sight of one hardly got Orick's pulse racing, not after all the things that he had been through.

"You'll not make a living robbing bears," Orick said. "Or is it drunk you are – too damned drunk to tell what species we are?"

The highwayman peered about, as if searching for witnesses, then pulled back his hood.

A young man stood there, with pimples on his face and stringy blonde hair. He grinned widely. "Orick, it's me – Race O'Mally. You don't really think your old friends would be forgetting you?"

Orick laughed. Race had been working at the inn for as long as Orick could remember.

Orick rose up, and gave the lad a bear hug, crushing him until ribs popped. Race laughed.

"I knew it was you as soon as I laid eyes on ya," Race said. "You've grown, but that ugly muzzle hasn't changed a bit."

"Aye," Orick said, "and you've filled out, too."

"I'm married now," Race said. "I've got a daughter even."

"Someone was desperate enough to marry you?" Orick said in mock disbelief. "She must be ugly, or maybe weak in the brain."

"No, she's a looker, and smarter than both of us put together. She's got personality, too. I can't figure out what she sees in me."

"You've got a fine heart," Orick said, and that was true. Race didn't just work in the inn, he saw to people's needs, and he anticipated them before they did.

"What happened to you?" Race hissed, still glancing into the darkness. "When you and Gallen left, where did you go?"

"Oh, you know, traveling to faraway places."

Race focused tight on Orick. "You left this world. I *know* it. I followed your tracks afterward, and they took me into Coille Sidhe, into the darkest heart of the woods, to Geata na Chruinne – the Gate of the World. You stepped under the gate, and you never came out."

It wasn't a statement exactly. It was almost a question. The young lad was quivering with excitement

"I can't talk about where I've been," Orick said.

"Yet you've been to other worlds. I know it! I... I spoke with my wife. I want to come with you when you leave."

"Oh, lad," Orick said sadly. "Once you leave, there's no coming back."

Race smiled victoriously, a grin spreading across his face. "I knew it. I knew it. There really is life on other worlds."

"Life, and death," Orick agreed.

A twig snapped in the shadows under the trees, and Orick spotted another cowled figure – a woman. Race's wife stumbled forward a bit, and she stood bouncing her newborn babe in her arms. "We both want to go. I know others who will want to go, too."

From the shadows came a voice, "Oh, lass, you're in more than a wee bit of trouble here."

The artef came around the corner of the building, sporting his lamb-chop sideburns and holding his pipe. His eyes smoldered. He didn't walk like a regular man, but instead seemed to float in the air.

Orick's heart froze.

The artef looked toward the young woman, a pitiless gaze in his eyes. The creature showed no emotion, had none. He was more like a machine.

"Come," the artef said, and two more artefs rounded the tree.

Their leader stared hard at Orick. "You should never have come back here, lad."

"Let them go," Orick pleaded. "They've done nothing wrong. They only ask to leave."

"'Tis a pity," the artef said. "That carries a death penalty."

"We'll leave," Orick said. "We'll never come back."

"Who knows how many other folks in town recognized you," the artef said. He stepped toward Orick, and as he did, he expanded, growing taller so that he reached nearly twice the height of a man. "What queer notions might other townsfolk be hiding? You're a plague, master bear, an illness, and all that you've touched must be burned away."

In that instance, the artef lurched toward Race's wife. She turned to run, but the artef caught her shoulder, and he blazed, actinic lights flashing.

Smoke and fire filled the air, and Orick was momentarily blind. Orick smelled the woman's flesh sizzle. She shrieked and tried to flee.

Race shouted and leapt to his wife's aid, but the other two artefs caught him, one on each arm, and they blazed too, flashing red like whirling fires while golden sparks leapt from them.

Smoke roiled from human skin, along with the reek of cooking meat.

Tallea made a "whuff" as she charged the artefs, and Orick shouted, "No!"

But in the last second she leapt incredibly high. Orick had never seen a bear leap like that, though he recalled how Tallea had jumped when still in human form. At the height of her arc, she caught a silver streamer and brought it down in her teeth, then bit the lead artef.

The creature shrieked and shrank in size, tried to flee.

329

She bowled past the other artefs, carrying the streamer in her mouth. As she bit into a second artef, sparks flashed from the streamer. The last artef yelped and sped away, racing into the woods.

But Tallea circled the two artefs wrapping them in silver foil, as if in chains. The transformation that overcame them was astonishing, for one moment, they looked like men, and the next their noses and chins twisted and bent like melting wax. Dents appeared in their faces. The artefs cried incoherently and tried to run, but their legs melted like butter in the hot sun, and they floundered.

Tallea yanked the silver streamer tightly around the creatures.

Soon, the artefs lost all human form, becoming puddles on the ground, like magma boiling within a volcano.

Orick rushed over to Race, found that his skin was badly burned where the artefs had touched him. His wife had fared worse. Her left arm was a grisly mess. The fire had all but burned through the bone. There was surprisingly little blood, for the wound was cauterized. Here on Tihrglas, she'd soon get gangrene.

But on most worlds, re-growing flesh and skin would take only a few weeks. He had to get her off planet.

Fortunately, the baby had not been touched.

Folks had heard the screaming, and now they began to stumble from the inn, or open the windows in their house trees.

Orick peered at Tallea. "What did you do?"

"Long radio waves," Tallea explained. "They interfere with an artef's thoughts, make them stupid. On a backwater world like this, the only radio waves are emitted by the sun during the day, but there are plenty of them bouncing off the ionosphere, even at night. So I used the silver foil in the streamer to create an antenna."

Orick had only the vaguest notion of what she was talking about, but it sounded good. "Och, my sweet, smart wife."

Orick's escape from Tihrglas was made by the heat of the day, when the sun shone its fiercest, and the artefs abandoned even the darkest recesses of Coille Sidhe.

Orick and his friends simply walked out, with Orick hooked up to a goat cart that held Race O'Mally's family.

Orick took his few refugees to a planet called Dobsinfree, a pleasant place ruled by a council of kindly Bocks – treelike creatures that had been engineered from humans. The tech level was high on Dobsinfree, but not so high as to leave a bear baffled.

Tallea woke the next morning to find that Orick was not in bed at their hotel. She went out into the sunlight, a strange red sun made the morning sky especially glorious, dying everything in rose, and found him standing up, walking carefully, aiming a strange device that looked vaguely like a gun into a pile of rocks and bushes.

"What are you after doing?" she asked, coming close.

"The artefs gave me an idea," Orick said. "They asked if we had any rayguns, and I wondered why they're so afraid of them. Did you know that every creature creates an electric field – not just the artefs? And if you hit a creature with just the right amperage, the charge can cause the creature pain, or even disable it?"

"Of course," Tallea answered. "Such weapons are banned on most worlds."

"Well, it got me wondering about Saint Paddy..." Orick said. Tallea walked around the rock, and found out what he was doing.

Down on the ground, herded into a pile, were half a dozen angry-looking gopher snakes.

Within a week, Orick went to visit his mother. He didn't go with empty paws this time. He took her a gift – a pregnant gopher snake, and he made sure to spread dozens more across Tihrglas. His mother was delighted by the visit, and even more delighted by the holos that he showed her of her grandchildren, and of some of the worlds that one could visit if they stepped through the arches at Geata na Chruinne.

He left a gift near the gate – a powerful radio transmitter that destroyed every artef within a hundred miles. It wasn't like killing people, after all. It was more like turning off a light.

But Orick, being Orick, had to justify what he did.

"Some people like to live in the past," he told his mother, "while others put more hope in the future. The folks who created Tihrglas had a right to cling to the past, but they didn't have the right to damn their children to it, for all of the future."

So he left the world gate open, and told a few folks how to use it, and soon there were odd folks – inventors, the curious, those seeking their own ideas of paradise – who dared to walk into someone else's dream of the future.

Orick never returned home to Tihrglas after that, but he was long remembered. Soon tales spread of a bear who never did join the priesthood, but in time became known as Good Saint Orick, who drove the snakes *back* to Tihrglas, and put an end to the infestation of mice.

A memorial was put up in his honor in the town square at Clere, a statue with a few words carved into its base of white granite: "Leave the world better than you found it."

THE LEGEND OF RAE RAYGUN

Legend tells of a hallowed gun
And the lass who slung it, Rae Raygun.

Her story ends in just one way:
A blaze of glory at the end of the day.

But the telling of whereby and thereby and such
Could drain a bar's stores and only have scratched

The thousands of planets she's said to hail from
Where she's lauded a hero bested by none.

A princess, an orphan, a waif on the run
A sailor, a soldier, a spy, or a nun –

And wherever, whenever, however she comes,
She comes with that hallowed gun.

At the end of the day, it ends just the same –
The gun in both hands, her eyes all aflame

I know, I was there, and would like to have done
But the story's the thing, it has to live on.

And on goes the torch, that symbol of right
That inexhaustible fount of justified might

And so here you are, your story's your own
But I've got that gun, and the songs can go on:

Something somewhere's some horrible wrong,
And we need you there, in front of the throng.

It's the end of the night, the beginning of day;
so step yourself up and enter the fray...

It'll all end the same but the end's never done:
say you'll be Rae, the lass with the gun.

Kaolin Fire

Acknowledgements

First, thanks must go to Camille Gooderham Campbell, Jordan Ellinger and Steven Smethurst of Every Day Publishing for giving me the opportunity to do a project like this. And, along those lines, I must also thank *Ray Gun Revival* overlords/founders Johne Cook, L.S. King and Paul Christian Glenn, on whose vision and work I piggybacked a bit. It's not easy to let someone else carry on with something so precious, but in the end, I think we came up with something all of us can own and be proud of. Not just theirs, it's also mine and EDP's and, I hope, the start to new opportunities for all of us.

In the end, though, all errors and mistakes are mine and the authors', although we've done our best to eliminate them, of course. And in that regard, here are some people who have helped with that process:

Thanks to a great group of writers, headlined by Seanan McGuire, Mike Resnick, Kristine Kathryn Rusch, Allen M. Steele, Robin Wayne Bailey, David Farland, Brenda Cooper, Sarah A. Hoyt, and A.C. Crispin, who despite a difficult battle with cancer, pushed herself to write and revise her story for us. I grew up reading books by A.C., and I can't say enough how honored I am to get to work with her. Thanks to you all and the rest for trusting me with your stories, even when I pushed you to polish stuff that had already been printed once. It was all about making it the best it can be and I'm sure readers will reward the efforts.

Thanks to Paul Pedersen for blowing us away with an awesome cover. We knew you could do fantasy but had no idea what you'd do with science fiction. You far exceeded our expectations, and I am so thrilled to have this cover on a book that bears my name. You're just getting started. Here's to many great successes ahead.

Thanks to our Kickstarter backers for their faithful support, enthusiasm, and belief. We hope the result of your sacrifice will be something you treasure as much as we do.

Thanks to fellow editors Alex Shvartsman, Cat Rambo, Ellen Datlow, Rich Horton, Paula Guran, Gardner Dozois, Jennifer Brozek and David Lee Summers who have always been free with their advice and support.

Thanks to all those who introduced me to space opera and the authors who paved the way. Especially my childhood favorites Alan Dean Foster, A.C. Crispin, James Blish, C.S. Lewis, and Robert Silverberg. Their work continues to inspire me, and I met so many other fine authors thanks to their own mentions of their inspirations and favorites.

Thanks to EE "Doc" Smith for inventing space opera with "The Skylark of Space."

Thanks to Camille for doing a great job organizing, handling legal stuff, and making a really good looking book out of all our disparate parts. She cheered me on through many trials, from the stresses of the Kickstarter wait, to selecting stories, and more. This book is in many ways hers as much as mine or any author's. Camille, it's an honor to call you friend, and I'm so glad we got to work together. Let's do it again.

Last, but not least, thanks to my two little buddies, Louie and Amelie, who keep me laughing, smiling, and going with their devotion and love even when I'm exhausted. Man's best friends indeed.

Bryan Thomas Schmidt

About the Editor

BRYAN THOMAS SCHMIDT *is an author and editor of adult and children's speculative fiction. His debut novel,* The Worker Prince *(2011) received Honorable Mention on Barnes & Noble Book Club's Year's Best Science Fiction Releases for 2011. A sequel,* The Returning, *followed in 2012 and* The Exodus *will appear in 2014, completing the space opera* Saga Of Davi Rhii. *His first children's books,* 102 More Hilarious Dinosaur Jokes For Kids *and* Abraham Lincoln: Dinosaur Hunter—Land Of Legends *released in 2012 and 2013 from Delabarre Publishing. His short stories have appeared in magazines, anthologies and online. In addition to* Raygun Chronicles: Space Opera For a New Age, *he edited the anthologies* Space Battles: Full Throttle Space Tales #6 (2012), Beyond The Sun (2013) *and is working on* Shattered Shields, *a military fantasy anthology with co-editor Jennifer Brozek for Baen Books in 2014. He hosts #sffwrtcht (Science Fiction & Fantasy Writer's Chat) Wednesdays at 9 pm ET on Twitter as @BryanThomasS.*

About the Cover Artist

PAUL PEDERSON *was born August 11, 1980, in Bessemer, Alabama and raised in St. Augustine, Florida (the oldest city in the nation). Art and history were prominent features in the small tourist town and had a tremendous influence on him. From an early age, he loved to draw and paint. Paul and his older brothers were always fascinated with works of fantasy and science fiction. Subsequently, he leaned more towards fantasy illustrations. Paul's parents established a private school known as Taldeve (Talent Development) School of the Arts that Paul attended through middle school and high school. This gave him the rare opportunity to study one-on-one under professional artists in the North Florida area. After high school Paul moved to Australia for two years spending much of his time learning the Aboriginal culture and doing freelance art. He later studied Art and Design at Dixie State College and has worked for over ten years as a Graphic Designer, painting murals, and doing illustrations. He currently resides in Salt Lake City, Utah and can be found online at www.paulpederson.com.*

About the Contributors

in alphabetical order

A life-long science fiction reader, LOU ANTONELLI's first story was published in 2003 when he was 46. Since then he has had 80 short stories published in the U.S., U.K., Canada and Australia in venues such as Asimov's Science Fiction, Jim Baen's Universe, Dark Recesses, Andromeda Spaceways In-Flight Magazine, Greatest Uncommon Denominator (GUD), and Daily Science Fiction, among others. He has received honorable mentions in The Year's Best Science Fiction edited by Gardner Dozois in 2010, 2008, 2006, 2005 and 2004. His steampunk short story, "A Rocket for the Republic", was the last story accepted by Dozois before he retired as editor of Asimov's Science Fiction after 19 years. Published in Asimov's in September 2005, placed third in the annual Readers' Poll. His collections include Fantastic Texas published in 2009 and Texas & Other Planets published in 2010. A collection of collaborative short stories co-authored with Oregon-based author Edward Morris, Music for Four Hands, was published in 2011. He is a professional journalist and the managing editor of The Daily Tribune in Mount Pleasant, Texas.

ROBIN WAYNE BAILEY is the author of numerous novels, including the bestselling Dragonkin series, the Frost saga, Shadowdance and the Fritz Leiber-inspired Swords Against The Shadowland. He's written over one hundred short stories, many of which are included in his two collections, Turn Left To Tomorrow and The Fantastikon: Tales Of Wonder. He is a former president of the Science Fiction and Fantasy Writers of America and was a 2008 Nebula Award nominee. He lives in Kansas City, Missouri.

KEANAN BRAND grew up on the West Coast then the South, attended college in Missouri, and now resides in Oklahoma. Writing under another name, Brand also produces fantasy, general fiction, and poetry. He keeps an intermittent blog, Adventures in Fiction (keananbrand.wordpress.com), covering life, the writing process, the occasional book or movie review. He is also a freelance editor, and an *associate fiction editor for an independent press.* Thieves' Honor *is Brand's first long-form science fiction endeavor, originally serialized in* Ray Gun Revival *and now available on the blog. A short experimental work ("At the end of Time, When the World Was New") was the last story in the final issue of* Dragons, Knights & Angels, *and remains one of his favorites. But that's probably because story and author are both a bit sideways.*

JENNIFER CAMPBELL-HICKS *is a writer, journalist, wife, mother and lifelong science-fiction fan who lives in Colorado. Her fiction has appeared or is forthcoming in* Daily Science Fiction, Fireside Magazine, Abyss & Apex *and many other magazines and anthologies. She blogs at jennifercampbellhicks.blogspot.com.*

JOHNE COOK *is a technical writer by day and creative writer/editor at night. His interests include prog rock, film noir, space opera, and racquetball. His short fiction has appeared in* Deep Magic, The Sword Review, Wayfarer's Journal, *and* Digital Dragon *magazines. In 2006, with L. S. King and Paul Christian Glenn, Johne founded* Ray Gun Revival *magazine, devoted to space opera and golden age sci-fi. They refer to themselves collectively as the Overlords, and are often vaporizing someone's puny planet for various arbitrary infractions.*

BRENDA COOPER *has published fiction in* Analog, Oceans of the Mind, Nature, *and in multiple anthologies. Her most recent novel is* The Diamond Deep, *from Pyr. By day, she is the City of Kirkland's CIO, and at night and in early morning hours, she's a futurist and writer. See more at www.brenda-cooper.com.*

A.C. CRISPIN *is the author of the bestselling* Star Wars Han Solo *trilogy and four top-selling* Star Trek *novels as well as the 1984 novelization of the television miniseries* V *and two follow ups in that series. Crispin and noted fantasy author Andre Norton wrote two* Witch World *novels together. In her own original universes, her major science fiction undertaking was the StarBridge series for Berkley/Putnam, centering around a school for young diplomats, translators and explorers, both alien and human, located on an asteroid far from Earth. StarBridge Book One was placed on the American Library Association's Young Adult Services Division's list of Best Books of 1991, and* Silent Dances *(Book Two, co-authored with Kathleen O'Malley) made the 1991 Preliminary ballot for the Nebula. Her newest work is an original fantasy trilogy for Harper/Eos,* The Exiles of Boq'urain, *and the first tie-in novel for Disney's* Pirates Of The Carribbean, The Price Of Freedom. *In recognition of her outstanding work, The International Association of Media Tie-In Writers named her Grand Master earlier this year. She can be found online as @anncrispin on Twitter or via her website at www.accrispin.com. Miss Crispin sadly passed away in September 2013.*

DAVID FARLAND *is a New York Times bestselling author with over 50 novel-length works to his credit. His lastest novel,* Nightingale, *won the International Book Award for Best Young Adult Novel, the Next Gen Award, the Global E-Book Award, and the Hollywood Book Festival Award for Best Novel of the Year. This tale, "Saint Orick," is set in the world of his popular* Golden Queen Series. *Dave says, "For years now, I've wanted to write more about the adventures of Orick, a genetically engineered bear living in the far future. Hope you love it!"*

SHAUN FARRELL *interviewed science fiction and fantasy professionals for 8 years at Far Sector SFFH and the Parsec Award winning* Adventures in Scifi Publishing *podcast. His nonfiction has been published in* Clarkesworld, Strange Horizons, Gateworld *and other non-genre publications. "Conversion" was his first short story sale some 6 years ago... he hopes it doesn't show! Shaun recently retired from* Adventures in Scifi Publishing *to focus on ministry, his two beautiful children and supporting wife, and his writing. He also helps people buy and sell homes in the Sacramento area. To learn more about Shaun, please visit www.facebook.com/ shaunfarrellrealestate.*

KAOLIN FIRE *is a conglomeration of ideas, side projects, and experiments. Outside of his primary occupation, he also develops computer games for desktop, iPhone, and iPad; does cover art and design; and very occasionally teaches computer science. At six months old, his latest project is teaching him more about the nature of existence than he imagined. Kaolin graduated with his Bachelors in Electrical Engineering and Computer Science from UC Berkeley, with a specialization in Bioelectrical Engineering. He dreams of androids dreaming.*

MILO JAMES FOWLER *is a teacher by day, speculative fictioneer by night, and an active SFWA member. His work has appeared in* AE Science Fiction, Cosmos,

Daily Science Fiction, Nature, *and* Shimmer, *and many of his stories are now available wherever eBooks are sold. Learn more at www.milojamesfowler.com.*

SARAH A. HOYT *was born in Portugal (where her birth family still lives) and English is her third language (second is French). This possibly explains why she's on the kill-list of most copy editors. To avoid them, she lives high and dry in Colorado with her husband, two sons and a variable clowder of cats, reading and writing, with an occasional leitmotif of pastel painting, sewing or carpentry thrown in when someone complains she's been at the keyboard too long. Her most recent books are* A Few Good Men *and* Noah's Boy *from Baen books, and upcoming* Night Shifters, Through Fire, *and* Darkship Revenge, *also from Baen books, along with indie* Witchfinder, *a Regency fantasy.*

T. M. HUNTER *has always had a fascination with travel to other worlds, earning a B. S. in Aerospace Engineering from the University of Kansas. His works have often been compared to the great pulp writers of the past, which made his multiple appearances in* Ray Gun Revival *seem almost destined. He mainly writes in his Aston West universe, with three novels in the series (*Heroes Die Young, Friends In Deed *and* Death Brings Victory*) and a novella,* Seeker. *His short stories have been featured in various online magazines and in several short story collections (including the* Dead or Alive *collection from ResAliens Press). T. M. Hunter currently lives in Wichita, Kansas with his wife and their two feline masters, also known as the demon-spawn. Find out more about his body of work at AstonWest.com.*

ROB MANCEBO *keeps churning up stories out of the endless landfill of his brain. In particular, he likes to take actual bits of history and project them out into the future, then see where it takes him. His stories have appeared in* Ray Gun Revival, Heroic Fantasy Quarterly, *and the anthology* Rage Of The Behemoth, *among others. His novel* Born To Trouble, *a shoot-em-up Western, is out from Eternal Press.*

SEANAN McGUIRE *writes things constantly, and has done so since she was very young, resulting in a truly daunting number of letters sent home by teachers who wanted her to pay attention. Luckily for her, she grew up to be a writer, where writing things is basically required. She has written several books, and even more short stories, and shows no signs of stopping. Seanan lives on the Pacific Coast with three large blue cats, a lot of books, and her machete collection. You can keep up with her at www.seananmcguire.com. Seanan doesn't really sleep.*

MICHAEL MERRIAM, *an author of speculative fiction and spoken-word performer living in Hopkins, MN, has published two novels, two short story collections, three single-title novellas, over 80 pieces of short fiction and poetry, and edited two anthologies. His novella,* Should We Drown in Feathered Sleep, *was long-listed for the Nebula Award in 2010, and his novel,* Last Car to Annwn Station *was named a Top Book in 2011 by Readings in Lesbian & Bisexual Women's Fiction. A working actor and storyteller, Michael is also the co-organizer of the Minnesota Speculative Fiction Writers and a member of the Artists with Disabilities Alliance, the Steampunk Artists and Writers Guild, and Story Arts Minnesota. Visit his homepage at www.michaelmerriam.net.*

MIKE RESNICK *is, according to* Locus, *the all-time leading award winner, living or dead, for short science fiction. He is the winner of five Hugos, a Nebula, and other major awards in the United States, France, Spain, Japan, Croatia and Poland, and has been short-listed for major awards in England, Italy and Australia. He is the author of 68 novels, over 250 stories, and 2 screenplays, and is the editor of 41 anthologies. His work has been translated into 25 languages. He was the Guest of Honor at the 2012 Worldcon and can be found online as @ResnickMike on Twitter or at www.mikeresnick.com.*

MICHAEL S. ROBERTS *lives on a sailboat with his wife of 20-plus years. Unlike most authors, they have no cats. Or air conditioning. His hot stories have appeared in* Ray Gun Revival *and some old college papers, if you can find them.*

ALICE M. ROELKE *has been writing since the age of eight in various genres but got her start in the publishing world with a fiction contest win in the Young Salvationist Creativity Contest for teenagers. Alice enjoys writing science fiction, fantasy, children's fiction, YA, romance, short stories, and more. She can always be found at work on a current story. Her fiction has so far been published by Young Salvationist,*

About the Contributors

GateWay S-F, Ray Gun Revival, Tower of Light Fantasy, Wayfarer's Journal, Haruah: Breath of Heaven, Mindflights, Residential Aliens, Stories That Lift, *Whortleberry Press*, Ethereal Tales, Every Day Fiction, Digital Dragon Magazine, Daily Science Fiction, The Nonsense Society, *and MuseItUp Publishing. Alice's Author page on Amazon is www.amazon.com/A.M.-Roelke/e/B00A2AV9BW.*

KRISTINE KATHRYN RUSCH *has won awards in every genre for her work. She has several pen names, including Kris Nelscott for mystery and Kristine Grayson for romance. She's writing two different science fiction series,* The Retrieval Artist *and the space opera* Diving *series. Her next novel, the standalone* Snipers, *a time-travel thriller, appeared in July, followed by* Skirmishes, *the next* Diving *novel, in August. WMG Publishing is releasing her entire backlist. She's also editing the anthology series* Fiction River. *For more on her work, go to kristinekathrynrusch.com.*

JENNY SCHWARTZ *is an Australian author. Her high school yearbook predicted she'd be a writer – something about always having her nose in a book. When not living up to others' expectations, she enjoys lazy days in the suburbs and indulging her fascination with steampunk. Her website is authorjennyschwartz.com.*

Before becoming a science fiction author, ALLEN M. STEELE *was a journalist who'd worked for newspapers and magazines in Massachusetts, New Hampshire, Missouri, and his home state of Tennessee. After ditching journalism to focus on his first love, science fiction, Steele has published eighteen novels and nearly a hundred short stories. His work has received numerous awards, including three Hugos, and has been translated worldwide, mainly in languages he can't read. He serves on the Board of Advisors for the Space Frontier Foundation and the Science Fiction and Fantasy Writers of America. He also belongs to Sigma, a group of SF writers who frequently serve as unpaid consultants on matters regarding technology and security. Steele lives in western Massachusetts with his wife Linda and a continual procession of adopted dogs. He collects vintage science fiction books and magazines, spacecraft model kits, and dreams.*

A. M. STICKEL, *author of the fantasy novel* Alat *and the* Napper's Holler *short story series, edits* Black Petals *e-zine and is former Managing Copyeditor for* Ray Gun Revival, *with many prose, poetry and art publications. She has had works in Santa Cruz County papers and Fair, and winners in California Chaparral Poets contests.* Yellow Mama *has published her fiction and nonfiction. She has edited for Brian Royer, B.T. Robertson, Jeremiah Edwards, Jeff Wheeler, Jeremy Whitted, Lynda Williams, Nathalie Mallet, Steve Davidson, and Mike Mulvihill. Her "Honeymoon in Hayel" sequel to "To the Shores of Triple, Lee!" appeared in* Tales of the Talisman.

Possessing a quixotic fondness for difficult careers, Paula R. Stiles *has driven ambulances, taught fish farming for the Peace Corps in West Africa and earned a Scottish PhD in medieval history, studying Templars and non-Christians in Spain. She has also sold fiction to* Strange Horizons, Writers of the Future, Jim Baen's Universe, Shine, Futures, Hills of Fire, *and other markets, as well as a horror novel,* The Mighty Quinn, *out of Dark Continents, and a co-written supernatural mystery novel series,* Fraterfamilias. *She is Editor in Chief of the Lovecraft/Mythos 'zine and micropress,* Innsmouth Free Press. *You can find her on Twitter (@thesnowleopard) and Facebook, or at thesnowleopard.net.*

Throughout the course of his life, Peter J. Wacks *has acted (*Revenge of the Nerds *and others), he has both designed and written the story-lines for Games (the best-selling* Cyberpunk *CCG), written novels and other spec fiction (like* Second Paradigm, *which landed him a guest speaker gig at Mensa on how to tackle true nonlinear concepts in writing), and even gotten nominated for a Bram Stoker Award for his first graphic novel,* Behind These Eyes. *Currently, he is an editor for Wordfire Press, and he is working on his next three novels.*

Copyright Information

The Kickstarter Stars Who Made This Possible

Raygun Chronicles was made possible with the enormous support of space opera readers through a Kickstarter campaign. Thank you to all of our backers...

MUSCA

MARK YOHALEM
(WORMWOOD STUDIOS)
LESLEY RALPH
LOU ANTONELLI
CATHY SCOTT
GREGORY P. LEE,
ATTORNEY AT LAW
CAT RAMBO
STEVEN SMETHURST

CORVUS

BILL WARD
ANNE E. JOHNSON
AARON QUINTANILLA
MAX DEREMBOURG
JEFF RUTHERFORD
JOHN HEINE
SIMO MUINONEN
JAAKKO HEINONEN
J.W. ALDEN
JOSH BUSCHBACHER
MIKE "BLENDERMCCOY"
BUCKLEY
M.SHERLOCK
HUGH BLAIR
G. MARK COLE
HEATHER NORCROSS
RENZO CRISPIERI TH.
RICHARD SCOTT
STEVEN P MASHBURN
EMILIANO MARCHETTI
FRED MILANO
JAKE GNOW
PAUL WEIMER
DEBORAH WALKER
R.S. HUNTER
JONATHAN NORTHRUP
EDWARD LIPSETT
HUGH BLAIR
PAUL ALLAN BALLARD

DAVID ANNANDALE
JOHAN LJUNGMAN
HERBERT "VEGGIE" EDER
ANDREA SPEED
CHRIS HYDE
MILES MATTON
JASON MCGEE
SVEN OF THE DEAD
KARL GALLAGHER
DAVID SMALL
LYDELL CAPRITTA
WWW.TWISTEDSCIFI.COM
CASSI BAKER
SETH ELGART
ALYSSA RITCHIE
ANDREW J CLARK IV
JAAP WILLEM VAN DER
MEULEN
ALEX RISTEA
M HAROLD PAGE
ALDO OJEDA CAMPOS
JOHN SCHUHR
NATHAN ROSEN
JOHN M. PORTLEY
MATTHEW WALKER
JENNIFER STAPP
MICHAEL J. SULLIVAN
KARL O. KNUTSON
CHIP MEADOR
BEVERLY COOPER
DINO MASCOLO
CALVIN G. DODGE
BRIAN F
GEOFFREY KIDD
JOHN GREEN
ELIZABETH CREEGAN
BEN AMES
DANIEL NEELY
MIKE BARKER
TASHA TURNER
JOSH BLUESTEIN

CHRISTIAN BERNTSEN
ALEXANDER THE DRAKE
LI
DAN TAYLOR
JOE POW
MICHAEL B JONES
CAROLYN ROGERS
JENNIFER SCOTT
SWIFTONE
MATT HURLBURT
GARRETT MUNRO
AMANDA NIXON
MAX CAGE
JOACHIM FERMSTAD
MICHAEL BENTLEY
JULI GRIFFO
SAM KNIGHT
L. MEREDITH MCMULLAN
PETER NIBLETT
DAVID O MAHONY
STEPHEN HOPE
POPPY ARAKELIAN
CHANCE LEE
TROY PICHELMAN
KEVIN HEMINGWAY
KELLY STILES
LAURENCE O'BRYAN
JACKIE BOWER
THOMAS KRECH
NATHAN GLAESEMANN
J. CHRIS LAWRENCE
MATTHEW FARRER
IAN LLYWLEYN BROWN
FRAN FRIEL
KEVIN J. ANDERSON
MARK ASHER
GARY VANDEGRIFT
GREG JAYSON
SARAH HANS
DAVID EGGERSCHWILER

The Kickstarter Stars Who Made This Possible

Cindie Hurley
Demian Machado Walendorff
Tanith Korravai
Samuel Montgomery-Blinn
Pam Uphoff
M. Huw Evans
Brent Millis
Stewart C Baker
Traci Loudin
Kate Larking
Rawle Nyanzi
E.C. Myers
Kary English
Louise Sparrow
Kevin Shafer

VELA

Shervyn von Hoerl
StoryADay.org
Scot C. Morgan
Brent Knowles
Jeff Xilon
Brian J. Hunt
Daniel Lemire
Tom Warin
Jenny Schwartz
Aaron Hollingsworth
Thom Walls
Philip Harris
James Carlisle Holder
Robby Thrasher
Camille Griep
Beth Cato
Bill Crider
Cedar Sanderson
Christopher McKitterick

PAVO

Cindy Koepp
Josh and Kasandra Radke
C.S. Carrig
Richard Johnson
Sanford Begley

Gemini Wordsmiths
Martin L. Shoemaker
Laurelee Salter
Fred Kiesche
Angus Abranson
Angela James
Deirdre M. Murphy

PISCES

Janet Oblinger
John Devenny
Beth Tanner
Brian Mengel
Richard Leaver
Joey Gruszecki
James Elwood
Wendy Rogers
Rob Holland
Giovanni Grotto
Melanie Fletcher
Keith West
Holly Heisey
Tammi Miller
Margaret Bickers
Tim Salter
Michelle A Ristuccia
Eva Thompson
Yaron Davidson
Elizabeth McKinstry
Maryline Latorre
James Hancock
Earnie Sotirokos
Keith Martin
Kristian A. Bjørkelo
Karin Montemayor
Joelle Presby
Cory Cone
Jennifer Brozek
Mark Jednaszewski
Chris Emerson
Stephen Evans
Gil Pinheiro
Nick Tchan
Julia Stidolph
Martin DeMello

AQUARIUS

Kathleen Roberts
Jeffrey Boman
Charity Tahmaseb
Sandy Huff
Donald H Mark
Candice Greenlief
Pascal van den Berg
Andrew LeBlanc
Erin Kinch
Steve Ramey
Walt Rosenfeld
Peter Pollak
Jennefer Jones
Jose J Clavell
Jeff Michael
Ray Spitz
Damien Walters Grintalis
Sarah Troedson
Lydia Ondrusek
Kristine Rusch
James J. Kelly, Jr.
Jeff Soesbe
Gary Hayes
Katie Kearns
Gerald Warfield
Kate Shaw

ORION

Alex Shvartsman
Kevin Winter
Aaron Vander Giessen
Valerie Green
Michael Scholl
Kyle Pinches
Gerald Gaiser
David Gooderham
Lee Sweeney
Jocelyn Paige Kelly
Carol Guess
Guy Anthony De Marco
Andrew Foxx
Patricia Bullington-McGuire

THIS BOOK IS A WANTED BOOK

Every Day Publishing is committed to caring for the environment, and we choose print-on-demand technology so that every book is a wanted book – we don't warehouse wasted trees!

Please don't put this book in the trash; it was printed because someone wanted it, so keep it, share it, gift it, trade it or sell it, but don't throw it out.

CPSIA information can be obtained at www.ICGtesting.com
Printed in the USA
LVOW12s2213110214

373342LV00001B/156/P